T0355898

Pilgrim Through This Barren Land

A Novel

D.W. SNOW

Pilgrim Through This Barren Land
D.W. Snow

Copyright © 2025

ISBN: 979-8-35098-473-6

Also by D.W. Snow

Millstone Around the Neck

And Now the Vault of Heaven Resounds

At Concordia (short stories)

To

J.A.O. Preus II,
Trenton Parker,
Boulos A. Ayad
and
Bevelyn Williams

1

One September afternoon, three college seniors from Missouri Southern State University in Joplin jumped into a Chrysler convertible which belonged to one of them, and with some political flags and other political paraphernalia, they followed the campaign bus of the Democrat presidential candidate who was on a campaign trip through southern Missouri. The candidate and his glamorous wife, who was a lead partner of a powerful law firm, were traveling from a rally in Joplin to another series of political events and appearances in Kansas City. While the bus traveled north along Interstate 49, the Chrysler convertible with the three Missouri Southern students pulled along the left side of the bus and the students held up flags and signs which were insulting and inflammatory toward the Democrat nominee for president. Their signs accused him of being a baby killer, and of being disingenuous, and of being a serial abuser of women and being a sexual predator. The coed Missouri Southern student held up a sign that accused the charming wife of the Democrat nominee of being an enabler of her husband's countless trysts and rendezvous and sexual predatory exploits. The students in the Chrysler convertible yelled insults and provocations at the bus, and the driver of the convertible even engaged in a few attempts to abruptly change lanes in front of the bus – nothing particularly dangerous, as the media later accused, but it was the type of driving that could be regarded as rude and inconsiderate. There were members of the media, including television and newspaper reporters, aboard the bus traveling along with the Democrat nominee for president and his lovely wife. One of the media people on the bus was Jake Pepper who was working for National Public Radio at the time, but who would later become the White House correspondent for ABC News. Pepper was terribly offended by the antics of the three Missouri Southern students in the Chrysler convertible. To him they lacked decorum and were horrendously disrespectful of the soon-to-be elected president and his glamorous wife, who was promised the opportunity to serve as a co-president with her husband. In one of his famous, sanctimonious on-air lectures, Pepper filed his dispatch for NPR that evening to declare his outrage at the Missouri Southern students and their stunt of harassment to the Democrat presidential nominee and his dazzling wife, who worked as a partner with a large law firm in the South. About the three students, Pepper whined in his NPR report, "I wish. In my soul, I wish that these three people had a conscience, just an ounce of integrity."

The Democrat nominee for president was apparently very upset. His powerful and gracious wife told him not to worry. Once he was elected, she assured him, they would take some sweet revenge. The wife of the Democrat nominee talked to the Missouri State Highway Patrol officers who were accompanying the bus. "You need to detain the kids in that convertible," she directed the lieutenant who was in charge of the protective assignment. "They don't need to be arrested, but we need to obtain their names and addresses."

The intriguing and charming wife of the Democrat presidential candidate commented to Jake Pepper, who was slavishly riding along on the bus, "Remember, Jake, the primary lesson of Woodrow Wilson was that basically the American people are just a bunch of idiots, waiting for someone to show up and push them around."

Pepper was duly impressed by the wisdom shared by the wife of the nominee. "Yes, ma'am," he obediently blubbered. Pepper would go on to become a very valuable asset for the Democrat presidential nominee after the election. Untold to his listening audience – not that they would have cared anyway – Pepper had previously served as the press secretary to Pennsylvania Democrat Congresswoman Marjolene Moblies-Malivinsky – a close associate of the Democrat presidential nominee and his captivating wife. Pepper, who wishes in his soul that the idiots who populate the country had just an ounce of integrity, which he has luckily been blessed to possess, didn't believe his listeners and the consumers of his reporting needed to know about the minor details of influence peddling that dominate the symbiotic relationship of American politics and journalism. Congresswoman Moblies-Malivinsky was married to Iowa Democrat Congressman Edwin Malivinsky. Mr. Malivinsky was defeated by a Republican after serving two terms in Congress and then he conveniently just moved over to become the chairman of the Pennsylvania Democrat Party, even though he was from Iowa. It was a position he obtained because of the endorsement from his congresswoman wife. Malivinsky then went on to diligently coordinate a sordid operation of money laundering of more than $10 million. By the time Malivinsky was indicted and convicted of his crimes, the Democrat presidential nominee, who was so offended by three college students in a convertible while riding on the bus between Joplin and Kansas City, had been elected the president of the country. Congresswoman Marjolene Moblies-Malivinsky, who had been so ably represented by Jake Pepper as her press secretary, appeared before the Democrat president and asked the president to grant a pardon to her husband. The president refused to grant a pardon, presumably because Mr. Malivinsky failed a vital duty in politics – that is, to funnel any of that laundered cash into the president's personal charitable foundation. Yet, to show there were no hard feelings, the president gave his blessing to his daughter to marry the son of Marjolene Moblies-Malivinsky and Edwin Malivinsky. Their son, Morton Malivinsky, was a powerful New York investment banker and an executive with the president's personal charitable foundation. NPR and ABC News journalist Jake Pepper never found it necessary to report on any of these fetid details, presumably because he was too busy fawning over his own incredible conscience and personal integrity.

And so, the Missouri Highway Patrol indeed pulled over the Chrysler convertible. The three students were quizzed about their intentions and their identifications were obtained and the names and addresses were duly noted. The patrol officer advised them to be safe on the highway and he recommended that they return to the Joplin campus. Then the patrol officer dutifully contacted the amiable wife of the Democrat presidential nominee and provided her with the identities and addresses of the three college students.

"Thank you, officer," she said. "Job well done. I think we may be able to find a position for you in our administration after we are elected."

They were indeed elected under the promise that the American people got a real bargain – the new president, who so ably served as a governor of a small southern state, would bring along his charming wife to serve as a figurative co-president at his side. The new first lady rarely forgets anything, especially when it involves settling scores – perhaps training from her years as a partner with the powerful law firm. She contacted the nation's new attorney general and ordered the attorney general to file federal criminal charges against the three students at Missouri Southern State University.

"What is the offense?" the attorney general asked.

"These three students are members of the Ku Klux Klan," the first lady pronounced. "They need to be charged under the Ku Klux Klan Act of 1871, also known as the Enforcement Act of 1871."

"And what did they do?"

The first lady explained the merciless harassment of the president, while he was a candidate campaigning in Missouri.

"Luckily not everyone in Missouri is a Klansman, because we did carry that state," the first lady reflected.

At the time of the discussion with the first lady, the newly appointed attorney general didn't know that the three Missouri Southern students were black – and that it might be difficult to convince a judge or a jury that black students could have violated the Ku Klux Klan Act of 1871. When the U.S. attorney general learned the three culprits were black, she changed gears slightly in order to accommodate the first lady's request; the attorney general transformed the matter into a civil complaint against the suspects, using the civil procedure provisions of the Ku Klux Klan Act. It will be considerably easier to make this stick if it is pursued as civil matter, the attorney general reasoned to herself, and as a civil complaint we can engage in endless delays and continuances and thus create enormous legal expenses for the defendants. By the time the federal civil complaint was filed, the three offenders had graduated from Missouri Southern and all three had moved back to St. Louis, their original home.

One of the student suspects from Missouri Southern was Michael Holden. Michael grew up in a conservative Christian family in north St. Louis, lifelong members of an historic church body, known as the synod, which has its origins in medieval Saxon Germany. He went to a synod parochial elementary school with a student population of nearly all black children. After the Civil War, the synod, based in St. Louis, sent missionaries into the South to introduce the gospel and the traditional synod style of worship to former slaves. Part of this process was to plant churches and parochial schools in rural areas and small and large towns in a concerted effort to appeal to former slaves. Because of this history, the synod has always had a large membership of black people, with many parishes composed predominantly of black members. By 1922, there were so many black synod members in the South – sixty-six thriving black parishes and parochial schools in Alabama alone – the synod opened a college for black synod members, Concordia College in Selma, which became one of the country's one-hundred-four historically black colleges and universities. There were eleven other synod colleges which were open to black synod members, but it was discovered that many black people prefer predominantly black institutions for their higher education. The synod is a traditional, liturgical church body and has found that it has always had a particular appeal to conservative, disciplined, reserved, and conventional black families. Synod churches do not celebrate their Sunday liturgies with loud choirs swaying to the beat, or fire and brimstone sermons, or spirit-filled whoops, hand clapping, and amen shouting. Rather, the synod's liturgical worship is very formal, dignified, stately, ceremonial events with slow processions down the main church aisle, incense being swung by the pastor in a gold-plated censer, J.S. Bach Baroque processionals and hymns on the organ, ritualistic prayers and responsorials, bowing, genuflecting, kneeling, a quiet, dignified and ceremonial celebration of the Lord's Supper. Some observers have said synod church services seem like a Catholic mass – but more reverent. The synod has found that this style of worship is particularly appealing to certain types of black families whose worship proclivities are dispassionate, low-key, constrained, earnest, staid and reserved. Because of this appeal, the synod has a total membership of about 25 percent black people. The synod has its origins in medieval Saxony – church people drenched in ancient, traditional and conservative religious customs. Because of their conflict with the progressive Saxon prince in the early 1800s, the synod people escaped Germany and made their way to St. Louis in 1839 when a group of about a thousand immigrants crossed the Atlantic Ocean and arrived in New Orleans; then they came aboard steamships up the Mississippi River to St. Louis. These traditional Saxon immigrants believed they were escaping a persecution from the Saxon prince, who had married a Calvinist and embraced liberal, progressive, ecumenical Protestant practices. The prince ordered the conservative Saxon medieval worshippers to adopt liberal and nontraditional religious behaviors. These Saxon synod believers openly refused the intimidation and instead escaped to the United States to express and retain their solemn, traditional, liturgical religious customs without interference.

Part of synod tradition has been for individual parishes to operate their own primary schools. In black neighborhoods, these parochial schools are primarily composed of black children, reflecting the racial composition of the neighborhoods and the parishes. Beginning in the mid-1960s the bureaucracy at the St. Louis synod headquarters decided that predominantly black parochial schools were practicing a form of segregation and consequently the synod school department ordered the parishes to shut down the schools if the student body was more than 75 percent black. The poorer black parishes, which did not have assertive pastors, complied and closed their schools. In the more middle-class black parishes, with more aggressive pastors, they defied the orders of the synod headquarters, and they kept their schools open. Michael Holden was a student at Ebenezer Synod School, with an assertive pastor at Ebenezer Synod Church in the Baden neighborhood of north St. Louis who refused to abide by the directive from the synod to close the segregated school. And because of this, Michael was able to complete his education through the eighth grade at Ebenezer's parochial school and then his parents insisted he attend St. Louis North Synod High School – a parochial synod high school with a student body of more than 50 percent black students.

After his graduation from St. Louis North Synod, Michael's parents encouraged him to pursue studies in college, and even asked him to consider attending one of the eleven synod colleges. After careful consideration, Michael instead chose to apply to Missouri Southern State University, a state-run college in Joplin.

While at Missouri Southern, Michael attended several concerts of the Missouri Southern Chorale. He noticed a beautiful female student, Carol Hudson, in the ensemble. He was drawn to her and believed he needed to introduce himself. They went out for coffee and he learned she too had grown up in St. Louis and was likewise a synod member. She attended a different synod parish in St. Louis and thus a different synod parochial school. Carol didn't go on to St. Louis North Synod High School, but rather attended a St. Louis public high school.

"It's just uncanny," Michael quipped. "And then we meet here of all places. I haven't seen you at Immanuel Church in Joplin. Where do you currently attend?"

"Oh, a friend of mine goes to a synod church in Carthage, so I go along with her to Good Shepherd parish."

"What is your home parish in St. Louis?" Michael asked.

"I grew up in St. Paul's College Hill."

"Isn't that where Alice Ploughmaster attends?" he asked, referring to the beloved former mayor of East St. Louis who had become a legend of resilience and dignity to all black people in the St. Louis area.

While at Missouri Southern, they made plans to attend church together – some weeks at Immanuel in Joplin, sometimes at Good Shepherd in Carthage. They became inseparable. During school breaks and the summer months they spent much of their time together in St. Louis, some weeks attending St. Paul's College Hill and other weeks at Ebenezer. After three years of courting, Michael asked Carol if they could make plans for marriage.

"It's important that you ask my father," Carol replied. "You know, this is a significant tradition in the synod."

"Of course, I know that, but I just wanted your permission."

Michael approached Mr. Hudson to ask for his blessing. Mr. Hudson wasn't surprised because of all of the time the couple spent together. "How will you support my daughter?" he obligatorily asked.

"I will work as an accountant here in St. Louis. That is my major at Missouri Southern."

"Of course, I give you my blessing, Michael. I am so proud that Carol has found a fine synod man."

After their engagement, Carol and Michael had one more year at Missouri Southern and that was the fall they interacted with the campaign bus along Interstate 49. Both Michael and Carol were opposed to the Democrat presidential candidate because of his support for abortion, as well as his other social and economic progressive ideologies. Carol was particularly offended by the governor's reputation as a serial sexual harasser, a cad, a sexual predator, and a boorish abuser of women. Along with another black student, Paul Mooney, a senior at Missouri Southern and the driver of the Chrysler convertible, they planned to follow the campaign bus with their signs and flags as a taunt to the Democrat nominee. The three students didn't display signs or banners supporting the Republican nominee, who was currently serving as an incumbent president. While all three intended to vote for the sitting Republican president, their gibe was purposely designed to display their objection to the Democrat governor – not to necessarily evoke support for the sitting president. When they were pulled over by the Missouri Highway Patrol, all three presented their identifications to the officer who took their IDs to his squad car and returned after about fifteen minutes to tell them they had not violated any Missouri laws and he advised them to drive with care and return to Joplin.

November arrived and the Democrat governor was elected president with only 43 percent of the national vote, but because he was a governor from a southern state, he was able to win in states from the

South and collect three-hundred-seventy electoral votes – a hundred more than necessary to secure a victory. The new president-elect appeared on stage with his dazzling and powerful wife, and their twelve-year-old daughter. He pranced around at his victory rally on election night, pretending to be engaging and grateful for the confidence of the American people. He appeared sallow, unctuous, smarmy, ingratiating, and artificially humble. He told the adoring crowds that they got a "two-for-one" with the first lady destined to serve as his co-president. The ravaging, glamorous wife glared out at the fawning crowds with her smug expression of contempt in her bold, blunt, trendy blonde flip-in bob hairstyle.

Carol and Michael graduated in May from Missouri Southern, Carol with a degree in art and Michael with a degree in accounting. After returning to St. Louis, they planned a summer wedding to be held at the synod parish of Carol's youth, St. Paul's Church College Hill – a stunning Gothic revival-Baroque structure built in 1925 by beloved St. Louis architect Albert Meyer. The wedding was a lovely affair – Carol dressed in a magnificent white gown with a moderate train. Michael was handsomely attired in his grey tuxedo. People whispered about how Michael was rather slight – just five feet, six inches. "But it is a match made in heaven," someone said.

At the wedding reception held in the parish hall of St. Paul's College Hill, Michael met Alice Ploughmaster, who attended the wedding as a guest. Mrs. Ploughmaster had once served as the mayor of East St. Louis, just across the Mississippi River in Illinois, and was revered by nearly every black person in the region as a symbol of dignity, respect, constancy, service, and humility. In addition to once serving as the mayor of East St. Louis, Alice Ploughmaster was a member of the board of directors of the Southern Illinois University Medical School Campus. It was at this time that Mrs. Ploughmaster wrote and self-published a children's book and signed a contract with the SIU Medical Center for the Medical Center to purchase 100,000 copies of her book to distribute them to children who came into the hospital or to one of its affiliates. Later, the attorney general of Illinois accused Mrs. Ploughmaster of not printing the full run of the books and double selling the books; she was indicted on several counts of fraud. To the astonishment of people in the area, she did not put up a fight, but rather accepted her punishment, resigned as mayor, and stepped down from the SIU Medical Campus board of directors. She asked for people to forgive her, and she was sentenced to five to ten years in the state prison. The governor of Illinois pardoned her after she had been incarcerated for nearly four months. When she was released, she shocked the residents of the region once again when she said she sought to redeem her reputation, and she engaged in a variety of volunteer projects; and then she became a member of the synod, ultimately devoting herself to St. Paul's College Hill, a small, poor, urban parish of mostly black synod members. She became a symbol for many black people in the St. Louis region as a beacon of integrity, modesty, humility, grace, and decency. Mrs. Ploughmaster, in recent years, spent much of her time in New Orleans organizing and leading an annual national conference at Xavier University, tackling issues involving global corruption and injustice.

"Michael, it is so nice to meet you. Congratulations. What is your home synod parish?" Mrs. Ploughmaster asked.

"It is my distinct honor, Mrs. Ploughmaster. You are so beloved in this city. I feel blessed to meet you. I grew up in Ebenezer parish."

"Michael, what will you be doing next?"

"I just finished my degree in accounting, and I hope to find a job in the field here in St. Louis."

The newlyweds didn't take a honeymoon to Haiti, as the new president and his captivating wife did when they were married in 1975. Carol and Michael made a trip to Puerto Rico, lounged on the white sand beaches; they took a couple of historic tours of the Spanish forts, and they enjoyed sipping on the famous Puerto Rican rum. After their return to St. Louis, Carol and Michael Holden were served a federal civil complaint by a U.S. marshal. They were being accused by the U.S. Justice Department of violating the Ku Klux Klan Act of 1871 – that they knowingly and willingly engaged in an act of harassment to violate the civil rights of the new president and his charming wife while they were campaigning in Missouri along Interstate 49 between Joplin and Kansas City. Also being sued was their friend Paul Mooney, who was with them at the time of the offense.

"Goodness. That is quite a wedding gift from the new president," Michael joked with Carol. "We will need to find an attorney. But, Carol, I can't let this get in the way of finding a job and starting my career."

2

Michael Holden met with an attorney, Larry Korhonen, at his office near downtown St. Louis about the federal civil complaint.

"Aside from the absurdity of the complaint, how is it possible for three black people to be conspiring with the Ku Klux Klan?" Michael asked incredulously.

"Well, the law doesn't specify the racial identity of the possible offender."

"But doesn't it just test the limits of credulity to claim that three black college students engaged in a conspiracy to deny the civil rights of a politician because the three black college students were Ku Klux Klan members? Something about that just doesn't make sense; maybe it sounds utterly preposterous."

"Perhaps. No doubt, it is peculiar, Michael; I will agree. But that will be a judgment by a jury after hearing the facts."

"But what evidence do they have that we are affiliated with the Ku Klux Klan? For heaven's sake!"

"It is a federal civil rights complaint. They are asserting the president's civil rights were violated and it was inspired by a conspiracy involving membership in the Ku Klux Klan. A jury will have to judge the facts."

"Good grief. How long will this go on?"

"Because it is not a criminal case – it is a civil complaint – it could go on for a while. If it were criminal, the speedy trial provisions would move it along at a more rapid pace. But since it is a civil matter, it could carry on for a while." The attorney, Larry Korhonen, was not inclined to share his personal interest in potentially keeping the affair going to be able to collect legal fees, but also, he didn't wish to share his suspicion that the government would like to keep the matter alive to make the lives of the defendants more difficult.

"Are we speaking of months?"

"Yes, possibly months." The attorney didn't share with Michael that it could go on for years – after all, the alleged victims were the president and his lovely wife.

"Aren't we protected by free speech – you know, the First Amendment?"

"The Ku Klux Klan Act clearly and specifically defines the offenses are not to be protected by the First Amendment." Korhonen didn't share with Michael that this is precisely why the Ku Klux Klan Act was invoked in this particular case.

"Will I be able to face my accusers – the president and the first lady?"

"You are not being accused by the president and his wife. The federal government is your accuser. And remember it is a civil matter; it's not criminal."

Attorney Korhonen collected the necessary details about the case. Indeed, if there had been another Justice Department under another president, the complaint would likely have been withdrawn after further review by the U.S. attorney for the district. However, when the new president took office, one of his first official acts was to direct his new attorney general to dismiss all ninety-three U.S. attorneys in the various states and districts, and to replace them with political appointees who would represent the interests of the new president and his glamorous wife. The new U.S. attorney for the eastern district of Missouri, based in St. Louis, was a devoted sycophant of the new president and the first lady, and this new U.S. attorney obediently took an interest in pursuing the Ku Klux Klan civil complaint against the three former Missouri Southern students.

At or about at this time, the new president and his lovely wife started giving regular interviews to the slavish, entranced media about the resurgence of activities of the Ku Klux Klan throughout the nation. It seemed they were planting a new narrative they desired the media to pick up and run with. The slobbering newspaper reporters and television personalities failed to probe into the claims by the president and the first lady. The members of the press conveniently failed to ask the simplest questions: Why is this suddenly the topic of conversation? Where is the evidence that the Ku Klux Klan has made a mysterious resurrection from obscurity after forty or fifty years? Mr. President, what really was the connection of the Ku Klux Klan to the Democrat Party and Woodrow Wilson? Surely, these were questions that weren't asked because there was no interest in obtaining the answers. The reporters merely repeated the president's and the first lady's persistent worries about a sudden re-emergence of the Ku Klux Klan in both the heartland and on both coasts. Just a month after the civil complaint was filed against Michael and Carol Holden and their friend Paul Mooney, the Madam Attorney General ordered the FBI to raid a remote cabin in the mountain wilderness of northern Idaho because she had reason to believe the resident of the cabin was likely a member of the Klan and could be in possession of unlicensed and unregistered firearms. FBI sharpshooters were called in and ordered by the attorney general to storm the remote property. The FBI snipers murdered the teenage son, the wife, and the family dog, and then arrested the owner of the property and his friend. Just nine months later, the attorney general ordered the FBI to storm the compound of an obscure Christian fundamentalist sect in Waco, Texas. The FBI then proceeded to fill the compound with highly flammable CS gas and then to ignite it, causing a conflagration which killed seventy-nine members of the group including twenty-one children. It wasn't but a few weeks later that the attorney general ordered the black mayor of Philadelphia to fly police helicopters over the top of a west Philadelphia rowhouse that was occupied by a group of obstinate black nationalists. The Madam Attorney General lectured the hapless Philadelphia mayor that the holed-up black nationalists were members of the Ku Klux Klan. The Philadelphia mayor replied in stunned disbelief, "But Madam Attorney General, how could they be in the Klan? They are all black people." The Madam replied, "Don't get impertinent with me. We have black Klan members all throughout the country." Just two weeks later, the mayor obediently directed police helicopters to fly over the tenement and firebomb the building, ultimately burning down an entire neighborhood – destroying sixty-five homes and killing four adults and five children. After the conflagration, Madam called the bewildered mayor and congratulated him on a job well done. "Good job," she pronounced. "We got rid of some more of the pernicious presence of the Klan."

Madam then followed up the three incidents by giving a gloomy speech detailing a resurgence of the Ku Klux Klan throughout the whole country. The president and his gracious wife repeated the same talking points, warning of a vast, dark conspiracy secretly roaming through the land. A new narrative had been created. Lacking any substantial interest in pursuing the matter or asking any probing questions, the media merely repeated the storyline being fed to them by the president, the first lady, and the diligent Madam Attorney General.

It soon became clear to Michael and Carol's attorney, Larry Korhonen, that there was a larger effort going on regarding the Department of Justice's civil complaint involving the Ku Klux Klan Act, but Korhonen didn't openly express his concerns and suspicions to

Michael or Carol or Paul because he didn't want to alarm them, and he perceived the matter had the potential to continue for quite some length of time. No need to interfere with the process while it is ongoing.

* * *

Michael began his search for a job in accounting. A fellow synod member at Ebenezer Church recommended that Michael apply for a position as an assistant accountant with the Alfred Sendahl Perfume Company, located on Goodfellow Blvd. in the North Pointe neighborhood of north St. Louis. The Sendahl Perfume Company was a venerable old company established in 1906 and did not specialize in the exotic, expensive fragrances, but rather focused on specialty bottles for their ordinary – some would say cheap or sweet – scents. The unique bottle designs were novelties, such as the shape of Cinderella's pumpkin carriage or clocks or telephones or birds or toy soldiers, and were commonly sold in dime stores or as seasonal features in the Avon catalog. Michael made a dignified impression on the management team, as well as the chief financial officer at Sendahl Perfume Company, and he was offered a position as an assistant accountant – primarily focused on recording and proofing account entries into the general ledger.

Michael was hired by the president of the Sendahl Perfume Company, Peter Selberg, who was the husband of the granddaughter of the founder of the company, Alfred A. Sendahl. Mr. Selberg was a courteous and dedicated man. He was particularly fond of black employees. He generally found black people to have wonderful senses of humor and could be self-effacing in a way that loosened tensions in the work environment. Selberg particularly liked black synod people because of the remarkable discipline and decorum promoted by the synod. While he was unable to ask about a person's religious affiliation because of employment discrimination laws, he would get around the prohibition by asking black employees who were members of the synod, already working for the company, to recruit fellow churchmen to join the company. And because of this strategy, Michael was able to learn about the accounting position at Sendahl Perfume Company from an Ebenezer synod parishioner.

With his new position, Michael shared with Carol that they could now qualify for a mortgage and buy a house. Michael's desire was to relocate to the suburban community of Florissant in St. Louis County, just north of the city and bordering the suburb of Ferguson. Florissant is a fully integrated community with a population of about 45 or 50 percent black residents. There are many older homes built in the early and mid-1900s, as well as subdivision housing constructed in more recent years. Carol wanted a home that was built within the past twenty to thirty years and she pleaded not to select a house near the creeks and streams in the region so they could avoid flooding which periodically occurs around St. Louis. Michael's preference was a house with a level yard without shrubbery and bushes so that he could maintain a proper, appealing suburban appearance. They finally settled on a ranch style brick home built in the late 1960s. Just to the north of their house was a residence that had a red cedar bush, a green juniper, an elm tree, and a dwarf mugo pine – all of which annoyed Michael because it would deflect from his desire to have a flat, level yard without unsightly obstructions. But Michael was able to convince himself that since the bothersome shrubbery was on someone else's property, he would merely ignore the disagreeable blockages. I'm sure I can convince myself to put these bushes out of my mind and pretend they are not there, he assured himself.

Carol, who graduated with a Bachelor of Fine Arts degree from Missouri Southern, wanted to open a small gallery with studio space that she could rent out to other artists. In addition, Carol's dream was to find a location that could accommodate a space for dancers. Her fantasy dream was to be able to have a dance venue that could host the Alvin Ailey Dance Troupe to appear in St. Louis. She searched ideal, and not-so-ideal, locations in the north St. Louis and the North County region and finally landed a quaint building to lease in the St. Louis Place neighborhood, not far from downtown and very close to the famed historic synod church – Zion Cathedral on 21st Street, a magnificent Gothic revival structure built in 1895 by revered St. Louis architect Albert Knell. Carol's building had about four hundred square feet which she planned to convert into a gallery, as well as about four hundred square feet which would become an art studio, and about five hundred square feet for a dance studio and venue. Quickly, Carol began developing contacts among area artists who were looking for studio space, and she spread the word about the gallery. She searched and found a few private dance teachers who were looking for studio and venue space. After months of searching, she found a group of painters, illustrators, sculptors, pottery and ceramics artists, and dance instructors who could occupy her space, pay rent, and help her to achieve her dream of a private arts venue for inner city St. Louis.

One August Sunday, Michael met his friend Paul Mooney to discuss their shared plight of being charged by the Justice Department in the civil complaint related to the Ku Klux Klan Act. Paul invited Michael to accompany him to his synod parish, a predominantly black church in the Carr Square neighborhood of north St. Louis – Transfiguration Church. The congregation sang the medieval German hymn by Paulus Speratus, *Salvation Unto Us Has Come*. A visiting pastor from another synod parish, a handsome, dignified man in his early sixties, led the liturgy in chant. After the Confiteor, Kyrie, Gloria, and Collect prayer, the pastor read the gospel of *St. Matthew*, chapter 16, wherein Jesus tells his followers that his destiny is to be arrested and sacrificed and then Jesus goes on to rebuke Peter for denying Jesus's pending suffering. This visiting pastor, a man named Father Richard Mueller, then delivered a quite remarkable sermon in which he told the congregation there is always a price to be paid for the events of life. Nothing is free, he counseled, and sometimes the price is much greater than what a person wishes to pay, but God's plan insists upon a sort of balance sheet – there is always a cost, and a price will be paid ... because life is an expression of fate – God's design of destiny.

Both American political parties try to spend their way to success. One party tries to solve problems by spending enormous amounts of money through debt. The other party counsels financial responsibility and fiscal restraint – yet that party finally has discovered that fiscal restraint will not achieve success at the ballot box and that party has jumped aboard the manic spending spree. The only question that remains is not whether wild, uncontrolled spending will occur – funds which will all be derived from mindlessly printing phony money in a fake printing press and borrowing from international bond markets and from nations that will exact a revenge – but rather, how will this insane indebtedness ever be repaid? Know this: someone will eventually have to pay this bill and it will be a very remarkable cost – the kind that causes a society to collapse.

From today's gospel, Jesus says to Peter, "Get thee behind me, Satan." But isn't that cruel of Jesus to say such a thing to a dear disciple and friend? What Jesus was expressing is that Satan is the one who constantly says, "You don't have to pay the price." In Jesus's forty-day fast in the wilderness, Satan tempted Jesus by saying he wouldn't have to pay the price. He wouldn't have to pay the price for disobedience to his Father's plan. He wouldn't have to pay the price for the sake of his Father's divine objective.

I am the pastor of a parish inside and bordering on a troubled area of St. Louis. I have presided at many funerals for young men who have died from drug over-doses, and dozens of funerals for young men who have been killed in gunfire in the war zone of inner-city streets of a large metropolis suffering from violence, thought-lessness, indignity, and crime. I can tell you that whoever introduced the life of drugs to these individuals never said that they would have to pay the price. And I can assure you the individuals who took the drugs firmly believed they wouldn't have to pay the price. I can also let you know the individuals who died from gunfire and violence in the troubled urban jungle also believed they would not have to pay the price for their participation in violent, thoughtless criminal activities. True, some were innocent bystanders, but they also never thought they would have to pay the price for the mindless violence surrounding them. None of them – whether participants in violent acts or the hapless victims – believed they would have to pay the price for pointless, shameful and premature deaths. "No," says Satan, "you won't have to pay the price. Not you."

I recently read a book about the final months of the Second World War. In those final days, the Nazis – the Gestapo, the SS, the collaborators – spent an enormous amount of energy at the end destroying written records, eliminating any evidence of their atrocities and despicable actions. They worked diligently in their final weeks to erase the savagery in the concentration death camps, the abominations in the small villages and towns and in the remote fields and forests. While they were committing their wickedness, they didn't believe they would ever have to pay the price, but when the jig was up and when they realized the end was looming, they attempted to hide the evidence of their offenses through obfuscation, deceit, lying, and covering up. With all of the energy they put into hiding their brutality and banality, they still had to pay the price. How about the promises of our consumer culture: you can lose fifty pounds by drinking a miracle fluid, or you can learn to play a Chopin Polonaise in five weeks, or you can learn a new language in just fifteen minutes a week, or you can earn $100,000 a year for only ten hours of work a week. These are hollow promises and are impossible because the true price was not paid.

To be the person you need to be, to follow God's plan, to sacrifice for others, to suffer and carry the cross, to live a life of discipline, resolve, righteousness and dignity – you will have to pay the price; even if your name is Jesus. The fancy theological term for this is atonement. As a way of demonstrating his shared humanity with us, Jesus tells us that his destiny is to pay the price – to reconcile us to a just and loving God, to remove the burden of our sin and degradation, to make God's kingdom a living reality in his presence, to renew God's covenant and usher in God's new creation, and to win for us the life of the age to come. He doesn't just talk about paying the price; on the cross he actually did pay it. He paid the enormous debt incurred by our unfaithfulness, our selfishness, our short-sightedness, our fallenness, our deceit, our lack of discipline, our thoughtlessness, our abomination, our indignity, our cluelessness. And the suffering, agony and indignity Jesus endured to pay this price defies belief and explanation. The misery and agony he suffered defies description.

But Peter appealed to Jesus, "Oh lord, you won't have to pay the price." Jesus knew otherwise and clearly he understood the price always, absolutely must be paid. This is the divine principle of God's creation. Jesus bluntly replied to Peter, "Get thee behind me, Satan." Jesus knew the price must be paid, and it will be paid.

3

While working at her art studio and gallery, Carol would frequently visit Zion Cathedral since it was so close to her gallery. Zion, a huge Gothic structure with a stunning marble interior, is a predominantly black synod parish; the church holds matins and vespers services, usually on five midweek days. Carol tried to attend as many of these services as possible and often she went to the Thursday eucharist liturgy because the chrism was sometimes given at those services in commemoration of Holy Thursday. Almost every time she was at Zion, she would see a distinguished man, along with several other regular congregants. He was a dignified black man in his sixties – he always wore a shirt and tie with a suit jacket. Over the months, Carol finally had the opportunity to meet this gentleman. His name was Keith Newland. Keith worked as an accountant for an auto and truck parts supply company in the neighborhood.

"Oh, my husband is an accountant also."

"Where does he work?"

"He is an accountant with the Alfred Sendahl Perfume Company in the North Pointe neighborhood."

"Oh, yes. That is a fine old company. They have been in business in St. Louis since the early 1900s."

Carol became fond of Keith and she invited Keith and his wife to come to meet Michael at their home in Florissant and share a dinner engagement together. One Tuesday evening, Keith and his wife Doris came to the Holdens' home in Florissant for a meal. They brought a gift to Carol and Michael – a beautiful Saxon Meissen porcelain, likely from the seventeenth century.

"My goodness," Carol exclaimed, knowing the high value of a genuine Meissen. "I don't think we can accept this. It is terribly valuable and expensive."

"Please," Keith said. "It was given to me by a synod church worker many years ago. I will be retiring soon, and Doris and I will begin to separate from our belongings. I can think of no one more deserving of a Saxon Meissen. And Carol, you have become such a dear friend, and you are a devout synod believer. I just feel called to share this gift with you and Michael. Please accept it as a gift of gratitude from my heart."

"Goodness. I just feel ashamed to take such a priceless possession," Carol said.

"Please," Doris interjected. "Keith treasures your friendship, and he is so moved by your devotion to the synod. It would touch both of our hearts to know you will accept this token of our relationship. And Carol, Keith has watched your pregnancy with such anticipation. He has kept me up to date every time he sees you. He has told me how much bigger you are each week. He is so excited about your upcoming new child."

Indeed, Carol was expecting and both she and Michael were thrilled about the prospects of becoming parents. Michael had prepared the baby's bedroom; the anticipation of the new baby was a thrill for both Carol and Michael.

At the dinner engagement, Keith talked about his reverence, awe and joy each time he enters Zion Cathedral. The massive Gothic revival church was built in 1895 and has long been regarded as one of the treasured architectural gems in St. Louis. It has a colossal spire, stunning ceiling vaults, beautiful stained glass, an intricate Gothic altarpiece, and four remarkable sections of staggering wooden pews in the enormous nave. Inside the gigantic church, a person's voice echoes, shrouded with a sense of mystery, as if somehow returning in time to the Saxon Baroque era.

"It was a memory I will cherish for my lifetime to have been able to go to Zion to see President Probst installed there, and Bach's gorgeous *Magnificat* was performed in the church during that service," Keith shared. "What a glorious memory for Doris and me. Every time I go into that church I am always touched by memories, recollections, and experiences I have had there. The church seems like an advance preview of what heaven could be like."

As they enjoyed their dinner of manicotti made with ricotta cheese, they laughed and shared stories. Keith said to Michael, "Carol has told me you are an accountant at Sendahl Perfume Company. That is a venerable old St. Louis outfit. How do you like working for them?"

"It is a good company. The president is the husband of the grand-daughter of the founder, Alfred Sendahl. He is a very decent man to work for. One of the most interesting things about him is that he likes black brothers and sisters to work for him – particularly if they are synod people. I think he trusts us and believes the company to be in good hands because of the synod traditions of discipline and decorum. He's not a member of the synod; it's just something he has learned over the years."

"How's business?" Keith asked.

"Business is good. You know, people buy the perfume because of our novelty bottles. We do a lot of business with Avon Products. Every month the Avon catalog features one of our bottles. They are our largest customer."

Michael asked where in St. Louis Doris and Keith live. Keith said they live in the neighborhood of St. Louis Place, near Zion Cathedral, which has gone through a difficult phase – rundown properties, increased crime, vandalism, abandoned homes. However, he shared that they would never leave because of their advanced years, but also because they didn't want to abandon Zion Cathedral.

"Have you ever been a victim of crime?" Carol asked.

"Our garage was broken into twice," Doris said. "Our car was broken into once. Our front porch window was broken once. Irritating, but nothing terribly serious."

"I love St. Louis," Keith said. "We have our problems. We have our crime and some blight. But I love this city for a few reasons. We have an amazing history – a long, cherished, distinguished, proud history. On the whole, the city has preserved its glamorous architectural heritage. The buildings are stunning and beautiful, including the many amazing churches. And, most importantly, St. Louis is the home of our synod. I am very proud of that fact."

"How have you been treated by the police?" Michael asked.

"The police have always treated me with the greatest respect and dignity," Keith replied. "I freely speak very highly of them."

* * *

Carol gave birth to their baby who was named after his father. Thus, Michael Holden suddenly became Michael Holden, Senior. The baby was to be called Michael Junior.

Michael Junior was the most astonishingly cute, adorable child anyone could ever meet. Everyone wanted to be near him, cuddle him, play with him, hold him on their laps, kiss him, hug him, ask him questions and listen to his sweet, adorable voice. He was precocious and so outrageously endearing and precious. He loved to sing songs he learned from church. He said the most adorable things, such as, "Jesus is my best friend. He is my buddy." Or, "I think I'll go out and build a fence today." Or, "Papa, if you want me to mow the lawn, I think you might have to buy me a riding lawnmower." Or, "Momma, do you want me to do the laundry for you?" He always had a Matchbox toy car or truck with him to play with if he were alone or unoccupied. When he was four years old, while his parents were still asleep in the house on early summer mornings, he would get himself up, get dressed, walk to the front door and open it, pull out his low-rider flywheel tricycle and ride up and down the sidewalk pretending he was the mailman or the UPS delivery driver. There couldn't be a cuter and more lovable boy to be seen. He was adored by all.

Michael Senior and Carol, of course, enrolled Michael Junior into the parochial school operated by their synod parish, Salem Church in Florissant. When Michael Junior was in first grade, he worried to himself how difficult math class would be. "I wonder if we will be expected to count all the way up to one hundred," he said to himself. "That could be a real challenge. But I know I am up to the chore."

In third grade, there was another boy in his class named Steven. The teacher, Mrs. Bell, would tease Steven about the various spellings he used for his name when he wrote it on his assignments. Sometimes he would spell it Steven, other times Steve, or Stephen, or Stefan, or Stephan, or Stevie, or Stevon, or Stephaen, or Stevin, or Stevers, or Stevenson, or Stephian. Mrs. Bell thought it was all rather clever and witty. Michael Junior explained to his mother the situation with Steven and the alternative spellings of his name.

"Momma, I wonder if I should have some other spellings of my name, just in case. Who knows, maybe someday I will need them. They would come in handy."

"What do you think those names would be?"

"Well, I already have Mike and Mikey. But maybe I could have Mick, Micky, Mikael, Micha, Mikhail, Micah, or Michel. And, of course, I can always rely on Junior, Number Two, the Second, JR, Deuce, Chip."

"Those are good. But I'm still going to call you Michael Junior."

When Michael Junior was in fourth grade, he noticed homeless people in tents in some areas of St. Louis, and he worried about it.

"Momma, those people are Jesus's children too. We must do something for them."

"Yes, Son. But we need to understand they have other problems too, which is why they are on the street. Problems like addiction and mental problems."

"But, Momma, they are Jesus's children too. They need to be helped."

"Okay, Son. What do you think we can do for them? Let's try."

"Maybe they need money."

"I don't think we should be handing money out to them. I don't think that will solve their problem. Do you have some other ideas?"

"Maybe if we bought clothes for them."

"Okay, Michael Junior. I think that's an idea. But rather than just spending our family money to buy clothes for them, maybe you can think of a way to earn some money on your own to help buy them coats or warm clothes."

And so, Michael Junior came up with an idea. He decided to make some wooden crosses that could be tied to a string or thin leather tether cord; he could then sell the crosses to Salem Church parishioners in the narthex of the church and tell people how the proceeds would go to buy clothes and coats and sweaters for the homeless. He obtained permission from the pastor at Salem to start his project. He worked diligently in the family garage making different sized crosses. He painted some, he stained others. He drilled a small hole on the top of the upright post. He brought a folding table to the church narthex, put up a sign and sat at the table before and after the liturgy. After several months, he collected a few hundred dollars. With his mother, Michael Junior took the money to a thrift store in St. Louis and he purchased coats, sweaters, blankets, long-johns, mufflers, and caps. The following day they drove to the neighborhoods where the homeless people were and he handed out the warm clothing. Many of the homeless people looked at the gear and said, "I don't want that crap. Show me the money," or, "I need money, not that stuff." A few people took the clothes and warm apparel with smug expressions. After Michael Junior had distributed the clothes, he and his mother walked to the car. Michael looked back at the homeless people and he noticed how the people threw the clothes in the street or in the gutter.

"But, Momma, why are they doing that? Don't they want to be warm?"

"Son, we cannot force people to accept what we think is helpful to them. They have a choice too. As you noticed, they said they didn't really want our help. They wanted money so they could spend it the way they wanted. You know, Michael Junior, Jesus himself said, 'The poor we will always have with us.' What he meant is that people with problems, or who are on the downside of life, will be there whether we help them or not. He was not telling us to ignore them, but to realize they are always among us, and we cannot make their problems disappear with a simple formula of handing out money or food or clothes. Surely, we are supposed to help people in need, but sometimes they don't really want our help. And even when we give people help, that doesn't necessarily change the things in life that are creating their difficulties. It is okay, Son; you did the right thing to try to help people who are hurting. But we need to remind ourselves that our attempts to help don't always make their problems go away."

Carol gave birth to a sister for Michael Junior – a beautiful little girl named Andrea.

"Momma, since Papa will be at work, I will help you bring up little Andrea when Papa's not here."

"Oh my, thank you, Michael Junior. I am so grateful for all of your help. She will grow up to be a fine young lady with you as her big brother and her example."

Michael Junior loved to accompany his father on his trips to the hardware store, the gas station, or when they took the dog on a walk. Michael Junior listened attentively to his father's wisdom about proper behavior, decorum and discipline. Michael Senior spent a lot of time teaching his son about the synod and how the synod had played such an important part in the lives of black people. These were the same lessons that Michael Senior had learned from his father when he was a youngster.

"In the 1840s and 1850s, many people were terribly upset about the presence of slavery in America. In July of 1854, a group of a thousand people gathered in Jackson, Michigan under the oak grove. They met to put together plans to bring slavery to an end. No man should ever be chattel property. Is not a man a human being, a son of Jesus? It applies to all people no matter the color of their skin. The people who gathered in Jackson, Michigan began a process of forming groups to agitate for change to force slavery to be abolished. The group that gathered under the oak grove in Jackson organized and established the Republican Party – and at least three hundred of that one thousand people under the oak grove were members of the synod. They pressured to find new political candidates to win office to force this change in the country. Abraham Lincoln was a lawyer in Springfield, Illinois – less than two hours from here in St. Louis. Lincoln was a close friend of the synod, and he became a member the board of trustees of the synod's university in Springfield. In 1860, Abraham Lincoln was elected as the first Republican president of the United States with the promise to end slavery. The southern states left the union of the United States when

Lincoln was elected, and war was declared between the North and the South. Many synod people joined the army of the North to fight against the South to bring an end to slavery. After the end of the Civil War, the synod sent many missionaries to the South to bring the message of the gospel and to introduce the synod to the former slaves. The synod planted many churches throughout the South for black people. And because of this, the synod became an important part of the lives of many black people. We, as black people, are grateful for the synod. We must always work to defend and protect the synod. The synod established two colleges for black people – one in North Carolina and one in Alabama; this was when we as black people didn't have a way to obtain a higher education elsewhere. The synod is important to the black people – even to black people who do not know this history."

"Papa, was Abraham Lincoln a synod person?"

"No, Son, Abraham Lincoln was not a member of the synod, but we respect him dearly. He was a dear friend of the synod. In the late 1850s, Lincoln served as a member of the board of trustees of the synod's university in Springfield, which later became Concordia Seminary, and he helped organize and establish the synod's Memorial Hospital in Springfield. He served as a trustee of the synod's university until he was elected president of the country in November of 1860, and he then stepped down as a trustee."

When Michael Junior was in the fifth grade, he was asked by the pastor of Salem Synod Church if he wished to serve as an acolyte on Sundays. He looked so conscientious and charming, wearing his surplice, as he walked in the processional holding up the gold-plated scriptures, or the processional cross, or the incense censer, or the processional candlestick torch. One Sunday during the entrance, while the congregation sang Hans Hassler, J.S. Bach, and Paul Gerhardt's poignant hymn *O Sacred Head Now Wounded*, Michael carried the processional crucifix down the central aisle in front of the deacon and the pastor; a friend of the Holdens whispered into Carol's ear, "Young Michael is so proper and reverent. We are all very proud of him. He may end up having a calling."

4

In the meantime, the Justice Department's Ku Klux Klan civil complaint against Michael and Carol and their friend Paul Mooney remained on the court docket of the eastern Missouri district of the federal district court. Two years had passed since the complaint was lodged against the defendants. Delays were persistent. The defense filed motions to set a schedule for discovery – the opportunity to collect evidence and open all records for analysis. The U.S. attorney's office dragged their feet and sought slower schedules for the discovery process. When any discovery was executed, not all information was immediately revealed and there wasn't obvious transparency. When defense attorney Larry Korhonen sought confirmation that the president and his charming wife were actually aboard the bus, the U.S. attorney's office obfuscated and avoided providing clear information. New and ongoing discovery procedures were scheduled months away. Larry Korhonen made a motion with the court to prompt a more timely discovery schedule and to enforce transparency. The judge denied the motions. The wheels of justice moved very slowly. Orders come down from the Madam Attorney General in Washington to the U.S. attorney's office in St. Louis to slow-walk the process including discovery.

"Under no circumstances are you to allow pursuit of the passengers on that bus," the Madam Attorney General directed the U.S. attorney in St. Louis. "This is a federal civil complaint by the Justice

Department against three members of the Ku Klux Klan. It is not a complaint from the passengers of that bus. Do you understand me?"

"Yes, Madam Attorney General," the U.S. attorney for the eastern district of Missouri obediently replied. "But Madam Attorney General, don't we lose some credibility by claiming that three black college students are members of the Ku Klux Klan?"

"Now, you listen to me now. And you listen carefully. Do you understand?"

"Yes, Madam."

"This is not a criminal case. This is a civil action. It is your job to pursue this matter seriously and diligently, and to establish the possibilities that these three Klan members were involved in the Klan. We have several hundred agents with the FBI who are members of the Klan who can be expected to fabricate enough evidence to support the claim that the three students were in the Klan. The FBI does this for us all the time. We can always rely on the FBI to come forward with the necessary evidence to pursue federal legal matters. That is their job. There is no requirement to develop this entire case beyond a reasonable doubt. This is a civil matter – it is driven by the preponderance of the evidence. You need to establish enough doubt to make a credible possibility that these three people are members of the Klan. These three individuals are all conservative Republicans who are members of a sanctimonious church cult which has long been associated with the Republican Party. That cult was instrumental in starting the Republican Party in 1854. Look, we're halfway to proving they're Klan members: they're in the Republican Party. We have enormous circumstantial evidence. I expect you to follow this thoroughly and pursue every angle. One of the primary purposes of this entire administration is to find the Ku Klux Klan in every closet, under every stone, hiding behind every bush. I will settle for nothing less than a guilty verdict. Do you understand me?"

The U.S. attorney for the eastern district of Missouri was an obedient sycophant of the new president and his brilliant wife, and readily agreed to diligently participate in the legal strategy established by the Madam Attorney General.

Michael Holden and Paul Mooney met with their attorney, Larry Korhonen.

"This has gone on for more than two years," Michael complained to Larry Korhonen. "Don't you think we can get on with our lives without this cloud hanging over us?"

"This is a federal civil complaint," Korhonen replied. "It is not unusual for cases like this to continue for a lengthy period of time. Michael, just move forward with your life. We are diligently monitoring everything. No need to worry. And Paul, same for you; carry forward with your life." Korhonen, conscious of their frustration, avoided talking about the much-appreciated diligence of the two men regularly paying the monthly fees for legal services for Carol and Michael and Paul.

Michael and Carol were active in the Republican Party. Both had gained their allegiance to the party from their parents who taught them the Republican Party was, to a large degree, the creation of the synod people, dating from July, 1854 when one thousand people gathered under the oak grove in Jackson, Michigan to organize a party to fight against slavery. In the 1960s, when President Lyndon Johnson created his war on poverty spending blitz, he famously said the new program of handing out welfare and government subsidies to black Americans would keep them voting for the Democrats for a hundred years. It seemed to have an impact on the political orientation of many black Americans as they started shifting their traditional allegiance and began voting for and supporting Democrat candidates. Prior to Johnson's welfare state, black people tended to support the Republican Party – dating to the Civil War and the Reconstruction era.

Nevertheless, in St. Louis County, especially the area known as North County, many members of the Republican Party were black and most of those were black synod people.

Michael and Carol became Republican precinct committee leaders in their neighborhood and hosted the party caucuses each year. They also canvassed the neighborhood during election seasons, helping to generate support for party candidates. As precinct committee leaders, they were elected to attend the county convention, and frequently they were voted to be delegates to the congressional district convention and the state convention. This gave them a front row seat to observe some of the sordid corruption the party had to deal with. "While I support the party and the principles of the party, we need to be honest with ourselves. Corruption and malfeasance worm their way into any institution," Michael once said. "It's right out of Shakespeare – the fall of the most esteemed." Michael and Carol observed this several times.

One self-serving man named Bill Willburty was a real estate broker in St. Louis County. He would have given anything to negotiate real estate contracts and deals in Clayton, or Town and Country, or Kirkwood, or Des Peres – the big payday types of deals, but the reality of his prowess in real estate needed to be a little more muted. He was lucky to close deals on small houses or properties in Fenton, Sunset Hills, Mehlville, Lemay, or Arnold. He purposely avoided pursuing any deals in St. Louis City or in North County because the crime rate was higher and the demographics – that is, too many black residents – didn't fit into his vision of the ideal life. Willburty was someone who could be called an establishment Republican – inclined to turn over the actual workings of government and policy to the Democrats and have the Republicans merely play a back seat, secondary role. He generally always supported higher taxes, more government spending, greater regulatory controls, more spending on public education, and stricter

gun controls – which made him a supporting player to Democrat policies. When people would complain if the Republicans lost an election
to a Democrat, he loved to recite, "Oh, the Republicans do much better
as the minor partner in power politics. That way we don't have to bear
responsibility when things get screwed up or go wrong."

Bill Willburty found a way to weasel his way into being appointed
to minor roles of bureaucratic responsibility in the St. Louis County
party apparatus – serving variously as the chairman of the sample
ballot printing committee, or the chairman of the county meeting
refreshments committee, or serving on the county convention logistics
committees which rounded up folding tables and chairs, or serving
on the rules or the credentials committees for the county convention.
Many people found him to be a distasteful character – a bit of a bully,
highly self-impressed, and smug.

Willburty's primary goal in politics was to find a way to become
the Republican National Committeeman for the Missouri State
Republican Party. Each state and U.S. territory elects one national
committeeman and one national committeewoman every four years.
These individuals are the elected officers who make all policy and
operational decisions for the national party. The national committeeman campaign is very competitive since it is a statewide race, and
thus Willburty knew he would need to diligently build a name for
himself and give himself greater appeal state-wide. Consequently, Bill
Willburty decided one year to put his name forth as a candidate to
become chairman of the St. Louis County Republican Party. He had
already developed adequate contacts in the party through his minor
bureaucratic roles; therefore, his identity was already known. He made
some additional outreach by calling every county precinct committee
leader, including Michael and Carol Holden.

When Willburty called Michael, he boasted and implied that
he had worked so diligently for the county party operation and

furthermore he had been a central contributor in building the party's strength in North County and Florissant. Michael, of course, knew Willburty had done the opposite – actively working to diminish North County and ignoring the party presence in Ferguson and Florissant.

"So, Michael, can I count on your vote for me to be county chairman?"

"Well, to be frank, I haven't made a decision about who to vote for in the county chairman race. But I will consider you as an option." Of course, Michael and Carol had no intention of voting for Bill Willburty, whom they perceived as a vile opportunist.

There were four people running to become county chairman, each with his or her own appeal. One was from the southern part of the county, two were from the western part of the county, and Willburty was from the southwestern suburbs of the county. During the election, the vote was split in such a way that Willburty was able to edge out his opponents and he won the election by plurality to become the new chairman of the county party. In the same election, Kimberly Stratton was elected to be county party secretary. Because the chairman and secretary worked so closely together, one thing led to another, and the couple began a romantic relationship. After four months of the affair, Miss Stratton began to have a guilty conscience, not to mention her internal repulsion from Willburty's irritating and priggish personality. She came to the conclusion their relationship was morally wrong, even disgusting, and it must end. She told Willburty she was calling it off, and to avoid conflict, she decided she would resign from her position as county party secretary. Willburty became so enraged he took his pistol and shot Kimberly Stratton in the head and killed her. "There. That will teach her a lesson," he reassured himself. Knowing that his aspiration to become a national committeeman had been destroyed because of his necessity to teach Miss Stratton a thing or two, Bill Willburty decided the most logical and dignified thing for him to do was to kill himself, and so he put the barrel of his pistol up to his head and pulled the trigger.

And then there was the time when Carol and Michael observed the antics of Republican State Representative David Barth, who campaigned as a staunch supporter of family values and even reached out to the members of the synod to rally behind him. Rep. Barth lived a secret life as a participant in orgies with young, supple, nubile girls and boys – and to ensure his proclivities could be saved for posterity, he filmed the escapades. The prosecuting attorney in Jefferson City apparently wasn't sufficiently amused, perhaps because he had not been invited to participate, and so he negotiated a plea deal with Rep. Barth which required the morally upstanding legislator to resign his seat in the state legislature and plead guilty to indecent exposure.

It's not that the Republicans were the only culprits of sleaze and corruption. There was enough to go around – among the Democrats also. George Leach, who served as the Democrat prosecuting attorney in St. Louis City for thirty years, maintained a campaign against pornography and prostitution, proudly shutting down businesses that engaged in the sale of smut including movie houses, bookstores, and shops dealing in indecent sex products and paraphernalia. He enthralled himself by jailing the operators of these businesses for destroying the morals of the community. Mr. Leach regaled in having prostitutes, pimps, and customers of prostitution arrested, tried, convicted and sentenced to prison for dealing in smut and contributing to the moral degradation of life in St. Louis. While vigorously enforcing the laws to protect the city from immoral activity, a peculiar feature of his integrity and personal behavior was discovered: Mr. Leach himself maintained a series of private checking accounts which were filled with money from the city's treasury, and he was able to use these accounts for his own personal use. Later it was discovered dozens of these checks were written to purchase thousands of dollars in pornographic materials. In addition, Mr. Leach was a regular customer of prostitutes and was once even discovered to be renting a hotel room with prostitute companions. And to make matters worse, it was shockingly discovered he personally was a regular customer of pornographic movie houses, outside the borders of the City of St. Louis, of course – in Belleville across the river, and in various towns in St. Louis County. Eventually he was arrested, convicted and served a short time in jail for his missteps and indiscretions.

A group of three Democrat aldermen in St. Louis City were arrested, convicted and sentenced to time in federal prison for accepting bribes over the course of at least ten years; and there is sufficient evidence that the Democrat congressman representing St. Louis City knew all about the sordid scheme and even participated in it. The Democrat county executive in St. Louis County, Steve Schlenk, operated a kickback scheme for at least four years. Contractors for the county were expected to be generous donors to his political campaigns. In some cases, Mr. Schlenk would grant sham contracts to companies who actually performed no services and merely collected payment from the county – with the requirement the companies kicked back large sums to Schlenk's political campaign treasury. Schlenk was known to be arrogant and abusive to political operatives in the county. If Democrats weren't sufficiently obeisant and sycophantic to him, he would publicly humiliate and ridicule them. "The best way to build an empire is to know how to properly use intimidation," Schlenk once confided to one of his toadies. He was eventually convicted for his corruption and served nearly two years in jail.

Limney Grantham, the Democrat St. Louis City prosecuting attorney, following in the footsteps of her one-time predecessor, Prosecutor George Leach, directed one of her staff attorneys to concoct and create evidence which could be used to bring charges of official misconduct against the sitting Republican governor of Missouri. In addition, Miss Grantham continually refuses to file charges against persons who happen to share her political agenda. Frequently, she purposely refuses to bring charges against persons who commit serious violent felonies in the city because they are members of racial groups who she regards as victims of discrimination. As part of her conspiracy to use the prosecuting attorney's office as a vendetta enterprise, she regularly quashes subpoenas, disregards evidence, refuses to press charges, and fails to make serious arguments on cases she wishes to influence, including obtaining results which reflect her political prejudices. For instance, residents who possess firearms for self-defense purposes are consistently charged with firearms infractions, but criminals who use firearms during the commission of violent crimes are never charged with possessing a deadly weapon.

And then there were the discoveries by writer Lincoln Steffans in his 1904 book *The Shame of the Cities*. In his chapter "Tweed Days in St. Louis," he describes the legacy of contemptible abuse by the Democrat Party in St. Louis at the end of the nineteenth century and beginning of the twentieth century. Everything in St. Louis was for sale by the Democrats – justice because courtroom judges were paid off by the Democrats, city services because each city department was controlled by Democrat operatives on the take, the city legislative assembly because nearly every member was a Democrat collecting bribes; all elections held in the city – whether it be a federal, state or municipal election – were corrupt because the election commission was controlled by Democrats with a $30 million rigging and bribery fund. Steffans says only Chicago and Philadelphia could qualify as being more corrupted by Democrats.

"Surely both parties have their failings – it is the nature of politics," Michael Holden, Sr. said to a neighbor in Florissant. "But I believe in the Republican Party, for reasons related to its history and being founded by synod members, as well as the principles it has generally championed. It concerns me that black people have been treated like we are on a plantation operated by the Democrat Party. I hate to see the brothers and sisters going from one historic plantation onto another."

Richard Gephardt was the Democrat congressman representing St. Louis for years in the U.S House of Representatives. He managed to develop a constituency in the Democrat Party by appealing to labor unions and by maintaining a strong anti-abortion position which he calculated would appeal to the large number of Catholics and synod people living in his district. A little more than four years before Michael and Carol and Paul Mooney had their incident with the campaign bus belonging to the Democrat presidential candidate on Interstate 49, Richard Gephardt had a short campaign as a candidate for the Democrat presidential nomination. When he made his announcement that he was declaring his candidacy, he opportunistically declared he was no longer pro-life and that he, from now on, supported abortion. He had been informed by his consultants and handlers that he could never obtain the Democrat presidential nomination if he maintained a pro-life position. Since the position against abortion was not actually part of his personal beliefs, he had no problem changing his views – sort of like turning off a light switch. While campaigning in Iowa, he steered his campaign to the traditional Democrat obsession: how many new spending programs could he come up with? Traditional Democrat voters met together in coffee shops, diners, agriculture implement retailers, feed stores, and other venues to talk about the Democrats running for the nomination.

National Public Radio and Public Broadcasting System set up their cameras and recording devices at one gathering of Democrat voters in a Des Moines diner.

"I like Gephardt. He has a lot of programs. He brings a whole list of new spending," one voter said.

"I agree. What are the programs that Dukakis has, or Paul Simon, or Bruce Babbitt, or Gary Hart? They don't have any programs."

"We need more programs. And, also, they need to show us what their programs are. It's just got to be Gephardt. He has so many programs, too many to enumerate."

Gephardt spent his lengthy career in Congress directing his massive staff to research ways to expand or create new government programs: welfare and assistance to the needy, universal guaranteed income, newspaper industry subsidies, electric vehicle and battery production subsidies, solar panel and windmill subsidies, nutritional assistance and food stamps, utility payment subsidies, disability assistance funding, rent controls, housing vouchers and subsidized public housing, sustainable gardens, higher education tuition assistance and grants, parental paid leave, unemployment subsidies, paycheck protection subsidies, Agriculture Department guarantees, public school grants, health care subsidies, children's health funding, refugee resettlement, funding for job training, disaster recovery, research grants, loan guarantees, law enforcement agency funding, federal employee incentives and retirement pensions, defense industry subsidies, insurance industry subsidies, energy rebates, Planned Parenthood funding, urban renewal grants, financing political campaigns, increasing foreign aid, launching vaccination campaigns, expanding public health plans, launching equity and diversity social engineering, expanding federal land confiscation, expanding EPA restrictions including designating mud puddles on private property to be wildlife wetlands, funding for computer network expansion, medicating all school children for behavioral disorders, subsidizing the sugar industry, liability indemnification for pharmaceutical companies, requiring fluoridation of all water supplies, subsidizing genetically modified food development, subsidizing and promoting use of high fructose corn syrup in 50 percent of food products, perpetual and revolving student loans, guaranteeing pensions for government employees. The list is endless; this comes along with the existence of a large government. The congressman never saw a program he didn't like and he consistently advocated for more bloat.

Gephardt did well in Iowa and won the state caucuses, and even won the South Dakota primary, and finished a strong second place in New Hampshire – all based on his long list of programs. After that, he only won the Missouri primary and was forced to drop out. He sought the Democrat nomination again sixteen years later. He rolled out his enormous list of new programs, but even with his mind-boggling collection of programs, he couldn't gain any traction and made the decision to just get out of electoral politics altogether and pursue a more lucrative enterprise of planning the development of more programs to be promoted to politicians – that is, running a large lobbying firm in Washington.

Since Michael and Carol were active in the Republican Party in St. Louis County, someone from the county party operation told the Holdens they could talk to Missouri Senators Kit Bond or John Ashcroft, both Republicans, about the curious and unbelievable Ku Klux Klan case being pursued by the Justice Department. The chairman of the Missouri Republican Party arranged for Michael and Paul to speak to Senator Bond. They explained the whole affair, the utterly preposterous claim that three black college students were members of the KKK, and the strange civil complaint under the Ku Klux Klan Act of 1871.

"This is truly unbelievable," Senator Bond said. "I am a close friend of the chairman of the Senate Judiciary Committee, Senator Orrin Hatch, and another member of the committee, Senator Chuck Grassley. They will both be interested in this matter, and I think they could start an investigation. In addition, Chuck Grassley has a lot of synod members in his state of Iowa. I think he would be interested in pursuing the possibility that the Justice Department has a goal of targeting synod people. The administration wants everyone to be focused on how concerned they are about the struggles of black people but look at what they are doing to you."

Senator Bond talked to Senator Orrin Hatch about the matter. Hatch, a Republican senator from Utah and the chairman of the Senate Judiciary Committee, had a large, influential senatorial staff. After Bond talked to Hatch about the Ku Klux Klan matter, one of the members of the staff then happened to mention the entire incident and court case to a senatorial aide to Senator John McCain, a liberal senator from Arizona. Quickly, McCain's famous rage and anger erupted – but his anger was not about the Justice Department's pursuit of the case against the Holdens and Paul Mooney. What upset McCain is that the three black residents of Missouri had the audacity to think they could bring some untoward influence into the hallowed halls of the Senate – an institution of immense dignity and integrity. After McCain heard the three suspects were members of the synod, the senator called a close personal friend who had once been the president of the synod's seminary in St. Louis, Dr. Jon Dismashoft. McCain had become associated Dismashoft years before when he needed a religious figure to give him an ecclesiastical pass for an affair of sordid political corruption when the senator tried to protect a California bank that was involved in a massive money laundering scheme. Subsequently, Dr. Dismashoft was investigated by the leadership of the synod because Dismashoft had permitted the seminary to become filled with activists who were spreading political propaganda and controversial dogmatic postulations in their theology courses. Dismashoft was asked by the seminary's board of regents to sign a commitment that he would abide by official church doctrine and prevent faculty agendas which were in conflict with church teachings. Dismashoft flatly refused to comply, and he left the seminary and resigned from the synod under a cloud of ignominy and disgrace. However, he maintained his close friendship with Senator McCain.

McCain said to Dr. Dismashoft, "Jon, I just heard there are three members of your synod church who are being charged in a civil matter for being members of the Ku Klux Klan, and they want the U.S. Senate to intervene on their behalf."

"First of all, Senator McCain, it's not *my* synod church any longer. I left the synod precisely because it is filled with these types of people who are in the Ku Klux Klan."

"Do they actually have Ku Klux Klan members in the synod?" the liberal senator asked.

"They're all over in that church organization. It's essentially a cult of backwoodsy country bumpkins roaming around with pitchforks in hand. That's why I left them."

After hearing the report from Dismashoft, Senator McCain contacted Senator Orrin Hatch and pressured the Utah senator to avoid any investigation or involvement surrounding the three Missouri defendants. He encouraged Hatch to not entertain any publicity from people who think they are victims of the Justice Department's Ku Klux Klan investigations. McCain assured Senator Hatch that he had good sources who indicated the attorney general's actions were well-founded and that there are Klan members in the defendants' church. And then McCain went to the floor of the Senate and gave one of his memorable speeches.

> It has come to my attention that the Justice Department is pursuing legal matters related to a pernicious presence of the Ku Klux Klan in this country. I am aware of one such situation involving three members of a religious cult in Missouri. We have already seen how the Ku Klux Klan burrows into church cults – the situation in Waco, Texas

comes to mind. Fortunately, our very able attorney general tracked down that cult and eliminated the Ku Klux Klan slinking around in their Texas church compound; they were hiding behind the cover of being self-righteous church people. These people were rightly and properly burned to a crisp. We cannot allow the Ku Klux Klan to invade churches all over this country as a cover – a means to hide – their nefarious activities. We need to trust our able and dignified attorney general to track down these sinister forces that wish to commit crimes and insurrection. Our attorney general is a true patriot. Thankfully, we have the wisdom of the Ku Klux Klan Act of 1871 to help track down these offenders and put them out of business. I am certain there is not a senator in these hallowed chambers who does not want to eliminate the Ku Klux Klan from infiltrating our churches. Let's get behind the Justice Department and our wonderful attorney general, and let us support their brave actions.

5

Michael had a reputation in his neighborhood for having one of the nicest, neatest, trimmest, most prim and proper yards in all of Florissant. As a child, he had always taken pride in maintaining his parents' yard in the Baden neighborhood with the greatest attention and care. These habits came with him when he and Carol bought their house in Florissant. He assiduously fertilized in both the spring and the fall. He carefully and diligently tracked down weeds and crabgrass. He devotedly monitored for the presence of lantern-fly and Japanese garden beetles and other pests. He conscientiously grew fresh sweet basil plants in potted planters along his patio every summer, yet constantly worried that the Japanese garden beetle grubs would get into his beloved sweet basil plants. He methodically mowed his show-like yard three days a week and painstakingly brought out his edger after each mowing to ensure the sides of the lawn were perfectly straight. He fastidiously used a leaf blower to clear off any grass clippings from the sidewalks – and to remove any offensive leaves that could have blown onto his property. While Michael had nothing really against trees, he certainly didn't want any of them on his property, nor the litter and refuse they so carelessly generate. When he and Carol selected their house in Florissant, Michael was sure to find a property without any trees, bushes or shrubs. The house to the north did have a few bushes and trees, which Michael did his best to ignore, but he carefully monitored any leaf or needle debris that would make its way onto his pristine lawn.

Some neighbors found it all a bit too finicky and overdone. Others thought it was simply magnificent. Those who did find it over the top, would occasionally tease Michael about his perfect yard – but it was all good-natured humor, meant to poke a little fun with him. On rare occasions, high school pranksters in the middle of the night would bring trash or a bag of grass clippings to dump on his yard – just providing Michael another reason to indulge his seemingly award-winning landscape. Whenever anyone asked Michael about how to control Japanese beetles or other pests, he would happily go through an entire lecture and presentation about garlic, vinegar or soapy applications, or even using traps to capture the irritating insects.

Michael knew pride wasn't an honorable or an upright virtue, and so he resisted the temptation to have too much self-satisfaction in his yard. He reminded himself it had more to do with discipline – the treasured, most notable feature of the synod people. Generally, synod people in the neighborhood did not have pristine lawns like Michael's, but another characteristic of synod people is to resist the temptation of envy – so the synod residents of the area looked at the Holden property with a sense of awe and respect as part of the abiding synod tradition of recognizing a life that is meet and right – that is, salutary and a "job well done."

Michael frequently enjoyed sitting on his front porch along with Carol, or sometimes with Michael Junior and Andrea, and peacefully resting in contentment – presiding over his neatly manicured yard. One early evening, while sitting in peace, observing his front lawn, Carol took a phone call and burst into hysterical sobbing. Michael quickly approached Carol to discover the problem and commotion.

Earlier in the day on that June Tuesday, Keith Newland, the synod friend of the Holdens who worked as an accountant for an auto and truck parts supplier, took a Metropolitan Transit Agency bus from the auto and truck parts company to the location of one of the company's vendors. Keith needed to pick up some documents for the purpose of accurate record keeping in his accounting files. After he had obtained the records, Keith left the business and was waiting at the street corner to cross so that he could catch the bus for his return trip. The sidewalk had a fair amount of pedestrian traffic and noise. While Keith was waiting for the traffic signal to change to be able to cross the street, a Metropolitan Police squad car wildly and frantically pulled up next to Keith, screeching to a stop. The police officer jumped out of the squad car and rapidly, aggressively and abruptly approached Keith – yelling, "Stop! Don't move! Put your hands up!" Keith raised his arms.

"What is this about, sir?" Keith asked.

"Quiet! Don't resist," Officer Sean Holland replied.

"I'm not resisting. What's going on?"

"Stop! Don't resist. I'm warning you."

"Sir, I'm not resisting. What are you doing?"

"Stop arguing. Why are you arguing and resisting?"

"I said I am not resisting. What is going on?"

A passerby observed the exchange, and he spoke to the officer. "Are you here about the robbery at the bookstore? That is not the man. That's not him."

Officer Holland interrupted and responded to the passerby. "Shut up! Now! Stop interfering."

"But officer, that's not him."

Quickly, without warning, Officer Holland took both of his hands and began choking Keith's neck, strangling him. He didn't let go until Keith's body went limp and he dropped to the pavement.

"Excuse me, sir," the passerby called out. "That old man is not the suspect. The guy who robbed the bookstore was much younger – maybe twenty-five or thirty, and he was big and muscular."

Officer Holland replied in a shout, "Shut up! You don't know what you're talking about. This man was resisting arrest and preventing me from obtaining information about the situation."

The clerk at the bookstore came out of the store to see the commotion. "Are you here about the robbery?"

Officer Holland replied that he was responding to the robbery call. A full twenty minutes before, the clerk had called the police to report a robbery which had just occurred. With this timeline, Officer Holland made it to the location between twenty and twenty-five minutes after the reported robbery of the bookstore. The clerk had reported the robber was a black male, between twenty-five and thirty, a muscular build, wearing jeans and a hoodie. Keith Newland, who had been detained and strangled to death by Officer Sean Holland, was a black male, elderly in his late sixties, was slender and potentially frail, and was wearing dress trousers, a dress shirt, a necktie and a sport jacket.

The clerk at the bookstore immediately returned to the store and called emergency services for an ambulance to be dispatched. Keith was already dead – asphyxiated by Officer Holland. An ambulance arrived and took the corpse to the Barnes-Jewish Hospital for medical evaluation.

Doris Newland was beside herself and couldn't understand what occurred. The Metropolitan Police would not answer her questions and said the matter was under investigation. The media, including the *Post-Dispatch* and the area television stations generally had a servile relationship with the police department and were hesitant to pursue the incident with too much interest or investigatory fervor. Carol Holden immediately went to Doris Newland's house to provide comfort and consolation. Carol called the pastor of Zion Cathedral, where Doris and Keith attended. Carol explained Doris had not been given enough information to know what occurred to Keith. The pastor suggested Carol call her attorney who had been handling her Ku Klux Klan case and maybe he could obtain some rudimentary information from the police.

Carol's attorney, Larry Korhonen, contacted the Metropolitan Police Department and was not provided with much information. Korhonen spoke to a reporter from Channel 5 who explained he had sources that told him this is what occurred: The bookstore had been robbed twenty to twenty-five minutes before the police arrived. The suspect was a young, muscular black man wearing jeans and a hoodie. While Keith was waiting to cross the street to catch his bus, the police arrived – twenty to twenty-five minutes after the robbery. Because Keith was a black man standing near the bookstore, the officer jumped to the conclusion he must be the suspect – not taking into account the unlikelihood a suspect would linger around outside the store he had just robbed. The police report suggested Keith resisted arrest and the officer strangled Keith to subdue him.

Doris was beside herself and was unable to communicate clearly.

"What in the world can be done?" Carol asked Korhonen.

"Let me speak to my source at Channel 5," Korhonen said. "Perhaps we can get the media to ask the commissioner of police to call a press conference."

Police Commissioner Arthur Dillard, who had previously served as the chief of police in Belleville, Illinois, just across the Mississippi River from St. Louis, agreed to hold a press conference to address the situation surrounding the death of Keith Newland.

"The decedent died after he resisted arrest while our officer was responding to a robbery at a bookstore," Dillard told the media.

"Why was it assumed Mr. Newland was the robbery suspect when it had occurred twenty minutes before, and he didn't match the description?"

"That is under investigation"

"Why was Mr. Newland detained by Officer Holland?"

"That's under investigation. It appears the suspect was resisting arrest."

"How did Mr. Newland die?"

"That's under investigation. He apparently had a breathing problem, perhaps he suffered from pulmonary disease."

"Has the police officer been involved in other incidents where suspects have died?"

"I have no comment on that."

A reporter from *The Monitor*, the newspaper in East St. Louis, asked, "Didn't you have a similar incident like this in Belleville when you were the chief there? A drunken man was murdered by a police officer when he entered the police station for booking."

"That's not accurate. And the grand jury did not make the conclusions you are asserting. Are there any other questions?"

"What has happened to Officer Holland?"

"He is on paid leave while this is investigated."

Dillard was peppered with a few other perfunctory questions, and he said, "Okay. That's enough. I have nothing more to say."

The matter was turned over to the St. Louis City prosecuting attorney for review. A grand jury was called to assess the information, the narrative, medical records, and the evidence to determine if an indictment should be presented. The grand jury concluded there was not sufficient evidence to bring forth an indictment and determined that Officer Holland used appropriate force to subdue a suspect who was resisting arrest.

Doris Newland was devastated, and after Keith's funeral, she decided she would put her house on the market and move to Ste. Genevieve, Missouri, about one hour south of St. Louis, where her daughter lived. Since Doris's home was in the St. Louis Place neighborhood, housing sales are slow, and it took a year for her property to find a buyer.

* * *

Anne Newland, Doris and Keith's daughter, was an artist who participated in the artists' colony of Ste. Genevieve – a small town founded in the mid-eighteenth century along the banks of the Mississippi River. The town always had a population of black residents; in the early years, they worked in the lime quarries and kilns in the region. In 1930, there was a race riot – a four-day disturbance that ultimately forced nearly three hundred black residents out of the town. In more recent years, as the village became an artists' colony and a hub of the arts – including clay work, pottery and tile-making crafts and ceramics, painting, and sculpture – there has been a resurgence of several notable black artists into the area, pursuing the goal of rediscovery of the black cultural heritage of the region. The winding roads near Ste. Genevieve are filled with small, quaint cabin-like structures built in the French creole colonial style. Particularly notable are the vertical wooden post-style and the posts-on-a-sill style which cause the buildings to be on slightly elevated lifts or stilts – allegedly to avoid river flooding, however, they were not always able to protect the structures as the Mississippi regularly overflows its banks. The walls of the buildings are made of upright posts which do not support the floor. The floor is supported by separate stone pillars and joists. This style of construction differs from American colonial cabins which were built with horizontal logs.

The creole colonial cabins all have steeply pitched roofs, high interior ceilings, and quaint wrap-around porches. The dozens of artists' cabins are used as living quarters and studios – commonly used by painters, sculptors, and pottery artists applying their skills outside in their front lots abutting the county roads. It's a unique opportunity for people driving on the roads to watch the artists performing their vocations in front of their cabins and studios. The cabin Anne Newland lived in once belonged to Charles Nerinckx, a Belgian missionary who lived in Ste. Genevieve in 1810 before establishing a Catholic order of nuns who called themselves the Weeping Sisters at the Foot of the Cross, housed near Lebanon, Kentucky. He sought to establish an order of nuns who could compete with a rival order of nuns – the Beseeching Sisters of Everlasting Sorrow – who came to Berea, Kentucky from a convent in Leavenworth, Kansas. The Beseeching Sisters laid claim to eastern Kentucky as their domain and even opened a hospital and were not interested in being under the autocratic control of missionary Charles Nerinckx. So upset was Nerinckx by the flippantly indepen-dent, disrespectful, and rebellious attitude of the Beseeching Sisters of Everlasting Sorrow that he organized the Weeping Sisters at the Foot of the Cross, and he ordered his newly established order of nuns to open their own hospital to compete with the Leavenworth-based invading nuns, but the Weeping Sisters were never able to successfully initiate a medical facility.

Anne Newland's arrival in Ste. Genevieve was a circuitous venture that took her from her youth in St. Louis, to a city on the outskirts of Kansas City for her college studies in art, and then into downtown Kansas City for her first foray as a professional artist. Anne studied art at St. Mary's College of Leavenworth in Leavenworth, Kansas – a college founded by the famed, or infamous, Beseeching Sisters of Everlasting Sorrow, who were the order of nuns who defied missionary Charles Nerinckx. Once Anne completed her studies and her degree in art at Leavenworth, she discovered an opportunity to go to Kansas City and help build the Crossroads Art Community. Anne opened a studio for her own painting, and she invited sculptors and Arts and Crafts designers to join her in her space. In a city with its primary signature being its endless miles of urban decay, ghetto, slum, overcrowded and crumbling tenements and hovels, there are a couple of areas that have been rebuilt from the horrendous distress started in 1835. Massive swaths of the decaying, run-down, decrepit city are filled with collapsing structures, squalor, blight, and poverty with streets and sidewalks that haven't been repaved or rebuilt in more than seventy-five years, and public infrastructure, such as powerlines and water and sewage systems, that haven't been upgraded in nearly a century. In the early 1980s, a group of artists attempted to set up an arts district near the old, decaying train station and the dilapidated freight warehouses. Anne Newland was one of these pioneers.

On one July evening, Anne Newland was in downtown Kansas City with her boyfriend, and they witnessed the collapse of a large hotel, the Hyatt Regency, which killed 114 people and seriously injured 216 bystanders. Anne immediately thought to herself, "Even the new buildings in this god-forsaken rathole of a city are collapsing." The Hyatt Regency, while having the appearance of a fancy, new, modern building, was in reality just another slapdash structure – seemingly the universal principle of Kansas City's architectural design and construction practices. The forty-story building was constructed with a cheap, bargain-basement, low-budget, ill-conceived design approach. Engineering principles of weight-bearing load were not applied, mimicking the same design schemes used for the hundreds of slums and destitution of the 1840s and 1850s that Kansas City is so well-known for – once again proving the famous Kansas City adage that "the newer slums are not really distinguishable from the older." During construction of the Hyatt Regency, there were many design and engineering faults including the collapse of a roof, the pulling apart of structural walls, and the precarious, unsupported skywalk balcony, but the city fathers and the inspectors were driven to achieve some much-needed eyewash for their pathetic, grimy, worn-out town and they just overlooked the flaws – once again applying a reliable Kansas City principle that a new coat of paint will adequately cover over all the destitution and distress.

After the tragedy, Anne told her boyfriend that she would go ahead and open her Kansas City studio because of previous promises and commitments, but once she had the studio running, she intended to escape the misery, agony, and gloom of the vast, rundown plantation shantytown of Kansas City. That is what brought her to Ste. Genevieve, and while she was heart-stricken by the unjust murder of her father, she was delighted to be reunited with her mother in her southern Missouri art enclave.

6

When Michael Junior was in fifth grade, his parents took him to see a concert of J.S. Bach motets performed at the synod church the Holdens attended – Salem Church in Florissant. Daphne Probst, the wife of the president of the synod, was a world-renowned performer of J.S. Bach vocal music and she regularly organized and sang in Bach concerts in synod churches throughout the country, which were frequently broadcast on the synod's radio station KFUO. Mrs. Probst scheduled a performance of the motet *O Jesu Christ, meins lebens licht,* BWV 118, as well as two other motets for the Salem Church concert. Mrs. Probst was accompanied by a small ensemble from the Forte Orchestra of St. Louis and a choir. The motet *O Jesu Christ, meins lebens licht* features performances by three sackbuts, which are similar to the modern trombone. During Bach's lifetime, it was probably performed with an instrument Bach identified as the *lituus* – a brass instrument that no longer exists and there aren't even any drawings of it. It is presumed the *lituus* was a horn that was six-and-a-half feet in length, with a flared bell on the end. Michael Junior was so thrilled to watch the sackbuts play, he asked his parents after the performance if he could learn to play one.

While at the concert, the Holdens had the opportunity to meet Mrs. Probst, who was endearing and reached out to talk to both Michael Junior and Andrea. Also in attendance was Alice Ploughmaster, the former mayor of East St. Louis. Michael Senior approached Mrs. Ploughmaster.

"Mrs. Ploughmaster, I don't know if you remember me. I'm Michael Holden. You came to my wedding at St. Paul's College Hill."

"Oh, yes, I remember you. I have known Carol and her parents for years from St. Paul's College Hill. How are you, Michael?"

"I am well, thank you. This is my son, Michael."

"So, there are two Michael Holdens," she said to Michael Junior. "What did you think of the concert?"

"I loved it," Michael Junior said. "And I am going to learn to play that horn. And then maybe I can play in a Bach concert."

Mrs. Ploughmaster whispered to Michael Senior that his son was so adorable and precious. "The world is in such good hands with a sweet young man like that – ready to lead us into the future," she said.

"Thank you, Mrs. Ploughmaster." He thought to himself, no wonder everyone loves her; she is so charismatic and charming to each person she meets.

The synod parochial schools in the northern areas of St. Louis City and in North County share an instrumental music education program, and one of the teachers is a brass instrument instructor. Michael Senior was put in touch with the brass instrument teacher and Michael explained his son saw a Bach motet played on the sackbut and he wanted to learn to play it.

"Well, we don't really teach the sackbut particularly, but the trombone is a close relative of the sackbut, and your son could certainly begin to learn to play the trombone. Let's set up a lesson."

Michael Junior began learning the trombone and he studied and practiced diligently. Generally, Carol had Michael Junior wear button dress shirts and nice slacks. The trombone teacher once said to Carol, "Michael is so proper. What a fine young gentleman. He sits up serious and straight; he is so correctly focused and conscientious. And he is attired like a true gentleman. The synod will be in such good hands with a young man like that to lead us. You are obviously devout synod parents and you have brought up a model Christian young man."

When Michael Junior was asked by people at church what musical instrument he was studying, he would reply, "I am currently studying the trombone, soon to be the sackbut."

One day after classes ended at Salem Synod School, a friend in Michael Junior's fifth grade class asked Michael to visit his house and they could do some things together.

"Do you mean play musical instruments together?" Michael asked.

"No, I was thinking of catching butterflies or exploring at the creek."

When the school day ended, the pair rode their bikes to Freddy's house. Freddy's mother set out glasses of milk and graham crackers as a snack for the boys. After they had eaten, the boys went out with butterfly nets to see if they could catch some butterflies. After the butterfly hunt ended, without a single catch, only a moth, they headed to the creek. They explored to see if they could find some crawdads but didn't come up with any. However, they did get their trousers and their shoes muddy. When their adventures concluded, Michael Junior rode his bike to his home. As he came in the front door, Carol was frantic.

"Michael Junior, where have you been? I've been so worried about you."

"Oh, I'm sorry, Momma. I completely forgot to call you. I went to Freddy's house, and we hunted for butterflies, and we went to the creek to see if we could find crawdads."

Carol began to cry.

"Momma, what is wrong?"

"I was so worried about you. I didn't know what happened. I don't want anything bad to happen to you. You are my precious gem."

"Is Andrea your precious gem too?"

"Yes, dear, I am a very lucky woman. I have two precious gems."

"Is Papa a precious gem?"

"No, he is not a precious gem because he is not my child." She continued to sob quietly. "He is my husband. So that means he is my sweetheart."

Two weeks before Christmas, four students from Michael Junior's class decided on their own to walk through the neighborhood and sing Christmas carols, going door-to-door. Michael, Freddy, Tina, and Marie made plans to do caroling on a cold winter evening. Michael Junior told his mother that he wanted to dress nicely in a tie and a sport jacket.

"And you will need to be bundled up to stay warm," Carol advised.

The foursome walked through the neighborhood with an effort to be sure to stop at as many synod families as possible. They sang the standard fare – *Angels We Have Heard on High, Silent Night, Joy to the World, God Rest Ye Merry Gentlemen, We Three Kings.* Nearly every house invited the young, ardent quartet into their homes to share hot chocolate or treats. The synod families, in particular, were very welcoming and even gave gifts to the singers.

After the caroling, one neighbor, Monica Hamilton, called Carol to share her impressions.

"Carol, I can't even express to you what a sweet young son you have. What an amazing young man. Not only is he the cutest boy I can think of, but his demeanor, his disposition, his personality, his poise – everything about that boy – is simply adorable. He is the most astonishing young man I can think of. If I had a daughter his age, I would be hoping and praying she could find a way to be around him. You and Michael should be so terribly proud. Our synod, and the world in general, is in such good hands with your son at the helm. Carol, how did you do it?"

"Oh my, Monica, thank you so much. We did nothing extraordinary. I give all the credit to God and the synod."

* * *

When young Michael was finishing second grade at Salem School, it had been more than seven years since the federal complaint against Carol, Michael and Paul was filed, accusing them of civil violations of the Ku Klux Klan Act of 1871. The wheels of justice turned very, very slowly. Every four to six months the federal judge presiding over the case in the St. Louis federal courthouse would schedule a pretrial status conference to assess the progress of the case. Usually, at those times, the assistant U.S. attorney would file motions for a continuance or a delay of some kind. Occasionally, the U.S. attorney would file requests for additional evidence or discovery. For instance, during the course of the seven years, the U.S. attorney's office requested all information related to the defendants' participation in political activities including memberships in political, social or activist organizations, as well as specifying any events they may have attended over the past twenty years. The prosecutors wanted details of the defendants' political views on a scope of topics – ranging from economics, education, environmental activism, feminism, sexual orientation, abortion, class consciousness, Marxism, equality and equity, criminal justice, carbon pollution, welfare and public assistance, health care, government spending, and so forth. The prosecution demanded the defendants define the synod's doctrinal or teaching positions on a plethora of moral and social agendas. The defense attorney, Larry Korhonen, made boilerplate objections that the defendants' political, speech and religious views were protected by the First Amendment. The judge, Hedrick J. Winters, noted the objections, but overruled these procedural objections because the Ku Klux Klan Act of 1871 specifically exempts First Amendment protections including those related to freedoms of speech, association, the press, assembly, religious beliefs, or redress of grievances.

At several conferences in the courthouse, defense attorney Korhonen filed a series of motions as part of the defense discovery to collect evidence. One request was to discover the identities of the people aboard the campaign bus. Judge Winters denied the discovery request because the current president was invoking executive privilege over that information. Korhonen argued the discovery should apply to those who were not the president or his lovely wife. The judge denied the request to identify any passengers aboard the bus.

During one of the pretrial deposition phases, the government presented several witnesses who claimed to be FBI undercover agents who had allegedly infiltrated the Ku Klux Klan. The U.S. attorney's office insisted the agents remain anonymous and that during their depositions they would be shrouded behind a screen so their identities could not be revealed. In addition, the prosecution requested the voices of the undercover agents be electronically modified so their identity would not be revealed. The defense objected and insisted such anonymity would make the credibility of the witnesses suspect and questionable. Judge Winters, in short order and in standard routine, denied all of the defense objections.

During the secret witness depositions of the undercover FBI agents – a lengthy process that went on for many months – the witnesses were asked hundreds of questions about Ku Klux Klan membership.

"How many people are members of the Ku Klux Klan?" Korhonen probed.

"I don't know," the witness said in an electronically altered voice.

"How many would you estimate – nationally and in the State of Missouri?"

"I don't know."

"Would you say that it is more than five?"

"I really don't have any idea."

"Isn't it true the Ku Klux Klan was created as an enforcement arm for the Democrat Party during the Reconstruction era?" Korhonen asked.

"I have no idea. I don't know the history of the Ku Klux Klan."

"Did you have contact with Ku Klux Klan members in multiple states or only in the State of Missouri?"

"I am not certain because I didn't ask what state people are from."

"So, that implies that you met with more than one person. Correct?"

"Not necessarily."

"Did you ever meet any other Ku Klux Klan member who was *not* an agent of the FBI?"

"I don't know, but I don't think so."

"So, in other words, every other Ku Klux Klan member was an undercover agent with the FBI. Correct?"

"That's possible, but I am not certain," the witness replied.

"By what information do you have knowledge the defendants are members of the Ku Klux Klan?"

"I am aware they attended certain political meetings and gatherings where there were Ku Klux Klan members present," the witness answered.

"What were those meetings? What organization or group? How was it identified?" Korhonen asked.

"The Republican Party."

"And you know for a fact there were members of the Ku Klux Klan present at these meetings?"

"Yes," the FBI witness said.

"How do you know?"

"I was present in the meeting."

"In other words, because you, as a Ku Klux Klan member, were in the meeting, there was at least one member of the Klan present. Is that correct?

"Yes, at least one," the undercover FBI witness responded. Because of the electronic voice modification, it couldn't be determined if the witness had any appreciation for irony.

The absurdity of these deposition interviews continued for months, even years. The defense attorney, Larry Korhonen, was convinced the FBI undercover agents were the only members of the Ku Klux Klan and every meeting or event they attended – simply because they were present – transformed the event into a Klan event. It seemed so preposterous he didn't see how the case could move forward. Korhonen made detailed motions to dismiss based upon the "guilt by association" argument – and to make it even more ludicrous and farcical, the only Ku Klux Klan members were undercover FBI agents – implying the entire affair is a very sloppy form of entrapment. The judge denied the motions to dismiss and lectured the defense attorney that the charges were so serious, the case must move forward. However, the judge was never inclined to see to it that the case move forward with any urgency.

7

Immediately after the murder of Keith Newland, Carol and Michael made arrangements to pick up Doris Newland every Sunday morning and bring her to Zion Cathedral for church services and on alternating weeks to drive her to the Holden family's parish, Salem Synod Church in Florissant. One Sunday morning, while driving along West Florissant Avenue to pick up Doris, Michael drove past an old, abandoned gas station – just a tiny, cinderblock, square building with white paint peeling off the exterior walls, probably constructed in the late 1930s. Likely, it had not been in business since the 1960s. However, the entire flat roof of the building was covered with shiny, new satellite dishes – it looked like eight or ten dishes of various sizes. In the fenced-in lot surrounding the building, there were a dozen other new satellite dishes on poles with cables running from the satellite dishes into the small, empty gas station building. The windows on the building were fogged with grime and dirt accumulated over the years of abandonment. There were no vehicles in the lot.

"That's quite a sight," Michael quipped.

"Papa, what is that all about?" asked Michael Junior.

"That, Son, is a Korean CIA transmission station. Not only does the Korean CIA have satellite transmission stations in the United States, but Cuba has spy operations all over America, and the Chinese Communist Party even operates their own private police stations throughout the country so they can arrest Chinese people and kidnap them and take them back to China. And China also has a network of secret bioweapons labs in America."

Michael Junior had a stunned, perplexed expression on his face. "But, Papa, I thought the South Koreans were our friends. Why would they be spying?"

"Yes, Son, they are our friends. But you need to know how government intelligence agencies work. Their view is that everyone is suspect. In their method of thinking, your friend is the first object of your suspicion. It's not just the totalitarians and communist countries in the world doing this. The American intelligence system does the same thing. The Democrat Party in America created a secret terrorist enforcement group to target and terrorize black people in this country and then a few years after it was created, President Wilson endorsed this terrorist group. That was the Ku Klux Klan. Years later, President Truman ordered American spies to destroy the reputation of General Douglas MacArthur to prevent MacArthur from stopping the communists in China during the Korean War. President Truman liked what the communists were doing in China, and he thought it might be a good idea to try something like that in America. Later, the FBI spied on Martin Luther King, Jr. and tried to sabotage the civil rights movement in the South during the 1960s. In the 1950s and 1960s, the FBI was secretly giving people brain-altering psychotropic drugs without their knowledge as part of a plot to transform the population into a bunch of mind-numbed zombies and listless puppets. The FBI and the CIA spied on President Kennedy and probably arranged to have him assassinated in 1963. The CIA spied on and arranged to assassinate presidents of countries in Central America and South America and Vietnam and Greece. This is the danger of secret intelligence agencies. All government intelligence operations – whether foreign intelligence or American intelligence operations – have a voracious appetite for data and information. Their systems cannot work without data. If they are going to succeed in controlling everything in the world – determining who has power, who makes money and who does not, manipulating what people think and what they believe, who will have freedom and who will be slaves – they must endlessly collect every ounce of information in existence. That's what those satellite transmission stations are all about, Son."

Michael Senior carefully avoided mentioning his own experience with the FBI after the incident on Interstate 49 north of Joplin. They arrived at Doris Newland's house to pick her up for church services.

During the divine liturgy at Zion Cathedral, while the congregation sang Johann Cruger and Paul Gerhardt's touching hymn *O Lord How Shall I Meet You*, Michael Junior drifted off into some daydreaming, prompted by his father's lesson in the car about intelligence organizations and influence peddling. It was only a couple years ago that the board of governors of Northeast Missouri State University in Kirksville, just three hours northwest of St. Louis, voted to change the name of the university to Truman State University and Michael Senior went into a private verbal tirade, accusing the bureaucratic board of governors who run the college of being a "bunch of liberal toadies trying to slurp up the leavings of the elite plutocrats who run the country." He claimed the board of governors changed the name of the old, venerable college so they could heap cringing obeisance onto the sordid, shameful memory of Harry S. Truman – the vile character the Democrats yearned to be the most substantial native son of Missouri. Michael Holden, Sr. was outraged that the conspirators sought to diminish and belittle the state's true heroic figures in the slavish attempt to recover the tarnished reputation of one of the most despicable, self-serving political crooks to ever live in the state – a deceitful, mean-spirited, racist man who steered his way into the office of the presidency of the country.

Michael Senior evoked the glorious memory of Mark Twain, John Pershing, Laura Ingalls Wilder, Scott Joplin, George Washington Carver, Daniel Boone, William Clark, Augustus Tolton, Omar Bradley, T.S. Eliot, Tom Organ, Homer G. Phillips, Dale Carnegie, Calamity Jane, Kit Carson, Thomas Hart Benton, Langston Hughes, Josephine Baker, Chuck Berry, Yogi Berra, Joe Garagiola, Casey Stengel. Speaking of the Northeast Missouri State University board of governors who were in an entranced stupor over Truman, Michael barked, "And these sniveling, whimpering, simpering fools are driven by the urge to somehow rehabilitate the tarnished stature of that scoundrel and change the fine, upstanding name of a college in his honor. Contemptible!"

Truman was driven by two primary interests – himself and the Democrat Party. In the eccentricity of the county government structure surrounding Kansas City, the executive branch of Jackson County is called the "County Court." In most counties in the nation, this body would be called the board of county commissioners or board of county supervisors. In Jackson County, the members of the county court are called "judges." Presumably they invoked these self-impressed, elite-sounding names because they would possibly conjure up the images of the southern plantations that the power brokers of Kansas City were so enchanted by. Truman gained the confidence of the Pendergast boss-style machine of Jackson County, run by a corrupt godfather named Tom Pendergast. It's not been made clear why Tom Pendergast selected Harry Truman to become a judge for the county – it most likely stems from a pledge Truman must have made to filter hundreds of thousands of dollars in kickbacks and bribes to the boss, which is how others obtained political positions or appointments in Jackson County. All things considered (as NPR's Jake Pepper might put it), it doesn't matter what the reason is that Truman was handpicked to be a Jackson County executive, because what becomes completely clear is that Truman was a tool and obedient sycophant of the elite power brokers in the Democrat Party – and this is the reason they selected him as the Democrat candidate for the Senate from Missouri. Truman soon became a close associate of the segregationists and racists who dominated the Democrat Party from the Deep South, because that represented his personal pattern of behavior and his own political views. In Washington, Truman quickly became friendly with Colonel Edward M. House, the one-time chief of staff of former President Woodrow Wilson. President Wilson himself had been a rabid racist and a sponsor of the Ku Klux Klan. Many of the racist proclivities of Wilson were presumed to have been encouraged by Colonel House. After Wilson's death, Colonel House remained in Washington to ply his racist influence within the Democrat Party, and Truman was naturally entranced. During his sordid association with Colonel House, Truman was drawn to the nostalgia of his own working relationship with the Ku Klux Klan in Kansas City, as well as during his senatorial campaign in Missouri. President Roosevelt was in ill health before his 1944 presidential campaign and White House insiders were aware that Roosevelt wasn't likely to live through a fourth term. With knowledge that the vice president would ascend to the presidency, panic ensued because Roosevelt's sitting vice president, Henry Wallace, was a socialist and held radical views about politics, economics and social policy. While Roosevelt wasn't particularly alienated by Vice President Wallace's political preferences, he was pressured by Democrat Party dignitaries to at least allow another vice-presidential nominee to be nominated at the upcoming Democrat National Convention in Chicago. Roosevelt was partial to White House adviser James Byrne to be a nominee. Byrne was a committed racist and white supremacist from South Carolina and would have faced a difficult time generating enough delegate votes at the national convention. When Truman resisted initial promptings that he allow his name to be put into nomination for the vice presidency, Roosevelt called and told Truman that if he refused to run, it merely proved that Truman didn't care about the health of the Democrat Party. That comment hit a raw nerve for Truman since his only personal interests were himself and the party. Vice President Wallace remained the favorite at the Chicago convention; in the first round of voting, Wallace received the greatest number of votes, but not the necessary majority. Rumors spread through the convention hall that Truman was associated with the Ku Klux Klan which would cause certain factions of the party to be inclined to abandon Truman. To ensure the predetermined outcome, and using age-old tactics employed by the corrupt Philadelphia and Chicago party machines, the Democrat overlords at the convention reliably returned to their standard practices, and they locked out of the convention hall enough delegates to be able to arrange the adequate number of votes to ensure Truman would be able to win the majority after two more rounds of ballots.

When Truman ascended to the presidency because of Roosevelt's death in April of 1945, just two months after the inauguration, Truman quickly turned to like-minded supporters to fill his new adminis- tration, including racist and Ku Klux Klan supporter James Byrne from South Carolina to serve as secretary of state and segregationist Fred M. Vinson from Kentucky, a former colleague from his days in Congress, to become treasury secretary. Truman ordered the U.S. government to secretly develop an apocalyptic weapon to be used against the Japanese, but even by the time the nuclear bomb had been created, Japan was on the verge of defeat because of the toll of the Pacific war and the ongoing military struggles with the Soviet Union and China. Truman directed the U.S. military to simply ignore the precarious and unstable condition of the Japanese regime: just move forward with the nuclear weapon as a means of executing revenge for the Pearl Harbor catastrophe. The decision by Truman in August, 1945 to use two nuclear bombs on Japan could be history's most extreme, outlandish, unparalleled, inappropriate, disproportionate, and incongruous action in international political affairs. Human civilization was vaporized in mere seconds for the sake of revenge – when the victims were, by all accounts, already at the edge of defeat and prepared to surrender. Churchill's military advisor, General Hastings Ismay, was revolted by Truman's decision and said it was clear to all military strategists that Japan was tottering and was on the verge of surrender. To General Ismay, it was purely about vindictive, hateful revenge. Truman will need to face his maker for that decision, Ismay mused. Bob Caron, the tail gunner of the aircraft that dropped the bomb over Hiroshima, said the horror he witnessed was a "peep into Hell."

Truman was a follower of Woodrow Wilson, partially because of the training he received from Wilson's adviser, Colonel Edward House. Roosevelt himself was a devotee of Woodrow Wilson and followed Wilson's admonition that Congress was no longer necessary in a modern country – a nation should be run by an elite cadre of experts and unelected bureaucrats. Truman was also a believer in Wilson's concept that the American people are a herd of idiotic sheep waiting for someone to come along to push them around. In response to this vision, Truman created his proudest achievement in 1947 – the national intelligence security state. With the National Security Act, Truman was able to have available to himself a new, supersecret, powerful spy agency – the CIA – which could roam through the globe assassinating people at will and clandestinely collecting private and sensitive information from individuals, companies, and governments. When the Korean War was nearing a victory by General Douglas MacArthur, Truman ordered his Secretary of the Air Force, Stuart Symington, to surreptitiously collect information about MacArthur and his plans. When MacArthur believed the U.S. forces could successfully invade China and eliminate the communist takeover there, Truman instantly fired MacArthur because Truman held his own admiration, awe, and respect for the small cadre of Chinese Communists and their merciless ability to terrorize and manipulate the pathetic masses – a view about people that Truman harvested from Woodrow Wilson.

Truman's natural tendency of harboring contempt for black people was demonstrated by his vocal disapproval of Martin Luther King, Jr. Truman encouraged J. Edgar Hoover of the FBI to put Dr. King under surveillance and to sabotage his civil rights efforts. In April of 1952, steelworkers went on national strike in a labor dispute with nine large steel companies. Truman, inspired by the Chinese and Soviet communist approach to the existence of industry, naturally responded by attempting to nationalize the steel industry. After all, a government should just control everything, as Wilson had previously advocated. By this time, Truman had appointed his ideological sycophant, Fred M. Vinson, to be the chief justice of the Supreme Court. Truman believed he could rely on Vinson to rubberstamp Truman's effort to nationalize the steel industry. Indeed, Vinson supported Truman's power grab, but Vinson was only able to bribe two other members of the Court to go along with Truman's totalitarian dream. Truman lost the court case and private enterprise, at least in the steel industry, prevailed for the time being. However, Chief Justice Vinson did pay his reverence to Truman with the notoriously racist rulings in *Sweatt v. Painter* and *McLaurin v. Oklahoma State Regents* that held black people shouldn't get too uppity in a modern society and instead they should just sit quietly and be satisfied with separate but equal access to facilities and opportunities.

As part of Truman's personal commitment to the Democrat Party, he saw himself as the godfather of the party after Roosevelt's demise. To reward his former Secretary of the Air Force, Stuart Symington, for spying on Gen. MacArthur, Truman arranged for Symington to be elected to the U.S. Senate representing Missouri, even though Symington was from Massachusetts and had never set foot in Missouri. He later asked Symington to run for the Democrat presidential nomination in 1960, and when Symington did not collect enough delegates for the nomination, Truman refused to endorse anyone else. In the 1952 presidential campaign, Truman asked his reliable bootlicker, Chief Justice Fred M. Vinson, to step down from the Court and run for the Democrat nomination. Vinson demurred and Eisenhower went on that year to win as a Republican.

Truman was always in fine form as a performative actor in his effort to display himself as a common man. He loved to trot out the fable that he was just a "simple haberdasher from Independence, Missouri." It had a Barney Google and Snuffy Smith flavor to it. Just a down-home boy from backwoods, small town Missouri. There is only a thin film of truth to that story. Truman and a partner, indeed, operated a small dry goods shop inside the Glennon Hotel in Independence for two years. The business was not successful and went bankrupt. However, to Truman's credit, he insisted that he pay off his part of the debts rather than rely on bankruptcy court protection. The image of a simple haber-dasher serving as a president fulfilled his personal desire to live a stage act and be perceived as a common man of modest means. He knew how to play the role well: he constantly complained to Congress that he was in dire financial straits, nearing impoverishment. In response, Congress voted to increase his salary as president and to furnish a $50,000 annual tax-free expense budget without accountability. He pocketed the annual $50,000 and methodically saved every penny of his salary. He loved to complain he was being "allowed to starve" while in the White House. Truman adored rolling out the legend that when he left the White House, his wife Bess was forced to take out a bank loan just for them to find enough money to put a few meager ounces of food on the table back in Independence. Members of Congress, particularly Democrats paying homage to their beloved former leader, became alarmed by Truman's claim of penury, and passed the Former

Presidents Act, which provides a lavish post-presidential salary and other perks including rent or mortgage reimbursements, travel allowances, office and security expenses, spending cash, and a full staff. In truth, Truman was a very wealthy man when he left office in 1953. When he departed the White House, his net worth was $660,000, or $6.6 million in today's money when adjusted for inflation. Truman later went on television to moan and complain about his poverty and spoke with feigned alarm that in the U.S., former presidents are just abandoned and turned out onto the grass. "They're just allowed to starve," he exclaimed. In truth, by 1959, Truman's net worth was $1.1 million, or $9.7 million when adjusted for inflation. Truman and Bess blubbered that their house in Independence had to be sold to find enough money for simple survival – they didn't even have the money to pay their auto insurance. The Democrat Party responded by locating wealthy donors to purchase the real estate and donate it back to the former president. After reacquiring the house for free, for some reason the Trumans performed no preventative maintenance or upkeep on the house – a peculiarity discovered when Bess died in 1982. The house was found in a completely dilapidated state – making it just another typical property amidst the miles of crumbling blight in the Kansas City area.

* * *

Michael Junior roused himself from his daydreaming.

"Michael Junior, it seems like you were occupied with something else during the church liturgy. What was on your mind?" his father asked.

"Papa, I was thinking about what you taught me about that satellite station and also when Truman was around in Missouri and as president."

"Yes, Son, that was a disgraceful, sad, and abhorrent period in the country, and in Missouri too. We still bear the burden of that shameful time."

8

After almost eight years of the Ku Klux Klan pretrial procedures, there weren't any changes in the progress of the legal action. In the case, Judge Hedrick J. Winters generally dismissed any motions or requests filed by Larry Korhonen, the attorney representing Michael, Carol and Paul. Korhonen again requested that the FBI's secret, undercover agent be identified. The motion was denied. Korhonen filed a motion for dismissal on grounds that the deposition wasn't dispositive of Ku Klux Klan membership of the defendants. The motion was denied. Korhonen filed a motion to dismiss because no definitive relationship was established between Republican Party membership and Ku Klux Klan membership. Judge Winters denied the motion and said it was a matter for the jury to decide. A motion was filed to compel testimony regarding the total number of black people who are members of the Ku Klux Klan. The judge denied the motion. All of the government's motions for protracted discovery, more time for evidentiary processes, and additional witness depositions were uniformly granted by the judge. Complaints from the defense about the prolonged timeframe of the action were dismissed by Judge Winters with a lecture that the charges were substantial, and the case merited careful attention. During one pretrial status conference, Korhonen informed the judge he wanted to conduct at least one deposition with the lead agent of the FBI's Ku Klux Klan Task Force.

"What will be the nature of that questioning?" Judge Winters probed.

"We want to discover if there are any members of the Ku Klux Klan who are *not* agents with the FBI."

The prosecution didn't need to overly react to tactics or strategies of Korhonen in the courtroom because the judge protected the government's interests adequately.

"I will not allow that line of questioning," the judge responded.

"May I ask why, your honor?" Korhonen replied.

"Those questions will likely bias the jury."

"How, your honor? It will merely provide background details about how the FBI's Ku Klux Klan program is able to detect members of the Klan. We would like to know if all members of the Klan are actually working for the FBI. This will help us put on a defense in this court."

"That line of questioning will reveal sources and methods of the FBI. That is not permitted. I will not allow this line of questioning."

It was at about this time that the U.S. Madam Attorney General ordered a raid on a private home in Florida that she believed was harboring a kidnapped six-year-old Cuban national. Elian Gonzalez was aboard a raft with his mother and fourteen other Cubans, escaping the Cuban communist paradise. Their raft capsized off the shore of Florida and everyone drowned except Elian. The boy clung onto the raft until he was rescued by the U.S. Coast Guard. The boy was ultimately taken in by an uncle who granted him refuge in his Miami home. In the meantime, the boy's father in Cuba was pressured by the ever-paternalistic communist Cuban government to request that his son be returned to Cuba. The Miami relatives refused – out of respect for the boy's perished mother's sentiments, and because they didn't believe the boy should have to grow up in the demeaning mind-control of a communist dictatorship. The U.S. Madam Attorney General professed the belief that the relatives who were caring for Elian and providing him refuge were secret members of the Ku Klux Klan. Because of the administration's commitment to track down and eradicate the pernicious presence of the Ku Klux Klan wherever it can be discovered, the attorney general ordered FBI agents to raid the Florida residence and forcibly remove the child. When the FBI agents charged the house, dressed in camouflage and carrying loaded assault rifles, Elian's uncle ran to hide the child, frantically attempting to protect the boy from the invading storm troopers. The youngster and his uncle were found in abject fear, cowering in a coat closet. After the Madam Attorney General had achieved the rescue of the boy from the dangerous influence of Ku Klux Klan members, she immediately ordered the child to be sent back to Cuba to live in harmony in the sublime, blissful utopia of Cuba. The alluring first lady called the attorney general and said, "Good job, Madam. You saved a child from the insidious influence of the Ku Klux Klan."

During this period of time, the president ordered the Air Force to engage in a lengthy and merciless campaign of carpet bombing over Yugoslavia, allegedly to rout out hotbeds of white supremacy and the persistent influence of the Ku Klux Klan in the small Balkan country. At a press appearance, the president said one of the primary objectives for his administration was to eliminate the pernicious influence of the Ku Klux Klan throughout the world. One naïve reporter for *The New York Post,* who also wrote articles for William F. Buckley's opinion journal, drifted off the reservation and came out of the constant media trance long enough to skeptically ask the president, "But, sir, how is it that the Ku Klux Klan is even in Yugoslavia of all places?" The president glibly replied in a play-acting sort of southern accent, "Well, it is a proto-Ku Klux Klan." It has been speculated that the media was unable to muster up the energy to ask any pertinent questions about the president's carpet bombing campaign on a sovereign foreign country because the members of the press were in a stupor and were paralyzed in a state of awe as they gazed at the astonishingly glamorous $17,000 Kiton Neapolitan custom-tailored business suits worn by the president's secretary of state, who was always in the room whenever the president was trotted out to talk about Yugoslavia. Generally, the members of the media reserved their curiosity to asking the president what his favorite color was or what his favorite flavor of ice cream was.

Rarely did Michael Holden ever talk to anyone about the Ku Klux Klan charges that he, Carol, and Paul were confronting. Carol and Michael never talked about the matter with the children. They never discussed it with fellow synod church members and only talked about it to their pastor on rare occasions, usually during confession. Among themselves, they marveled that the United States government was so adamant and willing to promote the notion that three black people were active members of the Ku Klux Klan.

And Michael never mentioned the Klan case even one time to anyone at his job with the Alfred Sendahl Perfume Company.

Alfred A. Sendahl founded his perfume manufacturing company in 1906, and it set up shop on Vernon Avenue in St. Louis. In 1934, the company had outgrown the Vernon Avenue location and found another building on Goodfellow Blvd. in the North Pointe neighborhood of St. Louis. After moving into the Goodfellow Blvd. facility, new telephone lines needed to be set up in the building. Southwestern Bell and Telephone Company of Missouri was contacted so that a telephone technician could come to the building to complete the job. The first black man to be certified as a PBX (private branch exchange) telephone installation technician with Southwestern Bell was Bartholomew L. Philigrew. Southwestern Bell was incredibly proud of Philigrew and sponsored a reception for him after he obtained his certification because he represented a proud moment in the company's history for a black man to achieve full PBX certification. Mr. Philigrew was an unassuming, very modest and humble man; he expressed his gratitude for the acknowledgment but downplayed all of the attention. Philigrew received the assignment to install the PBX phone system at the Sendahl Perfume Company building on Goodfellow Blvd. During his initial review and assessment of the job, Philigrew told the maintenance manager of Sendahl Perfume Company that some pipes needed to be removed and a box needed to be constructed to cover over the cut-off pipes and thus make it possible to install the phone system. While the maintenance manager was supposed to work on the project, Mr. Philigrew took his lunch break and went to a small Chinese restaurant around the corner on Natural Bridge Avenue to enjoy a delicious order of chop suey. When Mr. Philigrew returned to the Alfred Sendahl Perfume Company, he found that the pipes had indeed been cut off, but the box had not been built. Mr. Philigrew went to the maintenance manager's room to clarify the preparatory phase before the PBX installation and while Philigrew was discussing the matter, five large boxes fell onto Philigrew. The boxes were filled with empty glass bottles for perfume products which had been shipped to the Goodfellow Blvd. factory from a glass manufacturer in Illinois. Just before the boxes collapsed onto Mr. Philigrew, someone yelled, "Hey, look out!" But it was too late, and the boxes landed on Philigrew's back and legs. Each box was estimated to weigh at least one hundred pounds. It was clear Philigrew was seriously injured. An ambulance was called and Mr. Philigrew was transported to DePaul Hospital on Kingshighway Blvd. – an elegant Romanesque structure built in 1930. The injured Bartholomew L. Philigrew, while in serious pain, had enough awareness to be able to call out to the ambulance attendees, "Take me to City Hospital Number Two." Black residents in St. Louis before 1937 were consistently taken to the basement unit in City Hospital Number One or to segregated floors at City Hospital Number Two because part of Jim Crow practices in the area prevented black people from being treated in other hospitals. The ambulance attendees told him they must take him to DePaul Hospital since it was so close to Goodfellow Blvd., and the injuries were very serious. However, the DePaul emergency room personnel weren't inclined to be so accommodating to the ambulance attendees when the ambulance arrived, and they reacted with an indignant sense of alarm as Mr. Philigrew was taken out of the vehicle and rolled into the ER.

"What's going on here?" an ER doctor exclaimed to the ambulance driver. "That man is a Negro. He can't be in here. Take him to the basement of City Hospital Number One."

"But, sir, this is pretty serious, and we were just a few blocks away where the accident occurred."

"That doesn't matter. He's black. Take him to the basement of City Hospital Number One. Certainly, you know the policy."

A byproduct of the type of thinking championed by a long litany of American political leaders, including Missouri's own Harry S. Truman and his protégé, Fred M. Vinson, who would soon become a chief justice of the Supreme Court, asserts that separate but equal facilities are the most logical way to keep colored people in their place and prevent them from becoming too uppity.

The medical director of DePaul Hospital, Dr. Robert Fischer, by chance was in the emergency department at the time Mr. Philigrew was delivered to the hospital by the ambulance, and Dr. Fischer overheard the confrontation with the ambulance driver and the emergency room physician. Dr. Fischer happened to be a member of the synod, and he was morally offended and mortified by the whole notion that black patients could not be treated in any hospital other than the basement of City Hospital Number One or the segregated floors of City Hospital Number Two. For Robert Fischer nothing could be more offensive and disrespectful – a flagrant assault on the teachings of the gospel of Jesus. However, Dr. Fischer also knew he couldn't single-handedly change such vile practices which had such a lengthy history. However, Dr. Fischer was able to observe that Philigrew was seriously injured, and he intervened.

"Bring him into the unit immediately. If he needs to be transferred to one of the City Hospitals, that can happen after he is stabilized."

"But, Dr. Fischer, he is a Negro. He belongs in the basement of City Hospital One or on the segregated floors of City Hospital Two."

"I understand. But let's stabilize him first. And then he can be transferred. Admit him immediately and treat him."

Only two years later, in 1937, the Homer G. Phillips Hospital was opened for black residents in St. Louis. It was a treasured institution by the black residents of St. Louis for the forty-two years of its existence – seen as a symbol of achievement, pride and possibility. But since the accident occurred before Homer G. Phillips was opened, Mr. Philigrew's treatment – primarily pain control and stabilizing his broken bones – started at DePaul Hospital prior to transferring him to one of the City Hospitals.

The day following Bartholomew Philigrew's treatment in the DePaul emergency department, the nursing staff began planning Mr. Philigrew's transfer to the basement of City Hospital Number One, an institution which was allowed to treat black people in St. Louis in compliance with the principles of Jim Crow separate but equal – a legal concept later clarified by the U.S. Supreme Court under the leadership of Fred M. Vinson as the proper and valid application of the United States Constitution.

Bartholomew Philigrew made it clear he did not want to be in the basement of any hospital and, thus, he made a scene.

"I want to be at City Hospital Number Two. I do not want to be in the basement of any hospital. Take me to City Hospital Number Two."

The head nurse in the emergency department was an author-itarian type who had absorbed her dictatorial approach to health care during her training at St. Mary's College of Leavenworth in Leavenworth, Kansas and later at the college's affiliated hospital, Leavenworth General Hospital. Both the Leavenworth nursing school and the eponymously named hospital are run by a rigid, autocratic order of thrifty Catholic nuns, the Beseeching Sisters of Everlasting Sorrow, who constantly stressed that the entire purpose of health care is to cut costs and to enforce all rules with a commitment to rigid prin-ciples of administration from the top-down. The head nurse proceeded to engage in an argument with Mr. Philigrew.

"You belong in the basement of City Hospital Number One," she told Mr. Philigrew, thinking him to be just a bit too insolent.

"As I understand the rules, I can go to either City Hospital One or City Hospital Two. I want to go to City Hospital Two."

"No. We are sending you to the basement of City Hospital Number One. That is a good place for you."

"I need to make a phone call, please," Mr. Philigrew replied.

"We cannot allow a black man to use a telephone in this hospi-tal," the head nurse lectured. "Certainly, you should know that."

"Then I need to talk to Dr. Fischer."

"Dr. Fischer is the medical director here. You don't need to talk to him."

"Dr. Fischer has been involved with my care before. I insist on being able to talk to him."

"What do you mean Dr. Fischer was involved in your care?" His impertinence had evolved into very irritable uppityness.

The head nurse had Dr. Fischer paged and requested his presence immediately in the emergency department. Dr. Fischer arrived at the emergency department and proceeded to ask the head nurse why he was paged.

"This Negro patient said you have previously been involved in his care."

Fischer recognized Philigrew. "Oh yes, how are you doing, sir?" The head nurse was sickened that Dr. Fischer referred to Bartholomew Philigrew as "sir."

"Thank you for coming, Dr. Fischer. I wanted to use the phone, but the nurse said a black man cannot use a phone in the hospital."

"Okay. I think we can get through this," Fischer responded. "Do you mind if I make the call for you. That way you will not be violating the policy of who can use the phone, but the call can nevertheless be made."

Bartholomew Philigrew was emotionally moved and began to weep. "You are a fine Christian man, Dr. Fischer. May I ask you, sir, where do you attend church?"

Fischer was a bit taken aback, but replied, "I attend Trinity Church; it is a synod church."

"Thank you again, Dr. Fischer. Can you please call my supervisor at Southwestern Bell? Because I want him to intervene so that I can be sent to City Hospital Number Two."

Dr. Fischer called Southwestern Bell and spoke to Bartholomew Philigrew's supervisor in the PBX department and explained that Philigrew wanted to go to City Hospital Number Two but there was some confusion, and a plan was being executed to send him to the basement of City Hospital Number One, but Bartholomew did not wish to go there.

"Thank you for calling, doctor," Philigrew's supervisor said. "We are so worried about Bartholomew. What can we do to help?"

"Perhaps, you could have someone in your personnel department call City Hospital Number Two who can then call DePaul's Emergency Department to request that Mr. Philigrew be transferred to City Hospital Two."

The head nurse stormed out of the room, and as she departed, she exclaimed, "Well, I'll be!"

The ambulance attendees transported Mr. Philigrew to City Hospital Number Two and then moved him onto the black patients' segregated floor where orthopedic care took place. Mr. Philigrew sustained a broken spine and a broken femur. He was forced to undergo treatment in the hospital for nearly two months including two surgeries. He was later transferred to his home and went through post-surgical care and physical therapy. Philigrew was on medical leave from Southwestern Bell for more than eight months. Since Bartholomew L. Philigrew was so beloved by his department at Southwestern Bell, he was encouraged by his supervisor, and even an executive with the company, to pursue a personal injury lawsuit against the company where he sustained his injuries – that is, the Alfred Sendahl Perfume Company. One of Southwestern Bell's executive vice presidents put Mr. Philigrew in touch with a St. Louis personal injury attorney. After a jury trial in St. Louis, Philigrew won a personal injury negligence lawsuit and was awarded a $19,500 judgment against the Alfred Sendahl Perfume Company. When adjusted for inflation, the award would be about $400,000. The perfume company's attorneys believed the award was excessive and appealed to the Missouri Supreme Court. The Supreme Court concurred and ruled that Philigrew was only entitled to receive $16,000 and he was ordered to repay the Alfred Sendahl Perfume Company $3,500 plus interest. After being adjusted for inflation, $3,500 is about $72,000. All of the lawsuit award money was used up by attorneys' fees and his ongoing medical care and therapy. The whole affair tremendously upset Philigrew, and while he did repay the perfume company, he remained indignant and believed he had been slighted, insulted and mistreated. He remained in pain for the rest of his life.

The storied history of DePaul Hospital would have scandalized Dr. Robert Fischer, however, the conscientious doctor passed away before the hospital spiraled into a seamy tale of woe. The building itself is a stunning specimen of Richardsonian Romanesque revival architecture, designed by the esteemed architects Patrick M. O'Meara and James B. Hills and it was completed in 1930 for the Sisters of St. Mary. Gradually, the neighborhood along Kingshighway Blvd. degraded and became unsightly. The Sisters, following in the footsteps of their rival operator of hospitals – the Beseeching Sisters of Everlasting Sorrow – decided a troubled urban environment was not suited to their pristine image of themselves, and in 1977 they opened a replacement hospital in Bridgeton in North County of St. Louis, just a few miles west of Florissant, and they took the DePaul name along with their move. The Sisters arranged to have the large hospital on Kingshighway Blvd., still in very fine condition, sold to two investors and two financial trusts, who converted the sizeable building into a nursing home – the region's largest long-term care facility. The nursing home operated for decades, but as the neighborhood continued to collapse, the task of reaching full occupancy goals became more and more of a struggle. A majority of the residents were poor black occupants on Medicaid. One Friday night in December, without warning and while the employees were in the midst of holding their annual Christmas party, the owners barged in unannounced and declared the facility was closing at that very moment. While employees were shoveling cake and treats into their mouths at the holiday party, they were told the nursing home was immediately closed and everyone should instantly vacate the premises. Friday was payday and instead of paychecks, they received pink slips.

"What about my pay?" said Gwen, a nurse at the facility.

"You're not getting paid," the administrator replied indignantly. "We don't have any money. Get out now!"

"What about our residents?"

"We have buses outside. We will put them on buses and take them somewhere."

The families of the residents were not informed and the whereabouts of their loved ones were unknown. Nursing home administrators told the families they didn't know where their family members had been placed. The sister of one resident said the building was abruptly evacuated without anything, other than the residents, removed. The Christmas party was abandoned in the middle of the event with food and drink still on the tables. Nurses' stations were deserted with records and medications still on top of the counters. Resident rooms were left with television sets still on, clothes and belongings remaining on top of beds and in chests and closets.

The Missouri Department of Health and Senior Services said they hoped to find out where the 170 residents were now located, but information was sketchy, and nursing home administrators were difficult to locate, and legal representatives were refusing to comment.

Many years before the demise of DePaul, when Bartholomew L. Philigrew experienced his accident at the Alfred Sendahl Perfume Company and was then taken to DePaul Hospital, followed by his ultimate transfer to City Hospital Number Two, because he was black and didn't qualify for treatment at DePaul, Mr. Philigrew had years to stew over his tragedy. Bartholomew was by all accounts a pleasant, dignified man, but his injuries and the insult of having to pay back the award he received for his physical suffering gnawed on him. It came to the point that he complained incessantly about his injuries, but more glaring for him was the indignity of having to repay the company when they were negligent. Bartholomew Philigrew's grandson, Chubbles, listened for hours to the moaning and grumbling of his grandfather. Over the years, Chubbles heard the story repeated endlessly how his grandfather suffered and was never able to live a life without pain and anguish. Chubbles listened to his grandfather tell about his indignity and the humiliation of being forced to repay the award for his debil-itating injuries to the guilty, negligent company who allowed such a ghastly incident to occur. The endless commentary from Bartholomew Philigrew had a psychological impact on Chubbles. Chubbles internal-ized his grandfather's pain and disappointment.

Chubbles Philigrew was an average student in the St. Louis Public Schools – not particularly memorable to anyone. A teacher once said Chubbles seemed rather sullen and had some kind of cause or score he was trying to settle. The boy never got into any trouble, disturbance, scuffle or legal conflict. Instead, Chubbles spent his time rehearsing in his mind the indignity of injustice and how one could be robbed of personal self-worth – because, at home every day, he continually heard his grandfather bewail and rehearse his destiny of having been slighted and scorned by the Missouri Supreme Court and the Alfred Sendahl Perfume Company. Finally, Bartholomew L. Philigrew died, presumably from age-related illnesses and a broken disposition.

Chubbles went on to high school – a forgettable, unremarkable student. A year after graduation, he enrolled at Webster University in St. Louis and studied business. Again, he was not a memorable student and was seen by his professors as merely average, but with a slightly defiant and disputatious personality. One professor said, "He certainly seems like he has a chip on his shoulder, but he never reveals what it is."

While at Webster, Chubbles met a fellow student named Ronald in a business class – a tall, dreary, awkward fellow with a large head and a dull, expressionless face. One day, Ronald asked Chubbles if he would like to come over to his house. Chubbles agreed to visit Ronald's place and when he arrived at the tiny brick house on a hill in the Hamilton Heights neighborhood, Ronald introduced his diminutive wife, Lisa. Lisa was constantly clinging on to Ronald in an almost suggestive, teasing, flirtatious way. Chubbles thought to himself, "What is this all about? Who is she performing for?" He couldn't calculate what the purpose of her coquettishness was – maybe to somehow impress her husband or the visitor?

Finally, Ronald said, "Well, Chubbles, I've really got something special to show you. Would you like to see it?"

Suddenly, Lisa almost became giddy with excitement, barely able to hold in her anticipation. It all seemed rather strange to Chubbles. It felt like it had suggestive tension to it all – Ronald's expectation verging on explosion and Lisa's panting, breathless excitement – and Chubbles wasn't quite certain how he was to interpret it all.

"We've really got something to show you," Lisa interjected with winded exhilaration; it seemed to be a hunger for satisfaction.

"Come into our bedroom," Ronald directed to Chubbles. Lisa could barely maintain her composure.

"Oh, I don't know," Chubbles replied.

"Yes, come into our bedroom," Ronald repeated. Lisa, in her animated state, had nearly reached her peak.

Chubbles entered their small bedroom. Ronald told Chubbles to sit on the edge of the bed.

"Oh, I don't know," Chubbles excused himself again.

"No, seriously. Sit!" demanded Ronald. Chubbles sat on the bed.

Then Ronald opened the bedroom closet while Lisa's body vibrated in sheer ecstasy. Ronald slowly removed six long rifles. One was a muzzleloader, another was a single shot, a bolt-action, a break-action, a lever-action, and a pump-action.

Lisa began to giggle and moan uncontrollably.

Chubbles said, "Oh, yes. I see. Very nice. Congratulations."

Lisa paused and exhaled, almost in a state of exhaustion. Chubbles thought to himself that the display of firepower was rather impressive and, perhaps one day, he would be able to make use of such fine hardware.

Chubbles left Ronald's house, never to make a return visit. After five years at Webster, Chubbles graduated with a degree in business with a 2.2 GPA – just barely an average, forgettable student.

Chubbles Philigrew, however, did have a plan.

There have been arguments for years about what makes a good leader. Business schools study the notion. Self-help programs try to assess the challenges. Seminars attempt to tackle the conundrum. Hundreds of books and articles are written about what makes a competent leader and to teach how a person can learn or obtain those skills. However, a reliable truism is that there are very few people who are true leaders, and there are even fewer who are able to learn it. Some theories have claimed that a leader must possess authenticity, empathy, a voice, or adaptability. Others have said a leader must have vision, critical thinking, future thinking, interpersonal skills, creativity, flexibility, patience, and be inspiring. These are all simplistic, formulaic suggestions, because a true leader is beyond these qualities. The true leader possesses a gift that is not easily put in a box. Maybe it involves charisma or larger-than-life qualities of personal character. In any case, the president of the Alfred Sendahl Perfume Company, Mr. Peter Selberg, was not a true leader. He was a gentle and kind man – the husband of the granddaughter of the founder of the company, Alfred A. Sendahl, but a leader he was not. Customarily, Peter Selberg found the easiest way to serve as the president of the company was to delegate all responsibilities to managers of departments – office and business, accounting, shipping and receiving, chemistry and fragrance product development, bottle creative design, purchasing, sales and marketing, and so forth. He rarely had much to do with these various areas of the company. Michael Holden, Sr. had been promoted to accounting manager after working for the company for five years; he reinterviewed with Mr. Selberg and the chief financial officer for his accounting manager position. After that, he never spoke to Mr. Selberg again, other than perfunctory greetings. Michael was a disciplined, devoted worker and managed the bookkeeping and accounting proficiently, forwarding the journals and ledger summaries to the chief financial officer each month so the CFO could prepare the trial balance, balance sheet, P&Ls, and financial statements.

The company employed a substantial number of black synod members because of Mr. Selberg's appreciation for their diligent habits. Selberg learned over the years that black synod people consistently and reliably embodied the character of ideal employees: discipline, focus, dignity, dedication, commitment, and decorum. Selberg was not a religious person, and he did not possess the ability to understand the possible faith connection to the black synod people and their notable character, but he did know that he liked their temperament.

One summer, the office and business manager retired, and Mr. Selberg needed to find a replacement. He made one significant mistake – he failed to ask current employees for a recommendation prior to hiring a new office manager. It is not clear if Mr. Selberg thought he could figure it out for himself – to calculate and discern who could serve as an office manager, somehow mysteriously identify a black synod person through his own gut feelings or presumptions. Who knows. But the person Mr. Selberg hired to be the new office and business manager was not a member of the synod. Indeed, it is true he was a black man, but he had nothing to do with the synod. Peter Selberg hired Chubbles Philigrew to be the office and business manager of the Alfred Sendahl Perfume Company.

Chubbles was not particularly impressive during his interview with Mr. Selberg, displaying his customary glum, sulky and moody personality. Furthermore, Chubbles coifed himself in long, braided dreadlocks – something Mr. Selberg thought to be slightly unprofessional. Yet, Peter Selberg carefully read Chubbles's application and qualifications and determined the young Webster graduate could take on the duties of office and business manager – and maybe, possibly, hopefully, by chance he was a member of the synod ... so Mr. Selberg thought. Chubbles had an ulterior motive for working for the company that so thoughtlessly injured his grandfather and then petitioned the Missouri Supreme Court in order to steal his grandfather's negligence award. Mr. Selberg had no idea who Bartholomew Philigrew was – that was back in 1935 – and he had no awareness of Chubbles's relationship to Bartholomew Philigrew either. Why should he know about any of this?

As the office and business manager, Chubbles was charged with supervising all departments in the business. All business matters and activities passed by his desk for his review and approval. Quickly, Chubbles, whether by intent or merely a reflection of his surly disposition, began to behave in a petulant, moody and short-tempered manner with other employees. Unable to conceal his contempt for the company that humiliated and killed his grandfather, Chubbles was quick to become quarrelsome and argumentative with employees, belittling others, ignoring their suggestions. He frequently did nothing other than sit at his desk and instantly dispute anything that came before him with a smug putdown of the employee who took him out of his reverie. He ignored departments that needed constant supervision and direction to ensure work was being performed – such as the chemistry, testing and fragrance development department, or the shipping and receiving department. When work was not being performed in these areas, he simply ignored it. Chubbles was consistently rude and angry with the sales and marketing team. Some employees and department leaders approached Mr. Selberg and complained about Chubbles's difficult disposition. Mr. Selberg's inclination was to simply ignore these warnings and insist that a company with a black manager was a reflection of a modern, open-minded and farsighted business organization. Chubbles was on a mission of revenge. He began to disregard and destroy incoming orders; he would ignore customer requests for account adjustments. When calls would come through for account reconciliations, he would deflect the inquiries and fail to forward the requests to the accounting area. Customers found him to be temperamental and cantankerous and would refuse to speak to him. Slowly, customers began to cancel their orders or close their accounts with the Alfred Sendahl Perfume Company. Employees began to quit out of frustration and dislike for Chubbles. The sales and marketing department fell apart because so many accounts were leaving the company. Vendors stopped shipping supplies including chemicals and necessary materials. Department stores and dime stores that carried the Sendahl products ended their relationships with the company. One December afternoon, the company's largest account, Avon Products, announced they were stopping their seventy-five-year relationship with Sendahl. The company's CFO finally met with Peter Selberg and announced the company was bankrupt. The remaining employees of the Alfred Sendahl Perfume Company, including Michael Holden, as well as Chubbles Philigrew, were laid off and the company closed. Finally, Chubbles's subconscious mission had been accomplished.

Michael came home and told Carol about the news of Sendahl Perfume closing and his sorrow for the collapse of a venerable old company.

"Oh, Michael, I'm sorry," Carol said. "Let's go out to New Shanghai tonight and find an excuse to not dwell on it."

Michael and Carol's favorite restaurant was New Shanghai located in a rundown strip mall along Florissant Road in Florissant, across the street from another strip mall that was equally as decrepit and dilapidated, with a vacant storefront that was once a Kmart store, covered with graffiti. The strip mall that housed New Shanghai was what some people would call a dump – a parking lot filled with potholes and weeds sprouting up all over. About 50 percent of the storefronts were vacant and the occupied spots included a discount barbershop with a female Korean proprietor who claims she is studying to become a Muslim but is having difficulty because she can't get the hang of Arabic. A customer asked Mrs. Kim why she was studying Islam. "Is it because you have a Muslim boyfriend?" Mrs. Kim replied, "Of course not. It is because I like their wardrobe." Other tenants included a grimy tailor shop run by an immigrant woman from Chechnya. She took grave pleasure in belittling her customers by inspecting the crotch of the trousers to be repaired and then snorting, "What is *this* stain?" There was a vacuum repair shop that rarely had any customers, and a beauty supply store that sold chemicals for hair straightening. A beauty parlor kept intermittent business hours but offered eyebrow threading, which some customers find especially appealing. One business was King Solomon's Fashion Mine which has an owner who is controversial because he goes to wholesale fashion shows to select products but pays his vendors with counterfeit money. One vendor sent him a box full of uptown, faux designer fashion apparel as a COD delivery. Mr. Solomon paid with a check on a closed account and then refused to receive calls from the vendor.

Carol and Michael loved New Shanghai and Michael was tickled promoting it to friends, acquaintances, and anyone looking for a restaurant recommendation. Michael enjoyed calling in to the restaurant talk show on KSTL radio to rave about the chop suey, the wok stir fry with extra onions, miniature colorful bell peppers, sliced carrots and broccoli, lightly seasoned, or the bed of rice topped with the stir-fried vegetable combo, including the miniature corn cobs, and tofu.

Carol rounded up the children, and before they headed out the door to New Shanghai, the phone rang and Michael answered.

"Hi, Michael, it's Carla from three blocks east of you."

"Hi there, Carla. What's up?"

"Michael, I was driving down your street earlier today and I saw some suspicious people in your yard, next to your bushes."

"Carla, I don't have any bushes."

"Well, maybe it was the shrubs."

"Carla, I don't have any shrubs either."

"Oh, I'm sorry. Maybe I was mistaken."

"Hey, Carla, do you want to join Carol, the kids and me at New Shanghai?"

9

Chubbles Philigrew had a certain peculiar sense of contentment with the demise of the Alfred Sendahl Perfume Company, but as with all forms of psychological torture and internal haunting, there is never completion, consummation, fulfillment, or true satisfaction. He continued to be filled with the anxiety built up over years of listening to his grandfather lament over his physical pain and his mental suffering from injustice. Chubbles had not only become his grandfather's avenging angel, but he had become possessed with his own personal bitterness and stewing, and internal suspicions.

A few years before the demise of the Alfred Sendahl Perfume Company, Chubbles's sister, Tamika, went into her own crisis, which additionally helped fuel Chubbles's interaction with the world.

Tamika, an attractive, gentle, innocent young lady, was two years younger than Chubbles. She found a job as a bank teller at a small financial institution in the Dutchtown neighborhood. One Tuesday in June while Tamika was working the teller counter in the bank, taking deposits and processing withdrawals, she looked out the front window of the bank and witnessed an older black gentleman, attired in a dress shirt, necktie, and sport jacket, standing on the corner when suddenly a police cruiser raced up to the intersection and screeched to a stop. The police officer frantically jumped out of the cruiser, approached the older man and proceeded to strangle the man until the limp body dropped to the ground. In a matter of minutes, other police vehicles arrived, and the intersection was blocked for hours while an investigation occurred. That evening Tamika anxiously explained to her brother what she witnessed from her vantage point at the bank. The following morning, they both searched through the *Post-Dispatch* to see if they could find any news reporting on the incident. There was no information in the newspaper that day or the next or the next after that.

"Can you believe that?" Tamika quipped. "I guess something like that doesn't qualify as news."

The following week in the morning hours while Tamika was at the bank, two men entered the bank wearing ski masks on their heads, armed with handguns. One of the intruders approached her teller station with a gun pointed at her, and he told her to empty the cash contents of her drawer into a cloth bag. In accordance with bank policy, she emptied her drawer into the bag and returned the bag to the armed robber and watched both intruders depart. She instantly broke down and began to sob. Her supervisor, who witnessed the event, came to her side and provided comfort.

"Tamika, take a break. The police will be here shortly," her supervisor said. "Go to the back room. Sit down. Relax. The police will want to talk to you when they arrive."

When the police showed up, they interviewed Tamika, seeking descriptions of the two intruders. What was their height, weight, physical size? Could you distinguish the color of their skin? What were they wearing? What was his voice like? Could you estimate their ages? What clothing were they wearing? What direction did they go when they left? Did they go to a car or van? How long were they in the bank? Did anyone see them in the bank or outside? How many people were on the sidewalk? Did you talk to anyone outside the bank? How much money did he take? How much was in your drawer? The questions went on and on. Tamika began to become dizzy and disoriented. She could feel a sense of panic sweeping through her. She began to think they could come back and try it again. What if they thought she had a description of them and wanted to eliminate her because she could cause them trouble? She became stricken with paranoia and nervousness. Her supervisor told her that she should go home and rest.

When Chubbles came home, he found his sister sitting in the living room with an expression of stress and anxiety. She explained to Chubbles what happened to her at the bank.

"Chubbles, first it is the man who was strangled to death in front of the bank. And now it is the robbery at the bank. I'm having some troubles. I feel panicked and stressed. I don't think I can be in that area. I don't want to go back to the bank. Ever."

Chubbles, who was twisted with his own trauma and outrage, wondered if it were now, at this time, that his sister was readying her own soul to go down his same troubled path. He wasn't sure what to make of her beginning this trek of disappointment, discouragement, cynicism, outrage, requital. And he was unsure if he could tolerate watching his sister make this journey.

"See if you feel better tomorrow," Chubbles advised his sister.

Tamika didn't feel better when tomorrow arrived or the day after tomorrow. Or the day after that. Tamika began to drift into her own dark, foggy state of internal confusion and despair. Her feelings of helplessness, fear, anxiety and incapacitation built on themselves and fueled other fears. She began to feel she couldn't walk outside because someone could come by with a gun or a threat. What if a police squad car drove by, saw her, threw the car in reverse to park in front of her and then the officer would jump out of the car and approach her and strangle her until she was limp and dropped on the ground – perhaps dead from asphyxiation? What if she tried to walk across the street and suddenly a bus appeared out of nowhere and drove over her and paralyzed her and she suffered a serious brain injury and lost her ability to speak? And then she would have to hope someone would put the effort into teaching her sign language. Would anyone take the time to teach her sign language? What if she walked into the kitchen and the overhead light fixture exploded from some unknown electrical short and the burning embers of the fixture dropped right on top of her head and gave her a concussion and while she was unconscious the burning electrical object caused her to sustain second- or third-degree burns? The scenarios of disaster passed through her mind and returned in more exaggerated forms. She became paralyzed by fear. Tamika found if she stayed in her bed, she was safest and able to cope with her difficult state. Even while in the bed, she tried to not move because her movement could cause her to somehow fall out of the bed or accidentally hit her head on her bedside table or the bedframe and then she would possibly face post-concussion syndrome. Consequently, she laid very quietly and stiff without any movement. Sometimes her muscles ached because of the stiffness and inability to move.

Since she was in a state of psychological paralysis, she was on a leave of absence from the bank. Chubbles managed to convince Tamika to get out of bed, get dressed and come with him to Barnes-Jewish Hospital so they could see a doctor about possibly getting Tamika onto some kind of anti-anxiety medication. While driving to the hospital, they came upon a police chase rapidly in pursuit of a getaway vehicle. Because the chase was frantic and out of control with sirens screaming and fast cars racing in pursuit, some vehicles on the streets were forced to make quick lane changes to avoid the commotion and a collision. As one car was attempting to get out of the chase and fast-moving traffic, the vehicle drove into the side of Chubbles's car. Tamika burst into tears; her panic emerged in a flare-up. She began sobbing and shaking in terror. Chubbles wanted to blow up and engage in a confrontation with the driver of the car that hit him. "You stupid idiot," he wanted to say. "What is wrong with you? Can't you handle moving out of your lane and know where you're going? One of the first lessons from kindergarten is to look in both directions." But knowing that Tamika was unable to absorb the situation without a total collapse and meltdown, Chubbles decided to calmly and politely talk to the driver of the other vehicle.

"Listen, my sister has an appointment at Barnes-Jewish that we cannot miss," Chubbles told the confused and disoriented driver. "Let's exchange information from our licenses and our insurance cards. Give me your phone number; I'll give you mine. And we can try to sort this out tomorrow."

They made it to Barnes-Jewish Hospital and Tamika went through her appointment. She was prescribed a powerful anti-anxiety medication. Tamika became medicated and while her state of paralysis seemed to dissipate, she remained in a fog and was generally very quiet and unresponsive. She stayed in the house most of the time, living in a state of psychological disability.

Chubbles continued his mission at Sendahl Perfume Company, as the company slowly, gradually, methodically drifted into disarray. Production supplies were not arriving. The chemistry department had become dysfunctional. Production output had slowly reached a near standstill. The shipping department no longer operated. Employees were quitting. The sales department had dropped to only one salesman. Orders were not filled. Small, medium and large accounts ended their relationships with the company. It wouldn't be long, Chubbles pondered.

One day the supervisor of Tamika's bank called and talked to Chubbles. It seemed the police had arrested two men who were committing bank robberies, and the investigators believed the suspects were involved in the robbery that started Tamika's drift into a mental breakdown.

"The police may call and want to talk to Tamika," she said.

"Oh, I don't think that will work out. Tamika is not in the mental state to talk to anyone, especially about that situation."

"Chubbles, please talk to her and see if she could speak to them. We want to get these guys."

Chubbles talked to Tamika's physician and psychologist at Barnes-Jewish about the possibility of Tamika meeting with the police.

"Chubbles, she could talk to the police, maybe with a little advance warning to the police, but I don't want her being forced to go into court," the psychologist warned. "I think it would be a possible impediment to her mental state and recovery and it could even push her into a panic response. Let me talk to Tamika a little about this first."

The psychologist discussed the whole situation with Tamika, and they came to the understanding she could talk to the police briefly but would not be able to testify in a trial. The police did interview Tamika; the interview was uneventful and didn't cause her to panic. A trial was scheduled. The attorneys representing the two bank robbers were public defenders and they demanded that Tamika be subpoenaed for testimony at trial. The St. Louis prosecuting attorney, Limney Grantham, was not inclined to go forward with the charges and the prosecution of the two bank robber defendants in any case, because according to her judicial philosophy, it wasn't appropriate to be chasing members of racial minority groups as suspects on matters of little criminal significance. Her belief was that the pursuit of racial minority suspects was just perpetuating social inequity and systemic racism, and it needed to stop. Consequently, rarely did Limney Grantham pursue criminal charges against such suspects. And because Tamika Philigrew was psychologically incapable of testifying at trial, it was the perfect excuse to simply dismiss the charges against the two bank robbery suspects. Miss Grantham's staff prosecutors took the first opportunity to make a motion to dismiss the charges and to announce that the prosecution would not proceed forward because there were insufficient witnesses to be able to prevail at trial. The judge immediately dismissed the charges and released the two suspects. The whole legal process, from indictment to dismissal, had gone on for a year. What better usage of time, thought Miss Grantham. Shortly after the dismissal, St. Louis Prosecuting Attorney Limney Grantham requested the St. Louis Board of Aldermen to fast-track a proposal to increase remuneration for criminal public defenders in the St. Louis jurisdiction. Everyone was a winner, Miss Grantham reasoned: the psychologically fragile witness was allowed to not testify, the defendants were released to promote greater social equity, and the public defender lobby got a raise.

Chubbles's tenure at Sendahl Perfume Company was nearing completion with the certain pending closure of the business. Chubbles had observed a vibrant young woman with a life ahead of her turned into a paralyzed, petrified victim – essentially a vegetable for the sake of a social justice theory that made no sense. After observing the torture that Tamika had lived through and then the release of the two bank robbers because of the promotion of greater social equity, Chubbles decided the time had come for him to fulfill a part of his destiny which was planted when he met a fellow college student at Webster – a fellow named Ronald, with a quirky, excitable wife named Lisa. Chubbles contacted Ronald and asked if he could recommend some quality, effective firearms.

"What do you have in mind, Chubbles? What are you hoping to do?" Ronald asked.

"Self-defense," Chubbles replied.

"What is your level of experience with firearms?"

"Little, if any."

"Well, Chubbles, you may want to pursue some training at a gun range. I'd be happy to accompany you. But anyway, you could consider one of the semi-automatic pistols. I like the Baretta M-9, Baretta 92, or Baretta 418. Let's go to the range."

Chubbles set an appointment with Ronald to visit Sharp Shooters on Gravois Road and they did some target shooting with Ronald's firearms. After the time at the gun club, Chubbles purchased a Baretta 92 pistol.

Chubbles did some research at the St. Louis courthouse on Market Street. He studied the case against the two accused bank robbers who were now the beneficiaries of Limney Grantham's social equity program. He learned the addresses of the two social equity inheritors and made note. One Tuesday evening, Chubbles took his Baretta 92 and drove to the address of one of the suspects in the Greater Ville neighborhood in north St. Louis. When he was finished in Greater Ville, he would need to pay a visit to the Jeff-Vander-Lou neighborhood to complete his mission. He knew whom he was looking for because he saw a mugshot in the court records. Chubbles double parked on the street while he awaited his social equity champion to appear. After a five-minute wait, a police squad car pulled up behind him with emergency lights flashing. The officer approached the car. Chubbles's firearm was under the seat.

"What's going on?" the officer asked.

"Oh, I was waiting for someone I know, but I don't think he's coming out."

"May I see your license, please."

Chubbles handed his driver's license to the officer. The cop took the license to his squad car. Chubbles remained calm. The officer returned with Chubbles's license and handed it to him.

"I think you should move on if the person you're waiting for isn't going to come out."

"Yes. I agree." Chubbles drove away. Mission not accomplished, he thought. Isn't it something? he pondered. The police are surely able to pursue a problem like a double-parked vehicle, quickly and with focus and efficiency. Certainly, the City of St. Louis will not condone the very inequitable problem of double parking. I will need to find an opportunity to complete this task another time. A close call.

January arrived and the Alfred Sendahl Perfume Company closed. Mission complete, or perhaps a more accurate way to describe Chubbles's interpretation of the entire Sendahl affair was simply that events had reached an end. Chubbles received a call from his cousin in New Orleans who told him about a psychiatrist at Tulane University Medical School who was doing some experimental treatments for people with trauma. He thought Tamika could possibly qualify for the program. Chubbles talked to Tamika's psychologist and physician at Barnes-Jewish about the possibilities of Tamika participating in the Tulane program. The Barnes-Jewish doctors said they would look into it.

In the meantime, Anne Newland, who was living in Ste. Genevieve, about an hour south of St. Louis, in her art studio and cabin with her mother, talked on the phone to her former boyfriend who still resided in Kansas City. He told Anne he was planning to come to St. Louis at Christmas time before taking a trip to New Orleans, and he asked if they could meet in St. Louis for a short reunion of sorts. Anne believed the drive to St. Louis would give Anne and her mother a chance to see old friends, including Michael and Carol Holden, as well as Anne having a chance to reconnect with her former boyfriend. They planned to take the trip in the first week of January.

Anne Newland's former boyfriend arrived in St. Louis. Anne and her mother, Doris, drove up to St. Louis. Carol and Michael arranged for Doris and Anne to stay in their home while they were in St. Louis. Everyone, including Anne's ex-boyfriend, gathered at the Holdens' house in Florissant for an after-Christmas celebration. Carol served lasagna and salad. Someone, perhaps it was Anne's former boyfriend from Kansas City, exclaimed, "Best damn lasagna I ever ate!" Anne's former boyfriend asked Anne if she would like to accompany him to New Orleans – there is an art marketplace, and it could be an opportunity to make some excellent contacts.

"Let me talk to my mother about it," Anne said.

There was a lot of laughing and small talk. Doris was so enchanted with Michael Junior and Andrea. It had been a cold December and January, and a snowstorm was moving into the region. Anne decided she would not make the trip to New Orleans.

"I will not be going to New Orleans with you," Anne told her former boyfriend. "But I hope you make some quality connections at the art marketplace."

The following morning it was snowing hard in St. Louis. Anne spoke on the phone to her former boyfriend and asked him if the flight to New Orleans was still scheduled. He confirmed it was and Anne wished him a good trip. Also, that morning, Chubbles was packing up Tamika's luggage for her three-week stay at Tulane Hospital in New Orleans for the experimental psychiatric treatment for trauma. The weather was distressing to Chubbles and he called Lambert Airport to confirm the flight was still scheduled. Everything was on schedule, according to the airline representative. Chubbles took his sister to the gate at Lambert and assured Tamika that their cousin would pick her up when she arrived in New Orleans. Tamika was afraid and Chubbles talked to the gate attendant about his sister needing a little extra attention. He had purchased a first-class ticket for her to guarantee she would be appropriately cared for. As Anne's boyfriend boarded the plane, he looked at Tamika and smiled at her. Also on the flight was Alice Ploughmaster, the endearing former mayor of East St. Louis. Mrs. Ploughmaster spent a lot of time in New Orleans because she directed a series of conferences at Xavier University in New Orleans. Mrs. Ploughmaster sat next to Tamika in the first-class section and could discern the young lady was in distress. Mrs. Ploughmaster talked to the flight attendant about her concerns for the young passenger and the flight attendant explained the nature of Tamika's situation and how she was going to Tulane Medical School for some help with her psychological post-traumatic condition. Mrs. Ploughmaster engaged in some reassuring small talk with Tamika. It was about thirty minutes before take-off when a flight attendant approached Mrs. Ploughmaster and explained she was needed at the boarding gate to take a personal phone call. Mrs. Ploughmaster told Tamika that she had a phone call at the boarding area, and she would return shortly. Before she left the plane, she looked out the porthole and saw the snow was still coming down in a blizzard and the snow was rapidly accumulating on the apron and tarmac. I don't know as though this flight is going to happen, Mrs. Ploughmaster thought.

When Mrs. Ploughmaster went to the boarding gate, she took her phone call. It was her best friend, Eleni Malanatakis, who was the chairwoman of the classics department at Southern Illinois University in Carbondale, about ninety minutes east of St. Louis. Eleni Malanatakis pleaded with Mrs. Ploughmaster not to take the flight because she needed Alice's assistance for a special meeting in Carbondale.

"This is important," her friend Eleni said. "I have a special presentation at SIU and I need your assistance. Listen, Alice, I will pay for your flight. Don't worry, but I need your help in Carbondale this week. Please, Alice."

Alice asked the gate agent if it was too late to have her luggage removed from the plane. The boarding agent made a call and said it appeared the luggage could be removed. Alice also asked the boarding gate agent, "Can you ask the flight attendant to tell the young lady I was sitting next to in the first-class section that I am unable to make the flight?"

The pilot of the aircraft, a DC-9, was forty-three years old and had worked with the airline for about fifteen years. He had only been a captain for two weeks, having spent the prior years as first and second officer on Boeing 727s and DC-10s. He only had thirty-three hours of flying time with a DC-9. The first officer was a twenty-six-year-old pilot who had only thirty-six hours flying in any large commercial aircraft and had just received his qualifications for a DC-9 two weeks prior to this flight. In addition, the first officer had been previously terminated by two small commuter airlines for incompetent job performance. The two pilots had just met about one hour before the flight was scheduled for take-off and were not familiar with each other's practices and habits. Neither seemed concerned or bothered by the weather, the heavy snowfall, and the freezing conditions, nor did either notify the control tower that they thought another de-icing application was necessary. They agreed between themselves that the first officer would perform the take-off. Rules require pilots to physically walk through the cabin and look out the portholes every twenty minutes to confirm there is no accumulation of snow on the wings. Neither pilot executed this task. Accumulation of freezing snow merely the thickness of grains on a sheet of sandpaper can impede the aerodynamics of aircraft. Twenty-seven minutes had passed since the last de-icing of the aircraft and the pilot brought the plane toward the runway for take-off. Because of the blizzard conditions, the control tower was unable to see the plane and relied completely on radio contact. The plane sat on the runway for another fifteen minutes, collecting more snow and ice on the wings. There were about five inches of snow on the ground when the aircraft was ready to begin take-off. Finally, the first officer threw the engines into full thrust, hurling down the runway at 168 m.p.h. The plane made lift but only for a few seconds before the right wing dipped deeply and hit the ground surface of the runway; the pilot overcompensated and the aircraft rolled to the left, the wing slammed onto the ground and sheared off, and then the fuselage barreled into the runway. With the momentum of movement, the plane flipped over, and a long grinding skid ended with the aircraft bursting into flames.

There were no survivors.

Alice Ploughmaster arrived in Carbondale by car later that afternoon.

10

The funeral for Tamika Philigrew was scheduled for a Tuesday in January, two weeks after the plane crash. Chubbles made arrangements with a funeral home in the Vandeventer neighborhood and purchased a plot in the Bellefontaine Cemetery, where Grandfather Bartholomew Philigrew was buried. Chubbles wasn't a member of a church and so he relied on the funeral home to conduct the service, presided by a Presbyterian preacher who worked on-call with the funeral home. The funeral was attended by Tamika's friends from high school, coworkers from the bank, and some neighbors. St. Louis Democrat Prosecuting Attorney Limney Grantham didn't show up to pay her respects to Tamika, who turned out to be one of the hundreds of unwitting bystanders during Miss Grantham's criminal equity program.

When the funeral service concluded, the Presbyterian preacher announced there would be a funeral procession to the Bellefontaine Cemetery on West Florissant Avenue. The route would take Page Blvd. to Kingshighway Blvd. and then on to the cemetery. The hearse led the way, and more than a dozen cars followed.

Tamika Philigrew's inability to testify against the two career criminals in their trial for armed bank robbery, because of her fragile psychological condition, was the whole reason the two characters received the reward of equity justice from Miss Limney Grantham.

These two malefactors didn't know it was Tamika Philigrew's court-room absence that freed them; they wouldn't have cared if they did know, and they would have forgotten the link within ten minutes. The only thing that mattered is they were released back onto the street to continue their only known, and well-rehearsed, street enterprise. In reality, these two scoundrels didn't even know who Tamika Philigrew was, nor would they have given it a second thought if they were told.

The two bank robbers who were the beneficiaries of St. Louis Prosecuting Attorney Limney Grantham's obsession with awarding equity in criminal offenses were out on the streets of St. Louis plying their trade. These two individuals were the lowest, most vile inhabitants of ghetto, ratchet misbehavior. Even if they had been able to grasp the reward of equity they received from Miss Grantham, they would have been unable to resist the temptation of taking advantage of the next opportunity to execute some new offensive criminal act. The only lifestyle these two knew was the pursuit of degrading criminal activity – usually with firearms in their pockets and hands.

As the funeral procession continued down Kingshighway Blvd., two gun-wielding ghetto street thugs confronted the procession. While the hearse was stopped at a traffic signal, a car pulled in front of the limousine, pinning it in. Two masked bandits jumped out of the vehicle wielding their weapons – perhaps their visages were vaguely familiar to any of the bank employees who were also in the funeral procession. The gunmen approached the stopped cars in the caravan. They held out their guns and threatened to shoot if the drivers or passengers didn't open their windows or doors. One driver refused; the gunman shot a round at the door of the car. The driver quickly complied and opened his door. The intruder told the passengers to hand over their money, wallets, purses, watches, jewelry and rings. One man hesitated. The intruder shot his handgun into the floor-board of the car. Methodically, the two terrorists went from car to car.

One of the hoodlums approached Chubbles's car; this day Chubbles failed to bring his Baretta semi-automatic pistol. He belligerently refused to open his door. The gunman released a round into the side of Chubbles's car. Chubbles steadfastly refused to open his door. The gunman pointed his SIG Sauer 9 mm pistol at the window and released one round, however, Chubbles had thrown his body onto the surface of the car seat and avoided the penetrating bullet. The two assailants, along with their loot, took off in their car which had pinned in the hearse. The police arrived to start another investigation of street criminal activity which seemed to be the one true constant in the city. The funeral procession was called off. After one hour of police scene investigation, the hearse was allowed to depart, and it continued on to Bellefontaine Cemetery alone. Thus, the troubled, haunted, tormented, terrorized victim of the city's commitment to equity was buried in the Bellefontaine Cemetery grounds without a witness present, other than the grave diggers and cemetery workers who lowered her coffin into its hole. And the two bank robbers, who held a gun to her head while she scooped up cash into their cloth bag, and who then went on to other ventures of misdeed, lawlessness, armed heists and holdups, and felonies – these fellows ran away to perform their next escapade of conquest. Presumably, equity justice will be available for them again, if needed.

✳ ✳ ✳

The body of Anne Newland's former boyfriend was sent to Kansas City for his funeral and burial. Anne wanted to make the trip to Kansas City for the service, even though she dreaded having to see the dismal, rundown, decaying and derelict city. Anne drove from St. Louis and when she arrived in Kansas City, she noticed the city was abuzz with another scandal – apparently replacing the last one about a slum tenement which collapsed and killed fourteen people including a mother with her eight children. The newest crisis of the day involved a farmer at a horse farm in the rural parts of Jackson County. Perry Olmstead owned more than fifty acres along with twelve horses. Perry's property was a rural version of what much of Kansas City displays in its numerous urban neighborhoods – too much trash and detritus on the land. He had abandoned vehicles, used appliances, old farm implements, water tanks, lumber and construction materials, blue tarps and orange tarps covering up something or some things. The liberals who populate Jackson County found it to be an eyesore. These offended citizens went to the Jackson County Legislature and filed formal complaints about the public disturbance Perry Olmstead was causing for the uninhibited viewing pleasure of these residents. The County Legislature has twelve members, ten of whom are Democrats, representing the liberal, authoritarian, and nanny-state preferences of the bleating, sneering and conforming Kansas Citians. Several members of the Legislature drove past Perry's property and observed the offensive accumulation of junk. These members, conspiring to violate the sunshine law of the State of Missouri by meeting in private without advance public notice, determined among themselves that Perry Olmstead's property should be investigated by a county zoning inspector. Days later, the zoning inspector showed up at Perry's property unannounced and promptly left a zoning violation notice taped onto Perry's mailbox. He was ordered to appear at the Jackson County Zoning Court, pay a fine, and explain to a zoning judge when he would have his junk and debris cleaned up.

Perry Olmstead was an independent sort of person – perhaps misplaced in the trudge of history; maybe he was more suited to live in the mid-eighteenth century when a person's individual freedom and private property rights were treasured and protected. He didn't believe a "zoning court" should even exist, much less have any juris-diction over his rural property. But the problem is Perry Olmstead was confronted with a society composed of people who spend all day, every day "searching for the manager" to solve their problems and complaints.

Perry appeared at zoning court in Kansas City. The judge asked him why his property was filled with junk and debris. Perry replied that it was his property and he believed he possessed the right to use it as he saw fit including keeping equipment, vehicles, and construction materials. The judge believed Perry Olmstead was being confronta-tional, uncooperative, and not sufficiently deferential. The judge told Olmstead he was operating an unlicensed junk yard and slapped him with a $3,000 fine, and then ordered him to clean up the property within ninety days. Olmstead left the zoning court without paying his fine. He returned to his farm.

Perry Olmstead's fifty-acre farm was a property he inher-ited from his parents ten years ago. His parents, Anita and Norbert Olmstead, inherited the property from Norbert's parents who were among the first black people to own farm property in Jackson County – a notorious enclave which was once a slave region because of the Missouri Compromise which controversially admitted Missouri as a slave state in 1821. Anita and Norbert Olmstead were independent, defiant black people who were members of the synod, reflecting a family history of synod membership since the end of slavery. Surely, they taught Perry the same obstinate, bold, self-reliant values that they lived. The Democrats who control Jackson County became alarmed by Perry Olmstead's intransigence, defiance and behavior which was disrupting their desire to have a pristine county without junk yards, even though the neighborhoods of the decaying urban jungle of Kansas City are filled with yards containing used appliances and broken-down cars, not all that dissimilar from Perry's property. The Jackson County executive, a position much like a president of the county legislature, made a phone call to the U.S. attorney general.

"Madam Attorney General, we have a problem here in the Kansas City area. I would contact our state attorney general about this, but he is a Republican."

"What's the problem?" the attorney general asked.

Knowing the attorney general's obsessive interest in pursuing the Ku Klux Klan at every opportunity, the Jackson County executive cleverly raised the issue to entice her enthusiasm for what he was hoping to discuss with her.

"I know the administration is trying to eradicate the Ku Klux Klan and I don't think we have a particularly serious problem with the Ku Klux Klan here," the executive began.

"It's possible you have a Klan problem. It goes on everywhere," Madam replied.

"Well, Madam Attorney General, we do have a resident on a rural farm who is collecting junk on his property and the county zoning court even ruled he operates an unlicensed junk yard. But the culprit is simply ignoring us."

"Well, why don't you just arrest him?"

"We are worried because of racial sensitivity since he is a black person," the county executive continued. "And our prosecuting attorney is practicing judicial equity in our county – which we want to continue here because it is so effective in stifling any law enforcement."

"Yes, judicial equity programs are the latest trend and are just terrific. I know the prosecuting attorney in St. Louis has been using it very effectively. But how can I help you?"

"Is there some way you can pursue this junk yard culprit as a federal matter?"

"I suppose there could be some ways. He already sounds like he is in the Ku Klux Klan," said the attorney general. "After all, he is accumulating junk on his property. Do you know his political party affiliation?"

"He is a Republican."

"Well, we're halfway there. Obviously, he is very likely a member of the Ku Klux Klan. I think we can help you out. Don't worry that he is black. We go after black Klan members all the time."

"Thank you, Madam," the Jackson County executive blubbered.

Because Perry Olmstead refused to pay the $3,000 junk yard fine, the Jackson County zoning court judge ordered Perry to be held in contempt of court and to be jailed for ninety days in the county jail. Perry responded to the contempt order by saying he would kill all twelve horses. The animal protection lobby heard about his threat and went into a panic. It so happened their annual animal protection fund-raising banquet was scheduled to be held the following weekend at the recently rebuilt Hyatt Regency Hotel. During the star-studded event, with appearances by Hollywood and Democrat Party glitterati dining on servings of medallions of veal, chicken fricassee, glazed roast pork tenderloin, liver pâté, and roasted goose, an appeal was made to save the twelve horses on the Olmstead farm. The animal protection charity petitioned the county district court to have the horses removed from Perry Olmstead's property and placed in a horse rescue shelter program. The judge issued the order immediately without even allowing Perry Olmstead to appear and respond to the petition. "I like this fast-paced justice," quipped one Jackson County Democrat activist.

The horses were removed. The same day the horses were taken away, a Jackson County sheriff's deputy arrived at Perry's home to arrest him and take him to the county jail in Kansas City to serve his contempt of court sentence. When Perry Olmstead was released from the county jail and returned to his farm, there was a notice placed on his front window with chains wrapped around the door. The notice was a property forfeiture seizure notification. As Perry read the notice, it said the FBI was seizing the farm because of criminal activity taking place on the property including violations of the federal Animal Welfare Act, violations of federal statutes related to the possession of firearms and dangerous weapons, and violations of the Ku Klux Klan Act of 1871. Perry Olmstead contacted a Kansas City attorney, Jack Aiello, who told Perry he was lucky to be alive.

"Perry, the FBI generally shoots first and asks questions later. Look at what happened in Idaho and in Waco, Texas. In any case, I think we can get a stay on the forfeiture seizure of your farm. Perry, if we are able to get the property seizure reversed, I think you should consider selling the farm and moving to a more sympathetic, hospitable county – and no longer live in Jackson County. Use the money from selling the farm to buy a property elsewhere in the state."

While all of this was going on, another disturbing incident took place in Kansas City. One February afternoon, Patrick Simms, a seventeen-year-old black student who lived in Kansas City, was playing a video game at an upscale video arcade in the Country Club Plaza Shopping Center. The teen became upset with the game because it failed to give him credit for winning a round, and in a frustrated response, he threw a bottle of soda at the game and broke the screen. In a panicked response, Patrick ran out of the arcade and was quickly pursued by two Kansas City police officers. The police caught up with Patrick in the parking lot and responded to his flight from them by shooting him in the chest and instantly killing the unarmed boy. The two officers were placed on paid administrative leave and after a short investigation by the Jackson County prosecuting attorney's office, it was determined there was insufficient evidence to pursue the matter further. The Kansas City chief of police noted that Patrick violated a valid police order by fleeing and he should have expected that he would get shot. The prosecuting attorney was alarmed that Patrick Simms had vandalized and caused property damage to expensive equipment inside the Fun Province Arcade and then he fled from the police. "Let this be a warning to young blacks who choose to come to our special Plaza shopping center," the prosecuting attorney lectured. "Kansas City will not tolerate criminal behavior from you thugs. Just keep out of our city. Stay on your basketball courts. We don't want your type here."

11

In Washington, the administration's second term came to a merciful end. On the last day of the administration, the president and his glamorous first lady stripped nearly all of the furniture out of the White House, likely to be sold on the black market with the proceeds deposited into the treasury of their personal foundation. In addition, on that last day, the president issued one thousand pardons, a constitutionally specified right of the president. Most of the pardons were handed out to individuals who had engaged in flagrant money laundering, and presumably these individuals had generously funneled some of their sordid gains into the president's personal foundation. The president and the first lady had previously announced that they thought their greatest accomplishment was the ardent, steadfast campaign against the pernicious presence of the Ku Klux Klan. The president was even boastful that he had targeted the Ku Klux Klan in Yugoslavia – thought to be a proto, or perhaps it was a paleo, remnant of the much-despised racist organization. There were no media personalities or reporters who ever quizzed the president or the first lady about the slimy connection of the Ku Klux Klan to the Democrat Party and Woodrow Wilson. There were a few Republicans who thought the departing president's most memorable legacy was his constant proclivity to be a skirt chaser and a cad, and famously engaging in various lurid sexual predatory activities inside the oval office with a

White House intern barely two years older than his own daughter. But, at least, the Republicans never found the necessity to express the sentiment that the president was a threat to democracy. The president's most significant contribution to his legacy, aside from his obsession with bombing Yugoslavia into the Stone Age, was when he demonstrated his mastery of Descartes as he explained away his obsession with predatory conduct with women by saying, "It depends on what the meaning of 'is' is." One of the president's aides even attempted to rationalize the president's predatory behavior by shaming the women he targeted by saying, "You never know what you'll attract by hanging a two dollar bill out of the window as you drive through a trailer park." Famously, the first lady lashed out at the continual commentary about her husband's rapacious appetite for women and young girls when she said that these assertions were part of "a vast right-wing conspiracy which controls all of the world's information ecosystem algorithms that force everyone into rabbit holes to endlessly watch car crashes all day and night." Her most memorable glib response was, "At this point, what difference does it make?!"

With the departure of the Madam Attorney General, because of a new Republican president, there was some hope that the Ku Klux Klan program would be shuffled off to the back burner. While everyone understood the FBI would not end the Ku Klux Klan Task Force, since the esteemed agency had never previously been known to stop one of its task forces, it was hoped by some that the Justice Department might suspend the courtroom prosecution of frivolous cases. The Madam Attorney General gave an ominous departing speech at the Justice Department before she left office, declaring the department's "eternal commitment to rout out white supremacy and the Ku Klux Klan in every corner of the world as the most dangerous, insidious presence on the globe." Many interpreted her comments to mean the Ku Klux Klan project had a life of its own and would slither along without regard to who occupied the office of attorney general.

It was the desire and expectation of Michael and Carol Holden and Paul Mooney that the whole charade could finally stop. Their attorney, Larry Korhonen, wasn't nearly as naïve and unrealistic. Korhonen was an experienced attorney and knew that the government never discontinues a pursuit – especially if it is already in the litigation phase. But he did not openly diminish their hope and dream. He merely said, "Well, let's see how this comes along." In addition, subconsciously he certainly wasn't wishing for the monthly fees from the three defendants to end.

The new attorney general was a former Republican senator from Missouri, of all places, who had served as the governor of Missouri before being elected as a senator. He was a popular figure in Missouri Republican circles, and Michael Holden hoped the Missouri connection and his party affiliation would finally bring an end to the Ku Klux Klan case. Michael asked activists in the St. Louis County Republican Party to contact the new attorney general and discuss the absurdity of the Ku Klux Klan case in the Missouri eastern district. A St. Louis County party official indeed spoke to the new attorney general who said he would look into the matter.

Months passed. A new status conference was called by the judge hearing the case, and no word came down from the Justice Department in Washington. Michael asked his acquaintance in the St. Louis County Republican Party operation if anything had been heard from the new attorney general. Nothing had been heard. Michael continued to ask about the new attorney general's decision about the case. Finally, after nearly a year, word came down that the new attorney general would not interfere and would not ask for the case to be dismissed. Michael, Carol and Paul were disappointed and began to realize that the wheels of justice are not only slow, but they are part of Wilsonian bureaucracy and just continue plodding along without any connection to reality or what is happening in the actual existence of living, breathing people. It was a discouraging realization for the three of them. It seemed to them that everything is on autopilot, that once something is set into motion – even for nefarious reasons or for malintent – it just keeps going. Michael realized this was the entire purpose of the Wilsonian, Rooseveltian, Trumanite, and Johnsonian systems of bureaucracy: the elites and experts are mere functionaries, serving no one, controlled or limited by nothing, answerable to nothing, merely cogs in a huge perpetual motion machine, dishing out regulations and rules and supervision and decisions without any checks or limitations. He began to realize the Ku Klux Klan case would go on and on until it ran out of gas on its own – there was nothing that could be done to stop it or interfere with it. Essentially, this is what their attorney had been trying to get them to understand.

"I don't want to be fatalistic, but I am fatalistic," Michael shared with Carol. "The justice system is purely about serving itself. It is not about justice or right or wrong. It is only about itself and its ownership over its own bureaucracy – to ensure the proper shuffling of paper, and sorting of pencils and paper clips, and filing the proper forms, and saying the proper and right words. How many people do you think have had their property confiscated or been thrown into jail and lost their liberty because this bureaucratic, faceless system has just plowed over them as it mercilessly lumbers along – dispensing its justice?"

Michael Junior's eighth-grade year was rewarding. He was remarkably dignified as he served as an acolyte at Salem Synod Church. People constantly came to Carol and told her how handsome, and proper, and reverent, and solemn, and disciplined he was. Michael Junior's trombone teacher wanted him to play a trombone recital for the end of his eighth-grade year. Michael Junior prepared J.S. Bach's *Air from Suite No. 3*, Montbrun's *Aria*, and Ropartz's *Andante and*

Allegro. But his teacher had a special surprise for the boy. Michael Junior's teacher arranged for him to play the trombone with the Forte Orchestra in Daphne Probst's cantata performance at the synod's Trinity Church. The group was to perform J.S. Bach's cantata *Es ist nichts Gesundes an meinem Leibe*, BWV 25. Michael Junior would play alongside two other trombonists from the Forte Orchestra of St. Louis. After the performance of the cantata, Michael Junior would play his three solo recital pieces. The entire concert would be recorded and played on the synod's radio station KFUO.

Es ist nichts Gesundes an meinem Leibe, BWV 25.

There is nothing healthy in my body because of your anger

And there is no peace in my bones

The whole world is nothing but a hospital

Where in numbers too great to count

People and even children in their cradles

Lie down in pain and sickness.

One person is tortured in his breast

By a fierce fever of vicious desire;

Another lies sick from the detestable stench of his own honor;

A third wastes away through his obsession with money

And before his time is thrown into the grave.

The first fall has stained everyone

And infected them with the leprosy of sin.

Ah, this poison rages through my limbs!

Where in my wretchedness may I find a cure?

Who stands by me in my misery?

Where is my doctor, who can help me again?

Ah, where in my wretchedness may I find counsel?

My leprosy, my boils.

O Jesus, beloved master, I flee to you;

Ah, strengthen my weakened vital spirits!
Take pity, you doctor and helper of all who are sick,
Do not drive me away from your face!
My healer, make me clean from the leprosy of sin;
Then to you I want in return my whole heart
To dedicate as a constant offering
And for all my life to be thankful for your help.
Open to my simple songs, Jesus, your merciful ears!
When there in the choir above
I shall sing with the angels,
My song of thanksgiving will resound better.
All my days I shall praise your mighty hand
Because by your mighty hand
Because of you my trouble and distress
Have been turned aside with such love.
Not only in this mortal life should your glory be spread abroad:
I want to bear witness to it hereafter also
And there forever praise you.

Michael Junior practiced diligently. He rehearsed the Bach cantata with the Forte Orchestra five times before the concert – one rehearsal with the full choir and soloists. Michael and Carol rented a tuxedo for their son. He put it on and took it off several times, doing a fashion show for his parents and his sister.

"Andrea, what do you think?" he asked his sister.

"It looks like you're ready to get married," she teased him in response.

"Momma, I'm nervous."

"Of course, you are, Son. But you will do very well, I know. Lord knows, you have been practicing with every ounce of your attention and dedication."

He practiced his three solo pieces over and over with piercing focus.

The concert was held at Trinity Church, an old historic synod church built in 1865 with beautiful marble on the walls, the columns, and the altarpiece. The ceiling had stunning vaults in the nave and the apse. It was a venerable and beloved church that had hosted much of the synod's history over the past one-hundred-forty years. The church was filled for the concert including nearly all of the fifth-through-eighth-grade students from Michael Junior's school, Salem Synod School. Mrs. Probst brought her husband, Dr. Jacob Alan Probst, the former president of the synod. Alice Ploughmaster, the beloved former mayor of East St. Louis, attended also, because she was a close friend of Dr. and Mrs. Probst. When Michael Junior saw the large audience, he was nervous. He observed the members of the orchestra tuning their instruments and playing through small parts of the cantata. One of the trombonists whispered to Michael Junior that this was the time to loosen up on the horn and be certain his embouchure was flexible and ready. "Play some scales, and even some of our parts of the piece," he advised. "That's what we do now." Michael Junior looked out into the nave and located his mother, father, Andrea, and his grandparents. He smiled and waved at them.

The conductor of the Forte Orchestra walked out to his podium. He turned to the audience and bowed. He then pointed to the side of the church and acknowledged Mrs. Probst and the bass and tenor soloists. Then the soloists came out and bowed. The soloists took their positions with their sections of the choir. When everything was quiet, the conductor stood and eyed each section of the orchestra and the choir. He nodded his head and raised his arms. The cantata begins with a short string and woodwind opening joined with a choral fugue and then the trombones and recorders enter with a dirge chorale. The trombones and the trumpet along with the soprano section bring the first movement chorale to a crescendo. The tenor moved to the front and sang a recitative with continuo accompaniment from the cello and harpsicord. Then the bass stepped forward and performed a very special aria with a cello continuo and an extraordinary lute part in continuo and counterpoint. The cantata moved to Mrs. Probst in front of the orchestra singing a lyrical soprano recitative with cello and lute continuo, and then a virtuosic soprano aria which features distinctive parts by the strings, the recorders, and the oboes in counterpoint. Finally, the cantata concludes with a chorus and the trombones briefly recalling and evoking the melody of the soprano's aria.

The audience burst into roars and cheers, as well as loud applause. The conductor acknowledged the three vocal soloists who came to the front of the orchestra and bowed. He then pointed to the three recorder players to stand separately, then the cellist and the lutist, then the trumpeter and the three trombonists. And the conductor concluded by pointing specifically to Michael Junior and had him stand alone. The audience reached a pitch and roared loudly just for Michael Junior. Carol began to cry. She was so proud of her sweet, adorable son. He is such a fine young man. She quickly remembered him as the angelic, sweet, innocent child. She briefly recalled his tender soul, his earnest desire to help the homeless, and how he busily and diligently built crosses and sold them in the church narthex to earn money to buy clothes for these people he so ardently wished to help. Here he was now playing with an orchestra and Mrs. Probst. She beamed with pride as tears flowed down her cheeks. The conductor announced there would be a brief pause and then Michael Junior would give his eighth-grade solo recital on the trombone. Michael walked down to the area next to the podium and played his three pieces, which seemed flawless to everyone, but he knew where he made his mistakes. When he finished, he was greeted with loud applause and cheers. Dr. Probst brought him a bouquet of flowers and said, "You are a wonderful talent, young man. You have a special future. The synod is very proud of you."

"Thank you, sir."

Mrs. Probst, who had just performed in the cantata, came up to him and gave him a big embrace and said she was so proud of him. "Michael, you are an inspiration to everyone. You are a very special model to every parent in this room. Everyone wants to have a remarkable young man like you to be their son. And you are a terrific blessing to the synod. What a fine young man you are."

"Thank you, ma'am."

Then Mrs. Probst waited in line to talk to Carol and Michael since they were surrounded by others in the nave. "Michael and Carol, you are so blessed to have such a wonderful son. What a special, special young man. He is an inspiration for the synod."

Mrs. Ploughmaster came to Michael Junior and told him she remembered him from when he was a younger boy. "You have turned out to be everything I thought you would be – a fine, inspiring, talented leader. Such a fine young gentleman. Congratulations. The synod is so lucky and blessed to have you. I know your parents are so very proud of you."

"Thank you, ma'am."

Teachers and students from his school approached him and congratulated him. Other audience members also came to him to give him their compliments and praise.

12

When the Alfred Sendahl Perfume Company closed, Michael began looking for a new job. After a three-week search he found employment as an accountant with the auto and truck parts company that Keith Newland once worked for. Following Keith's murder, the company used temporary accountants to perform the necessary bookkeeping and accounting routines, and they were delighted to find Michael to take on the permanent role. Michael's primary complaint about the new job was the salary was not as rewarding as his position with Sendahl Perfume. Michael and Carol were confronted with substantial financial stress from the ongoing legal bills stemming from the Ku Klux Klan case.

"I'm worried about our finances," Michael confided to Carol.

"It is going to be very tight," Carol concurred. "But Michael, I have a gallery exhibit that may generate a good commission. Some of the artists in Anne Newland's art colony in Ste. Genevieve are looking for a St. Louis gallery venue and we have made plans for the group to do a few shows at our gallery. I am hoping there will be excellent commissions."

"Congratulations. That's excellent. Any long-term prospects with this project?"

"It may develop into some lasting relationships."

Anne Newland was active with the Ste. Genevieve art colony. Several well-known black artists in recent years had settled at the Ste. Genevieve colony as part of an effort to rediscover the black heritage in the region. Ste. Genevieve always had a population of black workers in the quarries and the kilns near the town and by 1930 more than three hundred black residents lived in or around Ste. Genevieve. On an October night in 1930, two black men, Columbus Jennings and Lonnie Taylor, paid two white men for a ride in their wagon so they could get to the Mississippi River where a late-night and early-morning card game was scheduled to occur. While at the river, a fight broke out between the four men and after the conclusion of the melee, one of the white men, Harry Panchot, was dead. The white survivor of the conflict, Paul Ritter, was badly injured and made accusations that he and Panchot had been attacked and robbed by the two black passengers in the wagon. Taylor and Jennings, the two black men, were brought to the courthouse for questioning. Taylor indicated that Ritter had offered a sum of money, perhaps as much as $50, for a sexual encounter, which is what caused the dispute between the four men. The allegations of a sexual nature conjured up age-old, cliché-ridden tensions, assumptions, and accusations between the races. To prevent a lynch mob from forming, the county sheriff removed Taylor and Jennings into protective custody and arranged for the pair to be transferred to the neighboring town of Hudson. Unrest among the white residents of Ste. Genevieve began to percolate. White residents went to the homes of black people and told them to leave Ste. Genevieve within twenty-four hours. By Monday, two hundred black families left the town and found refuge in neighboring counties. Only three black families remained in Ste. Genevieve. One of the remaining black residents was Louis Ribeau, the local mail carrier for Ste. Genevieve. Because Ritter, the surviving white man involved in the fight at the riverbank, finally died in the hospital from his injuries, the white residents decided they needed to express some type of revenge and attempted to kidnap mailman Ribeau. Hans Witt, a Ste. Genevieve white resident and a member of the synod, witnessed the kidnapping of Ribeau and was outraged by the racial discrimination and violence. He rammed his car into the mob of five hundred enraged, rioting white residents that was attempting to abduct Ribeau, and then Witt took the black mail carrier to his house and hid him in the basement. The county sheriff only arrested six rioters from the mob of five hundred, and they were released by the judge without any fines or punishment for illegal rioting and attempted kidnapping. Ribeau escaped to St. Louis and never returned to Ste. Genevieve. Hans Witt was charged by the county attorney and ultimately convicted of the misdemeanor of harboring a black man in his home. In the meantime, the two black men who were involved in the original riverbank altercation, Lonnie Taylor and Columbus Jennings, were tried for murder and were given life jail sentences. To prevent further violence, the sheriff in Ste. Genevieve issued an executive order that only property-owning black residents could be in Ste. Genevieve.

Beginning in the 1970s, black artists began moving to the Ste. Genevieve art colony in an effort to rediscover and reclaim the black heritage in the area. Because of the long-established kiln enterprises in Ste. Genevieve, many of the black artists were pottery makers, ceramics artists, and tile makers.

Back in Jackson County, Perry Olmstead awaited promises from his attorney, Jack Aiello, that the asset forfeiture seizure could be overturned. Perry Olmstead's attorney was just as drawn to collect attorney's fees as was Michael and Carol Holden's attorney, but Perry's attorney knew prompt action was necessary to rescue Perry's farm. Attorney Aiello petitioned the federal court in the western district of Missouri and made credible claims that the farm property was not subject to asset forfeiture. Fortuitously, the judge who drew the case was an appointee of President Reagan and was a staunch conservative, as well as a member of the synod. Judge John Langemeier found the entire asset forfeiture ploy to be exceedingly offensive and an overreach beyond comprehension by a police state. Judge Langemeier knew it was risky to reveal his tendency toward libertarian views about private property, so he kept his true beliefs veiled in judicial restraint. However, the judge took every opportunity from the bench, in all cases before him, to search for faults in the government's regular overreach and he would carefully excise government claims if he believed civil liberties or private property rights were under assault. Judge Langemeier ruled in summary judgment that the weapons charges against Perry Olmstead were not credible and dismissed them. He then ruled the Animal Welfare Act did not apply to Perry's horses. Judge Langemeier, however, did not dismiss the complaint related to the Ku Klux Klan Act of 1871 for two reasons. First, the judge knew the Justice Department was thoroughly committed to and entranced by the Ku Klux Klan Act and he didn't want to dip his toe into that murky quagmire. And, second, Judge Langemeier, as a member of the synod, was particularly outraged and sickened by an organization like the Ku Klux Klan – a creation of the Democrat Party as its enforcement arm and championed by Woodrow Wilson as a useful devise to push around the public which Wilson believed was a mass of annoying idiots. Judge Langemeier didn't want to make a ruling that could be interpreted as downplaying the vile, criminal, contemptible, and absolute offensiveness of the Ku Klux Klan – one of the prized creations of the Democrat Party. Consequently, Judge Langemeier let the Klan portion of the complaint remain – despite the peculiar and inexplicable curiosity that Perry Olmstead was a black man. However, Judge Langemeier did rule the charges related to the Ku Klux Klan Act did not give the FBI permission to attempt to seize Perry's farm. Jack Aiello, Perry's attorney, regarded the ruling as a tremendous victory and hoped Perry

Olmstead would invite him out to dinner, or at least to a fine restaurant or lounge at the Hyatt Regency for cocktails.

"Perry, you will need to sell the farm as soon as you can. I realize the property has been in your family for three generations, but I am giving you sound legal advice right now. You need to get the hell out of Jackson County. You need to look at this the same way black people were forced to face reality when the lynch mobs showed up on the porch of a black person in Kansas City, or Springfield, or the hundreds of other places in this state. They were wise; they didn't hang around and argue. They packed up their property and they went to safer refuge. Perry, it is time for you to see Kansas City and Jackson County as the hideout of the modern-day lynch mob. The liberals and the Democrats have their own up-to-date versions of the Ku Klux Klan – zoning courts, homeowners associations, public school boards of education, police departments, prosecuting attorneys who are practicing equity justice, the FBI, the Missouri Criminal Investigation Bureau, tax collectors, mothers enrolling their children in soccer clubs, the DMV, the FDA, the EPA, the State Department and the Labor Department, ballot harvesting, frivolous lawsuits; the list is endless. The fact that the federal government and the FBI want to pursue you for being in the Ku Klux Klan, I don't know what to tell you about that. I believe you should fight it, for principle if not to protect your liberties. I will be happy to defend you in that matter – I can assure you it will go on for a while. But in the meantime, sell your farm. You will need to clean out all the junk in order to obtain a sales contract. And, by the way, thanks for the beer."

Perry Olmstead contacted a junk hauling service and had them pick up the items on the farm he no longer needed. He hired a real estate broker who put the property on the market. A contract was offered, but before the closing on the real estate contract, Perry was contacted by the title company. The title company told Perry they were not able to release the title because Jackson County had placed a $10,000 lien on the property because of the county's assertion it was an unlicensed junk yard.

Perry Olmstead called his attorney about the latest assault. "Listen Perry, in other circumstances I would say we should just fight them in court," Jack Aiello said. "But you need to sell that farm and escape this hotbed of racist lynching immediately. Remember, lynching has a very long, established history in Jackson County. They love to lynch black people here. It is a form of entertainment by these characters. And you are now the target of a lynch mob. Just pay the damn $10,000 lien, then sell the farm, and then move out of this rathole before they lynch you during your escape."

Perry paid the $10,000 for the lien to be released. The property was sold. Perry Olmstead then searched for a more hospitable place to reside. He found a fifty-three-acre plot in Ste. Genevieve County in eastern Missouri.

* * *

While the new administration was considering what to do about the federal Ku Klux Klan case filed against Michael and Carol and Paul, another crisis erupted. Nineteen Al-Quaeda militant Muslim extremists hijacked four commercial jet airliners – two of them were flown into the World Trade Center skyscrapers, one into the Pentagon in Washington, and one crashed into a field in western Pennsylvania. Quickly, it appeared to be a coordinated, conspiratorial attack and the new administration immediately identified the militant group Al-Quaeda as the culprit. Years later it was discovered by an FBI agent, who was involved in tracking Saudi intelligence operations, that the nineteen hijackers were actually working for the CIA as secret agents.

Don Canestraro, who was the lead agent of Operation Encore, discovered years after the tragedy that all of the hijackers were working for the CIA, had their educational pursuits paid for by the CIA, lived in apartments paid for by the CIA, received allowances and payments from the CIA, and engaged in spying operations for the CIA. Apparently, the FBI had involvement in the program to protect the hijackers' identities and secret activities. Harry S. Truman's dream of an efficient, worldwide supersecret intelligence state, which would roam through the world killing people and collecting clandestine information, had finally reached its apex. Petrified by the backlash which would ultimately be unleashed by the Congress, as well as opponents of government overreach and the public, the CIA and the FBI engaged in a sordid, complex, secret coverup to prevent the revelations from being discovered. (It was assumed by both agencies that the lapdog media would merely ignore or discount the shocking findings. After all, their primary concern was the president's favorite flavor of ice cream.) When FBI officials discovered that Canestraro knew all about the hijackers' connections with the CIA, the FBI instantly ended Canestraro's investigation and encouraged him to take an early retirement. Since then, the FBI has forbidden additional investigation into the entire matter.

In a slightly feckless approach to the entire terrorist attack, the new administration sought Congressional approval to pursue the matter with military action – yet also avoid the constitutionally mandated requirement of a declaration of war. Apparently, the new administration thought a "declared war" would somehow upset the various foreign allies who had been such dedicated participants in pumping billions of dollars into the clandestine affairs of counterintelligence and developing lasting, excellent relationships with the terrorists who executed the attack. The new administration sought to launch a similar private war strategy that the previous administration had been conducting in Yugoslavia to rout out the proto- (or was it paleo?)

Ku Klux Klan. It's just that the new administration would be a little more open and obvious about their military campaign, as contrasted with the previous administration's secret war in Yugoslavia. At least the new administration didn't recycle the Ku Klux Klan excuse, so commonly relied on by the previous president, as well as the charming first lady, and the Madam Attorney General.

Despite the new administration not openly talking about the Ku Klux Klan obsession, the new attorney general, a former politician from Missouri, did insist the Ku Klux Klan federal cases continue without interruption. The judge in the St. Louis case involving Michael, Carol and Paul, called another status conference. The defendants' attorney continued to focus on the line of reasoning that the only known members of the Ku Klux Klan are FBI agents. Hedrick J. Winters, the judge in the case, became impatient and exploded without judicial composure or restraint.

"Now, you listen here, Mr. Korhonen! I have told you I will not tolerate that line of reasoning, that entire approach to your defense. I am warning you now, if you continue to pursue this, I will sanction you. I will not allow you to disparage the stellar reputation and impeccable integrity of the FBI. I am warning you that you are forbidden to pursue any of this in front of a jury. It will bias the jury. And I will order my bailiff to put duct tape over your mouth during the trial if you even imply or insinuate this line of reasoning. Do you understand me?"

The U.S attorney beamed with satisfaction; it's so nice to have the judge on your side.

* * *

Other dilemmas and troubles confronted the new administration, but the one that captured the imagination of the media was a devastating hurricane that hit New Orleans. There was some mild criticism of both the governor of Louisiana and the mayor of New Orleans for not taking the impending event any too seriously. The governor kept saying, "We have it handled." The mayor never invoked an evacuation order, and when he was quizzed why hundreds of school buses remained locked up inside a fenced-in lot when they could have been used to rescue residents, the mayor said the buses had recently been cleaned and the city couldn't afford for them to be soiled and furthermore, there was no one qualified to drive the buses since the insurance regulations are so restrictive.

But these criticisms of the governor and the mayor were purely perfunctory because the feigned outrage by the media was being saved up for the administration in Washington. Using the recycled tactics of the previous administration to magically see racism where it likely didn't occur, the media circusgoers flocked into New Orleans to point fingers at the administration in Washington for not doing anything for the poor victims of the hurricane. ABC News quickly sent their correspondent Jake Pepper and had him ensconced in the $500-a-night Four Seasons Hotel. The neighborhood around the Four Seasons didn't have an excessive amount of rain and storm surge – thus, keeping the sanctimonious journalist safe from the elements – and so Pepper searched around near the hotel until he found a puddle of water and carefully arranged to stand in the puddle while his cameraman set up for some quality film footage. And then Pepper announced to his audience that he had just witnessed several bodies of poor New Orleans residents floating down the flooded street which had turned into a river carrying hundreds of pathetic dead victims. "I wish. I just wish in my soul that the corrupt, racist administration in Washington even had an ounce of decency and integrity," he sanctimoniously whined. National Public Radio sent their rarified correspondent Tina Notenberger to New Orleans, and she whimpered on and on about how the New Orleans residents had been abandoned by the racists who run the administration in Washington. She told tear-jerking stories about poor residents forced to live on the roofs of their homes for days, or how small children were forced to live in dog shelters until help arrived.

There actually were some atrocities that defied explanation and could foster anger and abject disbelief. Trapped residents in New Orleans were encouraged to make their way to the Superdome, the city's domed professional football stadium. Thousands of people found refuge inside the building – estimated to be tens of thousands. Because of power outages, the building had no ventilation, and it became unbearable for the thousands of people crammed into the structure. Several men, using the inspiring ingenuity and finesse of the American spirit, climbed to the top levels of the stadium and these clever men, standing on each other's shoulders, began to hammer out holes and openings in the ceiling and the roof to be able to bring in some desperately needed fresh air. When the authorities – either from the Federal Emergency Management Agency or some other bureaucracy – learned of the numerous holes in the roof of the Superdome, they instantly dispatched repair crews in helicopters to land on top of the Superdome roof and execute immediate, emergency repairs to fill in and close the gaping holes. Jake Pepper didn't find this story worthy of his breathless reporting.

Memorial Hospital in New Orleans was flooded and lost electricity. A significant number of the 2,500 patients were poor black residents. Prior to the flooding, hundreds of hospital employees were unable to manage any type of organized evacuation – later discovered because their senses and rational minds were rendered incapable because they were high on marijuana. Dr. Anna Pou, a heroic and inspiring physician in the hospital, promised to guarantee care for all the patients who were trapped in the building. Dr. Pou marshaled physicians, nurses and other employees to care for the trapped patients.

After the disaster, the Democrat attorney general of Louisiana sought to track down various scapegoats for the tragedies from the hurricane. When it came to the Memorial Hospital crisis, where forty-five patients died, the state's attorney general started pointing fingers at Dr. Pou. He ordered the indictment of Dr. Pou and two nurses for murder. Later the state's Supreme Court ruled there were no grounds to blame Dr. Pou or any other health care professional for the tragedies resulting from the hurricane disaster and the indictments were dismissed. During the hysteria to blame Dr. Pou for the hurricane, Jake Pepper and Tina Notenberger were quick to jump aboard the bandwagon. "I wish. In my soul, I wish that a medical professional had just an ounce of dignity and conscience – especially when so many are suffering because of the thoughtlessness, hate and racism of the administration in Washington," Pepper bleated.

Alice Ploughmaster, the former mayor of East St. Louis, conducts a distinguished and esteemed conference every summer in New Orleans at Xavier University, where she received her college degrees and where she served as a visiting instructor one year. Mrs. Ploughmaster was in New Orleans when the hurricane hit the city. She observed the devastation of the flooding and the tragic consequences to the poor residents of the city – most of whom were black people. "It was heartbreaking and disturbing beyond belief," she reflected. "There is a significant population of poor people in New Orleans, and they clearly suffered tremendously. They suffered, not specifically because they were black, but because they were poor and had no way to escape. The city failed to evacuate these people. It was not the responsibility of Washington to execute an evacuation plan; that was the city's responsibility. If the mayor refused to allow school buses to be used to help get these people out, he should answer for it, not the bureaucrats and politicians in Washington."

Years later, during a subsequent Democrat administration, when a catastrophic hurricane swept through North Carolina devastating towns and roads and homes, the president and his sycophantic vice president, who was desperately clawing her way to replace the president in an upcoming election, said they had done all they could and furthermore, there just weren't enough financial resources remaining to help out; the entire federal budget had already been spent importing, transporting, housing, and subsidizing 21 million illegal, undocumented migrants over four years. There just wasn't any money left. The subservient and hypnotized media conveniently said nothing and pretended like they didn't notice anything was awry. For some reason, the television networks didn't find it necessary to dispatch Jake Pepper and Tina Notenberger to cover that disaster.

* * *

At the conclusion of Michael Junior's eighth-grade year at Salem Synod School, it was the plan of his parents to have him enroll at St. Louis North Synod High School, the alma mater of Michael Senior. There was a slight impediment, however. Once Michael lost his position at the Alfred Sendahl Perfume Company, the family's income took a significant hit. Carol's gallery was paying for itself and generating a small income for Carol, but certainly not enough to replace Michael's lost salary from Sendahl. In addition, Michael and Carol were paying a minimum of $1,000 each month to their attorney for the Ku Klux Klan case. These factors, in addition to the burden of confiscatory federal and state taxation, caused Michael and Carol to face significant financial burdens, and ultimately to decide to enroll Michael Junior in the public high school in Florissant. In hindsight, to give Michael Junior the synod high school education he deserved, and as was later understood, very desperately needed, the Holdens should have appealed to Dr. Probst and Daphne Probst for assistance, or they should have asked for a gift from Alice Ploughmaster, or they should have appealed to the synod itself, or to Salem parish for a financial scholarship. But Michael and Carol were black people with deep abiding dignity and self-esteem, imbued in them from their proud, noble, upstanding parents and grandparents before them. It never occurred to them to plead for help from the people who cared so much for them. They did not request financial aid and instead made a crucial decision that would later come to haunt them, as Jake Pepper would say, in their souls.

13

Chubbles Philigrew had occasion to visit a liquor store in the Baden neighborhood in north St. Louis. He wanted a 64-ounce bottle of Colt .45 malt liquor – the bottle with the image of Billy Dee Williams cryptically saying, "The dynamite power of Colt .45." While Chubbles was in the liquor store, two men walked into the business, dressed like bandits with ski masks and brandishing pistols. If employees of Tamika's bank were to have been present, they would likely have thought the two characters seemed familiar. Had Chubbles been more perceptive and observant on the day of Tamika's funeral, he might have been able to see a resemblance of the two liquor store intruders to the funeral procession hijackers. The two men, attired in light parka jackets and their ski masks, as if they were preparing to take a quick run down the man-made slopes at a ski area in Eureka on the outskirts of St. Louis, approached the sales counter and told the proprietor, "Gimme all you's cash."

Chubbles, armed with his semi-automatic Baretta, quietly approached the counter, behind the two equity recipients. The store proprietor looked at Chubbles with an expression of disapproval, and he said, "No! Hey, I don't want trouble. Please stop." The two hoodlums quickly turned around and were surprised to see Chubbles armed with a handgun. One of the robbers shot a round toward Chubbles, but it did not hit him and instead the projectile crashed into a shelf with vodka and bourbon bottles. The store owner announced again to Chubbles, "Let them go! I don't want a killing in my store."

The two robbers, with the cash in a paper bag, ran out of the store. Chubbles never pulled his trigger. The store proprietor called the Metro Police who arrived and immediately shifted the focus from the two armed robbers and onto Chubbles. They demanded his identification and wanted to see his concealed carry permit for his firearm. (At this time, all concealed firearms in Missouri required a permit if carried by a private individual.) Chubbles was placed under arrest, not for robbery, but for carrying a firearm without a concealed carry permit.

While Chubbles was being arrested and taken into custody to police headquarters on Tucker Blvd. for booking, the Metro Police were somehow able to locate and subdue the two men who had robbed the liquor store just twenty minutes earlier. The two suspects were transported to police headquarters and booked for aggravated armed robbery. Chubbles was informed that he would be released if he posted a five-hundred-dollar bail. Chubbles, a naturally ill-tempered and surly individual, was not able to maintain a network of friends who would be able to drive to police headquarters and post a bail for him. However, Chubbles had previously used an attorney for a few minor infractions, including the time a neighbor accused Chubbles of violating city zoning ordinances for keeping pigeon bird cages in his back yard. Someone told Chubbles about the prospect of raising pigeons as a hobby but also as an opportunity to sell the carcasses as meat to tiny Italian eateries and deli markets in The Hill neighborhood. His venture into pigeon farming never amounted to a payday because the proprietors of Italian dining establishments said they weren't interested, and the Italian delis and markets said they only purchased pigeon meat from Sicilian product import suppliers. When his neighbor filed a zoning complaint against Chubbles, it was necessary to hire an attorney to represent him at St. Louis Zoning Court. The zoning judge dismissed the case with the understanding that Chubbles would dismantle and remove the pigeon cages from his property.

"Charlie, it's Chubbles Philigrew," he said to attorney Charlie Walters, during his one allowed phone call. "I've gotten myself into some trouble, Charlie. I am being charged with carrying a concealed weapon without a permit. I'm being detained at police headquarters on Tucker Blvd. I need a five-hundred-dollar bail. I will repay you immediately on my release. Can you help me?"

Charlie Walters, a sixty-two-year-old black man who attended SIU Law school thirty years ago, drove to the police station and posted a bail for Chubbles and Chubbles repaid him from his personal stash that he kept hidden in his secondary socks drawer in his bedroom, which was on the bottom drawer of his chest.

An arraignment was scheduled at the St. Louis City circuit court on Market Street. Chubbles was charged with violating the state's concealed carry law without a permit. Charlie Walters, came to court wearing his standard flamboyant fare – an extra-large, red double-breasted suit jacket with extraordinarily wide lapels, oversized side pocket flaps, a pronounced back vent slit, large gold buttons, and a voluminous chest pocket square. The jacket could have been taken out of the *Captain Kangaroo* wardrobe. He wore a Victorian ruffled pink shirt with spectacular lace-ruffled cuffs, and a large bow tie. His hair was always coifed in a James Brown-style bouffant.

"I will talk to the assistant prosecuting attorney about obtaining equity justice for you, Chubbles," Walters said.

The assistant prosecuting attorney told Charlie Walters that equity justice was not available to Chubbles because he was *not* caught in the act of committing a crime. "Limney only allows equity justice when there is a criminal act taking place."

Democrat Prosecuting Attorney Limney Grantham maintains a strict policy that only individuals engaged in criminal acts or violent crimes are able to qualify for her prized equity justice program – and, thus, to be released back on the street to perpetuate more carefully rehearsed acts of criminal street theater.

Since it was Chubbles's first offense, Charlie Walters arranged a decreased fine of only a thousand dollars along with a guilty plea.

The same day of Chubbles's final disposition, the two liquor store robbers who brandished firearms and shot a round in the store in the direction of Chubbles, and then took off with nearly a thousand dollars in cash from the store register, appeared in the St. Louis City circuit court to face charges of felony aggravated armed robbery, attempted assault, discharge of a weapon, mischief and endangerment. Limney Grantham's equity justice program clearly applied to these two habitual offenders. The assistant prosecuting attorney made a motion to drop the charges and the judge instantly granted the routine motion – hardly able to conceal his delighted acquiescence. The two offenders committed at least one criminal act every single day in St. Louis – 355 days a year – only missing ten days a year because they happened to oversleep, or when it was a travel day on their way to Ste. Genevieve, Cape Girardeau, or Springfield. The two characters departed the courthouse free men, thanks once again to Miss Grantham's deeply held commitment to equity.

* * *

Carol and Michael were devastated that they felt forced to make the decision to not send Michael Junior to St. Louis North Synod High School. Michael Senior, in particular, was bothered because it was his alma mater, and he had such an excellent experience at the acclaimed school and wished for a similar opportunity for his son. St. Louis North Synod is a school with a predominantly black student body – more than 50 percent of the students are black or mixed race – with very high and competitive academic expectations. The school also maintains very motivated and determined athletic teams in football, baseball, basketball, softball, tennis, soccer, swimming, and track and field. The school is very famous for its acclaimed custom of highly intricate and solemn ceremonies, processionals, and rituals – pulled from medieval German observances – which are used to imbue character, reverence, devotion, and piety in the student body. In many of these solemn rituals, the entire grade – such as the junior class or senior class, both boys and girls – will file in an elaborate, reverent processional, attired in glamorous robes, some students carrying elegant wooden and brass staffs, some students wearing special caps, some carrying incense censers, all based on their ceremonial positions or their elected status in the school. They march in solemn dignity, sometimes with instrumental and choral accompaniment, often through the neighborhood surrounding the campus and then back onto the school grounds and into the chancel of the chapel. These dignified ceremonies – at least a dozen of them during the school year – carry the highest regard and respect by the entire student body and are regarded as one of the most distinct hallmarks of the extraordinary school. It broke Michael's heart to know his son would not be able to partake in the many fulfilling programs and traditions at St. Louis North Synod. When Carol finished her eighth-grade year at a synod parochial school, Bethlehem Synod School in the Hyde Park neighborhood of north St. Louis, her parents enrolled her in a public high school in St. Louis, and while it was not a particularly rewarding experience, she made the best of it and hoped the same would come to Michael Junior.

"Momma, do you think we should do some school clothes shopping before high school begins."

"Of course, Son; let's make a trip to the Boy's Shop." The Boy's Shop was inside the Jamestown Mall in North County just outside of Florissant. At one time, Jamestown Mall was considered to be one of the hottest retail spots in the St. Louis area. The residents of Kirkwood and Des Peres sneered and wrinkled their noses when they heard anyone boast about Jamestown Mall; it was just a little too plebeian and diverse – which was another way of saying (a sort of code language) that the racial composition was slightly more mixed than considered desirable. Des Peres was the elite and upscale town which was home to the West County Center, where all the trendy people, the upwardly mobile, and fashionable suburban *nouveau riche* shopped. Jamestown didn't have elite oyster bars and chic taverns and taprooms for the stylish and sophisticated lawyers and MBA graduates to prance about like peacocks impressing one another. Jamestown Mall was the home of a Sears and a J.C. Penney, with a food court and dozens of small shops selling apparel, candles, bath merchandise, shoes, and jewelry. Instead of trendy, highbrow bars and brewpubs and elegant New York jewelers and boutiques, Jamestown merely offered up a Jared's, a Cinnabon, a Wetzel's, a Chick-fil-A, a Taco Bell, and a Panda Express. Carol and Michael Junior shopped for school clothes and the new ninth-grader obtained the kind of apparel he liked best and was accustomed to wearing – button down dress shirts, dress slacks, Levi's 502 jeans.

"Thank you, Momma. I will feel like a new man."

"You will look like a new man, but you will still be my special boy – my gem."

When they came home from Jamestown Mall, Michael Junior asked Andrea if she wanted to see a fashion show. After the fashion show, Michael Junior practiced his trombone for two hours, and then he sang synod hymns for an hour with Andrea.

* * *

The Ku Klux Klan case in St. Louis federal court continued. Pretrial status conferences were called by the judge every few months and the defense was regularly warned not to take the case off the very narrow path blazed by Judge Winters. The prosecutor sought a deposition with an official from the Alan Guttmacher Foundation as a way to establish the grounds that the victimized Democrat president and his lovely wife were actively and deeply concerned about women's health issues. And, according to the prosecutor's reasoning, the anti-abortion placards displayed by the defendants during their drive on I-49 caused grave disturbance, threat and upset to the president and his gracious wife. The prosecutor argued to the judge that the anti-abortion signs were perceived by the president to be a threat not only to him but to the civil rights of all women – one of his beloved and established constituencies.

The defense attorney, Larry Korhonen, challenged the prosecution's interpretation of the events on I-49 and the president's feelings of alarm. "Your honor, if the president has this sense of being under attack and is so deeply concerned about the civil rights of women, then he needs to make that case, in person as a witness, to the court and to the jury," Korhonen asserted.

"Your position is duly noted," Judge Winters responded. "But I believe the president had a reason to be upset and scandalized, and he believed his defense of women's health was under attack. And your request for the president to appear in this case is denied, as I have previously ruled. The president is afforded the protection of executive privilege. If the prosecution is able to use this witness to demonstrate a credible threat to women's health by holding up the offending placards, that satisfies the rules of reasoning, relevance, foundation and evidence. The prosecution may proceed with the deposition and then call the witness to testify at the trial."

Korhonen did not advance further objections with any vigor because he knew he could expose the flagrant hypocrisy of the prosecution's strategy in front of the jury during the trial.

14

After Perry Olmstead settled into his new farm in Ste. Genevieve County, he decided he would like to have his horses returned to him from Jackson County. Perry called his attorney in Kansas City to learn how he could recover his livestock.

"That's not going to be easy," Jack Aiello said. "Perry, remember you're dealing with the modern-day version of a Kansas City Ku Klux Klan rally. I can guarantee it is going to be a brutal lynching. Here's what is going on. Those horses have all been placed into animal rescue and these liberals are having a beach party with their new exotic creatures. Remember, we're dealing with the Klan here. Anyway, the rescue people have placed the animals into the care of do-gooders who have been lusting for a horse for free – and so you've got little twelve-year-old girls who finally are in possession of their ponies. All their fantasies are now being fulfilled – riding through the fields on their steeds, thrusting up and down on the back of the stallion as it thunders through the field, rubbing down the muscular flanks with shiny oils, massaging those big, strong hindquarters, fingering and caressing the sleek bodies of the large, supple studs. To steal this fantasy experience from these people would create a major crisis. Perry, I know those animals are your property – but the Klan has taken possession, and the mob is salivating to have another old-fashioned Jackson County lynching if you come along and try to remove their objects of desire. It's just not worth it, Perry. My advice is to start over. Don't poke a stick into the hornet's nest. Remember, Jackson County is a lynching party waiting to string someone up on a tree."

Perry's farm on the outskirts of Ste. Genevieve had a small house and a moderate-sized barn, both built in the 1930s. He traveled to Cooper County in central Missouri to attend a horse auction in pursuit of restoring his livestock operation. Perry was a devout synod member, learning his religious and spiritual convictions from his parents and grandparents. Ste. Genevieve has a robust synod community with a beautiful stone Tudor church, Holy Cross parish, built in 1867. While attending church services one Sunday, Perry had the good fortune to meet Anne Newland. She explained she was an artist in the Ste. Genevieve art colony, and she provided him with a short history of the art colony movement in the county, and the search among many black artists to rediscover the black heritage in the area. Similarly, Perry shared his history from Jackson County, a one-time hotbed of slavery and oppression of black people, how his grandparents were the first black rural farm landowners in the famously racist county. He explained how the liberals who control the county have established a new form of plantation governance in an effort to keep black people in their place and insist the "people of color" toe the line for the Democrat plutocracy. Perry told her about his travails on this farm, how the Jackson County plantation owners decided to lay claim to the farm built by his grandparents, how his livestock was stolen by the county, his time in jail for contempt, and the federal charges that he is a member of the Ku Klux Klan.

"Oh, my goodness. You have got to hear about what happened to friends of mine in St. Louis," Anne said. She explained the travails of Michael and Carol and Paul stemming from their experience in Joplin along I-49, and how they have been in federal court for more than ten years, accused of being black members of the Ku Klux Klan.

"So, apparently there is a campaign to accuse black people, who are not willingly abiding by the rules of the plantation, of being in the Ku Klux Klan?" Perry said.

"It seems that way."

Anne was very fond of Perry. She liked his large, burly body and his independent spirit. While she would have been pleased if he wore a tie and a sport jacket like her father – if only on occasion, such as on a Sunday morning in the church – she understood he was a farmer, and that type of attire was not natural to him. Soon, Perry and Anne became a couple. Perry enjoyed going to Anne's French creole cabin, visiting with Anne's mother, and watching Anne work on her paintings. Doris described to Perry how her husband, Keith, had been strangled to death on a street corner in St. Louis because a bookstore near the intersection had been robbed at least twenty minutes earlier, and the perpetrator was a black man in his twenties or thirties, but because Keith was a black man in his sixties, he was immediately presumed to be the suspect because he was near the location of the robbery – and Keith happened to have a similar skin tone – but the robbery incident had occurred at least twenty minutes prior to the police arriving at the scene.

"Doris, what was ever done about it?"

"Nothing, really. The Metro Police conducted an internal investigation. The matter was turned over to the prosecuting attorney's office who determined Keith could have died because he possibly could have had a breathing disorder. Of course, Keith never had a breathing problem. How preposterous. And that's not even the point; he was strangled to death. How is strangulation equivalent to a breathing disorder? What is going on here?"

"It almost sounds like St. Louis has a similar situation to Jackson County – I'm speaking of the county surrounding Kansas City. The whole system there is essentially a plantation run by the Democrats and the black people of the county are fulfilling the role of slaves on the plantation. The irony is that most of the Jackson County government is composed of black Democrats. So, the black politicians have become foremen and bossmen and overseers monitoring the black slaves on the Jackson County plantation. Think of it like Charleston, South Carolina in the 1850s and 1860s: there were the plantations with the slaves outside the city, and then in the city itself there were the merchants and traders, and the lawyers, and the financiers who benefited from the whole system. In Jackson County, it's a similar model: the white liberals – the affluent lawyers, the MBAs, the bankers, the computer and technology entrepreneurs – they keep a class of obedient black footmen and lackeys to efficiently run the plantation operation for them. Is that what they have in St. Louis?"

"Maybe it is like that," Doris replied. "But I never really thought of it quite in that way. I always knew it was corrupt and unscrupulous. But I never really thought of it as a remnant from slavery that you have described in antebellum Kansas City. I know Kansas City was more drawn into that kind of history because the slavery institution was more present there than in St. Louis. They even tried to import it into Kansas during the Bleeding Kansas era. We need to remember, however, the Union sentiment was very substantial and strong in St. Louis, and when the war broke out, the Union kept garrisons in St. Louis; it was regarded as Union territory. It is true there was slave trading in St. Louis earlier on, in the 1830s and before. But I don't think the St. Louis area was nearly as swept up in the antebellum culture as was seen in Kansas City. We should remember the St. Louis circuit court in 1852 found Dred Scott to be a freeman, which of course, was later overruled by Roger B. Taney in the U.S. Supreme Court. However, there is no question the government in the current era of St. Louis City is part of the corrupt liberal machine politics you would see in places like Chicago or Philadelphia or Kansas City."

"What's your perception of things here in Ste. Genevieve?" Perry asked.

"There is no tension here. That was not the case back in 1930. The area always had a population of black residents; in 1930 it may have been about 12 percent black. Anyway, in 1930, there was racial tension including a race riot and nearly every black person moved out of the town and the county. Beginning in the 1970s, there has been a renaissance of black people slowly returning to the area, especially artists, to rediscover the black heritage of the region. Because of the old kiln industry in the area dating to the late eighteenth century, many of the black artists are working with clay as potters and ceramic tile makers. This art renaissance is why Anne is here; I'm blessed to be with her."

Doris asked Perry to describe his farm business. He explained he is a horse farmer, breeding and raising horses for sale. At his Jackson County farm, at one time he had as many as twenty-four horses.

Perry was curious what Doris thought of the synod church in Ste. Genevieve.

"Oh, it's not of the traditional, confessional, discipline custom and observance that Keith and I loved so much back at Zion Cathedral in St. Louis. This Ste. Genevieve parish's practices are more like what you would find in a suburban Presbyterian church or one of those scores of crackpot Lutheran sects. You know, the church of what's-happening-now." She laughed. "I keep expecting them to burst out and start singing John Denver ballads. But I try to cope and just ignore it. There isn't another synod church around here."

Perry laughed.

One day when Perry was visiting Anne and Doris at their cabin, something disturbing occurred at Perry's farm. The two equity beneficiaries – that is, the pair who robbed Tamika's bank, terrorized Tamika's funeral procession, and robbed the liquor store in Baden – were accustomed to visiting Ste. Genevieve once or twice a year. Since

Ste. Genevieve always had a population of tourists and visitors, as well as the trendy artist colony, the two urban street thugs saw the town as the perfect target for some petty criminal enterprise. Ste. Genevieve is a mere one-hour drive south of St. Louis, making it the profitable object for a quick trip on a criminal escapade. While indeed, the art colony crowd – the artist entrepreneurs and the art customers – were terrific prey for the two heroes of equity (not that Ste. Genevieve could even dream of being in the same league with Moab, Sedona or Taos), the two boys liked to search for alternate quarry for their assaults. Perry Olmstead's horse farm looked like a possibility – there was not a vehicle parked in front of the house, it seemed there was no activity. The couple pulled into Perry's driveway, parked and exited their vehicle, and strolled up to the porch and promptly kicked in the front door. "Anyone home?" one of the boys called out. They rifled through the house, taking whatever looked valuable and searched for the most important find – cash. They found a couple hundred dollars but discovered something rather extraordinary – a find that would have significant consequences several weeks later. Their acquisition was a Saxon Meissen porcelain figurine from the year 1601. The figurine had been given to Perry's grandparents by a synod missionary who visited their Jackson County farm in 1880. The two equity champions knew nothing about Meissen china or porcelain, but merely thought it was special enough to take, and maybe to sell for twenty bucks in a pawn shop in St. Louis. They absconded with their loot and departed on their one-hour drive back to St. Louis. Mission accomplished.

Perry returned to his house later and discovered he had been the victim of a break-in and a burglary. He called the sheriff, not because he believed he would obtain any justice, but he did believe the incident should be officially recorded as a felony in order to keep the county's crime statistics accurate and up to date. Clearly, someone looking to move into Ste. Genevieve County would be entitled to the most

accurate and valid crime statistics before making the decision to relocate to the county. The loss of the Meissen broke Perry's heart because
he knew his grandparents and his parents were so fond of it and the
history that it represented. Something like that can never be duplicated,
he realized, even if there existed such remarkable talent as the Ste.
Genevieve art colony ceramics makers.

Anne Newland made plans to bring a collection of original
art from the colony to St. Louis to be displayed in Carol Holden's art
gallery. The art objects Anne would bring included some of her own
paintings but also ceramics, pottery, and paintings by other artists in
the Ste. Genevieve colony. Anne asked Perry if he could help pack up
the items and drive with her and her mother to St. Louis.

After arriving in St. Louis, when Anne and Doris were with
Carol in the gallery, Perry drove to Gravois Avenue in the Dutchtown
neighborhood; he pulled over for a cup of coffee at a small independent
coffee shop. Near the coffee shop was a pawn broker and Perry walked
to the store with his cup of coffee in hand. While he browsed through
the store looking at power tools, two young men walked in and engaged
with the counter salesman about a pawn transaction. The two men
would have been familiar to Tamika's bank employees or even the
liquor store proprietor in Baden, and they asked how much they could
receive for their Meissen porcelain, which happened to be the heirloom
taken from Perry Olmstead's living room. Perry, who always carried
a Smith & Wesson 9 mm Shield pistol, figured today was the day to
be able to take advantage of his friendly firearm. The two career street
entrepreneurs had become so brazen – likely because they understood
the generosity of the equity system, which was set up to protect them,
not punish them – they decided they would go ahead and rob the pawn
shop while conducting their pawn transaction, and not even obscure
their identity with ski masks because it didn't matter anyway. When the
counter clerk didn't make an offer for the Meissen, the pair then pulled

out their SIG Sauer pistols and demanded the cash in the drawer. The clerk complied, but Perry realized the situation demanded a response. While the pair was collecting up the cash, Perry approached with his firearm. The clerk quickly intervened and aggressively yelled at Perry, "Stop! Now! Drop your weapon! I don't need a shoot-out in this store!" When the boys realized what was going on, they fired a shot in the direction of Perry and ran out of the store with the cash and also with Perry's Meissen porcelain figurine. Perry was alarmed enough by the pawn broker's exclamation that he did not pull his trigger. The Metro Police were called, and they began an investigation, but quickly shifted their focus to Perry. "Do you have a concealed carry permit?" Perry was arrested for possession of a concealed firearm without a permit. Fortuitously, there was another customer in the store who was familiar with this entire scenario, an event that presumably repeats itself on a daily basis. Chubbles Philigrew was shopping in the pawn shop during the entire event, looking for another chest of drawers for his bedroom so that he could have a tertiary socks drawer to keep a backup stash – a nest egg, of sorts. Before Perry was removed from the store by the Metro Police, Chubbles approached Perry, handed him a small Post-it note, and said to Perry, "I have been through this experience myself. Here is the name and phone number of an attorney. You'll need it."

Perry Olmstead was taken to the Metro Police headquarters on Tucker Blvd. and was told he would be released on a five-hundred-dollar bail. Perry was able to pay the bail because he always carried cash for the necessities of daily shopping, pawn shop visits, and possible emergencies. Perry told the police officers on his way to the police station that the robbers were in possession of a valuable antique heirloom stolen from his home in Ste. Genevieve. The pair were picked up just a few blocks from the pawn shop. The police transporting Perry did send a radio message to the officers who were arresting the two street punks, recommending that they look for the porcelain antique. The Meissen was not recovered by the apprehending officers.

A month later Perry appeared in the St. Louis City circuit court, represented by Charlie Walters, who was wearing his standard flamboyant ensemble. A guilty plea agreement to the charges of possessing a concealed weapon without a permit was entered and Charlie comforted Perry with the knowledge he got a very good deal of only a one-thousand-dollar fine. Perry asked Charlie Walters to talk to the prosecuting attorney's office about the parallel crime by the two thugs who absconded with his family's Meissen heirloom. Charlie called Miss Limney Grantham's office and spoke to one of the staff attorneys and provided information about the purloined Meissen antique and even advised the prosecuting attorney's office to contact the Ste. Genevieve sheriff for corroborating details. Miss Grantham's assistant prosecuting attorney replied, "Charlie, we don't have time for that. And this will be an equity situation anyway. These boys will be released in the end. Don't waste our time on some memento missing from a fellow's farmhouse in Ste. Genevieve. The judge isn't interested, I can guarantee you."

And indeed, our two street entrepreneurs were released thanks to Democrat St. Louis Prosecuting Attorney Limney Grantham's equity justice program. The only real inconvenience for the two boys was their temporary incarceration while they awaited their equity release hearing. Their primary objection was the lost time and missed opportunities to ply their trade on the streets of the city.

15

Now comes the hard part of this story.

MacGyver High School is a large public high school, with a student body of more than four thousand students, on the border of Florissant and Ferguson. The school serves both cities. Michael Holden, Jr. had previously attended a synod elementary and middle school with a total student body of about one-hundred-forty students. His class, when he finished eighth grade, consisted of seventeen students. Most of the students when they graduated from eighth grade went on to St. Louis North Synod High School. Four continued to MacGyver and Michael wasn't particularly close to the others who went on to MacGyver. His best friends went to St. Louis North Synod, and so it was likely to be a solitary time for Michael, and an alienating and secular experience. The school day would not open and end with prayer. There would not be synod hymns sung during the day. There were so many students in the MacGyver building; the halls were crowded, the classrooms were filled with anonymous faces, the building was loud with aggressive students, the lunchroom was crowded, the bustling and rushing and pushing and shoving was impersonal and invasive.

When Michael first walked into the massive building, he was confused and disoriented. He began to cry. He realized he would make a fool of himself, to be seen as a wimp, a pansy, a babied and protected synod child coddled by a protective, old-fashioned, peculiar church group from medieval times. He pulled himself together and reminded himself that he would somehow manage to get through it – although he was thoroughly beaten down by an anonymous, faceless, mobbed, loud, overwhelming system he felt utterly alienated from. Each class had at least forty and sometime fifty students in huge, plain rooms without windows. Soon, he discovered he knew more than anyone else in each classroom – his synod education had filled his mind with much useful and applicable information, and he realized the students from the public middle schools were simply unprepared. When he performed well on class assignments or too quickly answered in-class questions, he was met with disapproval and resentment from other students – as though he were somehow showing off. He was viewed with contempt until he learned his role was to not answer questions in class and to merely hand in assignments with desultory effort. One of the things that stunned Michael, and made him feel so completely out of place, was the large number of boys with grown bodies – presumably juniors or seniors. They seemed like men to him, but their behavior was anything but manly. They generally behaved like delinquents – spoke poorly with bad diction, showed off with bluster and contempt, behaved defiantly and abusively with belligerence, dressed in unseemly ways, and were suggestive, indecent and aggressive to female students. The majority of students behaved as though all human interaction existed with a racial victimization undertone. Everyone seemed quick to jump to conclusions revolving around racial inequality or divisiveness. Michael had never been brought up with this perception or value system – either from his parents, or the synod, or the synod school. He felt isolated and disoriented by the stereotypical disaffection and constant racial grievance. It seemed to Michael that the aggrieved attitude was used as an excuse to not take responsibility for oneself. He was unable to make sense of the entire experience which seemed like a circus or sports arena filled with misbehaved, disorderly, defiant, and disrespectful miscreants. The entire escapade was all a big joke. While the thousands of students behaved like wild animals, they laughed and taunted anyone who disapproved. The teachers and administrators understood the whole charade and were forced to simply play along – just to get through the day. It was similar to the dynamic of a prison: the guards are perfunctory – the inmates ultimately run the operation.

He complained to his mother about the experience. "Momma, that school is not a good place. I feel so out of place."

"Oh, Son, you will do well. You are smart. You are a good student."

"Momma, it is not about being a good student or how smart I am. That place is inhuman. There are too many people trapped in that huge building all day long. There aren't any windows. The design of the building is big and vacant and alienating to humans. The people are misbehaved and uncivilized. The entire place does not treasure knowledge or education. It seems like the whole point it to push defiance and rebellion. And nobody cares."

Carol didn't really know what to say. She realized he was identifying the anonymous and broken world separated from the values of humanity – once promoted and championed by the Renaissance, Humanist, and the Scholastic eras. This is the secular world of impersonalism, socialism, victimization, dishonesty, abomination, and deceit. This is the modern world of uniformity and treating people like warehoused crabs or lemmings. What could she say to her precious boy, who had excelled in his young life, who lived with a tender, gentle spirit?

It didn't take Michael long to realize he could not change the system. It was exactly what it was, what it was meant to be – a huge impersonal, innominate, cacophonous, collective monstrosity. And complaining was not going to make it different. Here he was in a

massive behemoth of a faceless conglomerate that he did not understand, he was not able to influence, which purposely attacked and
imposed a vindictive torment on his own sensibilities and understanding of himself; he was entrapped and held hostage. Michael found
himself estranged and isolated. As each day and week passed, he went
into himself and became sullen and morose. Each minute of each day
he could feel a little bit of himself – the things that had always made
Michael Holden, Jr. who he was – slowly go away and disappear forever.
The innocent, pure, tender, sensitive, sober, touching boy was leaving
and going somewhere else.

After Michael's freshman year at MacGyver, he began to detach
himself from the world he had previously known. He spoke little at
home, whereas before he had been so talkative and gregarious. He
seemed to lack focus and purpose. He was not defiant or disobedient
or disrespectful, but he spent time inside himself, in pondering periods and introspective dwelling. During the family's evening meal, he
rarely spoke and when he was asked a direct question by his parents,
he responded with a one-word answer. He went to church with the
family but no longer served as an acolyte. When he was asked about
his choice not to serve at the altar, he said he had outgrown it. He often
had a sullen expression and rarely laughed or teased as had been his
previous demeanor. He no longer played with Andrea, nor sang hymns
with her, nor listened to her chatter. He slowly became less interested
in the trombone and only practiced once a week. His trombone teacher
talked to him about his poor lessons, and Michael said he was thinking
of merely taking lessons at school.

During Michael's sophomore year, he began the habit of wearing
very baggy pants like the other boys – that way he didn't stick out as an
outsider; he looked more like the other boys. He would wear his pants
so they would ride on the bottom of his buttocks, and he would need
to yank on them occasionally to prevent them from falling down to

his knees. He started laughing with the other boys at everything and everyone. Michael, whose diction had always been so proper, began to imitate the other boys and he started using a careless diction and words and phrases from hip-hop and rap music. He began to adopt the defiant attitude so popular among the other boys at MacGyver – sneering, leering, abusive, insolent, contemptuous, willful, stubborn, rebellious. Gradually, Michael began absorbing the common racial expressions of victimization and malevolence which were the uniform system of communication at MacGyver. He normalized the common behavior of disrespect to female students using sexually degrading expressions.

The other boys smoked marijuana in the parking lot during lunchbreak and Michael began participating in their daily rituals. He noticed the suspended alertness and fogginess caused by the marijuana would make the day more tolerable. He no longer participated in classroom activities or answered in-class questions. The only assignments completed, while poorly done, were in-class exercises. He never completed homework; however, the faculty rarely gave homework assignments since they understood it was pointless. At this stage, Michael avoided violent behaviors which he observed the other boys participating in, such as vandalism, stealing, threats, argumentation, fighting, or bullying.

At home, the family noticed significant changes in Michael's personality. He never used the expressions "momma" or "papa" which had previously been his standard communication for his parents. His surly, petulant, moody personality became glaringly apparent. His usage of poor diction and terms from the hip-hop culture shocked the family. He quit taking trombone lessons and did not study the instrument at school. He continued to go to church with the family but was very sulky and resentful during the church liturgy, even sleeping while in the pew.

"Momma, what is wrong with Michael?" Andrea asked. "He is so strange. He talks so weird. His clothes are so bad. Momma, what is wrong with him?"

"I know. I think it is a stage," Carol said.

Carol talked to Michael Senior about their son's transformation. "I know a boy needs to grow up, but this isn't what I would call growing up. It is growing down. I am worried about him."

"Maybe we should tell him it is time to get a part-time job," Michael said. "I know he wants a driver's license. If we tell him he needs to get a part-time job, then he can get his license. Perhaps that will help get him back on the track."

Michael talked to his son about getting a driver's license and finding a part-time job. Michael Junior thought it was a good idea and applied to be a backroom worker at King Solomon's Fashion Mine. He worked at the store for two hours a day for two weeks, but the owner never paid Michael. When Michael asked about his pay, Solomon said, "Oh, we can have that for you in a week or so." A week passed, and Solomon told Michael the checks weren't ready. Finally, after a month and a half, and Michael continuing to pester for the paycheck, Solomon gave him a check, but it was more than a hundred dollars less than what Michael expected. "Oh, well, we'll get you the rest in a week or so." Michael cashed the check at New Shanghai, the restaurant the Holdens enjoyed so much. In a week, Mr. Lee at New Shanghai called Carol and told her the check from King Solomon's Fashion Mine, which Mr. Lee cashed for Michael Junior, was written on a closed account. Carol explained the problem to her son and Michael said he would quit.

Michael went to King Solomon's Fashion Mine to complain about the check being written on a closed account. "And not only that, you still owe me more than a hundred dollars."

"Too bad you don't have a good work ethic," Solomon replied. "Anyway, I don't need you here anymore. No need to come back."

While Michael no longer had a part-time job, from which he never received any pay, at least he had a driver's license, and he could drive the cars belonging to the other boys' families and they could all go out and smoke weed together.

During Michael's eleventh-grade year, he joined the group of boys who were operating as a street gang. Michael went through a ritual initiation which required him to shoplift expensive cosmetics from a drug store which could then be sold on the street to make enough to buy weed. Next, he was expected to use a gun, belonging to another member of the gang, to rob a small café in the Jeff-Vander-Lou neighborhood. He got out of the restaurant with twenty dollars and fifty-five cents. The boys spent most of their time smoking weed and listening to racially offensive and sexually exploitative and aggressive hip-hop songs. None of the boys felt the need to continue to attend MacGyver, but by remaining enrolled they could avoid the prying eyes of Florissant or Ferguson social workers and the police. By this time, Michael had his hair in dreadlock braids and had obtained tattoos on his arms and his chest.

Michael decided he no longer wanted to attend church with the family and was certain to oversleep when it was time to get ready to go to church. After all, he smoked so much weed the night before, sleep was his only comforter. He would merely grumble when his mother came into his room to tell him to get ready for church. Carol complained to Michael Senior that she was unable to rouse the boy.

"Michael, what is going on here?" Carol asked her husband in desperation.

When they came home from church, Michael spoke to his son about missing church.

"I don't care. I don't need that," Michael told his father.

"What are you talking about?"

The boy's defiance was assaulting. He looked at his father with a glare and said, "Get da hell outta my's room."

"This is my house. You will not speak to me that way. You can just get out of the house."

The boy dressed himself in a baggy T-shirt and his low-hanging trousers and walked out of the house. He walked to the house of one of his gang buddies and spent the day smoking weed.

Carol was frantic. She called Anne Newland in Ste. Genevieve and explained what was happening to her son. "Anne, do you think Michael could go to Ste. Genevieve and spend some time with Perry on his farm. Maybe it could be like a boot camp experience for Michael and help to turn him around. I am so worried. I think we are losing him. Maybe we have lost him already. I just am at my wit's end. I don't know what to do." She sobbed.

"Of course, Carol. Let me talk to Perry."

Perry agreed to help and would arrange to put the boy to work on the farm. Anne called back to Carol and explained the arrangement would be fine with Perry.

Michael Senior and Carol spoke to their son about the plan. Michael Junior blew up and told his parents they were crazy, and he would do no such thing.

"You will, or you will move out of this house," Michael told his son.

"I is outta here, dude. I is outta here, now. Later."

And with that, Michael packed up a few items of clothing from his room and put them in a plastic grocery bag and he walked out of the house. Carol cried out in desperation, pleading with him not to leave. The boy merely ignored his mother and stormed out. He went to his gang buddy's house and slept on the floor.

During Michael's senior year at MacGyver, he rarely attended school. He lived in the house of one of the gang members, sleeping on the floor, and then went to another member's house and slept on the floor and continued on to other members' houses to crash for the night. They spent most of their time smoking weed and watching television reruns of *Star Trek, The Jeffersons, Gilligan's Island, Diff'rent Strokes,* and *The Fresh Prince of Bel-Air.*

Because each school district receives more than eight thousand dollars per student from the State of Missouri, it is very rare that a school will expel or flunk-out a student. Losing one student significantly reduces the remuneration from the state – thus making it nearly impossible for the school district to stay in business, despite collecting hundreds of thousands of dollars on each property within the county from confiscatory property taxes. Because of this symbiotic relationship of per-pupil funding and the imaginary existence of the pupil, students can simply fail to show up to school and remain on the enrollment records. After a year of smoking weed, engaging in petty theft, molesting girls and having sexual relations with any girl willing to step up to the plate for an opportunity for intercourse, Michael finished high school and a diploma was mailed to the last known address associated with his identity.

16

Carol became despondent about losing her son. She was beside herself and in a state of panic. She did not know where he was. Was he safe? What happened to him? She prayed and sought consolation with the pastor of Salem Synod Church. The pastor was understanding of her emotional vulnerability and told her to maintain her faith and confidence that Michael would find a way to turn his life around.

"Remain open to him. Don't judge him right now. Express your love and support for him. It is not a time to punish him."

Michael Senior was fond of the pastor at Salem, but he was a white man, and Michael felt the necessity to talk to a black man about the entire drama – particularly because the problems seemed to be more unique to a black boy. He talked to his friend Paul Mooney about what seemed to be a collapse of the Holden family.

"Listen, Michael, you can talk to our pastor at Transfiguration, or why not talk to the pastor at St. Paul's College Hill? That is Carol's home church, and that pastor is really a wonderful black man."

Michael set up an appointment to meet with Father Zachary Lucas at St. Paul's College Hill on John Avenue in the College Hill neighborhood of north St. Louis – Carol's home church when she was a youth.

"Michael, the world is fallen. No amount of attempting to fix it or bring it into an ideal place will ever repair it. And this culture is completely fallen and collapsed. How do we know this? Look at that school your son attended. The teachers and administrators know precisely what is going on, and they merely tolerate it or even promote it. No matter what the culture tries to do to address what seems to be the problems, it normally makes things worse: the welfare state, the sexual identity crisis, carbon pollution, promiscuity, abortion, accumulation of status or wealth, the obsessions of the hundreds of social reforms. The culture merely gets worse as each year passes. Or, how about looking at what is happening to you and Carol and Paul? Three black people are being tried in federal court for being in the Ku Klux Klan? What could be more preposterous? In the synod, we have three creeds that act as guideposts of our beliefs and what we can expect. We believe in the life of the world to come, and his kingdom shall have no end. These creeds don't even imply that the culture of this fallen world could ever provide us with any hope or expectation. The kingdom of God is not here and will never be here. It is only in the presence of Jesus that the kingdom is found. Let me tell you this about the fallen world and the culture your son is now in. It is difficult to be a young black man in our society. The influence of the popular culture is destructive and dangerous for a young black man. I see all kinds of insanity – street violence, gun violence, street crime, gang life, drugs, indignity to women. The music in this culture is very destructive and spreads a message of heroizing the urban jungle – disrespect, violence, and crime. This is not your fault. I know you brought up your son to be a devout synod believer. Surely, his transformation came from the public school he attended. Yes, Michael, he should have gone to St. Louis North Synod High School, there is no doubt, but it is too late to relive that life. First, pray and pray diligently. Then be open to your boy – don't embrace his behavior, but don't judge him at this stage. The time for judgment will come later. And it will come, I assure you. Reach out to anyone who knows him or is in contact with him and make a gesture of goodwill. At this point, that is about all you can do. Be open to receiving him – without commentary, without lessons to be taught, without judging him. You are not necessarily endorsing his decisions merely by being civil and welcoming to him. If you can have any direct contact with him, keep the conversation light, on the surface, and affable. I wish there were a magic formula, but we are at the mercy of the reality in front of us and sometimes it is very difficult and brutal."

Carol remained despondent and in despair. How could her adorable little boy, who just four years ago played the trumpet with Mrs. Probst and the Forte Orchestra, become a hoodlum, an urban street thug, a drug user, and a petty criminal? How is it possible that merely four years of exposure to a public high school in Florissant and Ferguson could transform a tender, sweet, sentimental boy with a devout synod character into a street thug and gangbanger? It made no sense to Carol that such an abomination could occur to such an innocent, pure child. Her devastation was thorough, and she thought of little else. Carol continued with her gallery which remained available to regional artists for shows and art sales. She found that she was unable to muster up the inspiration to paint, and so she rented her studio space to several area artists. The dance studio continued to be used as the teaching venue for several St. Louis dance instructors.

Michael Junior became a full-time street gang member, committing petty crimes and thefts, carrying a Ruger 9 mm pistol, smoking weed and drinking beer during the downtimes between shoplifting, breaking into cars, committing minor robberies, engaging in casual sex with any girl who happened to pass by, and sleeping in past noon each day. He never talked to his parents or to Andrea. He had no interest in their Oreo lives.

Paul Mooney, Michael and Carol's co-defendant in the federal Ku Klux Klan case, watched Michael struggling with the awareness his son had become a street thug and a gang member. He advised Michael to attempt to release his worries and help occupy his mind in another way by considering attending community and neighborhood activist meetings.

"Michael, this is an opportunity to change your focus, your internal anxiety, and self-questioning, and to look outward. These meetings aren't going to make your pain go away, but they will help change the subject a little bit. I want to warn you, however, the people who attend these neighborhood activist meetings are usually a little annoying – liberal, do-gooder types, dingy and not rational, complainers, people who like to hear themselves gripe, people who are constantly championing the perceived underdog and the victim. But, besides this slight irritation, it is a great opportunity to meet some people in the neighborhood, listening to what's on their minds, getting your own mind off your current worries. I recommend that you not talk initially; just listen to the people. After some time of getting to know the people at these meetings, then you can start to speak up; you can do a little educating, expose them to a point of view that these ardent social engineers have never thought about before. These meetings are all over the area, including right there in the North County area. I think Florissant and Ferguson probably have a half dozen of these groups who meet once a week or so. Try it out. Brother, I think it could help change the recording in your mind, so you are not replaying the same song over and over again."

Michael found a neighborhood meeting that took place once a week at a Presbyterian church basement in Florissant. He attended the meetings and only listened and attempted to understand the points of view being shared by the people. Nearly everyone in attendance was a liberal embracing the standard fare of social consciousness and justice causes: greater rights for people with sexual identity concerns, advocacy for transgendered persons, worries about carbon pollution and global warming, promoting the causes and concerns about the homeless, advocacy for drug legalization, a hypersensitivity about racism, defending abortion rights and feminist causes, promoting the construction of more bike lanes as a way to curb automobile driving, advocating for public transit, seeing police brutality everywhere, advocating for more social spending and tax increases, and so forth. However, he noticed they often shifted their allegiance when it came to protecting and defending their own personal turf, property or causes: strict zoning regulations, the safety of their homes, their trendy cars, their pricey bicycles, the elaborate toys for their children, their expensive personal devices like Pelotons or other exercise equipment. He noticed their vitriolic criticism of national retailers such as Walmart, but their spirited defense for the businesses they perceived to reflect their own ideologies, such as Starbucks or Ben and Jerry's. While Michael listened to them complain and whine and carp about the parts of the American capitalist society they found so offensive, he also heard them come to the protection, defense and cover for the social conditions that disturb so many other Americans: homelessness, illegal immigration, urban blight, drug abusers and addicts, facility overcrowding, urban congestion, social engineering through public schools, gender modification, public health clinics and soup kitchens strategically placed inside residential neighborhoods, or harboring the carriers of infectious diseases.

One regular attendee named Omar Clift, a black man in his mid-forties – who Perry Olmstead would have said was a bossman or a lackey or a footman on the plantation – made it a point to always complain about the unfair treatment of black people during the course of their partying or street barbecues. He was always quick to see racism in every event that occurred in the city or in North County. Omar whined on for twenty minutes about a brother who was shot by the police at Bellefontaine Cemetery because the man was involved in armed robberies at the cemetery. The Metro Police said the suspect would approach elderly visitors at the cemetery and attempt to rob the mourners at graves. Omar said it was obvious that the black suspect was the victim of racism by the visitors to the cemetery. "We must assume the 85-year-old couple visiting a grave must have engaged in racial slurs and abusive racist language. And then the police assassinated the black brother just because he had been verbally abused by racial slurs."

Michael noticed that none of the attendees disputed Omar's claims, but instead accepted the accusations and calumny merely because it produced the image of victimization. Jumping to conclusions without logical connections seemed to be one of the ground rules of the group.

Omar then went on to howl about how the Metro Police beat a black man senseless because he failed to move himself across the street in Delmar Loop when a group of white bar hoppers were passing along the sidewalk. "This poor brother was just trying to get out a little after being cooped up in his shack," Omar complained. "And then some white woman sees him walking down Delmar Loop and reports him for not moving to the other side of the street, just because he's standing around near a liquor store. And then the cops show up and beat the poor guy into a bloody pulp."

Again, Michael observed not even one of the liberals asked a solitary question about the veracity of Omar's story. The tale was simply accepted as accurate because it had successfully created a victim and a narrative.

Omar stood up and explained that people are claiming they are so disturbed because the Missouri Department of Corrections is planning to release prisoners before their sentences are complete because of a limited amount of prison space. He said the corrections department is planning to release more than two thousand prisoners because of over-crowding. He said one released prisoner has been accused of murdering someone after his early release. Omar, however, didn't happen mention that just last Saturday, Cornelius Haning, who had been released early from his ten-year sentence for armed robbery, went on a wild, violent weekend escapade after his release and he decided to murder a twenty-one-year-old woman who happened to be sitting on her front porch. "I feel bad when someone is murdered in cold blood," Omar moaned. "But keeping a prisoner cooped up in a shed isn't helping anyone. And the only way we can make room for more people is to clear out the prisons filled with the brothers who are already there. That will make more space. C'mon people, we need to just calm down and go out for some chop suey. Let's all just chill out a little."

Then a woman named Neela stood up and said she was hoping the Missouri State Legislature will approve a bill to sanction, legalize and fund heroin injection sites in the state. These sites are locations set aside for heroin users to legally inject heroin, using free needles furnished by the state. Neela said in some cases the state will furnish the heroin free of charge to the user. She pointed to the success of legalized heroin injection sites in Vancouver, Canada, as well as Philadelphia and Seattle.

"This is just a terrific idea that we need to get behind. They work so well. These sites give young people and others the chance to experiment with drugs in a safe way, avoiding the dangers of bad heroin that some drug dealers peddle." Neela said one of the advantages is that the sites will encourage drug usage to take place in one centralized location rather than being used throughout the entire state. "It provides a compassionate way for young people to be introduced to drugs in a safe way."

Some brave soul interrupted Neela's libertine campaign and said, "Neela, just playing devil's advocate, but isn't this promoting drug use?"

Neela didn't miss a beat and obediently recited the liberal talking points she had been briefed on. "Studies have shown that these terrific opportunities to use and experiment with drugs actually helps reduce the use of opioids. And the great advantage is the heroin users will congregate in one neighborhood rather than throughout all of Missouri."

"Again, just playing devil's advocate," someone said. "What about discouraging drug usage, rather than promoting it?"

"That type of old-fashioned, closed-minded thinking is so racist and hasn't worked anyway. People should have the opportunity to freely use the drugs of their choice. For instance, you are able to drink coffee without interference. Why shouldn't a heroin user be able to do the same thing without judgment and humiliation?"

Jeanette Reilly, a white liberal, stood up and seemed to go into an emotional meltdown of sorts because when she recently shopped at a Walmart store, she had a confrontation with some of the customers. "When I was in the Walmart, it seemed all of the smelly, overweight, trailer park residents who patronize all the Walmarts were coughing and sneezing without putting their hands over their mouths. I can't believe it. How can they be so inconsiderate?"

Another white liberal, Elizabeth Britton, asked Reilly what she was even doing in the store. "That company represents the 1 percent – the capitalist ruling class – and all of their customers support Republicans," Britton lectured.

"But I am in an at-risk group," Reilly whined. "I have diabetes."

"If you're at-risk, you shouldn't be in a store or even in public," interjected Jim Walsenberg. "And, if you're at-risk, what are you doing in here with us?"

"I don't have time to listen to that kind of disinformation," Reilly snarled. "Look, I'm safe here. There are only progressives here. You know, our type of people."

Ethan Davidson, one of the popular liberals in the group, said he had a solution for Reilly's problem at Walmart. "Just burn down the store. All these capitalist structures should just be torched and burned to the ground."

Everyone in the room sat quietly with several people nodding their heads in affirmation.

Three of the most prominent white liberals in the group stood together to declare their support for the public schools in the area. "The public schools in Missouri are desperate for more financial support and are on the verge of closing because they have run out of money," whined Amy Eckhardt, who teaches political science at the University of Missouri-St. Louis at the campus in Normandy.

"We need to pressure the state legislature in Jefferson City to find ways to increase more taxes on the people of this state so the public schools can have just a few more pennies to be able to stay open," suggested Katrina Ziccarelli. "The poor, destitute public schools don't even know where their next meal will come from."

"Our public schools are completely impoverished," moaned Cathy Porterman. "Think of the children. This is about the children."

Omar stood up and said, "I agree with you three sisters. But I need to change the subject a little bit because of a police brutality problem going on."

He described what he thought was an over-the-top police response to a recent block party of three thousand revelers in Ferguson in North County. "These were all black people, of course, and what do we learn to expect? Police overkill. If it had been three thousand chardonnay sipping people in Kirkwood or Des Peres or Town and Country, there wouldn't have even been a response. This group in Ferguson, not harming anyone, was just having a block party that went on for twenty-four hours. Big damn deal. A lot of things go on for twenty-four hours, like your clock ticking. Someone called the police because of a 'loud spectacle.' Now, what's that supposed to mean? When the police showed up to harass these harmless people, some people in the crowd took out their handguns, which is completely appropriate. Don't we have a Second Amendment? The police became irrational and arrested some people at the block party – only black people, of course. It's just another case of racist police harassment. These people were just getting out of their sheds and shacks, which they are mercilessly kept cooped up in for months at a time. Who in the hell were they harming with a block party?"

Someone interrupted. "Just playing devil's advocate, Omar. But is it safe for block party participants to pull guns on the police? Just devil's advocate."

"What harm is that? Don't we have a Second Amendment? What's the big deal? The constant and continual abuse of black people by the police is just unacceptable. It has got to stop. Can't we even have a block party anymore? The brothers need to get out of their shacks and sheds and partake in some refreshing liquids and cultural herbs."

Michael whispered to the person sitting next to him, "Do you know what Omar does for a living?"

"Oh, he's an assistant principal at MacGyver High School," the woman replied.

17

Carla, a neighbor of the Holdens, who lived a few blocks to the west, saw Michael Senior in Schnucks at the Chop Suey Shopping Center. Schnucks is the popular grocery chain in the St. Louis area. They began to talk about the wet summer they were having.

"Michael, I was on a walk down your block the other day and I noticed how nice your lawn looked," Carla said.

"Oh, thank you, Carla. You know, I mow three days a week."

"But Michael, isn't it difficult to mow around the bushes?"

"What?! What are you talking about, Carla? I don't have any bushes."

"Oh, maybe it was the shrubs," Carla said.

"Carla, I don't have any trees, shrubs, bushes, hedges, thickets, brambles, vines, trellises, underbrush, scrubs, ferns, hedgerows, planter boxes, rocks, or flower gardens. Just plain, flat, green lawn. Isn't it wonderful?"

"Oh my, yes, Michael," Carla said. "How lovely. And how are your sweet basil plants doing in your patio planters?"

"I just can't seem to get the basil plants to take off. The leaves turn brown so quickly and then they just die and they always seem to get Japanese garden beetles. You know, Carol makes a fair number of Italian dishes, and she needs that basil. I just don't know what to do."

Since they were in the produce section, Carla walked over to the fresh-cut basil and handed Michael a bunch. "Michael, this fresh bunch of basil is about sixty-nine cents."

"But it's not from a growing plant. I like to pick it off a growing plant. It seems so much fresher to me."

Carla walked him over to the basil plants rooted in small plastic pots. "Michael, here is a basil plant. Schnucks's produce section has them nearly all year long. I think it's one-dollar-fifty-five cents."

"But Carla, I didn't grow this plant."

* * *

The federal Ku Klux Klan trial persisted. Judge Hedrick J. Winters called status conferences about every four months. The judge asked the defense attorney, Larry Korhonen, if his defense would involve calling witnesses at the trial. Korhonen explained the defense would call one witness and then rely on cross-examination of the prosecution witnesses.

"I want to warn you, Counselor, I will not tolerate you taking us off the rails in trial. I have established the trajectory of this case. There will be no references to the president or the first lady as parties to the complaint. There will not be any reference to the makeup of the membership rolls or records of the organization under question."

"What organization would that be, your honor?"

"That would be the organization your clients are members of – the Ku Klux Klan."

"Your honor, have you already summarily determined they are members of the Ku Klux Klan?"

"No, I have made no such determination. That will be a matter for the jury," Judge Winters replied. "Counselor, let's keep this trial on track. Please try to maintain the focus of the case that I have defined here. There will be no need to argue about who are on the membership rolls of the organization."

"Thank you, your honor."

"And I will not permit you to probe the FBI about their unique role as members of the Ku Klux Klan."

"Of course. Thank you, your honor."

* * *

Michael returned to the basement of the Presbyterian church in Florissant for the weekly neighborhood meeting. Omar Clift, one of the assistant principals at MacGyver, stood again, this time complaining about how the Missouri Department of Employment is discriminating against black persons who have been receiving unemployment benefits. "People who do not go back to work are being told by the government employment department that their benefits will be cut off. This unsympathetic position does not take into account the difficult conditions people are living with. People are suffering and they need to be given a break. What could be wrong with people collecting a little extra stash after all their pain? We have young brothers trapped in their sheds and shacks for months at a time. With a little extra stash, the brothers can finally get out of their sheds and start to stand around at the liquor stores, looking for some refreshing liquids and some cultural herbs."

The attendees sat in silence, clearly reflecting some type of agreement or concurrence with the MacGyver administrator. It all became so clear to Michael what was going on at that school, all too clear.

A white liberal woman named Martha stood up to give her thoughts. "NASA has finally discovered evidence that there are parallel universes where time actually runs backwards. NASA scientists were studying ghost particles in outer space above Antarctica, and they discovered the neutrinos were emerging upside down from the ground – which serves as definitive proof that there are parallel universes where time runs backwards." As Michael was listening to Martha share her impressions about the discovery, he thought to himself that this all sounded like some poppycock that was pulled right out of the F. Scott Fitzgerald story *The Curious Case of Benjamin Button.* Michael mused to himself: Because these eggheads found some teeny, weeny, tiny, itsy, bitsy particles are emerging from the ground turned upside down, whatever that means, they are now convinced there are parallel universes that can run backwards. How is that working out? Martha continued: "And Dr. Peter Caruthers, a NASA scientist and professor at Cornell University, has said the researchers are 100 percent driven only by science, and they could be able to use these types of discoveries to locate Kolob and other planets that we could emigrate to when the Earth becomes too hot to sustain life because of global warming."

The group seemed duly impressed and someone said she could hardly wait.

Jason Pagliarulo stood to tell the group he is a barista at Starbucks, and he has found an effective way to teach the pathetic and ignorant people who seem to populate so much of the country. "I use a Sharpie pen and write a message on the side of each cup for the customers to look at while they consume their drinks," the trendy progressive announced. "My messages are to promote our social justice causes."

He explained how he writes various short, pithy mottos such as, "Save our impoverished public schools," "No justice no peace," "Raise taxes for the children," "End white privilege," "De-fund the police," "Boycott Florida," "Joy and Brat and Vibe," "Unburdened by what has been," "Fall out of a coconut tree," "Significance of the passage of time," "Inspired by being inspired," "The time has come to do what we have been doing," "End the oppression, don't shop Walmart," "Listen to the 'Theme from *Ordinary People*.'"

Someone asked Pagliarulo if anyone objects to his reeducation efforts.

"I believe everyone loves it," Pagliarulo replied. "But those that don't like it will have their minds planted with our progressive seeds. That's what is important. They need to have their minds opened. It's just like what Ethan Davidson always teaches us – the mind is like a parachute; it only works when it's opened. And to open my mind, I try to hum the 'Theme from *Ordinary People*' every day."

The group seemed entranced by the wisdom from the young, ardent liberal.

Shandra Cordorvorano stood and praised the idealistic Starbucks employee. "Thank you, Jason, for inspiring us. And thank you for reminding us that we should listen to the 'Theme from *Ordinary People*.' Just think how the world could change if everyone listened to it. Some of the old-timers in here probably thought that listening to John Lennon's 'Imagine' could change the world – well, the 'Theme from *Ordinary People*' is at least as influential. And it's so beautiful."

The mesmerized group appeared to be in assent. But Shandra continued with her sense of outrage that there are people in the neighborhood who are not properly toeing the line for the various progressive causes. "I have had to tolerate and put up with people who don't agree with most of us in this room and it's been more than I can bear," Shandra whined. "And I don't even know how I am going to continue for the next year of my existence, much less the next three minutes."

Rodney Spear, one of the few skeptics in the group, interrupted and asked her what her main problem was.

"You don't even know!" she bleated. "How could you not care enough to just be so oblivious to all of my pain, and my rage, and my anxiety, and my misery, and my depression, and my hate?"

Spear said, "It really sounds like you've got a lot of problems."

"See! You don't even know how terribly difficult it is to be me. Sometimes I can't even move. I'm just paralyzed by all of this misery."

"Have you considered admitting yourself to one of the regional hospital psychiatric wards?"

"There you go! You're triggering me!"

"Well, please do tell us the specifics of your hurt," Spear gently prompted.

"There you go again! Triggering me!" Shandra complained. And then she went on to tell about her deep internal angst coming from sexism, transphobia, systemic racism, police brutality, capitalism, the nuclear family, the destitute public schools running out of money, so many Republicans in Missouri. And she continued on and on with a litany of gripes, as most of the people in the room found it difficult to concentrate and started drifting off.

"Well, Shandra, at least you've got the 'Theme from *Ordinary People*'," Spear suggested.

Lena Gould, a mixed-race woman and a friend of Michael and Carol, was at the meeting and approached Michael privately and out of earshot from the others in the room.

Lena approached Michael in confidence. "Michael, I have heard about the situation with young Michael and also Carol's pain. I am sorry. I am praying for you and Carol, and, of course, for Michael. It is a difficult situation in the world we live in; the culture is so off base. Listen, I will call Carol tomorrow; I'll take her out to lunch."

"Lena, thank you so much. You are one of the sweetest friends we have. One thing we have learned through all of this is that we have such wonderful friends. Indeed, we are worried about Michael."

Lena then rose to make an announcement. "The block I live on and the few around my house are having a prowling problem. Young black men, wearing all black clothing to hide their appearance, are traipsing through the area at three o'clock in the morning checking for unlocked car doors. I wake up every morning at three o'clock for my yoga routine, and today I heard my car alarm chirp. I looked out the window and saw a black-clad human checking my car door and others. A few minutes later another human came by and did the same thing. I yelled at the human and he ran off."

A white liberal attendee named David Reid, wearing a woolen beanie cap, stood up and challenged Lena. "Why do you keep calling them '*humans*'? That seems a little obscure to me ... maybe a little insensitive?"

"Oh, c'mon. I'm sorry this has gone over your head," Lena responded. "It's not about a term like human or even about race. It's about prowling and trying to get into cars in the middle of the night. I'm surprised you can't understand that."

"It just seems a little insensitive. Maybe a touch racist?" David continued.

Liberal attendee Sadie Rice echoed David Reid's implications. "It seems like code language to me. Why didn't you just call the police, if you're so worried about the '*humans*'?"

Omar Clift, MacGyver's assistant principal, saw an opportunity and jumped in. "The brothers out there are having enough troubles being cooped up in their shacks and sheds all day and all night. Maybe the brothers are hoping to get out for a little fresh air when there aren't as many cops spying on them. A brother has the right to walk through a neighborhood catching a little fresh air and all, in between tokes on the cultural herbs."

"Look, I always try to keep positive," Lena apologized. "I don't intend to demean anyone."

"You'd ought to try to keep a little more positive and stop judging the poor brothers," Omar scolded.

"I'm not trying to offend anyone. I just don't want my car burgled or anyone else's car. I'm not trying to judge the brothers."

Michael had finally heard enough and couldn't hold back, primarily because he knew Lena. "Excuse me. I'm Michael Holden. I happen to know Lena Gould very well. She has been a dear friend of our family for many years. I realize you cannot tell, because all of you in this room, whether you are white or black, are making judgments about people based purely on their skin color. Let me share a little surprise with you tonight. Lena is a mixed-race woman. Her father is black, and her mother is white. I presume to you she appears to be a white person, or perhaps of Italian heritage, or perhaps Hispanic. I happen to know Lena very well. She is a saintly *human* being – and I purposely used the word *human,* which some in here find so offensive. Lena attended St. Louis University and then went on to Washington University in St. Louis to study health sciences. She is a yoga and wholistic health and wellness instructor, and she only ever seeks the best – good health, good emotions, good spiritual state, good disposition, and good feelings – for everyone, regardless of your race. She was concerned about prowling and burglary. What in the world is wrong with that? While everyone seems to want to say how worried they are about the 'brothers,' let me just say Lena is every bit as much a 'sister' as anyone else in this room."

After the topic changed, Lena pulled Michael aside and with tears filling her eyes, she told Michael what a gentleman he is. "Michael, you are so valiant. Those things you said were touching. What I don't like about coming to these neighborhood meetings is they are so contentious, and the political agenda is always thoroughly vindictive. I know I am more of a progressive and I know you are not, but this is just plain venomous. I doubt I will ever come back here. Tell Carol I will call her tomorrow." She gave him a hug. "*Ciao.*"

The discussion shifted to one of the regular topics at the neighborhood meetings – the prevalence of homelessness. At the Schnucks supermarket in Ferguson, in the Chop Suey Shopping Center on North Florissant Avenue, an entire homeless encampment has formed in the shopping center. Donna French told the attendees she will no longer shop at the Ferguson Schnucks in the Chop Suey Shopping Center because of the homeless encampment and that at least 50 percent of the parking lot is the homeless settlement. Dirk Deckers said he notified the Ferguson Police about what he called a "homeless town" at the Schnucks parking lot.

Caitlin Flowers said she has seen a van at the Ferguson Schnucks in the Chop Suey Shopping Center which is being used as a homeless warehouse. "I think they are keeping their drugs and needles in the van. The homeless are lined up day and night waiting to purchase their fix." These complaints brought out a robust response and defense of the homeless town from the liberals at the meeting; and clearly, most of the attendees, being progressive types, were supporters of the homeless town.

Ethan Davidson, who was obviously a woman dressed up as a man, lashed out at the criticism of the poor, exploited victims of the capitalist system. "These people are suffering from your affluence," he lectured. "Leave them alone. They have it hard enough already, for Christ's sake. Look at the tremendous good they are doing. They contribute so much to Schnucks. They keep watch over the parking lot all hours of the day and night. They provide work for the cleanup employees. They use the restrooms in the store all day and until the store closes, and this helps make certain the plumbing still works. They ensure the fruit and produce are fresh by sampling it all day long. Stop hassling them and making their lives more difficult. Don't they have it tough enough?"

Caitlin Flowers asked Davidson if he even shops at the Schnucks in Ferguson. "No," Davidson replied. "I shop at Trader Joe's or Whole Foods."

White liberal attendee Tiffany changed the subject and told the group how proud she was of the Ben and Jerry's Ice Cream Corporation based in the liberal paradise of Vermont. "Because of racism and white supremacy, Ben and Jerry's is making changes to its products to promote the cause. From now on all ice cream will be chocolate. There will be no white or vanilla ice creams – even to be used as a base. All base ice cream must be chocolate and then other additives can be mixed in. This is according to orders from Ben Cohen and Jerry Greenfield. They are so progressive," she cooed. "All ice cream flavors are to carry an additional label that says, 'No Justice No Peace.' Ben even said the move will help eliminate racism in the country. Jerry said the move will bring justice to all people of color suffering from police brutality. And Ben even said this, 'Silence is not an option and so our company is not silent.'"

Omar quickly dropped in to the discussion and advised the assembled liberals, "Changing the contents of a carton of ice cream ain't gonna do squat for the brothas."

18

J ack Aiello, the perceptive Kansas City attorney representing Perry Olmstead, called Perry in Ste. Genevieve.

"Perry, we have a new appearance date in federal court in Kansas City for your Ku Klux Klan charges."

The Justice Department under the former president had filed a civil complaint against Perry, accusing him of being a member of the Klan. The U.S. attorney's office in Kansas City delayed bringing the civil complaint forward for a court appearance until now.

"Okay. What's up?" Perry replied.

"You will need to come to Kansas City for an appearance. It is a civil complaint so it will likely go on for quite a while – frankly, it is possible it could be years."

"I've heard about that," Perry said. "I know three black people in St. Louis who have been tied up in federal court in St. Louis for more than ten years under a similar type of case."

"I know about that case, and I have been following it," Aiello said. "But Perry, I need to talk to you about the challenge we are facing in federal court in Kansas City. The judge who received the assignment for your case will be no friend."

Moira Pembroke was appointed to the federal bench by the previous president. Miss Pembroke had been a close associate of the former, charming first lady. Pembroke worked for a while in the former first lady's law firm in Arkansas. And after her tenure at the Little Rock law firm, she found a staff attorney position with the Southern Discrimination Legal Committee, a public policy lobbying and fund-raising organization which likes to portray itself as a champion of civil rights. Having served as an attorney with the SDLC, Miss Pembroke was seen by the former first lady as eminently qualified to serve as a federal judge. Miss Pembroke had some difficulty overcoming an embarrassing exchange during her confirmation hearing in the Senate Judiciary Committee, but, in the end, scenarios like that rarely matter. Senator Chuck Grassley of the committee asked Miss Pembroke what are the five rights that are protected in the First Amendment.

"Excuse me, Senator?"

"Can you tell us what the five rights are that are defined and protected through the First Amendment?" Grassley asked.

"Senator, I can't say as though I am familiar with that," Pembroke replied.

"Can you name one or two of those rights?" Grassley continued.

"Thank you for that question, Senator. Are you speaking of the right to a trial and representation by qualified counsel?"

"No. Can you try again?" Grassley persisted.

"Thank you, Senator. Are you speaking of the right to a speedy trial?"

"No. Try again."

"Thank you, Senator. The right to privacy?" Pembroke said.

"No, ma'am. And frankly, I don't know that you will be able to find a right to privacy in the Constitution," Grassley said. "Well, Miss Pembroke, what do you think about the First Amendment?"

"Can you repeat the question, Senator?"

"What do you think about the First Amendment?"

"Senator, I think it's something that is more reflective of the seventeenth and eighteenth centuries."

"Since it's something from the seventeenth or eighteenth century, do you think it has any applicability to our time?" Grassley pursued.

"Senator, I think it is an older provision, more definitive of the concerns and history of an ancient time, and less vital to the issues we are facing in modern times."

Jack Aiello told Perry that the incident at Judge Pembroke's confirmation hearing didn't prevent her from being confirmed by the U.S. Senate and the esteemed judge currently sits on the federal district court bench in Kansas City, and furthermore, she received the assignment to hear Perry's Ku Klux Klan civil case.

"Hmm. Because of her background at the Southern Discrimination Legal Committee, do you think she could have a favorable approach to our defense?" Perry asked Aiello.

"Well, Perry, that's not quite how it works. First of all, the Southern Discrimination Legal Committee has no interest in racism, Jim Crow, black codes, discrimination, separate but equal, racial intimidation, racial violence – any of that abuse to human rights that emerged as an outgrowth of the Democrat Party during the Reconstruction era. Frankly, it's in the interest of that organization to keep these offenses going, so they can collect more donations. That's what it's all about. It's called a shakedown. And organizations like this run elaborate shakedowns all over the country – just for the sake of collecting billions of dollars. They ply their schtick to the liberals, the Ivy League sycophants, the worried and nervous college students who are losing sleep because the world is destined to burn up into a crisp from too much carbon in the atmosphere. Judge Pembroke's SDLC is just a shakedown and doesn't have any concern about so-called justice. Their primary task, aside from collecting money, is to toss out insults and accuse people of being white supremacists. Consequently, Perry, that means she is already against you. She has been provided with a salacious, scandalous legal matter by the Justice Department that a federal judge will be required to hear. She is surely excited and looking forward to it."

"Sounds like we've already lost," mused Perry.

"Probably. She can get some prominence and standing among the liberal elites on the Kansas City plantation for having been the judge on the case of a black man who was a member of the Ku Klux Klan."

* * *

The neighborhood meetings in Florissant, at the Presbyterian church basement, continued to be absorbed with the problem of homelessness in the North County area. The neighbors remained in conflict with each other over the crisis. Several neighbors voiced their outrage that the homeless have set up towns and encampments at several Schnucks supermarket parking lots. A few attendees said they have stopped shopping at Schnucks because of the situation. Ferguson resident Ethan Davidson said the neighbors are in need of reeducation, just like how Mao did it during the Cultural Revolution in China.

"Why is this homeless situation such a problem for you bourgeois people?" Davidson asked, dripping with contempt.

"What in heaven's name are you talking about?" challenged resident Molly Markham, a friend of Michael and Carol from a few blocks down the street from their home in Florissant and who participated in Republican Party activities with the Holdens. "It is not hygienic, it is dangerous, they are using illegal drugs often with needles, they have serious mental illness problems, they get into fights and violent episodes. Not to mention that the purpose of a parking lot in a shopping center is not to house homeless people."

"People don't need to be driving cars which require parking lots," retorted Davidson. "Take public transportation. Then the homeless can have the parking lot and won't be bothering you."

"How can people conveniently function without mobility and vehicles?" asked Markham.

"Public transportation works adequately and furnishes you with your precious mobility – such a bourgeois obsession."

"Are you kidding me?" responded Markham. "Public transportation frequently just stops running without predictability. For instance, when the disgruntled masses you are championing go on their demonstrations and street riots and looting, public transportation does not run. When there are natural disasters, such as tornadoes or stream flooding, public transportation stops for days. But furthermore, public transportation is inconvenient; frequently it goes nowhere logical and certainly doesn't deposit people near their homes. Public transportation is not clean, it gives preference to the mentally disabled, and frequently, passengers are assaulted by mentally ill passengers."

"Well, then you should walk or ride a bike to your destination," lectured Davidson. "And truthfully, you shouldn't even be going to a store operated by a greedy multinational corporation or even an independently owned business that is focused on profits over people. These companies don't care about our neighborhoods. And not only that, you should also stop going to jobs that exploit people and merely enrich billionaires and trillionaires. Just stop going to jobs."

He was interrupted by a round of acclamation by the liberal contingent in the room, which was most of the attendees.

"Okay. Who is going to pay my mortgage? My utility bills? My insurance? My food? School tuition?" Molly replied.

"Those are rights," Davidson snapped. "You shouldn't have to concern yourself with paying for the necessities – although we shouldn't even have mortgages because they are a tool of inequity and promote ownership of private property. And, also, we should not have insurance – just another tool of the oppressors. Regarding tuition, education should be free. You need to have your perspective changed. You need to be reeducated."

Markham responded by saying the homeless create division, discomfort and danger to a community because of their abuse of property, drug abuse and addiction, and untreated mental illness. "Defecating in public is not acceptable. Stealing and robbery are not okay. Using heroin or methamphetamines is not normal."

"That is my point," Davidson replied smugly. "You need to be reeducated. Why are those things not normal and acceptable? Only because your bourgeois, entrapped thinking prevents you from under-standing that they are just as normal as anything. You need to alter your perceptions. There is no reason that any of the things that seem to offend you so much are not completely accepted."

The liberal attendees responded with applause.

Michael Holden had heard enough and stood up. "Homelessness is an indication of social collapse. It is not normal. It is caused by abuse of drugs and alcohol, or untreated mental illness, and these aberrations are not normal and should not be normalized. These are all people in need of treatment, or in extreme cases should be institutionalized. Those of you in this room who are enthralled with homelessness – I assume you live here in Florissant or Ferguson – are you proposing that they live on the parking grass in front of your homes? That eight-foot strip of land belongs to the city and consequently according to local ordinances, the homeless would be entitled to set up tents on that property. Do you want them living in front of your house?"

Ethan Davidson responded, "I have no problem with that."

"Do you want them relieving themselves, defecating, shooting up heroin, tossing their garbage in front of your house?"

"No problem," was Davidson's glib reply.

The liberals gave another round of loud applause.

Davidson then said, "I want to teach you simpler people in the room about hostile architecture. Once you open your eyes and open your mind, you will see it everywhere. Remember, the mind is like a parachute: it only works if it is opened," he said, reciting the primary principle of wisdom he learned at the University of Minnesota. "Hostile architecture is when design is purposely intended to target a population and make life miserable. Let's look at some examples. In a grocery store, for instance, the dairy is purposely placed in the back of the store. A person is forced to walk past all the useless bourgeois tripe that the greedy corporations want you to look at and buy. It's just putting more money into their voracious, greedy hands. Another example is the construction of sidewalks. Sidewalks are intended to make life miserable for people who don't have homes – making it impossible for them to sleep comfortably – they are made of concrete, they are narrow, they're stuck right out next to busy streets. Highways are built to purposely bisect through neighborhoods and generate loud noise and toxic pollution. Buildings are built with stairwells and bright lights which make it difficult for people without homes to comfortably sleep in them."

Molly Markham became indignant. "So, are you trying to tell us that highways shouldn't exist? How are we supposed to get around?"

"Highways should not exist. That's one of the primary lessons of the mayor of Muncie, Indiana – Alfred E. Neuman. He has embraced the understanding of hostile architecture and has advocated that all highways should be dismantled. And, as Mayor Neuman has advocated, cars shouldn't exist either. Look how cars have created the carbon cataclysm, putting all of that carbon in the atmosphere and heating up the planet into a burning crisp. There should only be bike and walking trails. This is something that has been promoted by the architecture school at Tulane. Everyone should get around by walking and riding their bikes."

"Thank you for teaching us about hostile architecture," announced Cathy Porterman in a grateful tone. "I have never thought about it before."

Davidson snidely replied, "Well, of course you haven't. Have you even been to college?"

Someone asked Michael Holden what he thought about the theory presented by Ethan Davidson.

"I don't think much about it at all, because it is all a steaming pile of crap."

Davidson was not to be deterred. He continued presenting other nuggets he picked up at the University of Minnesota. "Now, I want to introduce you all to an important concept that you city dwellers need to start to learn as part of your reeducation. By eliminating the police, we are then able to understand what systemic racism is and how people without homes are being purposely oppressed. Eliminating the police is the first step to expunging racism and oppression and bringing the people to power. The people must unite and destroy the oppressor. All we have to lose is our chains."

Michael thought Omar Clift, the assistant principal at MacGyver, may be impressed by such sentiments.

"Now just a minute," interrupted Molly Markham. "A society cannot exist without law and order. You would have bedlam without some type of presence from the police, especially in a large and complex society and big urban areas. There is an element of lawlessness and chaos that would take over without some type of check."

"There you go again," Davidson sneered. "Ignorance is so pervasive. You need to be reeducated in one of our camps."

"What about domestic abuse, child abuse, robbery, kidnapping and abduction, burglary, arson, pimping and child prostitution, human trafficking, drug trafficking, racketeering, murder, mayhem?"

D.W. SNOW

"We don't need police for any of that stuff," Davidson replied. "And who said any of that is necessarily wrong? That is the bourgeois influence of the oppressor. As Alfred E. Neuman, the mayor of Muncie, says, 'Common sense is the manipulation of the masses to make them comply with the demands of the powerful oppressors.'"

Omar Clift jumped in. "Yes. The police are the oppressors. They roam around harassing our brothers on the street – just like zookeepers to a bunch of animals locked up in cages for the rich folk to come by and stare at. It is the police who are keeping the brothers down, when they only want to come out of their sheds and shacks, after being locked up all the time, so they can get a breath of fresh air."

The group applauded the assistant principal of MacGyver High School.

Sadie Rice, a white liberal, stood up and said, "The problem stems from too many guns. We need to repeal the Second Amendment and then ban all guns. And then it will be easier for us to get rid of the police. And finally, that money can go to the public schools."

Omar Clift, the assistant principal at MacGyver, quickly responded, "Now just a minute here. The brothers need guns. When they's roamin' the streets after they's gettin' outta they's shacks and sheds for some fresh air, they's needin' some guns."

Molly turned to her friend, Michael Holden, and said, "Michael, what do you think of all of that?"

Holden was quiet initially. And then gently, with a barely audible voice, he said to the group, "What you are saying here is wrong and immoral – being promoted by dangerous agitators."

He took a deep breath. "Look, I know all about this kind of dangerous rhetoric. It is deceitful and causes social problems to spin more out of control."

He paused again and took another deep breath. His voice quivered. "My son became a gangbanger and a street thug because of this kind of perverse thinking. He is on the street now – probably robbing businesses, breaking into homes and cars, shooting at people during gang violence and gang wars."

Michael stood quietly, tears running down his cheeks.

19

Carol's despair had become overwhelming. The loss of her precious, tender-hearted boy to delinquency, street crime and gang lawlessness drove her into despondency. Michael finally convinced her to visit a physician at Sisters of St. Mary-DePaul Hospital in Bridgeton, just a few miles west of Florissant. The doctor prescribed a mild antidepressant medication to help her cope with her difficulties.

After seeing the devastation of Michael Junior's experience at MacGyver, it was decided Andrea needed to enroll at St. Louis North Synod High School. Anne Newland and Perry Olmstead watched the psychological collapse of Carol over her son's travails at MacGyver and the boy's drift into the underbelly. Anne expressed to the Holdens that she and Perry wanted to pay the tuition for Andrea to attend St. Louis North Synod. They assured Michael and Carol it would be the most meaningful gift they could give to the Holdens and to Andrea. Carol and Michael felt a sense of shame and initially turned down the gift, but Anne and Perry persisted, explaining it was their joy to help Andrea, whom they loved, and it would also be their way to pay a sense of acknowledgment and respect to Michael Junior – the belief that Andrea would be able to pull herself beyond difficulties while keeping her brother alive in her mind.

Andrea loved her experiences at St. Louis North Synod. She was a diligent and conscientious student and excelled in English, history, and science. She treasured going to chapel for prayer and the eucharist. She enjoyed singing hymns with the four hundred other students, as well as the deep spiritual traditions and intricate ceremonies and the historic, medieval rituals the school has devoted itself to and promoted over the years.

"Andrea, what do you think of St. Louis North Synod High School?" Carol asked.

"Oh, Momma. It is so excellent. I am so lucky to have this opportunity. I feel very blessed that Auntie Anne and Uncle Perry have made it possible for me."

"Andrea, do you see drugs at all?"

"Oh, no, Momma. It is a synod high school! It is just like Salem School, maybe a few more black kids than at Salem, which makes it truly feel like a family. But really, Momma, it is just like Salem."

When Andrea was in her senior year and was preparing for graduation at St. Louis North Synod, she was asked by the principal to give the senior talk at the graduation ceremony. She worked on preparing the speech diligently with sincere, fervent, passionate, and thoughtful consideration.

"Momma, I'm nervous."

"Do you know what you are going to talk about?"

"Yes. I am going to talk about my school experience and what it has meant to our family."

At the graduation ceremony, Elgar's *Pomp and Circumstance* was played by the high school band and the choir sang the lyrics. The congregation and students sang John Zundel and Charles Wesley's classic hymn *Love Divine All Love's Excelling*. After the invocation prayer and some introductory comments from the principal, Andrea was introduced as the senior class speaker, and she began.

Welcome! Congratulations, graduates! Thank you to the synod and this school's faculty and administrators. Thank you to parents, grandparents, brothers and sisters, aunts and uncles. More about the meaning and purpose of a family later in my talk.

I want to talk today about what makes St. Louis North Synod High School so very different from a public school. What is it that sets us apart? What makes us special, what makes us distinct? We get a lot of criticism and grief for being different from the popular culture; and it is true, we are different, very different. Some have said we are isolated, protected, innocent, sheltered, shielded, safeguarded, unsophisticated, not worldly, not part of the culture and the society. These are all probably accurate assessments. We are separated from the fallen world which surrounds us. Let's look at what has made us so different and how this school builds character. We have various unique qualities and characteristics that make us very different from what you might find in a public school. We are quite unique, and this has truly made us what we are.

St. Louis North Synod is famous for its academic rigor. More than 74 percent of the faculty have advanced and specialized degrees. More than 96 percent of the student body goes on to pursue higher education. Students here are required to complete a very demanding academic curriculum. In addition, the school offers high quality programs in art, instrumental and choral music, aesthetics, dance and theater.

We always have competitive sports and athletic teams. Our football, basketball, baseball, swimming, and track and field teams are frequently among the top teams in their conferences. The focus has always been to build both a competitive spirit but also personal character among the athletes. These athletes begin each practice and each game in prayer.

At St. Louis North Synod, we have a strong tradition of practicing our religious beliefs. We hold chapel every day. Eucharist is celebrated most days each week. Confession and absolution are given once a week. Each student, from ninth grade to twelfth grade, must attend the divine liturgy and all students, all four years, are required to take scripture class.

St. Louis North Synod builds character through our well-known traditions of service and community outreach. All four hundred students participate each year in the North County neighborhood and roadside cleanup, and the North St. Louis neighborhood cleanup. More than 50 percent of the junior class participates in tutoring at synod elementary schools. More than 25 percent of the senior class participates in the family crisis outreach, serving as counselors and mentors for synod families who have suffered tragedies or difficulties.

We have a proud tradition of teaching and nurturing the personal appreciation of ceremony and tradition among the students. These ceremonies and customs build our devotion to our synod's traditions, our values, our well-known history of discipline reflecting the synod's origins from medieval Germany. All four hundred students participate in the annual North St. Louis Processional and then the North St. Louis Retreat. The ninth graders celebrate the annual Freshman Ceremony of Initiation, the Ceremony of the Holy Trinity, and the Freshman Prayer Retreat. The tenth graders have the Eucharist Vigil, the Ceremony of the Holy Trinity, the Fraternity of the Oak Grove, and the Transfiguration Festival and Ceremony. The eleventh graders celebrate the Junior Convocation, the Ceremony of the Chrism, the Fraternity of the Oak Grove, the Saxon Palm Order of the Shrine, and the Procession of the Gifts. The seniors have the Senior Prayer Retreat, the Eucharist Vigil, the Saxon Palm Order of the Shrine, the Ceremony of the Chrism, Senior Convocation, Senior Processional, and the Congregation of the Discipline.

These old customs and traditions, derived from solemn medieval German practices and devotions, help make us aware that we are part of a larger, ancient community of believers which originated in the Middle Ages, and we as young people will be carrying forth this tradition and heritage in our synod and for the world.

St. Louis North Synod is a family of racial tolerance. Fifty percent of the student body is black or mixed race. This is a reflection of the synod's grand history. In 1854, a group of Americans famously gathered at the oak grove in Jackson, Michigan and established a commitment to finally bring an end to slavery in this country. We now know about three hundred of the one thousand participants at the oak grove were synod people. After that event in Jackson, Michigan, and the end of the Civil War, the synod sent scores of missionaries into the Deep South to spread the gospel and to plant churches and parochial schools among the former slaves. And then the synod built and opened two colleges for black people to help promote racial equality – Immanuel College in Greensboro, North Carolina and Concordia College in Selma, Alabama. Because of this splendid and impressive history of the synod, about 25 percent of the total synod membership is composed of black people. We have a proud tradition of having predominantly black parishes – several right here in the St. Louis area.

We – the synod people – are a conservative, traditional, disciplined, reserved, orthodox, conventional, constant, dignified, reverent, confessional, liturgical, and solemn community of believers. This school teaches those values; these are the values of the synod.

And finally, I want to talk about one of the most important aspects of what St. Louis North Synod represents – that is, family. This school institution builds and protects the values of the family. That is one of its primary purposes. The family is the foundation of a society, a people, a nation. This is most notably symbolized by the Holy Family, that is, Mary, Joseph, and Jesus. It is the family that represents stability, love, devotion, sacrifice, convention, decency, innocence and purity, leadership, vulnerability, and the foundational principles of morality. While the school is not the family itself, it does everything it can to support the family and to imitate many of the characteristics of the family unit. If you will indulge me, let me tell a story of my own family. My Papa attended this high school as a boy. He is a proud graduate of St. Louis North Synod. It was my parents' intention to send their two children to St. Louis North Synod, to follow in the footsteps of my Papa. But when it came time to send my older brother to this school, my Papa had lost his job and found it financially impossible to send my brother to this school. My brother was the gentlest, sweetest, cutest, most adorable and innocent boy. Because of my parents' financial difficulties, it wasn't possible to send him here and he went to a large public school of more than four thousand students. Let us not forget, St. Louis North Synod tries to imitate a family – we don't have four thousand students; we have four hundred students. Over the course of just a year, he was literally transformed into a street gang member. He became a street thug, carrying a gun, committing petty theft and criminal activity, smoking weed, sleeping until the afternoon each day. He has left the synod. My family has not seen him in more than five years. My Momma, who is a devout synod woman, who prays incessantly, attends matins or vespers at least three days a week, professes the adoration of the eucharist, attends the consecration of the chrism every year, she is now completely heartbroken. She has asked endlessly, why has a devout synod family been subjected to this torment, this terror. After this nightmare, my family decided that their daughter, me – Andrea Holden – must attend St. Louis North Synod. They would have been unable to bear witness to that same torture for their remaining child. Luckily, my Auntie Anne and Uncle Perry – they are here today – stepped up and made my enrollment in this wonderful school possible, so that I could have this terrific, rewarding, character-building experience.

Let us celebrate, defend, and protect our families. And that importantly includes our synod's particular family of St. Louis North Synod High School.

After Andrea's graduation from St. Louis North Synod, she enrolled at St. Louis Community College at the Florissant Valley campus in Ferguson. Again, Anne Newland and Perry Olmstead helped Andrea by paying her tuition at the college. While a college student, one day she attended a vespers service at Zion Cathedral with her mother, and during the vespers she had the opportunity to meet a charming, tall black man who also attended the service. William Birmingham grew up in St. Louis and attended Zion Cathedral since his youth. William attended Webster University, received a degree in business and he then landed a job as a salesman of aftermarket parts and accessories for Harley-Davidson motorcycles. While Andrea was still in her first year at St. Louis Community College, William and Andrea decided they wanted to get married. William, according to synod custom, asked Michael for permission to propose to his daughter. Michael obediently, according to synod custom, asked William how he would support Michael's daughter. William explained the nature of his sales position with the Harley-Davidson aftermarket accessories supplier. Carol and Michael were supportive because Andrea found a devout synod believer and William Birmingham was a responsible, reverent and dignified man. The wedding, a beautiful and solemn, traditional ceremony, with a eucharist celebration, was held at St. Paul's Church College Hill on John Avenue in the College Hill neighborhood. This was the church of both Carol's youth and where Michael and Carol were married. Carol and Michael obtained permission from their pastor at Salem Church, their home parish in Florissant, to hold the wedding at St. Paul's College Hill. The congregation sang Johann Cruger and Paul Gerhardt's hymn *Rejoice My Heart Be Glad and Singing*. After the entry of the bride and groom, the pastor led the congregation in the Confiteor, Kyrie and Gloria, and then sang the Collect prayer in chant. Then, as part of ancient tradition, Father Zachary Lucas celebrated the chrism as a blessing for the young newlyweds. At the conclusion of the vows and before the consecration of the eucharist, Father Lucas opened the chrism ambry to the right of the high altar to bring out the chrism vessel. He approached the kneeling young couple, and then he dipped the chrism spoon into the vessel to moisten the spoon with holy oils, and he proceeded to dab the chrism oils on the foreheads, necks, lips, eyelids, ears, noses, hands and arms of Andrea and William. Andrea quietly wept with joy, yet also haunted in the back of her mind as she thought of her missing brother.

Alice Ploughmaster, the adored former mayor of East St. Louis and the inspirational symbol for nearly all black people in the St. Louis area, was a wedding guest and she took time during the reception to talk to Carol and Michael about their missing son. Mrs. Ploughmaster broke down and cried with Carol about the lost boy.

"I wonder nearly every day, how this could have happened in a devout synod family," Carol said in tears. "He was such a tender boy. He was such a sincere believer. He often told me Jesus was his best friend."

"I will never forget him playing his trombone during the cantata at Trinity, and his adorable recital," Mrs. Ploughmaster consoled. "What a tender, sweet boy. Truly, one of the most memorable children you will ever see in a lifetime. In any case, Carol, pray – pray ceaselessly."

Andrea and William planned to move to an apartment in the Forest Park Southeast neighborhood of St. Louis.

* * *

Michael and Carol customarily visited New Shanghai Restaurant on Fridays. They particularly enjoyed bringing along a neighbor to enjoy their favorite restaurant. This particular Friday they weren't able to find anyone to come along. They drove to the dumpy little strip mall with King Solomon's Fashion Mine on Florissant Road, just down the road from the Chop Suey Shopping Center with the Schnucks supermarket. As they pulled into the rundown parking lot filled with weeds, Michael had to slow down to a crawl because of all the massive potholes and mounds of trash. Michael loves the delicious Chinese fare, even more than one famous, wealthy Democrat California congresswoman loves her $65-per-piece frozen chocolate confection that she keeps in her $10,000 elegant refrigerator. This esteemed, elderly San Francisco congresswoman enjoys the ritual of spearing her expensive ice cream treat with a fancy, golden charm that is shaped like a snake with a carved golden buzzard perched on the top of the head of the snake. After she has pleasurably popped the chocolate ice cream confection into her mouth, she marvels in the delight of its flavor and then affectionately rubs and caresses her treasured snake charm and whispers to her dear snake talisman friend, "There, there my precious; we have had our special treat."

Michael is tickled by the Chinese owner of New Shanghai, Mr. Lee, who is so clever and kind. It was a lunch date for the Holdens. When they arrived, Mr. Lee greeted two of his favorite customers.

"Herro, Michaer."

"Oh, hi, Mr. Lee. Can you put us in one of those back booths."

Mr. Lee sat Michael and Carol in the back corner booth. In just a few minutes, Mr. Lee came to their booth to take their order. Michael ordered moo goo gai pan, vegetable chop suey, sesame shrimp, and two large glasses of iced tea. Their order arrived and the Holdens engaged in one of their favorite rituals – the Friday casual dining treat of delicious Chinese food and interacting with the quaint Chinese owner. What could make a better end to the week? Suddenly, two young men entered the restaurant – two men who would have been familiar to Tamika Philigrew's bank coworkers in Dutchtown, or familiar to the funeral procession mourners on their way to Bellefontaine Cemetery, or recognized by Perry Olmstead and the clerk at the pawn shop on Gravois Avenue, and even remembered by Chubbles Philigrew and the proprietor of the liquor store in Baden. As they burst into New Shanghai with their dirty dreadlock braids dangling on the side of their heads like a den of dead snakes, they yelled and brandished their SEI Sauer semi-automatic pistols. One of these equity boys, this time, was carrying a sawed-off shotgun – a weapon which is illegal under the Bureau of Alcohol, Tobacco and Firearms regulations because it is a wickedly powerful weapon which lacks the civility of any control when it is fired; the shell sprays out in a broad circumference with massive power and can easily blast a hole ten inches in diameter. "Y'all muthas, shut up, y'all hears me's," one of the equity gentlemen announced to Mr. Lee. "Now, we's here to collect everythang in you's regista. Y'all hears me's now, ya mutha." Mr. Lee was suddenly taken with a case of paralysis and was frozen; the blood drained from his face. "Now! You's mutha chinaman. Gimme all da dope in y'all's draw. Y'all hears me's? Now!" Mr. Lee for some reason was unable to move, petrified in fear. Certainly, by now one would logically have thought Mr. Lee would have already experienced something like this, being in such a prime location along Florissant Road, just a few blocks from the homeless encampment of heroin addicts who live in the parking lot in front of the Schnucks in the Chop Suey Shopping Center. The other equity brother yanked up his SEI Sauer 9 mm, a brutal but elegantly powerful weapon, and he pulled the trigger. A bullet flew across the room at 1,709 m.p.h. and plowed straight into a glass framed picture of a lotus flower that Chinese restaurants are able to purchase as part of a decorations package from the restaurant supply warehouse. The picture of the lotus flower exploded and fell into hundreds of tiny pieces to the floor. This event seemed to have the effect of awakening Mr. Lee from his temporary paralysis. He quickly opened the register and emptied the contents of $456.68 into a bag politely handed to him by one of the equity conquistadores sporting his lovely dreadlock braids. The two visitors rapidly exited the door they had entered just sixty-nine seconds before, and one of the boys yelled out, "Power to our's peoples! Smash da man!"

Mr. Lee, in a rush and a panic, picked up the phone and dialed 911 to report the disturbing incident. After Mr. Lee made the obligatory phone call, he walked around to customers' tables, asking if everyone was alright. He came to Michael and Carol's table. Carol was panicking and breathing heavily; tears ran down her cheeks.

"You okay?" Mr. Lee asked.

"Yes, this chop suey is delicious," Michael replied.

"You okay? The wobbels here," Lee persisted.

"Oh, I didn't see that," Michael replied. "I guess I missed that."

When Mr. Lee departed, Carol, in tears, whispered to Michael, "Good Lord, Michael. I thought it could have been Michael Junior initially. I keep expecting that is how we will ultimately discover him."

"I know, Carol," Michael quietly replied. "When will the nightmare end?"

20

Michael Holden, Jr. had taken up a job as an occasional driver of a shuttle van, despite living the life of a street criminal. He found that the street life didn't generate quite enough income for some of his obligations – including funneling enough cash into the hands of the baby momma who was always demanding money. The baby momma even just today hit Michael in the forehead, causing a cut and a bruise, because she was upset the money wasn't coming down the pike. He only worked one day a week, and frequently wasn't able to show up on the days he was scheduled because of the necessity to sleep in after a late night of smoking weed with the boys. Michael slept on the floor of the apartment of one of his gang buddies. The apartment was a grimy, small one-bedroom unit in a dingy building in the Jeff-Vander-Lou neighborhood of north St. Louis. Crime was common in the neighborhood and on most nights, gunfire was a regular background noise. Michael and his gang friends, on occasion, contributed to the gunfire background sound effects. While Jeff-Vander-Lou is a poor, rundown neighborhood in St. Louis with high crime, in comparison, the area is the peak of dignity and decency when contrasted with the uniform, endless, subhuman blight that dominates Kansas City. The predominating feature of most of Kansas City is the utter collapse of human civilization – miles of neglect, squalor, disrepair, deterioration, decrepit abandonment, seediness, crumbling and decaying hovels, derelict and tumbling buildings, blight and total decay, a complete and thoroughly bombed-out war-zone rampant with street crime, drug trafficking, constant shootings, burglaries, assaults, larceny, rapes, and armed robbery.

At least in St. Louis, the rundown and decaying areas reflect a certain remnant of civilization that is simply not visible in Kansas City – which is a blighted city of old, decaying, dumpy, shabby leftovers of a slave plantation settlement. St. Louis still displays the dignity of beautiful nineteenth and early twentieth century architecture, even in the troubled areas; the overwhelming number of these historic, old, stately homes and buildings, despite the despair in some of the neighborhoods, represent Craftsman designs, Victorian elegance, charming red brick construction, and attractive brownstones. In Kansas City, the endless miles of ghetto are purely slapdash, ramshackle, cheap, thoughtless detritus in abject ruin.

When Michael would wake up at noon or later, he would meet up with the other gangsters in his group and they would either watch television reruns and smoke weed, or they would haphazardly plan their next venture into street crime – perhaps an armed robbery of a liquor store or convenience store, a break-in into a small business, burglary in homes or businesses, armed robbery, and assault of a motorist or pedestrian. During these years, Michael never made any contact with his parents or his sister. He was part of a new family with a new code of living – the thug code.

There were times that Michael was able to muster up the energy and concentration and he would go to the shuttle van company and receive an assignment for a transport run. Sometimes he would deliver a product to a location in the metro area. Other times he would be assigned to pick up a passenger for drop-off to the airport or another business location, or do a pickup of a passenger at the airport and take the individual to the appropriate destination – usually a hotel.

One Tuesday in early June, the shuttle service told Michael they needed him for a few late evening and early morning runs. The shuttle company manager promised good pay to Michael if he drove all of the assignments – delivery of official documents to a business in the southern part of the county, picking up a passenger at Lambert International Airport, and finally at midnight picking up a passenger at a hotel in downtown and delivering him to the airport. The prospect of earning more than two-hundred dollars plus tips interested Michael and he agreed to the assignments – which would begin in the evening and finally conclude in the early morning hours, perhaps two o'clock. He told the boys in his crew that he was unable to participate in the regular routine of smoking weed and executing some street banging that evening. He got into the more respectable clothes he kept for his shuttle driver assignments. He even put on some Hugo Boss cologne to make himself have the scent of a serious and sincere shuttle driver. At about five-thirty in the early evening, Michael jumped aboard a Metro Transit bus and took it to the shuttle service near downtown on Market Street. When Michael arrived in the office, he was given his assignments. The delivery of the business documents was to be carried out at about six-thirty or seven o'clock, taking the documents to a construction company in Green Park, south of the city. Then at about nine o'clock, Michael picked up a passenger at Lambert International Airport and transported the passenger to the Magnolia Hotel in downtown St. Louis. He then waited for a couple hours before he was scheduled to pick up a customer at the Pennywell Hilton in downtown. Michael's assignment sheet said the passenger would be a Korean man who didn't speak much, if any, English. He was to pick up Mr. Hyuk Soon Kim at about midnight and deliver him to Lambert International Airport. When Michael arrived at the Pennywell, Mr. Kim, a man in his mid-forties, came out to the shuttle van but it appeared to Michael that the Korean gentleman was drunk, or at least rather inebriated.

Mr. Kim had a small bag, which Michael placed in the back area of the van. Mr. Kim sat in the front passenger seat.

"To the airport, sir?" Michael asked.

"Airport, yes."

Michael wrote down in his logbook the time, ten minutes after midnight, and the mileage on the van odometer. Michael took I-44 which turns into I-70 and then he drove west to Lambert International Airport. Before reaching the airport, Michael asked Mr. Kim what airline he was boarding so that Michael would know where to drop off the passenger. However, Mr. Kim was sound asleep. Michael believed he may have fallen asleep due to the consumption of too much liquor. Michael yelled at Mr. Kim to wake up.

"Chinaman! Hey! You! Hey, Chinaman! Wake the hell up! You stupid son of a bitch!"

Mr. Kim did not wake up. Michael then drove for more than seventy minutes through St. Louis County – North County, the western sections of the county, even into the southern sections of the county. And then Michael Holden, Jr., fortuitously, drove into St. Louis City. It was especially fortuitous because what happened next would, indeed, make it very beneficial for Michael to be inside the city limits of St. Louis City. It was especially fortuitous for Michael because Miss Limney Grantham is the prosecuting attorney in St. Louis City. Michael pulled over along the shoulder of I-64, also called Hwy. 40 by the people of St. Louis. In a state of complete irritation and frustration with his drunken, sleeping Korean passenger, Michael exited his driver's door and walked around to the passenger door. He opened the door and yanked at Mr. Kim, and he must have roused the passenger because Mr. Kim was able to move his body at this point. Michael took out his Ruger 9 mm semi-automatic pistol from his holster and shot Mr. Kim ten times at point blank range and then returned the firearm to his holster. Mr. Kim died instantly from the gunshots to his chest, his neck, his arms, and his lower torso. A driver on I-64/Hwy. 40 who witnessed the shooting immediately called the Metro Police. After Michael shot and killed Mr. Kim, he walked back to the driver's door and pulled out a six-inch knife with a metal handle from under the driver's seat. He walked back to the dead Mr. Kim and placed the knife into Mr. Kim's right hand, making certain the decedent's fingerprints were on the knife. The Metro Police arrived, and Michael stood next to the van. The police found ten spent 9 mm bullet casings and found the firearm in Michael's holster on his body. One officer asked Michael what happened, and Michael relied enough on his knowledge of criminal activity to say, "I don't know" and then he said no more. The police found Mr. Kim on the floor of the passenger's seat curled up into a fetal position, with his arms and hands pathetically pulled up over his head as though he would somehow be able to protect himself from an impending deadly assault from ten rounds which would soon pummel into his body in a deadly assault and promptly kill him. Photographs were taken of the victim, and of Michael, and of the scene of the crime. Michael was placed under arrest for suspicion of first-degree murder and advised of his rights. Interstate 64, also known as Hwy. 40, was shut down for nearly six hours while an investigation proceeded by the Metro Police Department including the detective bureau, and investigators from the St. Louis prosecuting attorney's office. Michael was taken to the St. Louis City Justice Center jail on Tucker Blvd., and he was booked into the jail for pending charges of first-degree murder.

In the morning, Michael was brought into the jail's circuit court arraignment facility. He was informed he was being charged with first-degree murder, reckless endangerment, discharging a weapon, deadly assault, and possession of a concealed weapon without a permit. He was assigned a public defender who spoke with Michael for two minutes prior to his appearance before the city magistrate.

"You need to plead not guilty. I recommend you find an attorney for these charges; they are serious and substantial. I am only here now to represent you during this arraignment."

The judge withheld the granting of bond because it was a first-degree murder charge. The magistrate indicated when the defendant appeared for his next arraignment in the St. Louis City circuit court on Market Street, the judge in the case will be able review any possible orders for a bond.

Michael was remanded to the city jail on Tucker Blvd. He was allowed to make one phone call as a collect call, charges reversed. He called his parents. Michael Senior answered the phone and accepted the charges. Michael Junior was not certain what to say, but nevertheless he said he was in jail, being held on charges of first-degree murder, there is no bond, and he would like advice about finding an attorney to represent him.

Michael Senior knew he couldn't say anything in front of Carol at that moment because of her fragile state. He asked his son if he would be able to visit Michael at the jail. Michael said he didn't know and said he thought his father should call the jail for confirmation.

"Have you talked to an attorney?" Michael Senior asked his son.

"Not really. Only a public defender who entered the plea of not guilty. He told me the charges are so serious I will need to find an attorney who knows how to handle homicide."

"Okay. I will call the jail to find out about visitation. I will work on finding an attorney."

Michael decided, before he talked to Carol about the situation, that he wanted to consult with their pastor at Salem Church to see if they could be in the presence of the pastor when the situation was revealed to Carol. After Carol went to her gallery, Michael called the pastor and explained over the phone what was going on and his desire to have the pastor present when the situation was explained to Carol. They agreed that the pastor would come to their home when Carol's day at the gallery ended.

Michael called the office at the auto and truck parts company where he was an accountant and explained he had a family emergency and would not be able to come to work that day. Carol came home from her gallery and the pastor was already at their house.

"Oh, Father, good to see you," Carol greeted him.

Michael asked Carol to take a seat and they had something to share. Carol felt panic come over her. Michael announced all he knew – Michael was in jail, charged with first-degree murder, and is not qualified for bond at this time.

Carol felt all of the blood flow out of her head. She burst into tears, collapsed and she fainted. Michael positioned Carol on the couch in the front room and brought in a cool rag and placed it on her head. She awoke and began to sob. The pastor consoled her and asked her if he could pray with her. She wept. They prayed together. Andrea, who was visiting her parents before she and her new husband moved into their apartment, came into the room and Michael explained the situation to his daughter. She wept alongside her mother. Carol went to her bedroom and fell asleep on her bed.

Michael called Carol's physician at DePaul Hospital in Bridgeton and explained the situation to the nurse practitioner. The nurse practitioner asked Michael to bring in Carol the following morning to see if they needed to change her medication.

Michael called the jail and learned about visiting policies. He then called Larry Korhonen, the attorney who represented Michael, Carol and Paul Mooney in the Ku Klux Klan case.

"Michael, I don't handle homicide cases. I will give you a recommendation. I need to tell you homicide representation is very complicated and expensive – because the type of law is specialized but also because case preparation and evidence review is expensive and very time consuming."

Korhonen provided the name of Kiera Salzman to Michael as a homicide attorney who could help with Michael Junior's situation. Michael called Miss Salzman and briefly explained what was going on. She told him she would review the police report initially before a consultation meeting would be arranged. Miss Salzman read the police report and called Michael Senior to invite him for a consultation.

"Nice to meet you," Miss Salzman said to Michael. "I have read the police report. The first thing we need to talk about before we discuss anything else is the cost of providing representation in a case like this. I only bring this up now, because if you are not able to accept the fees, it would be best to look for another attorney immediately. The bare minimum fee for this case will be two-hundred-fifty-thousand dollars. We will have to hire a private investigator, and we will need to go through extensive evidentiary review. There will be depositions, interrogatories, discovery, motion hearings, evidence analysis, negotiations with the prosecution, and pretrial conferences. And then there is the trial with jury selection, hearings, trial preparations, legal research, witness interviews, and the trial itself."

"I am familiar with some of this because of a case I am currently involved with. Larry Korhonen is handling that for us."

"Okay. So, we need to arrange payment for services. If you don't have the cash readily available, I recommend you contact a banker and see if you can obtain a second mortgage on your house or any other property you may own. You can call me back and let me know if you wish to proceed, or if you wish to find other representation. It has been nice to meet you." She walked him to the door of her office and said, "Bye now, take care. Give me a call."

21

Michael learned about visitation at the City Justice Center on Tucker Blvd. – which days are permitted, registration of the visitor, time restrictions, and so forth. Because only one visitor is allowed at a time, Michael went as the first visitor so he could observe all the routines and regulations. He visited his son and saw how demeaning the entire place was – the overcrowding, the prisoner's dress and shackles, the rigid restrictions, the echoing noise, the surly and indignant inmates. Michael Junior was distant and gloomy. Michael understood and realized that anyone would be that way under the circumstances, but the breach between Michael Junior and the family certainly was part of the detached and dispassionate attitude. Michael explained to his son that an attorney had been found, a woman named Kiera Salzman, and she would make contact with him soon – before his next arraignment hearing. Michael Junior replied without any particular reaction – certainly not gratitude or satisfaction. He merely said, "Good." They said little and primarily sat and stared at one another separated by a thick plexiglass wall, with Michael maintaining a peevish, distant, disgruntled expression. Finally, the guard announced the visitation had concluded. As Michael Junior left the room his father said, "Goodbye, Son, your mother will come next time." And as another guard approached the boy, who was shackled and handcuffed, he was removed from the room.

Michael explained to Carol what the routine was and said he would accompany her into the building the following week, although he would not accompany her into the visitor's waiting area since only one registered visitor was allowed. Carol was anxious and nervous. Her medications helped control her peaks of emotion. After Carol entered the jail, she went through the metal detector and was patted down by a female guard. She was directed to the visitor's waiting area, and Michael returned to the car until Carol was finished with her visit.

When Carol was brought into the inmate visitation area and sat in her chair with the plexiglass wall in front of her, she realized the impersonal, institutionalized setting would be alienating to anyone – even the most hardened, cynical criminal. Michael came into the room, with handcuffs and loose ankle shackles on. He looked at his mother and did not smile. Carol saw him as so much more detached and distant. She had not seen him in six years, and he appeared sour, petulant, cold, sullen, embittered. He looked so much older, rougher and streetwise. He observed Carol with a sense of detachment and disregard. His face was blank, expressionless. His eyes – which had been so warm, endearing and alive as a precious little boy – were cold, ambivalent and impassive. Carol couldn't control her emotions and began to quietly weep. She couldn't help having her mind dwell on that darling, adorable, sweet, tender little boy – so innocent and pure – sincerely loving his parents, his sister and his grandparents, ardently telling about how Jesus is his best friend, conscientiously playing his trumpet, performing with Mrs. Probst and the Forte Orchestra. After minimal talking between mother and child, the visit ended when a guard arrived to take Michael out of the room in his shackles and hand-cuffs. Carol left the area and entered the main lobby where Michael was waiting for her. She wept. "When will the nightmare end?" she asked her husband.

When they arrived back at their home in Florissant, there was a reporter from the *Post-Dispatch* waiting for them on their porch.

"I wonder who that could be?" Michael said.

"Hello. Mr. Holden? I'm Jason from the *Post-Dispatch*. I'd like to ask you a few questions about what has happened with your son."

"I really have nothing to say," Michael replied.

The reporter began asking questions anyway. Michael responded again that he had nothing to say. The reporter turned to Carol. She looked distressed but desired to express something – a reflection of her sorrow over the whole affair.

"I am sorry about what happened. I am particularly sorry about what occurred to Mr. Kim. I know he has a wife and parents who are grieving and are pained in a way none of us could ever grasp. I want to extend my deepest condolences to them. Their pain and agony can never be understood. I hurt for them – deeply. My family is hurting also; I don't wish to compare the pain. Let's leave it there."

The reporter persisted, asking question after question about Michael's life, his history, his participation in crime, his ownership of a semi-automatic pistol. How could he mercilessly, in cold blood, kill a man in the front seat of his van? What could he have thought pummeling a man in the fetal position with ten bullets from a semi-automatic weapon? And then there was a series of questions intended to humiliate Carol and Michael as parents. What do you think about your own parenting of a son who would do this? Has he always been violent and volatile – even as a child? When he obtained his weapon, did you provide guidance and gun safety training? Did you motivate your son to do something with his life? Did you ever ask him what his plans were for his life? Did you ever ask him who he associated with?

Carol quickly understood what her husband meant when he said he had nothing to say. Any comment would be taken out of context and would ultimately be used to manufacture or prop up a predetermined narrative.

"I have nothing more to say. Would you now leave us alone?" Carol said.

The reporter walked around to other houses on the block to ask about Michael and Carol's parenting habits and qualifications to serve as adequate caretakers of the next generation – which was actually the human capital belonging to the government ... people who are supposed to live up to the expectations and designs of the secular culture. The interest of the media was purely to assign blame on such a disappointing and culpable family – clearly living outside the norms and expectations of the approved secular culture and society. Most of the neighbors refused to comment, instinctively knowing that the questions were intended to elicit guilt, blame, culpability, recrimination, disgrace, stigma. Two neighbors told the reporter that the Holdens were the paragon of decency and decorum – "After all, they are in the synod, don't you know!"

When it came to writing up the story about Michael and Carol, there was nothing revealing other than a smug comment about the family being churchy people in that pious, sanctimonious, cult-like synod.

Michael asked Larry Korhonen, his attorney, about the prospect of obtaining a second mortgage to pay for his son's legal defense. Korhonen provided Michael with advice and recommended a good bank which would likely provide the loan, especially with Korhonen's reference. Michael was able to obtain a one-hundred-thousand-dollar loan in a second mortgage, which was not even halfway to his goal. He redeemed one-hundred-thousand dollars in his retirement savings account. Although Michael didn't want to do it, he contacted Perry Olmstead and explained the nature of his problem. Perry and Anne were able to loan Michael fifty-thousand dollars. Michael now began the life of being a debt slave – a character taken right off the plantation in Kansas City.

Michael talked to Korhonen about the wisdom and advisability of putting his entire life into a two-hundred-fifty-thousand-dollar debt – with an unknown likelihood of repaying it.

"Should we have merely turned it over to a public defender?" Michael asked.

"That's just not a good idea," Korhonen said. "The job of the public defender is to avoid trial – only to find a way to a guilty plea. So, a jury never hears the case. With a public defender, Michael will be found guilty through a plea – likely second-degree murder – and will spend many years, perhaps thirty or forty years or more, in prison. The risk you have taken with the large loan debt is that with proper representation he may be able to avoid that negative result, and possibly be exonerated or merely found guilty of a much more minor offense. Your defense attorney will need to negotiate all those guardrails through the pretrial and pleadings phase. And then you will still have the unknown conclusion of what happens at the trial. It's all a risk, a chance. I think you made the right decision. Paying back your debt will likely be a lifetime proposition. Sorry, but that is the truth."

"It's daunting, dispiriting and disconcerting. None of this would have happened if I had taken on the debt to send him to the synod high school in the first place."

"Michael, we don't know what life has in store for us. You can't second guess any of this."

"Very depressing. So much despair. I made very poor decisions when he was heading to high school. I am now paying the price."

"Michael, I have one other thing to say. You and Carol and Paul Mooney have done the right thing with your Ku Klux Klan case – you and Carol have been paying a thousand dollars a month for your defense, and Paul has too, and all three of you have kept on top of it all. Who knows what the trial outcome will be, but at least you don't have the burden of a massive legal debt hanging over your head from that case. It turns out you had good foresight and made the right decision."

Michael called Miss Salzman and indicated he had the cash to begin his son's defense. He went to her office and signed a contract and paid her the two-hundred-fifty-thousand dollars for Michael's defense. She said it was now a waiting process. She would appear at his next arraignment, begin discovery, prepare pleadings, conduct depositions, hire the private investigator, carefully research the case, plan the defense strategy, work with the prosecuting attorney's office to find out what their plan is and do some negotiating. She indicated Michael could not obtain a bond because it is a first-degree murder case.

✳ ✳ ✳

Michael went to the neighborhood meeting at the Florissant Presbyterian church basement again.

Ginny Valasco de Azuelos stood up and made an appeal to help locate her stolen trailer which was parked near North Florissant Road and Frost Avenue in Ferguson. She said it was stolen over the weekend.

Ethan Davidson said the trailer could likely better serve someone else, such as the person who took it.

"What do you mean? That's my trailer," Valasco protested.

"That's what you think. That property could better serve another person other than you," Davidson shot back.

"What are you talking about? That trailer doesn't belong to another person."

Davidson patronizingly glared at Valasco. "Private property is merely a social construct. It was better able to serve another person."

"What is this crap?" she fumed. "You sound like a propaganda commissar from China or the Soviet Union. Or, perhaps, a district attorney in San Francisco."

Alex Liebovits, who came to the U.S. more than thirty years ago from the Soviet Union piped in. "When I lived in the Soviet Union, it was necessary for my cousins and me to learn that property was interchangeable based on how the Party needed to use it at any point in time. So, I think Ethan is correct."

Indignant, Valasco responded, "Excuse me, Comrade Alex. We don't happen to live in your communist paradise right now, in case you have forgotten."

Their disagreement was interrupted when neighbor Lani Woodlawn, who works as a child psychologist, announced there was a guest speaker who had been invited to the meeting. Woodlawn introduced Marcellina Killups who lives in Kirkwood and works as a clinician in the Child Gender Transition Clinic at Children's Hospital, an institution operated by Washington University of St. Louis. Mrs. Killups also serves as a life coach in the western suburbs of St. Louis County. Killups said she has written two self-published books, *You Too Can Amount to Something* and *Making a Life for Yourself When Nothing Else Works Out.*

"So how can I help you all out today?" Killups said.

Several of the earnest liberals in the room said they were worried about so much police brutality and the thousands of black people killed by the police every day and they hoped to find ways to de-fund and abolish the police.

"These are great suggestions," Mrs. Killups said. "Keep trying to de-fund them. That will help unify the city around one main important issue."

Somebody in the back of the room asked about the homeless town which has developed at the Chop Suey Shopping Center with thousands of people living in an encampment in front of the Schnucks supermarket.

"Those types of situations add a little spice and variety to a neighborhood, don't you think?" Mrs. Killups said. "We don't have that kind of diversity where I live in Kirkwood and Des Peres."

"Oh, yes," Danny McGuire interjected. "We should think of ourselves as lucky to walk through the mountains of trash and needles and human waste, and to walk over the bodies just to get into the store, here in Florissant and Ferguson. We should consider ourselves to be lucky to be so very diverse."

Killups smiled and walked over to McGuire and patted him on top of his head. "Good job, Danny. You're starting to get the picture."

Alex Liebovits wanted to talk about the homeless town at the Chop Suey Shopping Center. "When I go to Schnucks, it is hard to find a parking place in the lot because almost every space is used by the homeless residents there in their tents and they congregate around while they are shooting up heroin. After I find a place, I must walk through all their supplies and their garbage. That's okay, I guess; it sort of reminds me of my days in the Soviet Union when we had to march through all the nuclear and radioactive waste after an accident at one of the nuclear power plants. But, anyway, when you get up close to Schnucks, it is necessary to walk over all the bodies sleeping on the concrete apron in front of the store. What I particularly like about this is that it brings back so many sentimental memories from the Soviet Union when it was necessary to sleep in front of the government store to be able to position yourself in a spot in the queue to get a single two-ounce tin of sardines."

"Oh, how wonderful, Alex," Mrs. Killups replied. "Bringing back some of the special memories of your youth to America. Aren't you lucky?"

Someone brought up that a Democratic Socialist member of the Florissant City Council has introduced a new housing proposal for the city and she is hoping Ferguson will adopt her idea. Kendra Blech has introduced a city ordinance that will help make a home within a neighborhood achieve its greatest efficiency. The concept is called Maximum Efficient Housing (MEH) and allows for as many unrelated occupants to live in a house as the front lawn can accommodate parked cars or pickup trucks.

"The point at which a house is not permitted to have any more unrelated occupants is determined by the available space on the front lawn for parked vehicles," the councilwoman told the *Post-Dispatch*. "If the front lawn can't fit any more parked cars or trucks, the house is regarded to be at full occupancy. This program has worked so well in Kansas City."

"Good grief. I think that destroys a neighborhood," complained Danny McGuire. "Just drive down any street in Kansas City and all you see are front yards crammed with cars and pickup trucks. That's one reason that Kansas City is so completely disgusting. There are many other reasons Kansas City is abominable, but cars parked on front lawns helps draw attention to why it is one of the most horrid ghettos in the entire world. Clearly, the whole proposal is to have thirty or forty people living in one house. That's not what a neighborhood is supposed to be. Just because a program to turn a city into absolute squalor has worked so well in Kansas City, doesn't mean we need to do it here."

"Oh my, Danny," replied Mrs. Killups. "This really gets you wound up, doesn't it? I hope you're watching your blood pressure."

Ethan Davidson interrupted. "Look, this whole city should just be burned to the ground. There is no need to even have these bourgeois areas with individual houses. Burn them all down and replace them with ten-story housing apartments, with one kitchen per floor that can be shared by everyone on the floor."

Michael Holden had heard enough and he replied to Ethan's suggestion. "While I realize you're trying to resurrect the housing system in the Soviet Union where everything worked so well, you probably aren't old enough to know that this idea has already been tried in St. Louis. In the 1950s, we had the Pruitt-Igoe public housing apartments. There were thirty-three high-rise towers packed into fifty acres in Carr Square, north of downtown. The complex housed ten thousand residents. And using your Soviet idea, the elevators only stopped intermittently every fourth floor, and the residents would have to get off and walk up the dilapidated stairway three or four stories to get to their apartments. The floors where the elevators stopped had garbage chutes which were always clogged and the laundry facilities which never worked. That was a real accomplishment because all of the thirty-three buildings were torn down in the 1970s. It seems logical to me that this concept for housing was probably hatched at your beloved University of Minnesota."

The group started to talk about a recent St. Louis police shooting of a street criminal, a black man, who died in the altercation. The police said the man attacked the officer and attempted to take a weapon away from the officer during an arrest. Instantly, as if on cue, the liberals in the room began calling for the abolition of the police as the most natural response to the tragedy. Sadie Rice stood and said, "Every single day the police are murdering thousands of black people all across the country, and St. Louis is no exception. Police must simply be abolished. It is the only logical answer."

"I don't like it when anyone is killed," Michael said in response. "But when a person attacks a police officer and attempts to steal the police firearm, it's not going to end well."

Wendy Sachlor became irrationally outraged. "You sanctimonious, lying Uncle Tom synod person," she squawked. "You are just a coon! What about your shameful family. Your son murdered a man."

Michael stood in silence. Then he gently spoke, "Yes, my son murdered a man." His voice broke. "I am ashamed of that. I stand here before each of you embarrassed and humiliated." Tears streamed down his cheeks. "My son was the sweetest, most adorable young boy. His little heart was so tender. We made a terrible mistake as his parents when we sent him to a high school right here on the border of Florissant and Ferguson." He didn't mention the name MacGyver because Omar Clift was in the room. "And suddenly, within a year, he transformed into a different person." He continued to weep. Trying to regain his composure, he cleared his throat. "That sensitive, tender little boy was transformed into a street gangster. I'm not making any excuses, but let me tell each one of you, schools are dangerous places. The influence that goes on there has a powerful sway over our children – especially vulnerable young boys. A young man can go in with sound and stable values – I am speaking of ancient Christian synod values … decency, respect, discipline, dignity, deference, reverence, decorum. You may ridicule our synod values, but they have stood the test of history – since the medieval era. And in just a few years, a young boy with a strong internal character is transformed by a sinister, devilish influence. This horrendous assault goes on elsewhere in this culture and society. I only know my son's change occurred during high school; he became a gangbanger."

Several people looked at Omar, curious to see if he would respond. But perhaps because he was too preoccupied, thinking about the brothers in their shacks, he said nothing.

Matt Drobney, a white neighbor who had become fond of Michael over the months, thought this was an opportunity to show some support for Michael's struggle and to draw attention to the hypocrisy of the group.

He stood up and said he wanted to do something about the crisis in the black family. "There is a violent culture in this country, and it has been systematically created from President Johnson's war on poverty which required black families to eliminate fathers in order to receive public assistance. Starting with the Johnson poverty program, black mothers were rewarded with more aid if the father was not present for their children."

The group was silent, and a few shifted uncomfortably in their chairs.

"Rather than just sit around and complain, I am willing to be honest about the problems in the black community," Drobney continued. "I will stand up right now and put myself on the line for this crisis. I am willing to help any young black child in Florissant or Ferguson or even St. Louis, no matter the age. Any child who needs guidance and a strong male role model, I am stepping forward right now."

The room remained uncomfortably silent. No one said a word. A few people cleared their throats.

"Unlike the woke progressives and liberals, I actually want to do something about this violent culture and help to find a way to end this fifty-year cycle of suffering, hopelessness, welfare, and lack of direction. I now step forward. I will be a strong male role model for any young black child floundering about in this unbelievable catastrophe."

The room remained silent. Finally, Wendy Sachlor spoke up.

"Well, Mr. Drobney, here in this very room, in living color so to speak, we have an example to look at," she said with a smirk. She pointed to Michael Holden. "Look over here at Mr. Holden. He was a role model for his very own son. He didn't need to go out searching for one like you are proposing. Mr. Holden was a role model from the very beginning. He would have us believe he was such a solid, upstanding, self-righteous moral role model for his son. After all, he is a member of that sanctimonious synod, don't you know? He didn't need you, Mr. Drobney. And yet, his son turned out to be a stone-cold murderer."

Everyone in the room looked at Michael. After what seemed like two minutes of silence, Michael stood up with tears running down his cheeks.

"Yes, what Wendy has said is true."

22

Carol continued with her regular devotion routine, attending matins or vespers at least three days a week at Zion Cathedral, which was near her gallery. She received the eucharist every week during the midweek service at Zion, and she received her confession absolution as often as possible, at least weekly at Zion and her home parish of Salem in Florissant. Confession was a soothing consolation for her and helped to relieve some of her internal pain and suffering from the nightmare surrounding her son. Carol was also a strong devotee of the adoration of the sacrament and frequently went to Zion Cathedral in the middle of the day to sit in prayer and contemplation before the exposition of the sacrament. She found it brought her peace during her internal struggles and anguish.

Carol was a devotee of the chrism – an old tradition from medieval Germany which has been preserved by the synod. The chrism is the holy oil used for anointing. The tradition originates from *Exodus* 25 and 30, *Leviticus* 8, and *Numbers* 4 and 11, and it is referred to as a vital and life-changing practice in *1* and *2 Samuel*, *2 Kings*, *Isaiah*, and the *Psalms*. The traditions in Christian beliefs and practices about sanctification with anointing oils are derived from all four gospels, the *Book of Acts*, and from the epistles of *1* and *2 Corinthians*, *James* and *1 John*. One of Carol's most treasured personal traditions was to attend the annual consecration of the chrism – a ceremony regarded as one of the most solemn liturgical events of the year in the synod. The service takes place in synod churches on Holy Thursday – that is, the Thursday before Easter.

During the consecration ceremony, olive oil, balsam, and aromatic resins are poured together into a vessel on the front part of the altar. After they are poured into the vessel, the pastor declares in a prayer that an odor of sanctity which is pleasing to the Lord has been created, referring to the fourth chapter of *Philippians*, and then he states that during the upcoming year, those who are touched by the chrism are counseled to strive in faith. The pastor breathes over the vessel and recites the words of the *Gospel of John*, chapter 20 ("He breathed on them and said to them, 'Receive the Holy Ghost'"). He then recites a series of prayers, invocations and blessings over the oil beseeching the healing and blessings for the sick and dying, providing strength to believers, the anointing of the baptized and those receiving the gifts of the Holy Ghost, as well as absolution, the anointing of newlyweds, and the anointing of the clergy and workers in the church. The pastor then places the vessel on the altar and recites the prayer of consecration; the vessel then remains on the altar for the remainder of the day to be viewed by anyone entering the church. And during the Holy Thursday liturgy, each person receiving the eucharist also receives the gift of the chrism, as the pastor dabs the new chrism oils on the forehead of each communion recipient. At the end of the day, the vessel of the chrism is then placed in the ambry.

A devotion to the chrism has developed over the centuries, and generally it is a tradition passed along through family practices and customs. Carol's parents were devotees of this sort and taught the tradition to their children. As a family, each year Carol, her parents and her siblings would anticipate the consecration liturgy with a great sense of reverence, and would walk solemnly through the neighborhood, dressed in their finest clothes, to the church. She treasured these memories and after she grew up and left her parents' home, she continued the devotion and looked forward to attending the consecration each year. Because of her devotion to the chrism, she attended the Holy Thursday liturgy at both Zion Cathedral and at St. Paul's College Hill, the parish of her parents and her youth.

The chrism is routinely applied to a recipient for anointing during baptism, when receiving the gifts of the Holy Ghost, during healing rituals, and at the ordination of a pastor. It is also commonly used during anointing at a wedding ceremony, last rites for the dying or the act of healing the sick, to set aside and designate church workers, teachers and missionaries, and on some occasions during the reception of communion or absolution. In some parishes, such as Zion Cathedral, devotees of the chrism are given anointing after the distribution of communion on various Thursdays during the year in memory and commemoration of Holy Thursday.

When Carol came home one Thursday evening after having received chrism anointing at Zion Cathedral, she said to her husband, "Michael, this peace which I have received today, it surpasses all understanding, and it has given me the ability to endeavor forward, even in this state of crisis in our family."

* * *

"I demand we immediately de-fund and eliminate the police," said Wendy Sachlor at the latest neighborhood meeting in the basement of the Presbyterian church in Florissant. Sachlor, a woman from Ferguson in her mid-sixties who looked uncannily like boutique tourist-revolutionary Emma Goldman in the early years of the twentieth century, was particularly fond of Ethan Davidson – the recent graduate from the University of Minnesota, who worked so diligently to reeducate the few holdout, ignorant, resistant, traditional thinking residents in the North County area. The majority of the attendees in the Presbyterian church basement were progressive, liberal types who spent most of their lives searching for a manager to whom to complain. Davidson was a woman who dressed as a man, presumably to give himself a more aggressive appearance and personality, and some gravitas. Many in the group found him to be over the top and moderately offensive with his doctrinaire approach to the issues of the left, yet, he had a fan club, and Wendy Sachlor was one of the leaders of his ingratiating followers. While the meetings were annoying and bothersome to his own conservative sensibilities, Michael simultaneously found the gatherings to be provocative and they helped him understand how lost and depraved the culture really is.

"I am so delighted that Ethan has made such persuasive presentations about the deplorable nature of the police," Wendy Sachlor lectured. "With the state's and this county's serious budget problems, elimination of the police would provide much more money for public education."

Omar Clift, the assistant principal at MacGyver, chimed in, "That's right, sister. Speak the word."

Miss Sachlor continued, "I am deeply concerned about rampant police brutality and systemic racism."

There was some mumbling in the room because of the emotional condemnation of police de-funding by Michael Holden at the meeting months before, when he lashed out against the de-policing efforts as mere anarchism and dangerous communist agitation. Michael's presence irritated Wendy Sachlor and he was beginning to get under her skin like a pernicious virus or a parasitical worm.

Sachlor raised her voice and glared at Michael and sneered, "As for you, Mr. Holden. Shame on you. Are you not a black man? Didn't your own son murder another man? And you, of all people, do not have the backbone to stand up. You are paralyzed and unable to stand up for your own people in this time of dire need."

The room was silent. Michael Holden said nothing with a feeling of humiliation and defeat, embarrassed and shamed by his son and the boy's life as a street gang thug. Not a breath could be heard.

Finally, Molly Markham, an old friend of Michael, who also knew Michael Junior, and was intimately aware of the deep emotional pain that Carol bore, stood up and she stared right into the cold eyes of Wendy Sachlor and she said, "Have you no decency, Wendy."

Not a soul in the room said another word at that meeting and the group slowly filed out quietly.

At the neighborhood meeting the following week, Molly Markham rose to make a short announcement. "Last week, something happened here among us that has haunted me a little bit. I don't want to stir up last week's stagnant, malaria-infested puddle that has now already flowed into the gutter and passed under the bridge, but I do want to say how much I respect a dear friend of mine for many years. He has also been a pillar of his Florissant neighborhood and made us all think seriously about what is happening in the area we call home."

At that point, Markham walked up to Michael Holden and threw her arms around him and handed him a bouquet of beautiful yellow roses.

Martha, a white liberal, who told the group at a meeting months ago, about alternate universes that run backwards and which could possibly reveal a planet which would be able absorb Earth's human population who will be trying to escape a climate cataclysm caused by too much carbon trapped in the atmosphere, quickly jumped up to take the attention away from Molly Markham and Michael Holden.

"Scientists from the Max Planck Institute have discovered a mirror image planet and sun, meaning that it is an absolute mirror to our sun and the planet Earth. And it's only 3,000 light years away from us. One light year is equivalent to eight trillion miles, so 3,000 light years is the number 24 followed with many, many, many zeros after it," she advised. "A mirror image Earth and sun is described by the Planck scientists as a planet that would imitate the Earth and our sun. And so, we will be able to emigrate to the mirror planet and sun to escape our carbon climate cataclysm. Some people have asked how we could know that it is a mirror if it is 3,000 light years away. The answer is simple. These are scientists and they know everything. Remember, believe the science!"

Not wanting to draw undue attention to himself because of the public display by Molly Markham, Michael didn't say anything about Martha's recent interplanetary discovery, but he thought flying through space for just one light year – or eight trillion miles – would take several hundreds of thousands of lifetimes of the travelers aboard the spaceship taking the residents to their new planet as they try to escape global warming, not to mention the daunting obstacle of 3,000 light years. If the rocket ship were to travel at 17,500 m.p.h., to reach the planet which is 240,000 trillion miles away, it would only take about 35,000 billion years to travel just one trillion miles. And thus, it would only take 38 billion years just to go about one light year. The trip to 3,000 light years away would take an unknown multitude of years – even going 17,500 m.p.h. "Hmm, I wonder how that's going to work out," Michael thought. "I hope they will be able to bring enough amaranth seeds to nibble on during their trip."

In response to Martha's description of a mirror planet, Omar interjected, "Yes, the brothers will be happy about that. Any chance to get out of their shacks and sheds for a little breath of fresh air."

The topic of homelessness came up again. Some of the residents began complaining about the homeless encampments surrounding some of the Schnucks stores, particularly the Schnucks in the Chop Suey Shopping Center on North Florissant Avenue in Ferguson. Patty

Hillinger and Jack Batchelette said they regularly see panhandling, vagrancy, public drunkenness and shooting up heroin. "It is rampant and ruining the livability of neighborhoods, causing crime and nuisances like litter, vandalism, loitering, petty theft, and break-ins," complained Doris Jacsmarek.

Katherine Sutton, who is a clinical social worker, jumped in with a sense of outrage. "Now, you pathetic, selfish, bourgeois elitists need to listen up. These are people. They need love, help and understanding. They have issues like all the rest of us. It is just that their issues are more glaring than our meaningless, selfish focus on ourselves. Don't assume you know their stories. Their lives are already hard. Let's be honest – every one of you in this room is only one or two paychecks away from being where they are ... homeless and facing other problems. Because of that reality, you all need to start seeing yourselves as homeless. Right now! You may as well just be homeless because you're just one paycheck away from it."

Jennifer Netanski immediately chimed in. "Homelessness is not a crime!"

The group of liberals paused and looked at Michael Holden. Michael slowly stood up and he said, "First of all, Jennifer, nobody wants to promote the idea that homelessness is a crime. Maybe what some of us are trying to say is there should be limitations to where it should occur. Maybe not in the Chop Suey Shopping Center, or on a residential street, or in front of a Schnucks."

Jennifer interrupted and shouted out loudly this time, as if she were reciting a slogan at a rally, or a chant at a football game, "Homelessness is not a crime!"

"Okay, I understand," Michael replied calmly. "Katherine, I know you're a social worker and you believe we are all just one paycheck away from being homeless and addicted to heroin. And because you believe that is what causes homelessness, we all need to start seeing

ourselves as homeless. But the facts are homelessness is not about missing a paycheck. Homelessness is about being addicted to alcohol, drugs,
or suffering from mental illness. That is what we should be addressing,
not paycheck protection. I agree with you, we should be compassionate
and caring in our lives. No question. But until we focus on these three
causes – alcoholism, drug addiction, mental illness – then nothing can
ever be done about homelessness and the Chop Suey Shopping Center
will continue to host a homeless town. To say every one of us is essentially already homeless because we are only one paycheck away from
being homeless and a heroin addict is a simplistic, illogical statement
which attempts to turn a chronic condition into the same thing as
walking across the street and stubbing your toe."

At the next neighborhood meeting in the Presbyterian church,
Michael stood up and made an announcement. "I have decided today
that I must do something that has been necessary for quite a while. Last
night, I was reading the Bible and I read the *Book of Matthew*, chapter
8 and the *Book of Mark*, chapter 5."

Suddenly, in the room there was a clearing of throats, shuffling, shifting back and forth, uncomfortable coughing among the
attendees.

"It became impressed upon me that we are told to call out the
demons by their names, and they are legion. So here goes." He paused
and then began, "Anarchy, communism, deceit, fraud, calumny,
violence, rioting, theft, queer consciousness, abuse, defilement, abortion, division, murder, atheism, avarice." He paused and looked at each
of the attendees. "That will do for this round."

He sat down quietly. Suddenly, the room erupted in a roar – a
burst of screaming, squealing, yelling, hollering, shouting, trampling,
bellowing, howling. The vocal progressives, led by Ethan Davidson
and Wendy Sachlor, were in a state of uncontrolled rage. It was as if
a tornado of indignation and fury had uncontrollably entered their

bodies and they wailed and howled and crowed like a creature trapped in a metal clamp. Some of their panicked cries were discernable while others were more like screeching squalls. "Traitor! Uncle Tom! Bigot! Homophobe! Transphobe! You pile of shit!" These words were mixed with shrieks and guttural howls from the deepest, darkest, hidden caverns of their troubled beings. Michael Holden remained in a state of complete, serene calm. He only looked at them with dignity and composure. As the calamity continued, Michael quietly left the room followed by Molly Markham, and she whispered to him, "Michael, that was so necessary."

Michael was beginning to enjoy the neighborhood meetings at the Presbyterian church, looking forward to them as an opportunity to turn upside down the magical fantasy-world occupied by the hand-wringing reformers, the ideological revolutionaries and opportunists, the ardent college students, and the Ivy League wannabes.

At the next meeting, Michael told the neighbors that citizens need to be wary of any calls to de-fund and abolish the police because it will end up provoking the necessity of creating a nationalized, federalized police force. "After people live in pure, total, devastating anarchy of cities without police, they will begin to beg and plead for the federal government to step in and mobilize the FBI and the Army to bring back law and order. Can you imagine a federalized police force under the direction of the corrupt FBI here in North County? For me, that is the blueprint for a complete dictatorship."

Instantly, Wendy Sachlor and Ethan Davidson rose to their feet.

"There you go again," cackled Wendy Sachlor. "What a lie! You're selling snake oil and fear again!"

Davidson accused Michael of trying to frighten people away from the freedom they would gain by being liberated from the domination of police. "Abolishing the police will allow us to provide more funding for public education!"

"I like the sounds of that," echoed Omar Clift, the assistant principal at MacGyver.

Sadie Rice, a white liberal and close friend of Wendy Sachlor, said, "We have so many programs that need more money which the police are so selfishly hogging up and stealing from the public – Head Start, public schools, welfare, food stamps, public housing projects."

Sachlor, her face turning red in a state of pure fury and rage, pointed her forefinger at Michael and she exclaimed in a fit of enraged animus, "I am so sick of you, you dirty, rotten nig–"

Sadie Rice quickly cut off Sachlor, "Please, Wendy, not here in front of the others."

The following week at the neighborhood meeting, twenty-three neighbors showed up in the basement of the Presbyterian church in Florissant. Ethan Davidson, the recent graduate from the University of Minnesota, was there to lecture the attendees about racism. Davidson, while a white person, nevertheless believed himself to be most qualified to teach the group, including the black attendees, about what racism is all about – primarily because he recently attended a university. Omar Clift was very willing to give Davidson the platform to do some educating since it was certain Davidson would protect the plantation and would guarantee that the plantation could continue without any interference. "That ninny cracker keeps going on – that's just fine," Omar thought. "Just keep the money rolling in."

"I'm here to teach you about the revolution for black liberation," Davidson intoned. The other white liberals in the room echoed his comments and sympathetically concurred that systemic racism is rampant through the country. Katherine Sutton, Wendy Sachlor, Sadie Rice and Katrina Ziccarelli all said they thought it was about time for white people to get down on their hands and knees in front of black people and beg for forgiveness, groveling on the ground and apologizing for being white.

Michael interrupted their ego-centered session of self-flagellation by saying, "Excuse me, white liberals, I'm just not too impressed. It's pretty clear to me that you are all doing this for your own selfish ego-gratification, because I don't think any one of you knows what black revolution even means."

Jesse Weir, a white liberal, interrupted, "What do you mean by that?"

"Not to steal Ethan's parade, but let me do a little educating," Michael quipped. "Black revolution is a Marxist communist program. It openly states in their manifesto that they yearn for the collapse of the capitalist system and the collectivization of all private property. They openly embrace queer consciousness and transsexual cross dressers. They insist on the annihilation of the nuclear family, replacing the family with villages, the abolition of religion because it is an opiate, the replacement of the proud black male with a government babysitting overlord which hands out a welfare pittance, and the substitution of the black church with more government-run clinics. No, as a proud black man, I don't believe that will do anything to improve our lives, no matter how much that makes white liberals feel better about themselves."

Wendy Sachlor boiled with rage. She leered at him. "Oh, Mr. Holden, you're so sanctimonious. Your own family has a big pile of sordid baggage. Just look at your son."

Jesse Weir said to Sachlor, "Wendy, I agree with you. I don't like how Michael is so sanctimonious toward us, but I do think Michael is extremely smart – even if I don't ever agree with him." Weir then directed himself to Michael, "I don't like how you think. And you don't use our language and our jargon that we are so comfortable with. But I actually do like that you express yourself. C'mon, Michael, let's change the world together."

Michael smiled at Weir. How quaint, he thought to himself. Then Michael directed himself to Wendy Sachlor, "Wendy, I'm just not inclined to respond to your insults." He then said to Weir, "Jesse, thank you for your thoughts, but perhaps you're not aware I am not really on a social crusade to change the world."

Wendy Sachlor decided to take another swipe at Michael. "Mr. Holden, I recently saw a news clip of Michigan Governor Gilda Whitman who made a poignant commentary about your self-righteous, medieval cult. And I happen to agree with her." Wendy was referring to a publicity stunt by Gov. Whitman, who enjoys asserting she is distantly related to poet Walt Whitman. The Democrat governor recently appeared at an adult porn video arcade in Detroit, dressed as a priest with a dominatrix flair; she was carrying a small package of Dorito snack chips. The governor approached a purple-haired transsexual who was suggestively kneeling in front of the governor. Whitman then placed a Dorito chip on the tongue of the kneeling transsexual supplicant – attempting to imitate the sacramental act of receiving the eucharist – and then the governor earnestly intoned, "The body of progress."

Gov. Whitman arranged to have the episode filmed and then distributed to news media outlets in an effort to demonstrate her trendy bona fides.

Michael refused to be drawn into responding to Wendy's provocation; he said nothing.

Then white liberal Katherine Sutton suddenly acclaimed her support for black revolution. "It's so healing to kneel down before African Americans and beg for forgiveness," she blubbered.

"Is that right?" Michael replied. "Well, good for you. I'm glad you have found something to do to find meaning and healing."

Sutton then challenged Michael. "Why don't you ever use the term 'African American'?"

"Well, Katherine, what does that term even mean? Does it mean people who came here from Africa? Does it mean Dutch people who came here from South Africa? Does it mean Arabic people from Egypt, Libya, Morocco, Algeria or Tunisia who come here?"

"No, Michael, don't be silly. It means black people. You know. You're black."

Michael smiled. "Yes, I do know. I've been black my whole life. That's precisely why I say black."

Wendy Sachlor sneered at Michael, a person she simply couldn't abide. She contemptuously glared at Michael. "You're so sanctimonious. You think you're so special because you have an excuse to not say African American."

White liberal Katrina Ziccarelli then announced that she wanted all the residents to get behind a Democrat effort in the state legislature in Jefferson City to raise taxes. "We just don't have enough revenue for the state to pay for all the services we need, like public schools."

MacGyver assistant principal Omar Clift perked up and smiled with glee. "That's right, sister. Speak the truth."

"Property taxes in Missouri are remarkably low," Ziccarelli whined. "We should be paying much higher property taxes to help our schools. We need more money. People are so selfish."

Omar broadly smiled. "That's right, sister."

"Why does the government need more money?" Michael asked. "Their appetite is voracious. They can never have enough."

"We need it for our public schools," Katrina moaned. "Our schools never have enough."

Omar grinned. "You go, sister."

"Your public schools have an insatiable appetite," Michael said. "You spoke wisdom when you said they never have enough. They are like a cancer. Once they have eaten the whole body away and the body dies – they need to find a new body to devour."

Wendy Sachlor was beginning to steam at Michael. "We're talking about the children here. This is for the children. The children!" she sniveled. "Mr. Holden, I'm sick of it. You are so sanctimonious. You're one of those self-righteous, moralizing synod people, aren't you? You people even have your own private schools, locked away from the rest of us. You pious churchy people."

Michael smiled at Miss Sachlor and replied by saying, "Please don't believe the empire of lies being peddled by the media, especially the *New York Times*, the *Washington Post*, or even the *Post-Dispatch*. They are spreading a canard, an empire of lies, that racial unrest is rampant, that the police need to be abolished, that taxes aren't high enough, that the government needs to regulate more of our lives, that China is the victim of discrimination because they haven't been able to take over the entire world economy yet."

White liberal Sadie Rice popped off. "How dare you. You are so sanctimonious. Everything you just said is a typical lie from a pious, conservative mole in that dangerous, self-righteous, medieval synod that slithers around and tries to bully everyone all over the St. Louis area. I am not surprised to hear lies like this from your type – you synod people, you arrogant wretches. There is rampant homelessness everywhere, in every neighborhood in the entire country. There is racial unrest everywhere in every city because of police brutality and thousands of black people are executed and murdered every single day by the police. Public schools are having to close down all over because they literally have no money. You haven't heard this?"

"That is all ridiculous distortion, untrue, or a complete fabrication," Michael replied calmly.

"You are a sanctimonious wizard of guile. A dangerous member of that deceitful, medieval synod. Everybody in here! Listen to me!"

Sadie Rice called out. "Vote Democrat! We need to find money for our poverty-stricken public schools. They have no money and need more money."

"You spoke a mouthful there," Michael responded with a sense of wry disbelief.

The group took a break for people to use the restroom. As Sadie Rice and Wendy Sachlor were heading to the restroom, they passed Omar Clift. "Sisters, don't forget the public schools. Remember, we need more money. And while you're at it, don't forget the brothers. All they're looking for is some fresh air after being cooped up in their shacks and sheds."

"Yes, of course, Omar," Wendy paternalistically replied.

"Wendy, you have to hear what happened to me yesterday at Tower Grove," Sadie Rice said to Sachlor, referring to the trendy, chic neighborhood in the Forest Park Southeast area of St. Louis. "While I was walking down the sidewalk, I approached some African American people, and I got down on my knees and asked them to forgive me for white supremacy. And do you know what the African American man said to me? He told me to stand up right away. He said he found my kneeling to be humiliating, patronizing, insulting, and a parody. Can you even believe it? What an ignorant person!"

"What in the world was wrong with that fool?" exclaimed Wendy Sachlor. "A pathetic slave boy! He reminds me of Michael Holden. How sanctimonious!"

Michael overheard the two liberals crowing about being scandalized by the occupants of their plantation. He thought to himself about Wendy Sachlor, "What a sach-lor of shit."

After using the restroom, Michael crossed paths with ardent liberal attendee, Jesse Weir. Jesse said, "Michael, you're a member of the synod, aren't you?"

"Yes, I am. I was brought up in the synod."

"It's the church with the beautiful stone churches built in the ancient style, high vaulted ceilings, fancy wooden and granite altars, statues, icons, crucifixes, tabernacles, ciboriums, fonts, paschal candles, incense, vestments, chalices, chancels, reredos, sacraments, confessions, consecrations, Gregorian chant, and all that. Right?"

"Yes, that's right."

"Well, I just want to say, personally I get religion when the sun comes up in the cornfield. I don't need all that fancy stuff and elaborate church buildings."

Michael paused and smiled. "Yes, I suppose that's right. But let me ask you this, Jesse. How often do you go into the cornfield to watch the sun come up, to get religion, to get that experience?"

When the restroom break ended, Ethan Davidson started lecturing the group about how hostile architecture is designed on purpose to make life miserable and horrible for everyone. Michael waited for Davidson to stop his never-ending tirade of misery.

Then Michael stood up and said, "Brother, we've now heard your seminar about how everything is designed to make us all miserable. Let me tell you a little story from Allan Seager. There were two men in a hospital room – both were suffering from tuberculosis. One was in a bed by the window, the other was away from the window. The fellow by the window provided a running commentary about what he was able to see by looking out the window. People would be walking and talking. Couples were holding hands. A couple paused for a cup of coffee together. A mother was instructing her child how to safely cross the street. A man was walking his dog and got all twisted up in his dog's leash. The patient in the bed far away from the window wished and pined to be able to be in the bed to see everything that was going on. One late night, the man next to the window took a turn for the worse. The fellow away from the window didn't say anything about his roommate's plummeting condition, thinking to himself if the man could end up dead, then the window bed would be open so that he would finally be able to look out the window and see what is happening down below. Subconsciously, he hoped for his roommate to die. When the man by the window did pass away, the other fellow asked the nurse if he could now be moved to the bed next to the window. The nurse quickly agreed and had him moved next to the window. When he looked out the window, he was finally able to see the view he had yearned for. It was merely a brick wall."

Michael paused. "Ethan, we can see as much misery as we wish to see."

That evening, everyone left the basement room quietly in reflection.

23

K iera Salzman, the attorney representing Michael Holden, Jr. for his first-degree murder charges, began the preparatory phase for the case. She hired a private investigator to collect as much information about the entire episode as possible. She worked with the prosecuting attorney's office to discern what turn the prosecution of the case would take. She pursued discovery to learn the timeline of the evening of the murder, the records of the shuttle company, the experiences and routines of Mr. Kim that evening including his airline ticketing, the mileage records and the logbooks for the shuttle van that evening, the police records. Depositions were conducted with the witness of the entire incident on the shoulder of I-64, also known as Hwy. 40 in St. Louis, as well as the responding police officer at the scene. Salzman conducted a deposition with the manager of the shuttle company. She interviewed the St. Louis City coroner and the hospital emergency personnel. Evidentiary requests were made so that Miss Salzman could inspect the pistol, the shell casings, the six-inch knife found in Mr. Kim's hand, the scene photographs including the photographs of Mr. Kim in a fetal position with his arms and hands desperately attempting to protect his body, photographs of Michael at the scene. Mr. Kim's autopsy results and blood alcohol content were reviewed. Since the Missouri Department of Transportation operates a highway camera system along I-64, and a camera did capture the entire incident on video, Salzman requested the video for complete review and inspection.

It was necessary for Salzman to interview Michael extensively to develop an understanding of what occurred and how a defense strategy could be developed. On initial assessment, Salzman's first reaction was that Michael drove the vehicle for seventy minutes to run up the shuttle charges to the customer. Perhaps a dispute occurred between the passenger and Michael because of the excessive driving, and possibly this resulted in Mr. Kim missing his scheduled departure at the airport. It appears the disagreement became so intense that Michael pulled over, got out of the van, walked over to the passenger, took out his gun, shot and killed the passenger, then walked to the driver's door, found the knife under the seat, and then placed the knife in the decedent's hand in an effort to ensure the victim's fingerprints were on the knife. The motivation could be perceived that Michael was attempting to rely on evidence and the presumption that the victim had a weapon and was threatening Michael. Salzman shared her impressions with Michael; however, Michael was not aware that he was observed placing the knife into deceased Mr. Kim's hand.

"How do you know he didn't already have the knife?" Michael asked Miss Salzman.

"Well, there are two reasons," Salzman said indignantly. "The shuttle manager said he was aware that you possessed that knife and carried it in the van. And also, the video shows you removing the knife from under the driver's seat and then taking it over to Mr. Kim's hands after he was already dead. The witness can corroborate that also."

"Oh."

"You will need to think through that whole scenario," Salzman said.

"Uh."

"It's okay. Think about it. Nothing is necessary right now. Tell me about the seventy-minute drive. Where did you go and why were you doing it?"

"How do you know it was seventy minutes?"

"Well, the logbook states your mileage and the time you began the pickup at the hotel. The incident finally concludes at the shoulder of I-64/Hwy. 40 about ninety minutes later. Ninety minus the twenty minutes to drive to the airport leaves us with about seventy minutes."

"He was drunk and was unconscious when we got to the airport. I drove around so he could sober up."

"Where did you drive?" Salzman asked.

"North County, West County, South County, and into St. Louis City."

"Did he wake up? Was he upset about the seventy-minute drive?"

"Not really. He just mumbled. He didn't even speak English," Michael said.

"What provoked you to pull over, and then walk around to his side and then shoot him?"

"I don't know."

"Okay, you will need to think that through," Miss Salzman said. "Not immediately. But you will need to put some thought into it."

It was obvious to Miss Salzman that Michael had not thought about what had occurred that evening – from the pickup at the hotel all the way to the shoulder of I-64.

"After Mr. Kim was shot, did you search his body for his wallet or money in his pocket?"

"No."

"Well, the detective forensics department has found your fingerprints on his wallet."

"Oh."

"You will need to think about that also. And there will be questions raised and doubts raised about the necessity of shooting Mr. Kim ten times with a semi-automatic weapon. There are ways to counter those questions and doubts, but you will need to think about that."

"Okay."

"And we will need to develop a defense. We need to ponder what it is that occurred that evening from beginning to end. We need to have a narrative that we can make believable – some kind of a narrative that explains the shooting and killing of Mr. Kim. So, you will need to think about that too. Just a comment, an observation – your act of placing your knife into Mr. Kim's hand after he was shot, perhaps because you thought it could implicate him, is not going to work out well for you. So, you will need to think about your reasoning and motivation for that action. Nothing right now, but it needs to be pondered."

It was clear from the filings with the court by the prosecutor that physical evidence from Mr. Kim's autopsy and blood alcohol would reveal the victim was four times over the legal limit for being too intoxicated to drive and he was likely unconscious, or barely conscious, at the time before the murder. His body did not suggest that he resisted or that there had been a physical altercation.

Because Miss Limney Grantham, the Democrat prosecuting attorney for the City of St. Louis, is generally willing to dismiss charges related to concealed weapons without a permit, Miss Salzman first began negotiations about the concealed weapons charge. The prosecuting attorney's office was immediately willing to drop the concealed weapons charge, as well as the charges related to the discharge of the weapon. Next, Salzman pursued a negotiation of dropping the reckless endangerment and deadly assault charges in exchange for adding a second-degree murder charge alongside the first-degree homicide charge. This would put the entire matter into the hands of a jury to decide between first- or second-degree murder. The prosecuting attorney's office agreed to Miss Salzman's negotiation proposal.

Salzman met with Michael again and informed him of the alterations to the criminal charges. And then she shared her interpretation of what occurred in the early morning hours of June 2.

"When you picked up Mr. Kim at the Pennywell Hotel, you noticed he was intoxicated, and he fell asleep in the van. When you arrived at the airport, Mr. Kim could not be awakened from his drunken condition. You drove around for seventy minutes, hoping he would wake up. He woke up as you were driving on I-64/Hwy. 40 and he attempted to sexually assault you by rubbing up your legs and even into the crotch of your pants. You resisted and told him to move away from you. He persisted. You became angry with him and told him to stop immediately. He became belligerent and used racial slurs and epithets toward you. While still on I-64, but inside St. Louis City at this point, you pulled over and said, 'That's it.' And as you attempted to exit the van, Mr. Kim assaulted you, hit your head, and yanked violently on your dreadlock braids. When you opened the passenger door, Mr. Kim again hit you in the face causing the cut and bruise seen in the police photographs. In a state of passion, you took out your pistol and shot him. You returned the pistol to your holster because you knew that to be the safest place for the weapon. Not certain if Mr. Kim were still alive, you walked to the driver's side and pulled out your knife from under the seat. You took the knife to Mr. Kim and placed it in his hand to check to see if he were able to grip the knife so you could confirm that he was still alive. You checked his wallet to see if you could confirm his identity and possibly find an emergency contact."

Miss Salzman was aware that her proposed defense had some flaws:

Mr. Kim's blood alcohol showed him to be
too intoxicated to react other than to sleep or remain

unconscious; and if he were conscious, he would have been incapable of an altercation.

Mr. Kim did not speak English, was unable to communicate with Michael, and did not know racial epithets or slurs.

Mr. Kim is unable to defend against any accusations about a sexual advance on Michael, and such an accusation would be perceived as character assassination. A dead Korean man's honor and reputation is blemished forever, with him being unable to recover it.

Placing the knife in Mr. Kim's hand to discover whether he was alive does not seem to be credible or believable.

The cut and bruise on Michael's head were caused by the baby momma when she was enraged about not receiving enough support money – not by Mr. Kim.

Returning the pistol to the holster seems cavalier and callous.

The seventy-minute drive seems irrational and perhaps diversionary.

Why did Michael keep a knife under the driver's seat?

Why does a shuttle driver need to carry a semi-automatic pistol?

Why would Michael search Mr. Kim's wallet for ID or an emergency contact when Michael did nothing to show he acted upon that information?

"That's the best defense I can put forth for you. It is based on the basic legal principles of self-defense under extreme circumstances, being forced to respond to a physical and sexual assault, and also responding to fears of a racially charged attack on you by someone who was using racial epithets and slurs."

She paused while Michael appeared hapless and reflective. Michael realized if he accepted the scenario described by Miss Salzman, he could never return to any form of the truth – whatever that was.

"Please think about this, Michael. Think it all through because I believe we will need to call you as a defense witness at trial. We do have a few things working for us – it is St. Louis City and the prosecuting attorney is committed to equity justice, and we will have a jury pool who will be sympathetic to our approach."

Michael, who had once been a devout synod believer – committed to the truth, free from ambiguity, because there actually is a truth – was now preparing to enter the realm of foggy, confused, devious duplicity and deception. In his soul, as ABC's Jake Pepper might put it, he knew that if he went down this road he would need to start to sincerely, in his soul, begin the long process of believing a lie for the sake of his own deceptive self-preservation. He wondered if living by a lie would ultimately impact his relationship with his parents – if he were ever to attempt to restore that contact. He did not reflect much, at this time, about the life of the streets that he had been living for nearly ten years – seven of those years away from his family. He did not contemplate what part of the lie that this sordid life had been.

24

"This will be an important way for St. Louis to show it has compassion and we will not be bullied by a federal agency that disrespects human rights," said St. Louis City Prosecuting Attorney Limney Grantham to a general session of the St. Louis Board of Aldermen. Miss Grantham was following the popular Democrat view promoted in cities and states throughout the country for local governments to disregard federal immigration laws by declaring themselves to be sanctuary jurisdictions. The pretext for the sanctuary status is for the local jurisdiction to refuse to comply with federal immigration laws as a way to provide equity justice – that is, not arresting suspects to prevent deportation of people who may be residing in the country without proper documentation. Since Miss Grantham had long been a staunch proponent of equity justice, it only seemed natural for the jurisdiction of St. Louis City to participate in the sanctuary movement. After listening to Miss Grantham's impassioned defense of the principles of equity, the St. Louis Aldermen obediently passed a resolution and ordinance declaring the city to be a sanctuary for undocumented migrants – stipulating that the city would not participate in any legal or judicial effort to identify or assist with the deportation of individuals who are in the country without legal permission.

Miss Limney Grantham was delighted by the decision of the St. Louis Aldermen to embrace her long-range equity strategies. With the vote by the Aldermen, she called the chairwoman of Democrat National Committee, Congresswoman Debbie Schultz, and crowed for twenty minutes about how progressive and cutting-edge the City of St. Louis is.

The Board of Aldermen sent a formal notice to the Metropolitan Police Department which specified the sanctuary status of any suspect who would have contact with the police. The police commissioner, Arthur Dillard, sent out a directive to the department that any individual who has contact with the police and who does not possess proper legal identification while appearing to be an undocumented alien, is to be released on the spot. No arrest is permissible. The only undocumented persons who may be detained are those who would face Class A, B, or C felonies. The Class A, B, and C felons may even be released through eligibility determined by the prosecuting attorney's office. All classes of misdemeanor offenses and Class D and E felonies are exempted from any detention for undocumented persons. Citizens of the United States are still to be detained for any felony – Class A through E – and any misdemeanor which would require detention.

"All misdemeanors and Class D and E felonies for undocumented offenders merely require the issuance of a summons to appear in court," Dillard advised.

Police Commissioner Dillard's pronouncement pleased Miss Grantham to no end, because it still allowed her office to release even the most heinous criminals by using prosecutorial discretion under the sanctuary provisions established by the Aldermen. True equity, Miss Grantham reassured herself.

The concept of equity in social theory is based on proactive corrective action. The notion is taken from the principles of Marxism and critical theory – that is, the belief that the current social order and legal system are so corrupted that they need to be demolished. Collapsing entire systems – a revolutionary concept – is generally regarded as alarming and disquieting. Consequently, the proponents of the equity movement are willing to approach the implementation of their changes incrementally. Instituting equity in the practice of law is essentially based on the demonstration of favoritism and ignoring infractions by perpetrators, because the population the suspects represent has been victimized through discrimination. The primary thesis is that the only correction for these past social errors and injustices is to give a free pass to the people who theoretically represent victimization from discrimination – even if the people are perpetrators of actual, current crimes and wrongdoing. Service of the greater theoretic goal is more important than addressing the actual misdeed or criminal act.

An undocumented migrant, also known as an illegal alien, by the name of Daniel Vasquez-Lopez was being held in the St. Louis City Justice Center on Tucker Blvd. for a series of Class A, B, and C felonies including aggravated kidnapping, sexual assault of a minor, aggravated assault, armed robbery, larceny, auto theft, as well as the misdemeanors of failure to appear, driving without a valid license, providing false information, and violating a valid police order. Vasquez-Lopez, who was twenty years old, engaged in an argument in the jail with William Anderson who was forty-two. Vasquez-Lopez challenged Anderson to go to the shower area because there are no cameras in the showers. During the altercation, Vasquez-Lopez shoved a razor-sharp shiv into Anderson's chest instantly puncturing and lacerating Anderson's heart who then fell to the floor dead.

Michael Holden, Jr. witnessed the murder but, knowing the code of the criminal, he said nothing. The rat who says anything, no matter how heinous or barbaric the offense, is destined to receive his just rewards according to the ethical code of the jailhouse. And, indeed, it may be possible that Mr. Anderson could have been receiving his in-house justice from some infraction or another that he committed in violation of the thug rules for quality living.

Jail authorities arrived to find the dead Anderson and thereafter subdued Vasquez-Lopez. When Democrat Prosecuting Attorney Grantham heard about the incident, she ordered the arraignment to be held at the main St. Louis courthouse on Market Street – an unusual request since initial charging appearances are customarily held in the detention center arraignment courtroom. When Vasquez-Lopez appeared in the circuit court on East Market Street to face charges of first-degree murder, Miss Grantham sent orders to her staff attorneys to drop the murder charges because the death was a result of "mutual combat" in a jail. The judge, by this time regularly accustomed to Miss Grantham's equity system, immediately dismissed the charges without asking a single question and then conveniently did not pay any attention to the defendant's six pending felonies and numerous misdemeanors. Without delay, once the charge was dismissed, an assistant prosecuting attorney quickly ushered Mr. Vasquez-Lopez out of the courthouse using a special prosecuting attorney's egress door on the backside of the building and told the career criminal, "You're free to go now." Another successful day in the blissful business of equity justice.

Only a week after the Vasquez-Lopez equity arrangement, there was another illustration of how well Miss Grantham's prized, well-oiled sanctuary system was operating in the city. Enver Villarreal had been arrested for armed robbery, aggravated assault, criminal mischief, attempted murder, and carrying a concealed weapon without a permit. After Villarreal was arrested and brought into the jail on Tucker Blvd., Miss Grantham ordered the defendant to be arraigned at the courthouse on Market Street. By this time, it had become standard practice to arraign all sanctuary jurisdiction criminal felons at the main courthouse because it is much more convenient to release them there, through the back door, rather than at the jailhouse courtroom, which doesn't have a secret exit door. Villarreal, who was nineteen, appeared before the judge, and the assistant prosecuting attorney moved to drop all charges because of a lack of evidence. The judge, accustomed to the standard routine by this time, instantly dismissed the charges. The defendant was taken to the secret side door and released into the welcoming, warm daylight. One day later, Enver Villarreal was arrested at the Skinker Blvd. Metrolink light rail station for murdering a commuter at the rail station because the man who was waiting for his train refused to give Mr. Villarreal twenty dollars. When Miss Grantham was informed by assistant attorneys in her office about Enver's latest arrest, she ordered the police not to book him into the Tucker Blvd. detention center, but rather transport him directly to the courthouse on Market Street so that she could arrange a quick arraignment for the accused murderer. During his arraignment, prosecuting attorneys requested personal recognizance, no-cash bail, for the defendant. After the no-cash bail was approved by the judge, in keeping with Miss Grantham's equity justice operation, the assistant prosecuting attorneys led Enver to their top-secret side door and set him loose onto the city.

The *Post-Dispatch* maintains a policy not to report any news stories involving the sanctuary justice program because the stories perpetuate stereotyping – an offense so disturbing to the purveyors of information – you know, "democracy dies in darkness" and all that. When the outrage or the backlash becomes too loud because the news isn't being reported, the *Post-Dispatch* takes it upon itself to print strange little twenty-word news briefs which do not name the suspects or perpetrators, followed by an accompanying disclaimer at the tail end of the story which says, "The identities of the subjects of this story have been withheld for the protection of the innocent."

Since the *Post-Dispatch* doesn't pursue stories which are not worthy of reporting, or which may offend the extraordinary sensitivities of the guardians of the stereotype, other people have been forced to ask questions of the illustrious prosecuting attorney. An official with the St. Louis County Republican Party quizzed the prosecuting attorney's office of the City of St. Louis to discover why they are not detaining undocumented immigrant criminals. Democrat Miss Limney Grantham, St. Louis City prosecuting attorney, snapped in response, "Are you kidding me? Aren't you a Republican from St. Louis County? I don't have to answer any questions from your racist, corrupt party – particularly if you aren't even in St. Louis City. You can take your concerns about your county to your county government or to your county prosecutor. My job involves St. Louis City only." And she promptly hung up.

In Missouri, judges for the circuit courts are selected by judicial appointment commissions which serve each of the state's forty-five judicial circuits. These appointment commissions love to show off and brag about being non-partisan, thus, ensuring that judges are appointed outside the stifling impact from political influence peddling – so famous in the Tom Pendergast and Harry S. Truman era in the cesspool of corruption known as Kansas City. The problem is this non-partisan hyperbole is all an elaborate charade. The process is incredibly partisan and incestuous: the people who are charged with selecting the commissions are themselves activists in the system they are trying to perpetuate. Consequently, only insiders are selecting other insiders to preserve and advance the agenda that has been anointed by the legal establishment. And if the legal establishment has embraced equity justice, that means only proponents of the social theory will be selected to be new judges. The forty-five commissions in the state universally select individuals who are partisan in some way to become judges – often through lawyer's associations or judicial activist organizations. The commissions themselves must be composed of members of the state bar association, which is notoriously partisan. Judges in higher courts are allowed to make two appointments and the commission members selected by judges are uniformly political or legal activists. The governor is allowed to make two appointments to the commissions and these people are always legal activists. Once the commissioners have been appointed, this group then selects who will serve as judges in their circuit. Universally, without exception, these newly appointed judges are legal professionals who are active in the politics of the law: professors at law schools, Missouri Bar Association activists, members of law journals, lawyers for philanthropic organizations, members of judicial reform groups, attorneys representing special interests who do lobbying, attorneys for public school districts, zoning lawyers and urban planning reformers, members of trial lawyers' and liability lawyers' associations. Consequently, in nearly all cases, the newly seated judges appointed by the judicial appointment commissions are Democrats, some independents with progressive credentials, and a handful of Republicans who are committed to keep the grift going.

Nevertheless, a member of the St. Louis County Republican Central Committee contacted one of the senior judges in the Twenty-second Circuit Court, which has judicial jurisdiction for St. Louis City. This Republican leader from St. Louis County asked the same question that he posed to Miss Grantham – the question about why illegal aliens are not being detained after crimes and are being released with dismissed cases or no review of their criminal records by the judges in the circuit. The judge politely responded, "That is a political question. Circuit judges do not step into the political arena. Furthermore, the Board of Aldermen in St. Louis City has already approved a resolution and an ordinance making the city a sanctuary jurisdiction. If you have concerns about enforcing federal immigration law, you would need to take that up with the Immigration and Naturalization Service." And then the judge politely hung up the telephone.

Democrat Miss Limney Grantham, the St. Louis City prosecuting attorney, was a disciple of the Cloward and Piven strategy, devised in 1966 as a revolutionary tool to be instituted by a wide variety of leftist radicals ranging from the Black Panthers to the Trotskyites, the Red Guard, and most grandiosely, the Democrat Party itself.

The primary thesis of the Cloward and Piven strategy is to overload the current political, social, economic, and legal systems with so much dysfunction that they simply collapse through their own weight and inability to operate. This complete implosion of all these systems will force a new political and social order to develop and to take over, which will reflect the goals of the Marxist-Leninist-Maoist frame of reference.

The ultimate goal of the Maoist equity revolution is the complete destruction, obliteration and elimination of society's oppressive systems at their very foundation. Young college students seem to be the ideal foot soldiers to mobilize this battle. Mao, in his Cultural Revolution in China, recruited hundreds of thousands of young people to roam through the Chinese countryside intimidating and humiliating people for behaving in ways that were in conflict with the equity objectives of the Communist Party. When intimidation didn't achieve obedience, the ideological youth moved to more severe tactics such as imprisonment and torture. People who wore eyeglasses were arrested because the vanity of wearing eyewear revealed bourgeois affinities. The children or grandchildren of medical doctors were detained and forced into reeducation camps because they had been exposed to thinking that would be contrary to the Party's equity commitment. In Neel Mukherjee's poignant novel, *The Lives of Others*, an idealistic college student is swept up in Maoist equity ideology and he joins a cell of revolutionaries in India's West Bengal. They hide and perch in trees so they can shoot and kill small plot farmers who happen to have accumulated a little more property, a few more tools, one extra cow or ox than the other peasants in the district. That farmer who possesses more represents the sinister evil of bourgeois accumulation in defiance of pure and uncompromising equity principles and he needs to be eliminated. The idealistic revolutionaries don't stop there. In their campaign to dismantle and destroy the oppressive system, they methodically remove the connectors and spikes on train rail tracks, ideally just before a trestle bridge, so that the train traveling along the tracks will derail and crash. Hopefully, hundreds of passengers will die – all for the sake of the equity revolution.

On a lighter note, this bizarre equity grift is cryptically described by Salman Rushdie in his novel *The Golden House*. In the book, the narrator becomes romantically involved with Suchitra, a woman whose parents were from India. Suchitra patiently explains her parents' utter befuddlement and bewilderment as they observed the development and evolution of the left-wing political and equity movements in India – particularly in West Bengal and the southern Indian state of Kerala. Suchitra slowly and gradually describes how the original Communist Party of India (CPI) becomes so doctrinaire and devoted to parochial concerns that over time it slowly grows and sprouts new wings and appendages which are obsessed with the tiniest, most intricate and minute ideologies of equity, so obscure that no one can grasp their meaning and within just fifty years there are hundreds of obsessive leftist political parties fighting among themselves over commas and periods and parentheses and apostrophes – and that's just about their mania to create their latest equity manifesto. When the arguing begins about where to place the public well in the town square to fulfill the aims of equity, then the real revolution begins, and the need suddenly emerges that two or three dozen more pure and even purer Maoist parties must be created. Just to clarify, it's all about the dialectic, after all.

This is the world of Miss Limney Grantham as she dispenses her equity justice – anything to collapse the current social order.

25

L imney Grantham maintained a policy in the prosecuting attorney's office that capital crimes normally need to go to trial. The only exception she makes is for undocumented migrants who are accused of capital offenses – they were afforded equity either before the arraignment or shortly after arraignment by using a secret side door in the courthouse. Other offenders of major capital crimes – such as murder, rape, kidnapping, attempted murder during a violent crime, arson resulting in death, brutal torture – in nearly all cases, go to trial. However, proceeding to trial does not mean her office abandons equity justice. The elected prosecuting attorney for the City of St. Louis, Miss Limney Grantham, is committed to equity justice for all cases which involve classes of people who can be identified as victims of systemic discrimination or racism. For Miss Grantham, Michael Holden, Jr. qualified as a candidate for equity justice – even though he was required to go through a criminal trial.

For criminals going to trial, Miss Grantham was able to rely on several factors to successfully achieve her equity program: depend on judges who share the equity commitment, require assistant prosecuting attorneys to argue cases in ways that benefit the equity goals, and finally, to trust that juries will, on their own, institute equity through their findings and the nullification process. Nullification is when a jury disregards the matters of law or even fact, including defying rulings made by a judge, and instead makes its own decisions which represent alternate agendas or interests. O.J. Simpson, for instance, was a beneficiary of the nullification process during his trial for the alleged murders of his former wife and her friend. While prosecutors generally abhor nullification, Limney Grantham depends on it to enforce her larger equity intentions. In the capital case for Michael Holden, Jr., Miss Grantham was comfortable in her assurance that the judge was in her pocket, her courtroom prosecuting attorneys would comply, and the jury would come from a pool of St. Louis residents who were adequately on board.

According to Missouri law, to use a criminal defense assertion of self-defense resulting in death, the judge presiding in the trial must give approval to use this defense strategy. The judge must first determine that the defendant was facing an imminent threat which would result in his own demise, the defendant had no other available option for survival, the defendant attempted to retreat, the defendant had a reasonable belief that his life was threatened, the defendant's response was proportional and reasonable for the circumstances, the defendant used no more force than necessary, the defendant's fear was substantial and reasonable. Clearly, most, if not all, of these requirements were not met in Michael's case. No reasonable argument could be made that Michael was in a situation that complied with these legal requirements for a valid claim of self-defense. However, after Michael's attorney declared to the judge, in a pretrial hearing, that she was intending to invoke the self-defense strategy, the prosecutor in the case raised no objection, nor even asked the judge to approve the self-defense claim. The judge, having been appointed by the equity-focused judicial appointment commission for the Twenty-second Circuit, of course, never raised the legal limitations of self-defense in the case. It was Miss Grantham's first victory in the case as part of her cause for equity.

The judge in the case was a former law professor at St. Louis University School of Law and had taught numerous classes on the principles of equity justice, had even invited Limney Grantham to give guest lectures in his classes, had been appointed to his seat by the judicial appointment commission which uniformly selects judges who share the equity agenda, and he had written no less than eight articles about the practice of equity justice in the American judicial system. This was Miss Grantham's second substantial accomplishment in achieving equity in the case.

Because Michael's crime occurred in the City of St. Louis, rather than St. Louis County, it would necessarily be adjudicated in the Twenty-second Circuit, at the courthouse on East Market Street in downtown St. Louis. This factor of location means the jury pool for all cases in the Twenty-second Circuit comes from residents of the City of St. Louis – not from South County, West County, or North County. What is the makeup of the population in St. Louis City – from whom a jury is selected? Forty-seven percent of residents are black, 43 percent are white, 3 percent are Asian, 3 percent are Hispanic, and 3 percent are mixed-race. The median age is 36. The poverty rate is about 20 percent. The median household income is $45,000. The median property value is $143,000. More than 81 percent of registered voters in the St. Louis City are Democrats; and 45 percent regard themselves as progressive, liberal, very liberal, or socialist.

The Urban Institute and the Brookings Foundation both have programs which rank communities on a scale assessing how well they are providing and executing equity. The components that go into calculating the score are complicated, but they include: the number of Democrats who are elected to office or are serving in appointed positions, the number of schools using deferred judgment, inclusive discipline or diversionary support programs, the number of schools eliminating zero-tolerance approaches to misbehavior among students

from discriminated populations, the replacement of Christmas celebrations in schools with Kwanzaa celebrations, the number of schools
promoting segregated graduation ceremonies which exclude white
students from the events, the number of police departments that
have been de-funded and number of police departments which have
replaced patrol officers with social workers, the commonality of schools
promoting anti-racism and revisionist history in the school curriculum, the number of schools denying admission of Asian students to
science and technology programs and saving admission places for
students from discriminated groups, the preponderance of community
judicial jurisdictions that have no-cash bail policies and alternatives to
detention for persons from discriminated populations, the percentage
of defendants from discriminated populations who have criminal
charges dropped, innovations used by the governments in eliminating
punishment for discriminated populations, practices in the community to build "bigger tents" to bring discriminated populations into
decision-making, the prevalence of carve-outs or saved opportunities
provided to discriminated populations, the frequency of police inac-
tion on complaints involving discriminated populations, the prevalence of diversity-equity-inclusion programs found in the government
and the private sector, the prevalence of gender inclusion and gender
affirming policies in government and the private sector, the prevalence
of restorative justice programs in the community, the prevalence of
affirmative action programs in government and the private sector, the
institution of sanctuary jurisdictions for undocumented persons, the
presence of "pride parades" and other sexual identity activities. There
are many other factors. The City of St. Louis has an equity score of 8
on a scale of 1 to 10.

The St. Louis Metro Police Department has been under the
supervision and control, at various times, by the State of Missouri since
the 1860s – primarily because of concerns about corruption. The city

has one of the highest crime rates in the country and many residents believe the police have not contributed to controlling crime. There have been racial tensions in the area – dating back to at least 1917 when a race riot broke out in East St. Louis and even spread into St. Louis City. Historian Walter Johnson claims St. Louis City has lived with an undercurrent of racism and discrimination against black people for many years. He says many black residents of the city have a sense of resentment that racism is tolerated in the area – particularly in the suburban communities to the west of the city limits. He also points to the destruction of black neighborhoods like Mill Creek Valley and the forced deportation of black residents from their neighborhoods and incarcerating them into a prison-like, high-rise concentration camp – the Pruitt-Igoe Housing Project. The housing project was so horrendous, humiliating and inhumane, the city was finally forced to tear down the thirty-three towers in 1973. In any case, there has been a general sense among many black residents in St. Louis City that racism, discrimination, intolerance, and unfairness have been tolerated, and even pervasive, in the city itself, as well as some suburban areas, particularly the western parts of the county. With a population reflecting these views, Miss Grantham was commonly able to draw juries who would internally share her equity vision, even if they didn't openly communicate it. It is this type of population who would be willing to use nullification when necessary. This constituted Limney Grantham's third achievement to find equity within the judicial system.

Finally, Limney Grantham depends on a staff of prosecuting attorneys who will argue cases in such a way that principles of equity will be ably served. She only hires attorneys to work in her office who can demonstrate that they share her commitment to equity. This requires attorneys to dismiss cases whenever possible when the equity objectives will be promoted. If a case must go to trial, the prosecuting attorneys are expected to present the cases in a way which will benefit equity principles. Consequently, staff attorneys will field questions which will benefit equity causes, select juries which will be composed of members who will serve the equity mission, construct cases in ways that promote equity, and conduct opening and closing statements and cross examination which benefit equity aims. Therefore, Grantham's attorneys steer their cases to the benefit of the defendant if the equity objectives necessitate this approach. Sometimes, cases need to be presented in the weakest way possible. Questions and interrogation will need to be kept superficial and without direction. Evidence may need to be ignored. It may be necessary to refuse to guide a jury toward conclusions and instead defer to the defense attorney to lead the jury to conclusions. Common sense and reasoning will need to be disregarded when the equity goals require greater deference. In many ways, this is Miss Grantham's greatest achievement on the road to equity. Incompetence can be equity's closest friend.

After more than fourteen months in the St. Louis City Detention Center, Michael was to appear for trial on a Tuesday in October. The judge had set aside the calendar for an anticipated one- or two-day trial. Jury selection was rapid, lasting only two hours. The jury was composed of twelve black members, four men and eight women. There were three alternate jurors; all three were white people. The staff prosecuting attorney was Linda Creech, a reliable functionary of equity justice who predictably lost so many prosecutions, she was assured to obtain certain promotion in the prosecuting attorney's office. Michael appeared in court with a buzz cut; his dreadlock braids were cut off.

Before the trial started, Michael Senior explained to Carol what the defense strategy was – self-defense from an Asian man who was making sexual advances on Michael and using racial epithets and slurs, and to protect himself, Michael shot the victim. Carol found the entire strategy and approach so dishonorable, objectionable, deplorable and beyond belief, even vile, she refused to go to the trial and told Michael she would instead spend the days of the trial at Zion Cathedral engaged in her own consolation in silent prayer and contemplation. Her prayer dwelt on her yearning that her son would find redemption.

"I cannot abide this," Carol told Michael. "Leave me out of it all. I am filled with humiliation and indignity."

As Carol sat in the pews at Zion Cathedral, the church choir was rehearsing the Heinrich Isaac and Paul Gerhardt hymn *Now Rest Beneath Night's Shadow*. She thought it was uncannily appropriate.

Michael Senior did attend the trial along with Andrea. Michael Senior met with Kiera Salzman, his son's defense attorney, before the trial started, and he insisted the jury and the media would not be interviewed by the defense team after the trial concluded. He told her he did not want the burden of the jury's deliberations or their thinking to be held over the head of Carol – that she would be unable to tolerate that entire discussion, and it would likely cause her to have a mental collapse.

"Whether it be guilty or not guilty, please let it rest where it will be. Whatever their decision, let us *not* discuss it with them or with the media. Carol carries so much internal pain over this whole affair – what Michael has done, and about what happened to Mr. Kim – she is pleading and begging that we just let it rest after the jury makes its decision. And if there will be a need for an appeal, that also does not need to be discussed with the media. No discussion with the jury and no comments to the media. Please, for Carol's sake, please."

Miss Salzman agreed to his terms.

Miss Creech delivered a brief opening statement. "Michael Holden, Jr., a shuttle driver, picked up Mr. Hyuk Soon Kim, a Korean who spoke little or no English, at the Pennywell Hilton Hotel in downtown St. Louis and drove him to Lambert International Airport, but because Mr. Kim was intoxicated, and he was not able to get out of the van when they arrived at the airport, Michael drove around the metro area for seventy minutes presumably to tack on higher shuttle fees. During the seventy-minute drive, Michael finally pulled over along I-64, also known as Hwy. 40, and he stopped. He got out of the driver's door walked around to the passenger door and then shot and killed Mr. Kim with his Ruger 9 mm semi-automatic pistol, hitting Mr. Kim with 10 bullets from point blank range. The victim was found by the police in a fetal position in the front passenger floor with his arms and hands trying to cover his head. The defendant returned the pistol to his holster. He then returned to the driver's door, pulled out his six-inch knife from under the seat, returned to the passenger door and placed the knife into the limp hand of dead Mr. Kim. He looked through Mr. Kim's pockets and removed Mr. Kim's wallet and returned the wallet to the decedent's body. He then stood calmly and waited for the police to arrive."

She explained Michael was being charged with first-degree murder – killing the victim with premeditation knowing and intending to kill the victim. And, in addition, he was being charged with second-degree murder – knowing his actions would result in the death of the victim. Miss Creech told the jury that the judge would clarify and explain how the jury would make the determination between first- or second-degree murder at the conclusion of the trial.

Kiera Salzman, Michael's defense attorney, gave an opening statement to the jury explaining Mr. Kim was intoxicated when he got into the van for the drive to the airport. Mr. Kim was unable to get out of the van at the airport, and thus Michael drove around for seventy minutes to allow Mr. Kim to sober up.

"During the drive, Mr. Kim made homosexual advances to Michael, even rubbing Michael's legs and moving his hand onto Michael's crotch. Michael told Mr. Kim to stop, but Mr. Kim did not cease his homosexual advances and attempts to sexually assault Michael. Mr. Kim even pulled on Michael's braids, which he possessed at the time of the incident, in an effort to bring Michael's head over to the passenger's side where Mr. Kim could kiss Michael. When Michael became angry and agitated, Michael said, 'That's it,' and he pulled over to the shoulder of I-64, also called Hwy. 40. Mr. Kim hit Michael in the face, beating Michael and continuing to pull on Michael's hair. We will show a photograph of Michael, taken by the Metro Police investigators at the side of the highway, which will show a cut and bruise on Michael's face, caused by Mr. Kim. When Mr. Kim realized his sexual advances failed, he used racial epithets and slurs toward Michael which roused greater upset and distress in Michael. When Michael walked to the passenger door, Mr. Kim continued to fight, punching and pulling Michael's hair and using racial epithets and slurs. In an act of defense, Michael pulled out his gun and shot Mr. Kim to protect himself from further assault. Michael placed the knife into Mr. Kim's hand to determine if he were still alive – that is, if his hand had enough life to be able to grip the object. Michael removed Mr. Kim's wallet to check and confirm his identification."

During the course of the trial, prosecutor Miss Creech presented evidence of Mr. Kim's stay at the Pennywell, his order for a shuttle to the airport, his luggage that was in the rear of the van, testimony from the shuttle company manager about the company's awareness of Michael's knife in the van. Creech presented Michael's logbook which showed the time of the pickup and the mileage of the van which demonstrated the number of miles driven during the incident. She called for testimony from the witness who observed the incident on the shoulder of the highway, as well as testimony from the Metro Police officer who responded to the incident, and testimony from a Missouri Department of Transportation employee who explained the video footage of the incident at the side of the highway. She also called the city coroner to testify about the results of the autopsy on Mr. Kim's body, the nature of his mortal wounds, his blood alcohol content, and the lack of physical bruising on Mr. Kim's body from a fight or an assault.

Miss Salzman put up a defense by asking the manager of the shuttle company if drivers had reason to be concerned about their safety in a city with such high crime, and what the policy was about a knife for defensive purposes, as well as a driver's possession of a gun. The manager replied that the shuttle company did not object to instruments of self-defense by drivers. Miss Salzman quizzed the Transportation Department employee about the failure of the camera to catch video of the assault by Mr. Kim on Michael which occurred prior to the incident on the shoulder of I-64/Hwy. 40.

"Did the video camera system record the passenger, Mr. Kim, assaulting the defendant, Mr. Holden?" Salzman asked the Transportation Department employee.

"Our video system is not able to capture the inside of a vehicle."

"So, it is your testimony that the video system was incapable of recording Mr. Kim assaulting Mr. Holden because the video system is not able to see images inside vehicles. Correct?"

"Yes, ma'am. Our video system is not able to capture images inside a vehicle."

"So, Mr. Holden was assaulted by Mr. Kim and your video system was unable to obtain that image because it happened inside the shuttle van?"

"Yes, ma'am."

Miss Salzman asked the police officer, and the motorist who witnessed the shooting, if either of them saw the assault by Mr. Kim against Michael that preceded the incident on the shoulder of the highway. They both testified that they did not observe the assault because it occurred before they became involved in the entire incident. She asked the police officer if, in his experience, he has noticed drunk or intoxicated people to be violent or combative. He told her drunk people are commonly combative. She asked the coroner if a person with Mr. Kim's intoxication level could be combative, and she asked if all physical altercations always resulted in noticeable bruising or injuries, which were not found on Mr. Kim's body. The coroner said people with Mr. Kim's level of intoxication could likely be combative, and not all physical altercations result in visible or detectible injury.

Michael was called to the stand to testify in his own defense. The judge forewarned him that he was not obligated to testify and told him of the possibility that his testimony could be used against his own interests by the prosecutor and by the judgment of the jury. Miss Salzman asked Michael to explain to the jury the occurrences of the night of the incident. She asked him about the seventy-minute drive, and he explained he did it to permit Mr. Kim to sober up. She asked him if it was a good idea to carry a weapon for protection in the city with such high crime. She asked him about the knife after the shooting occurred and he explained he placed it in Mr. Kim's hand to see if Mr. Kim could grip it to determine if he were still alive.

Michael then explained how he was threatened and feared for his life. He explained the sexual assault and how it was humiliating beyond any possible experience in his life; he felt so degraded, embarrassed and mortified. He was so ashamed and invaded, he didn't feel he could ever recover. Miss Salzman got him to talk about his sense of personal shame and degradation, his disgrace, his crushing discomfort, and his feelings of being demeaned and chastened. Michael even broke down and cried and his voice cracked.

Miss Salzman paused long enough for Michael to collapse in distress and sobs, and then for him to somehow pull himself together and recover. Miss Salzman then asked Michael to explain the feelings of having a person use racial epithets and slurs toward a black man. He talked about his feelings of being less than human, of being a slave boy, a bonded servant, nothing more than chattel property. He talked about the degradation of being victimized by racism, bigotry, intolerance, bias, hate, discrimination, of being shackled by a cruel, abusive society that strives to keep a black man in chains, of being shuffled off and assigned to occupy ghettos and slums, with raw sewage bubbling up in lawns and flowing out into places where children play and then the sewage effluent flowing down streets. He talked about the pain, sorrow, and heartbreak of watching poor, destitute black children destined and commanded to exist with pathetic, hopeless lives of poverty and desperation through vicious and cruel racism and the hateful language which leaves life-long scars to the simple dignity and the innocence of the human spirit.

In tears, he paused and somehow, he was able to regain a kernel of his composure.

"Am I not a man?!" he cried out in desperation as he sobbed and wept with tears generously flowing down his face.

Miss Salzman paused a long while allowing Michael to weep and gasp for breath. As the stunned jury watched the young black man suffer in his desperate anguish and agony, Miss Salzman waited patiently. Finally, she spoke as Michael continued to weep.

"The defense closes, your honor."

The prosecution had no questions for the defendant.

The judge remanded the jury to conduct deliberations. They were instructed that the jury was to find Michael guilty of first-degree murder if they determined, beyond a reasonable doubt, that he intended to kill Mr. Kim with premeditation. They were to find him guilty of second-degree murder if he knew his actions could have resulted in the death of Mr. Kim, but without premeditation. He then told them that their third choice was to find Michael not guilty, if the conditions of the first two charges did not apply to him.

The jury deliberated for three hours and returned to the court-room with its verdict. Michael and Miss Salzman stood and faced the jury.

The jury foreman announced that Michael Holden, Jr. was not guilty of first-degree murder and Michael Holden, Jr. was not guilty of second-degree murder.

And thus, Miss Grantham's equity justice had been served in St. Louis City once again.

26

After the verdict, Michael spoke to his attorney and then approached his father and Andrea.

"Yo," he said.

Michael Senior put out his arms for an embrace, but Michael Junior repelled the physical contact and stepped back. Andrea tried to hug her brother, but he receded once again. He told them he needed to take care of some business and quickly was swept away by the bailiff and the police officers in the court.

Michael and Andrea stood for a while, waiting in silence. Finally, Miss Salzman approached them and said Michael needed to sign some release documents in the court, and then he would need to return to the Tucker Blvd. detention center to pick up his belongings. She said they were welcome to drive to the detention center to pick him up if they wished.

Michael and Andrea waited at the detention center for ninety minutes and then Michael went into the building to ask about Michael Holden, Jr. He was informed that Michael Junior had already been released and had left the property.

Suddenly, Michael understood the wisdom of Carol's personal sentiments about the entire episode – from the boy's tragic and fallen transformation at MacGyver High School, to his irrational and sordid life on the streets, to the murder, to the deceitful defense strategy, all the way through the trial. He drove to Zion Cathedral in quiet reflection, and he approached Carol while she sat in silent prayer.

"Michael was found not guilty," he whispered to her. "And it appears to me he has simply gone back to the streets. He would not engage with Andrea or me after the verdict."

She began to weep. "Please, Michael, I want *not* to hear another word – not one more word – about any of this court antic for the remainder of my life."

✶ ✶ ✶

After nearly twenty-three years of waiting and endless preparations, the Ku Klux Klan case for Michael and Carol Holden and Paul Mooney was scheduled for trial. There was a new administration that had taken over in Washington now – an administration that wanted to renew the earnest pursuit of racism in the country. The new president, who was of mixed racial background yet claimed he was black, asserted there was no place for racism and discrimination and his new administration would pursue these matters with dedication. While the Justice Department in the previous two administrations had already been dedicated to chasing down the questionable presence of the Ku Klux Klan where it was unlikely to be found, the newest administration's Justice Department would now pursue it with even greater vigor. The absurdity of three black people facing a civil lawsuit by the federal government for allegedly being members of the Ku Klux Klan never seemed to be noticed by anyone. The newest attorney general, who was a black man, was preoccupied with an FBI effort to ship an entire arsenal of illegally obtained semi-automatic firearms into Mexico so the weapons could be carefully funneled to the drug and human trafficking cartels. And then, in a charade, the attorney general was planning to use the possession of these firearms by the cartels as a pretext to demand Congress pass a law to prohibit the production and sale of semi-automatic weapons. The new attorney general's entire approach to justice and the law was that it was a fast and furious enterprise. In addition, this new attorney general appeared at a Democrat Party fund-raising event to announce, "Republicans are reliably members of the Ku Klux Klan." It became obvious to Larry Korhonen and the defendants that there was no hope that the Justice Department under the new attorney general would ever consider setting aside the Klan case.

Before jury selection, Judge Hedrick J. Winters informed both parties – the federal prosecutor and the defense attorney – that the trial bore important and significant meaning which he held in the highest regard as part of the enforcement of federal laws dating from 1871 which relate to discrimination. Judge Winters repeated his expectation that the parties, particularly the defense, must be mindful of decorum and, more importantly, the court's insistence that the FBI's reputation not be impugned in any way and that the agency's sources and methods are not compromised and questioned.

He paused. "Do you understand me, Mr. Korhonen?"

Korhonen, the attorney representing Michael, Carol and Paul, affirmed the judge's request.

In accordance with federal rules of civil procedure, the judge selected the jury which turned out to be composed of all white members, and it was revealed in the *voir dire* that each juror was a member of the Democrat Party, and four of the jurors were very active in the Democrat Party – one having previously run for political office as a Democrat candidate.

Opening statements were made and the federal prosecutor said the trial would reveal that the three black defendants were members of a secret racist organization – the Ku Klux Klan – and that the three Klan members engaged in an act of harassment and intimidation of

the former president and his gracious wife when they were campaigning for the presidency in southwestern Missouri while the president
was in his campaign bus. The prosecutor, an unctuous, aggressive
and authoritarian woman, Miss Leila Shrewberry, who was likely
a Presbyterian in good standing, made a summary of the offensive
conduct of the defendants.

Miss Shrewberry told the jury how the defendants, who were
students at Missouri Southern State University, approached the bus in
a convertible car on I-49 and drove with an antagonistic and hostile
intent to torment and defame the president. They dangerously swerved
into the lane of traffic to force the bus to slow down and avoid a collision which could have threatened the life of the president and his
charming wife. The defendants held up offensive, insulting, truculent,
disrespectful, and derogatory signs which were intended to inflict pain,
suffering, affliction, discomfort, and torment on the president and
his glamorous wife. The defendants engaged in their offensive acts of
intimidation because they were driven by hate, loathing and detestation
for democracy and the president of the United States. And this hatred
is the result of their membership in the Ku Klux Klan. She told the jury
that the Ku Klux Klan Act of 1871 has a civil provision which allows
members of the Klan to be punished through civil procedures – levy-
ing fines and penalties and recovering costs to investigate and pursue
the members of the organization. She assured the jury it was not a
criminal trial, there was no punishment involving incarceration of the
defendants, and the civil provisions of the statute are merely designed
to fine the guilty through financial penalties. She then told the jurors
that because it is a civil trial, the verdict of guilt will be determined
through the preponderance of evidence not through the more stringent
requirements of "beyond a reasonable doubt" which would apply in a
criminal case. Miss Shrewberry then advised the jury that the judge

would clarify the differences when the trial phase concluded prior to the jury deliberations.

The jury of Democrat citizens seemed duly impressed.

Then Larry Korhonen asked for the members of the jury to apply the most essential aspect of being an American citizen – that is, common sense. He reminded the jurors that one of the founding fathers of the American Revolution was Thomas Paine, who appealed to the most important component of the American character – common sense. It defies the principles of common sense, Mr. Korhonen said, to claim that three black students at Missouri Southern State University were members of the Ku Klux Klan. He then reminded the jurors of the American tradition of peaceful protest, and he told the jury that the defendants were not and have not been charged with careless or reckless driving or changing lanes illegally. He told the jury that holding up political signs is not illegal – even if the signs are not complimentary to the political candidate running for office.

The prosecutor, Miss Shrewberry, called her first witness – the patrol officer of the Missouri State Patrol who pulled over the car with the three defendants.

She asked the officer perfunctory questions about his background and experience with the state patrol. The prosecutor asked the officer to describe the vehicle and explain why he pulled over the defendants. The patrol officer didn't explain the president's lovely wife had directed her Missouri State Patrol security detail to see to it that the suspects were pulled over, nor that the president's enchanting wife had ordered the state patrol to not detain the suspects but merely obtain their identifications and furnish that information to her. The officer only said he was on duty and pulled over the vehicle because it was following the campaign bus.

Miss Shrewberry asked the officer to describe the car, who was driving the car, and who was in the vehicle. She asked the officer to describe the convertible's aggressive driving. The patrolman described the swerving and rapid lane changes – failing to state that he never witnessed the driving but was only told about it. Shrewberry asked what the defendants were doing in the car. The patrolman described the taunts of the defendants and their inflammatory signs. He failed to say that he never witnessed the behavior of the defendants but instead was merely told about it by the president's lovely wife. Shrewberry asked the officer how he obtained the identification of the defendants, but she did not ask what he did with the information. She asked if the defendants were detained, ticketed or arrested. The patrolman said the defendants were not arrested, ticketed or detained and were simply told to return to Joplin. The officer did not testify that he gave the information about the defendants to the president's vivacious wife.

Mr. Korhonen asked in cross examination if the officer witnessed the interaction between the bus and the defendants' vehicle. The officer was not truthful and instead stated he did witness it. Korhonen asked why the driver of the car was not ticketed. The officer said it was law enforcement discretion and that frequently police officers do not always issue citations. The patrolman was asked if he witnessed the defendants holding up the so-called offensive signs. The officer was not wholly truthful and said he had seen the placards. The attorney asked what he did with the information from the defendants' identification. He said he used the IDs to track the information in the National Crime Information Center database and the Missouri DMV database. The officer was asked what he did with the information after that, and the officer said when he saw there were no outstanding warrants, he returned the IDs to the defendants. However, the officer failed to say the information was forwarded to the president's captivating wife.

The prosecutor then provided to the jury an exhibit which was a written summary of the contents of the placards and signs – statements which disparaged the character of the president and accused him of being a sexual predator, assertions that the first lady was an enabler of a sexual harasser and predator, and various statements about baby killing and abortion.

Miss Shrewberry then called Mr. Roderick Cronenberg to the witness stand. Mr. Cronenberg is an executive officer of the Alan Guttmacher Foundation. The prosecutor asked Mr. Cronenberg to describe the Alan Guttmacher Foundation. He explained it was a philanthropic organization which promotes health care for women – failing to explain that the foundation finances abortion and sterilization services throughout the world with a specific focus on the parts of the world which are populated by occupants with darker skin tones. She asked the Alan Guttmacher witness what his impressions were of the placards held up by the defendants.

"I found the abortion messages to be offensive, inflammatory, racist and defamatory," Cronenberg said. "A woman's health care is a human right and attempts to strip a woman from her rights to health care are deplorable, racist attacks on human and civil rights."

He then furnished statistics that black women and other women of color are the most victimized groups because they are denied health care. Miss Shrewberry asked Cronenberg if the signs were racist and defamatory. He said the signs were clearly racist because they sought to deny women of color their rights to health care.

In cross examination, Larry Korhonen asked Mr. Roderick Cronenberg what he regarded as the definition of women's health and women's health care. Cronenberg gave a circular statement that it is health possessed by women and care provided to women. He was asked if women's health generally would be interpreted to be things like heart disease, diabetes, chronic pulmonary disease, or other pathologies. Cronenberg said it could be those pathologies and others.

"Does your organization concern itself with these other pathologies or only abortion?" Korhonen asked.

"We are concerned about all health care."

"But does your organization focus on all health care or only on gynecology and abortion?"

"We only focus on gynecology and abortion."

"You said earlier you were especially concerned about discrimination and racism against black women and women of color. Can you tell the jury the percentage of abortions are being parlayed on black women and women of color? What is the percentage of abortions being provided to black women and women of color, as contrasted with white women?"

"About 70 percent of abortions are provided to black women and women of color."

"Can you tell the jury where the majority of Planned Parenthood abortion clinics are located? Are the clinics in black neighborhoods, strategically located across from black colleges and high schools with predominantly black students?"

The prosecutor, Miss Shrewberry, stood up and declared, "Objection, your honor."

"Sustained," Judge Winters replied.

Larry Korhonen resumed his questioning. "So, your organization is primarily concerned about executing abortion of black babies?"

The prosecutor again stood with a sense of indignation and exclaimed, "Objection, your honor."

"Sustained." The judge directed himself to Mr. Korhonen. "This questioning has now ended. There is no need for any re-cross examination. The witness is now dismissed. You may step down, Mr. Cronenberg."

The prosecutor called a witness who was not named because he was an undercover agent with the FBI. The judge informed the jury that because of the nature of the agent's sensitive job, he would remain hidden behind a screen and his voice would be electronically modified.

When the mystery witness was questioned by Miss Shrewberry and the witness began to speak, the electronic voice modification device malfunctioned in some way. Normally, the electronic voice modification system results in a deep, baritone, somewhat anonymous tonal quality. For some reason, the voice modifier was turning the witness's voice into a high-pitched, squeaky, squealy tone – somewhat like Alvin the Chipmunk. The prosecutor was clearly frustrated and announced to the judge that the voice modifier wasn't working properly, and she would like the audio-visual technician to check it before the witness's testimony continued. The judge concurred and the jury was asked to leave the courtroom and wait in the jury room.

The voice modifier could not be repaired, so the FBI witness would be forced to provide testimony with a chipmunk's voice. The jury returned. Miss Shrewberry asked the FBI agent what his relationship was to the defendants. He explained he was in the Ku Klux Klan along with the defendants. She asked the witness if he attended Ku Klux Klan meetings with the defendants. He confirmed he did attend Klan meetings with the defendants in both Joplin and St. Louis.

During cross examination, Mr. Korhonen asked what the nature of the meetings was, where they took place, how many people attended the meetings.

The judge interrupted. "Counselor, I am warning you to be very careful with your questioning."

Korhonen asked if the meetings were called Ku Klux Klan meetings. The witness said the meetings were not specifically called Ku Klux Klan meetings.

"How were the meetings identified?" Korhonen asked.

"They were called meetings of the Republican Party," the FBI agent responded.

The judge interrupted. "Please be careful, Counselor."

"Do you know how the Ku Klux Klan was established?" Korhonen asked the FBI agent. "What was the history of the creation of the Klan?"

"I don't know."

"Are you aware that the Ku Klux Klan was established during the Reconstruction era by the Democrat Party as its enforcement arm?"

"No."

"If the Ku Klux Klan were created by the Democrat Party, why would Klansmen be inside the Republican Party?" Korhonen asked.

The judge interrupted again. "Counselor, watch it. You're on thin ice here."

"As I understand it, there was a great switch that took place under Roosevelt," the agent responded to the defense attorney's question.

"Please explain," Korhonen said.

"The Democrat Party's issues and concerns became the interests of the Republicans, and the traditional Republican focus became the causes of the Democrats."

"Why would this have happened?" Korhonen asked.

"Because the Republicans became racists, and the Democrats were oriented toward fighting racism."

"Weren't the Democrats, who were so influential in the South during this period of time, fighting against civil rights legislation, maintaining and preserving the black codes, defending Jim Crow, and championing separate but equal?"

The judge interrupted again. "What is the point of this questioning?"

"I am trying to respond to the witness's claim that the Klan is in the Republican Party which impacts the defendants because of their membership in the Republican Party."

"I will only allow this questioning to continue in the most abbreviated fashion," Judge Winters said.

"Are you aware that President Johnson said, with the passage of the Civil Rights Act and welfare legislation in the 1960s, that black people would be converted to the Democrat Party and would vote for Democrats for one hundred years? Although President Johnson used a more inflammatory and derogatory expression than 'black people.'"

The judge jumped in. "That's it. No more questioning of this witness. The witness is dismissed."

Larry Korhonen called the lone defense witness, Doug O'Roarke, who was the chairman of the St. Louis County Republican Party.

"As chairman of the St. Louis County Republican Party, are you aware of any members of the party who are also members of the Ku Klux Klan?" Korhonen asked.

The judge interrupted, "I'm warning you, Mr. Korhonen. Be careful with this questioning."

Korhonen repeated the question, "Are you aware of any members of the Republican Party who are also members of the Ku Klux Klan?"

"Not that I know of," Mr. O'Roarke replied. "We would not tolerate it anyway. Anyone who was involved with the Ku Klux Klan would be expelled from the Republican Party instantly. The Ku Klux Klan was an invention of the Democrat Party as their enforcement arm."

Immediately, Judge Winters interrupted. "That's it. No more questions. This witness is dismissed. You may step down." Then the judge directed his comments to the jury, "You are directed to disregard any of that testimony, and it is not to be considered during your deliberations."

Then Judge Winters addressed Larry Korhonen and Miss Shrewberry. "The defense now rests," Winters said. "We can move forward to closing arguments. Miss Shrewberry, are you prepared?"

Closing arguments were made. The prosecutor told the jury it had been established the defendants intimidated the president, that they were all members of the Ku Klux Klan, and they attended Klan meetings. She asserted because the president's civil rights were under attack by members of the Ku Klux Klan, the defendants should be found guilty.

The defense attorney, Mr. Korhonen, told the jury that common sense tells everyone that holding up signs and engaging in political disagreement is not a violation of civil rights, and that membership in the Republican Party is not equivalent to membership in the Ku Klux Klan.

The judge directed the jury to disregard the defense arguments if they are based on theoretical assertions about historical activities in the 1960s, and Judge Winters told the jury to disregard defense arguments about Republican Party membership. He told the jury that an individual in the Republican Party clearly was capable of simultaneously being in the Ku Klux Klan.

Judge Winters described for the jury the difference between the standards of "beyond a reasonable doubt" and the preponderance of the evidence. He explained the jury was being held to the preponderance of evidence threshold. He told them the burden of proof is not as demanding as beyond a reasonable doubt – which is the threshold used in criminal matters. The burden for the jury was to determine the facts by being convinced there is a greater than 50 percent chance that the claims are true. The jury was remanded to the jury room to consider the evidence against the three defendants as members of the Ku Klux Klan, violating the civil rights of the former president, and acting in violation of the Ku Klux Klan Act of 1871.

The jury met for an hour. The jury of twelve white Democrats returned to the courtroom and announced they had reached a verdict. The three defendants – Michael Holden, Carol Holden, and Paul

Mooney – were guilty of civil violations of the Ku Klux Klan Act of 1871.

The judge announced the punishment phase would resume in six months.

27

As Michael Junior had transformed into a different person, so too had Carol changed – but in a very different way. She went more and more into herself, dwelling on introspection; she became significantly reflective, dedicated to solitude, and attracted to the role of lament in her life. While always a spiritual and religious woman, drawn from her devout synod upbringing, she became driven and consumed with her quiet prayer of grief. She spent hours in contemplation at Zion Cathedral on 21st Street and at St. Paul's Church College Hill on John Avenue. As part of her discipline of consolation and lament, she went to confession and received absolution weekly at either Zion, St. Paul's College Hill, or Salem. It frequently became difficult for Carol to work at the gallery, and she found she wasn't motivated to paint in her studio. Anne Newland was concerned that Carol would let the gallery and studio go, and she didn't want to lose the resource. Anne believed eventually Carol would return to focus on the business at a future time. Twice a week Anne would drive to St. Louis from Ste. Genevieve to monitor the gallery, studio and dance space, to keep the venture alive. She reached out to artists looking for a space – either gallery or studio – to maintain the operation. In addition, the gallery was valuable to the Ste. Genevieve artists' colony as a place to display and sell their art. Anne spent a lot of time with Carol on each of her visits and they prayed together at Zion or St. Paul's College Hill. Carol made it clear that she loved her son deeply but did not want to dwell on his fallen life and his court case. Together they prayed for Michael that he would find redemption. As part of Carol's absorption with lament, Anne and Carol frequently read together from the *Psalms, Book of Jeremiah* and *Lamentations*.

Carol talked about her struggles and expressed her desire for the nightmare to someday come to an end. She was disturbed about the loss of the Ku Klux Klan case and realized Michael Senior had been correct all along – the system of justice runs on autopilot with predetermined outcomes designed to maintain a convoluted apparatus plowing everyone under. The absurdity of three black people – or four, counting Perry Olmstead – being branded members of the Ku Klux Klan wasn't even considered or thought about as the system of justice methodically shuffles along. The narrative had already been written – law enforcement and the judicial system were set loose to impose the most irrational, insane, and preposterous causes. Nothing made any sense. And therefore, in this type of social order, it would only follow that three black people would be found guilty of violating the civil provisions of an 1871 law designed to prohibit organized activities which targeted and terrorized black people.

As Carol grieved her son, she sought retreat in her own internal privacy and solitude. Her sorrow and anguish at times was overbearing, like a heavy weight on her chest. "I made so many terrible mistakes that brought this on," she said to herself. She sought solace nearly every day at the two places that brought her peace and comfort. Zion Cathedral, the beloved church near her gallery, was the massive, sweeping, ornate Gothic church structure of white marble and enormous vaults. St. Paul's College Hill, the church of her youth, was the warmer, more intimate Baroque church with a towering barrel vault, and beautiful, huge oak interior buttresses intricately intertwining one another, yet the church is dominated by a subdued presence of deep, rich brown oak on the chancel walls, the pews, and the hand-carved wooden altarpiece.

One day while in prayer at St. Paul's College Hill, Carol met Alice Ploughmaster. Alice approached Carol and gently sat next to her.

"Carol, I know this is a deep, anguished pain for you," Alice said. "There are so many people praying for you during this deep hurt."

"I keep asking myself how this could happen to a synod family. We have always lived with such devotion and discipline. Yet, I know our actions brought this on to us."

"Carol, I understand what you are saying. He was the most precious boy. I do not believe all is lost. We must pray ceaselessly and keep our trust and our discipline. Carol, fate is the realm of God only. Keep your belief that what will come is all part of a larger plan. I have witnessed it myself. At Xavier, a young woman was abducted and disappeared for more than twenty years – she was presumed dead. But by some mysterious, inexplicable twist of fate, she was discovered; she had been held hostage in sex slavery – she was found by a man who didn't even know her, but he was driven by some mysterious, incomprehensible compulsion to rescue a woman he previously didn't have any knowledge of even existing. There is a distinct mystery to everything in life. Don't lose faith; all is not lost." She embraced Carol.

Carol often sought consolation from her husband and she would ask him over and over, "Michael, when will the nightmare end?"

Michael carried his pain and the loss of his son with his own internal reflection, inwardly praying and deliberating on how he could have made so many different decisions to protect that sweet, precious, tender boy. He realized more each day that the price to be paid in this life is so thoroughly overwhelming, devastating, and inordinate. He could no longer bear going to the Florissant neighborhood meetings in the basement of the Presbyterian church and he simply stopped showing up. Wendy Sachlor and Sadie Rice were relieved that he never reappeared.

One Tuesday in May, Michael, Carol and Paul appeared with Larry Korhonen, their attorney, in the federal courthouse for sentencing on the civil Ku Klux Klan case. Judge Hedrick J. Winters ruled that Michael and Carol Holden were to be fined $600,000 between the two of them for being members of the Ku Klux Klan and violating the civil rights of the aggrieved former president. Judge Winters ruled Paul Mooney was to be fined $300,000 for his membership in the Klan and violating the civil rights of the former president.

Larry Korhonen moved the court to suspend enforcement pending appeal. Judge Winters denied the motion, stating the entire matter had simply gone on much too long – more than twenty-four years – and the time had come to finally pay the price, as he put it.

Michael and Carol had no way to pay the judgment. Paul was in the same state – he had no means to pay $300,000.

The U.S. attorney's office began pursing ways of collecting on the penalty through a judgment lien. While researching the Holdens' real estate possessions, it was discovered the massive debt through the original mortgage and the second mortgage provided no value which could be claimed through a judgment lien. The entire value of the house was tied up in the first and second mortgages – the debt simply erased the equity. Their own personal property did not have significant value – one vehicle was indebted by a car loan, the other car had a resale value of less than a thousand dollars. They had no other discernable personal property. The U.S. attorney's office researched liens on intangibles – such as stocks, bonds, and retirement plans. Michael had previously redeemed his retirement plan for the sake of his son's legal defense. There was little left in his retirement account, and Michael and Carol had no significant savings. However, the government was able to make a garnishment on the salary of Michael – 50 percent of his income from his job as an accountant with the auto and truck parts company was subject to seizure.

The government promptly filed a garnishment on Michael's wages, taking one-half of his salary. Quickly, it became obvious to Michael and Carol that they were unable to pay their mortgage and loan obligations. They discussed their predicament and decided they needed to sell their house. With a sale, they would not gain any monetary value because the price of the sale would completely be absorbed by the bank to cure the mortgage and the loans. After the sale, they were still indebted to the bank, but the monthly payments were significantly less, and more manageable with 50 percent less income because of the garnishment. To find a place to live, without having to pay a new mortgage, Michael and Carol discussed their situation with Carol's parents, who promptly invited them to move into their house in the Hyde Park neighborhood – rent free. Their only indebtedness would be their remaining loan payments on the second mortgage loan which had been secured for Michael Junior's legal defense, some credit card debt, and their car payment.

Michael had a pronounced, very clear awareness of a principle he learned from a synod pastor in a sermon at Transfiguration synod parish in St. Louis many years ago. It was something he thought about regularly. There is always a price to be paid. Sometimes the price is very high and surpasses all understanding.

Jack Aiello, the Kansas City attorney representing Perry Olmstead in his federal Ku Klux Klan case, appeared before Judge Moira Pembroke during a pretrial status conference and motions hearing. Aiello presented several motions to dismiss the case based on arguments that Perry Olmstead is a black man, the civil lawsuit was a violation of First Amendment protections, and that membership in the Republican Party doesn't constitute proof of Ku Klux Klan affiliation.

Judge Pembroke denied Aiello's motions to dismiss. First, she said she wasn't familiar with how the First Amendment had anything to do with the matters before her – even making a veiled suggestion that she wasn't particularly familiar with the meaning of the First Amendment at all. Then Judge Pembroke announced she read the findings and the trial record of the recently concluded Ku Klux Klan case in St. Louis involving Michael and Carol Holden and Paul Mooney. Judge Pembroke interpreted the rulings of Judge Winters to allow the case to move forward despite the defendants being black people. She also noted that Judge Winters was very clear that Republican Party membership can validly be interpreted by a jury to be concurrent with Ku Klux Klan affiliation, if the jury were so inclined.

"This matter will need to move forward in exactly the same way the St. Louis case progressed," Judge Pembroke lectured.

Several months passed and Aiello called Perry Olmstead to tell him another status conference was scheduled on an upcoming Tuesday, and it would be a good idea for Perry to appear, merely to demonstrate to the judge that he was still engaged in the matter.

Although it was several years ahead of Perry, he too would eventually be confronted with his own price which would need to be paid.

Acknowledgments

Perception and hostile architecture. Allan Seager, "The Street." *Vanity Fair.* September, 1934.

Interpreting racism in St. Louis. Walter Johnson, *The Broken Heart of America: St. Louis and the Violent History of the United States.* Basic Books. 2022.

Harry S. Truman. B. F. LeBeau, D. M. Burke, J. Herron, W. Worley (eds.), *The Pendergast Years.* Kansas City Public Library. 2019. Bruce M. Russett, *No Clear and Present Danger.* Harper & Row. 1997. Michael J. Glennon, *National Security and Double Government.* Oxford University Press. 2016. Paul Campos, "The Truman Show." *New York Magazine.* 7/24/2021.

Ste. Genevieve. Patrick Huber, "Remembering the Ste. Genevieve Race Riot of 1930." *State Historical Society of Missouri.* 11/14/2017.

Democracy, information and the system of justice. Jacob Siegel, "The Guide to Understanding the Hoax of the Century: 13 Ways of Looking at Disinformation." *Tablet Magazine.* 3/28/2023. Ryszard Legutko, *The Demon in Democracy.* Encounter Books. 2018.

Equity and Maoism. Ting-Xing Ye, *My Name is Number 4*. St. Martins. 2007. Xi Van Fleet, *Mao's America*. Center Street. 2023. Ma Bo, *Red Blood Sunset*. Penguin. 1998. Jicai Feng, *Ten Years of Madness*. China Books. 2007. Ji-li Jiang, *Red Scarf Girl*. Scholastic. 1999. Christopher Rufo, *America's Cultural Revolution*. Broadside. 2023. Jack Posobiec and Joshua Lisec, *Unhumans*. Skyhorse. 2024.

Lament. Gregory P. Schulz, *The Problem of Suffering*. Concordia Publishing House. 2012. Gregory P. Schulz, "Pain, Suffering, Lament." *Logia*. Spring, 2015. Gregory P. Schulz, "Our Lamentable Lacuna." *Logia*. Winter, 2019. Dimiter Angelov (trans.), Medieval lament in "The Moral Pieces by Theordore II Lascar." *Dumbarton Oaks Papers*. Vol. 65-66. 2011-12.

The medieval mind. John T. Slotemaker, *Anselm of Canterbury and the Search for God*. Lexington Books. 2018. Benjamin Wheaton, *Suffering, Not Power: Atonement in the Middle Ages*. Lexham Academic. 2022. George C. Foley, *Anselm's Theory of the Atonement*. Legare Street Press. 2022. Damien Bouquet and Piroska Nagy, *Medieval Sensibilities*. Polity Press. 2018. J.W. Thomas, ed., *The Best Novellas of Medieval Germany*. Camden House. 1984. Roger Scruton, *The Aesthetics of Understanding*. St. Augustine Press. 1998.

The Author

D.W. Snow is a Michigan native who lives in the mountains of Colorado. The author's other books include *Millstone Around the Neck, And Now the Vault of Heaven Resounds,* and a collection of short stories, *At Concordia.*